THE DAY THE MONEY DIED
By

Will

Prologue

The room of the Central computer contained a mass of flickering screens which from moment to moment reflected the ever-changing myriad details of seemingly infinite financial transactions. From all over the Country, all over the World, a roller coaster of cash withdrawals, balance requests, deposits, were carried in a never-ending stream of ATM messages to and from the waiting millions out there in the cold and the rain in the dark of the night and the light and heat of the sun, all of which the massive computer system could, for the most part, handle with awesome efficiency.

24 hours a day, this automated juggernaut continued on its way, the flashing lights, the whirring and clicking from the relentless machines orchestrating a scene not unlike the *Krell* laboratory in *The Forbidden Planet*, eternally restless, in perpetual motion.

Today though, was different. Around these screens, monitoring them with unusual concentration were a group of men and women, clearly not the faceless operatives who usually stood idly by as casual servants to the mighty machines. Their eyes straining against the unremitting glow of the monitors, each person's face was etched with the tension inherited from their own experience of a harsher, more realistic climate, a raw place that was a world away from the abstract hidden life of the computer operators who were the natural inhabitants of this cold environment.

"Look!" said a man with a Scottish gravel voice as he pointed towards the screen,
"Here's another one!"

Although he spoke to the group in general, the man who could be easily identified as their leader, moved with swift economy to stand at the Scotsman's shoulder, peering at the screen, his dark eyes intense and alert.

"Yes, it's them all right" he said in a voice bristling with authority.

"Get someone down there right away, but no noise or fanfares, we want surveillance, not capture

There was a bustle of sudden activity, as a crowd of minions hurried to deal with his orders, bodies separating into corners as if from a rugby scrum, a confusing scramble of voices high and low intermingling as urgent messages sailed out into the ether. The Chief bit his lip anxiously, for this was not the first time in that evening he had given this order. There was no doubt about it, massive fraudulent withdrawals were being made from the banking system.

This in itself was not new, the Chief had seen massive fraud before, but this was something different, hundreds of thousands of these transactions seemed inextricably linked by *modus operandi* and in uneasy corroboration, sometimes-direct connection. Worse still, these known transactions being monitored could well be the tip of the iceberg. The conclusions to be reached from this seemed catastrophic. If true, there was no telling where it could lead. This *could* be paranoia, the Chief reasoned. He hoped it was, for if his worst fears were realised, the signs were ominous. Someone could be orchestrating an attack on the banking system itself.

PART ONE

CASH & CREDIT

1

In Finsbury Square, London, stands the impressive modern building whose marble and glass hallways house APACS, founded by a consortium of banks and financial institutions to oversee their joint interests including automated systems, security, and fraud, especially in relation to plastic cards and ATM transactions.

On this evening, the lights were burning late in these offices of the great and the good. In the main boardroom, a cloud of cigar smoke hovered above the long and elegant table where sat these modern knights of financial *Camelot*, the chairmen and major players who represented the banks and other financial institutions.

The meeting was chaired by the Director-General, Farquhar-Brown, a man who was sophisticated and clever, and not complacent. Yet time in this structure had taught him that his decisions must always be tempered by compromise, by the very nature of the institutions the consortium consisted of. They were competitors first and foremost, after all. He had position, but in reality he had little power, he was a virtual first secretary of a financial United Nations.

In this room with him, sitting at the long table among the most important financial people in the Country was a Junior Minister from the Treasury, something of a token gesture from the government at this stage.

"Gentlemen, this meeting is called to order," said the Director- General, and a gradual hush descended over the room, leaving his voice slightly echoing among the crystal chandeliers of the high ceiling.

"We have noted an unusually high level of fraudulent activity among our loans and credit card transactions. The volume of such transactions and of general defaults has risen by some 20% in the past year alone. At this rate of growth, we could be discussing a level of 50% by next year, and that is obviously unacceptable. I have asked you here tonight so that we may discuss what steps can be taken to neutralise this threat to our business. Are there any comments at this stage?"

The chairman of a major high street bank, who had only recently been knighted, was first to speak. Sweeping his hand and the cigar it held in an arc of acknowledgement towards his peers, he said unemotionally, almost like a *Mafia Don.*

"All of us have become used to levels of fraud ever-increasing, and after all, our business is also increasing at such levels, year in year out. So what is new?"

A murmur of agreement rumbled round the table, and the Director-General replied, trying to disguise the impatience in his voice.

"Fraud is indeed always with us, but I don't think you've grasped the figures we are talking about here. This is a 20% growth on what we may call 'normal' fraud. If this is allowed to go on and grow at its present rate, it will threaten our business to a very significant degree".

Lord Sefton, the chairman of a major building society signalled to the Director-General that he wished to make a contribution, and once again the room stilled, as the portly red-faced northerner spoke, his accent unchanged by his years of success and high society.

"So let's get down to brass tacks. Three questions for you - One - why is this happening? Two, what's brought the change? Three, what can we do about it?"

"I can answer questions one and two by saying that we believe - my investigating officers and I - that such activity is being led by an organisation rather than consisting of a random series of unconnected events" said Farquhar-Brown in a matter-of-fact businesslike voice. "This organisation must be very large, covering the whole country in fact, and it is growing week by week. In our opinion, this is fraud on a highly organised basis. The answer to the third question is more difficult. We could eradicate this problem at a moment's notice by closing down our loan and credit business......" A hubbub of protest drowned out the Director-General as he struggled to continue through the ensuing noise.

"Gentlemen, Gentlemen!" He was shouting now, the echoes of his voice carried by the cavernous room, the chandeliers ringing gently, like barely audible crystal bells.

"Gentlemen! *If* I could continue!" he said, calming himself down as the muttering voices reluctantly receded.

"Gentlemen, the fact is, that *is* the only certain way of eradicating this problem completely, but I accept it would be an operation which would nevertheless kill the patient".

A nervous ripple of laughter crossed the room as he continued.

"What could also be done is to ensure a much more rigorous examination of each application, so that only the genuine applicant would be successful".

"Hold on a minute!" said Lord Sefton, "What we're talking about here is a complete revamp of our existing systems. Everyone in this room knows that's impossible. The cost and time factors are just not on!"

A rumble and grumbling of assent punctuated his words. Farquhar-Brown had anticipated all of this, but had laid out the situation as he saw it mainly for the benefit of his own position at a later date. As a master of compromise - the very nature of his appointment - he had laid out the stall. No one could later accuse him of complacency, he had placed the onus squarely on his associates, who were virtually his employers. Now he was able to put forward the compromise solution he had in mind all along.

"Gentlemen, I propose that we set up a special body to deal directly with this problem. This virtual task force will comprise police officers of the highest calibre, as well as the best from our teams of investigators and specialised accountants etc."

Slouching languidly in his seat, his narrowed eyes fastening on the Director-General like a weasel, another captain of financial industry raised his voice.

"If this so-called task force is to have any real bite to it, it must be led by someone with teeth".

"Do we have such a man?" asked the recently

knighted banker, looking doubtful.

"Oh yes" said the Director-General, "I believe we have".

2

His life had been ordinary up to this point. There was nothing about him that made him seem different from the crowd, he was anonymous, he lived an anonymous life. He had drifted through school, through employment, through life, a notable underachiever; his youth had passed him by without incident. He lived in a typical house in a typical street with his Wife and 2.4 children. There was nothing visible to separate him from the great mass of humanity surrounding him. But he was different.

It had all changed that one day in autumn. Circumstances had forced his hand. Now he was proud of the system, though proud was perhaps too strong, for somewhere inside he still felt a deep regret that the system had proved necessary to his survival. Being respectable and successful would have meant so much more, but it was never to be, it never could be now.

It had all begun so slowly, but now its strength was frightening to behold, and yet it was all rooted in principles which had a simple premise - the institutions were vulnerable. They had no choice but to open themselves to abuse, and trust in the basic honesty of the great mass of the people. All it took to gain advantage from that belief was someone like him and the conjunction of circumstances that made his reactions inevitable.

Now, the network was indeed formidable. In every city and major town there were 'operatives' carrying out orders, taking over empty houses, moving into salubrious areas, opening offices in respectable business premises. Most of all, these operatives generated cash flow, withdrawing vast sums of money, yet in such small amounts at a time to be inconspicuous among the millions of transactions made daily by the honest section of the population.

His own distinctly dishonest transactions would only become obvious as such when the inevitable defaults began to appear, after all, there was no point to drawing money then paying it back again.

Some payments were indeed made. It was all a question of balance. While there were still opportunities to gain from keeping the account and the identity seemingly valid, there was reason to 'invest' in such an individual's illusory future as bait, in fact, to lure further income into the net.

The down side of these accumulating defaults was of course the growing visibility of the deception. Already, the system had accounted for some £10 million vanishing from the institutions. Around now, he knew, the authorities would begin to notice the unusual activity and take steps to monitor, identify any problems, and eradicate them, but he also knew that the nature of bureaucracy was slow to take action. It would be some time yet before his enemy began to take decisive steps against him. Defending the system would not be simple, for it had in effect become a bureaucracy itself. Controlling it, even with the swiftest of intentions, was like steering the *Titanic* away from the iceberg, so difficult for something of that size to make the manoeuvre quickly enough.

Another disadvantage was that his enemy had

the best of resources and could call on any such resource without fear or favour, whereas he had to make every move by stealth, hide every action by subterfuge and cunning. At the same time though, the system had all the facts at its disposal, the others were working in the dark, unaware of how the pieces of the jigsaw fitted together. Also, as vast as the system was becoming, it was still the size of a fly in relation to the elephant that was the banks and the treasury, but as huge and powerful as the elephant was, it would have great trouble standing on a fly. Nevertheless, even as things were, he had the capacity to do enormous damage, and he had every intention of doing so.

Lost in these thoughts, he glanced out at the night sky through the stained glass window of his elegant mansion. To the right of him, and slightly below, there on the one lonely road along the horizon, he could see the luminous glow of cars as they drifted through the darkness, on their way home perhaps, or enjoying the company of someone they loved.

An aching loneliness filled his heart as memories of another time pervaded his consciousness. The system he had planned was already spectacularly successful.

Why then, did he still feel so empty inside?

3

In a city far away, in the comfort of his home, with his wife Jane and their children safely tucked into bed, the Chief was trying to relax with a glass of whisky, but to no avail. His mind was full of the events of the day. His concern over this business was growing, yet his superiors did not seem to be taking this threat seriously enough, they were exhibiting typical complacency, and seemed to think that by drafting him into the spotlight, the problem had been solved.

The call had come a few weeks before. A somewhat officious lackey had loftily informed the Chief that he was hereby summoned to APACS to see the Director-General. The Chief was no stranger to that building, but calls like this were rare, they meant something big was on the cards. Despite his years of experience, the Chief still had butterflies in his stomach as he stood on the elegant escalator taking him up through the magnificent building symbolically to the upper echelons of the Director-General's suite.

"The Director-General is expecting you," the receptionist said, smilingly showing him through. He had not been kept waiting, another portent, he thought at the time.

"Come in!" said Farquhar-Brown in friendly fashion, another bad sign. Welcoming him in with a handshake and a few pleasantries, Farquhar-Brown had come straight to the point.

"We have a major credit fraud on our hands," he said, outlining the same facts he had

14

presented to the APACS committee. When he heard what was involved, the Chief whistled quietly to himself. This really is a challenge, he had thought. Even then he could already see that complacency from the APACS committee was likely to be a negative force in his investigations. Not that this was anything new, but it could be a problem if the scale of damage proved to be as bad as his instincts were already telling him.

"Anything you need is yours," Farquhar-Brown said, though both of them knew that wasn't strictly true.

"Anything within reason, more like", thought the Chief, but he was saying nothing. He too had long ago learned the nature of survival and compromise.

"I'll need to choose my own team" was all he had said, proceeding to name several of the APACS specialists, and in particular, as his personal assistant and number one, the woman who was in his opinion, the real expert in her field of credit systems, Susan Bryde. They had worked together on many cases, but only when 'big guns' were called for. Their individual expertise was deemed by their superiors too rare and too in demand to be left undiluted by working together on the vast bulk of cases, which in the main, proved to be fairly easy to deal with.

"Are you coming to bed?"

The voice of his Wife calling downstairs to him intruded into his thoughts.

"In a minute, Dear!" he said, guiltily taking another sip of whiskey. His mind wandered back to the case, and Susan Bryde. He remembered her reaction to his call.

"Bloody hell!" she had said, less than pleased to be summarily recruited, and he could understand that. He knew how annoying it was to be in the middle of a backlog of work and thoroughly involved in investigations only to be suddenly 'pulled' into something new. At the same time he knew that once Susan saw the basic facts, she would be hooked, as he already was. There was no doubt about it. This was the 'big one'.

Nevertheless, sitting here in his darkened room alone with his thoughts, a few weeks into the investigation he had to admit it was not going particularly well. After a promising beginning, it had stalled.

They had quickly identified some of the accounts that were fraudulently operating, and had taken steps to monitor applications and cash withdrawals, soon identifying a pattern of behaviour. From there, it had been fairly simple to keep surveillance on these individuals drawing the money and paying it into a series of accounts.   They had learned everything they needed to know about these individuals, including where and how they lived. Yet he did not move in and have any of them arrested, for he felt that it would simply be showing his hand to the enemy. Could any of these individuals lead him to the heart of the system? Somehow he doubted that, yet as he sat there, doing nothing, he was merely a spectator, a voyeur who was standing by doing nothing, just helplessly watching a constant haemorrhaging of the banks, a draining of their lifeblood by a financial vampire.

Susan had made it clear that she favoured a move against the system, even at the risk of showing their hand.

"At least it's doing *something*", she had reasoned, and who knows? - They might learn more than they thought? Surely it was worth the chance? He knew she was mad as hell at him, and he marvelled at her decisive certainty. But then it was easier for her than him, he was the one who would carry the can at the end of the day if it went wrong, she could walk away, her record unblemished. Still, he admitted to himself, she had a point. It was going nowhere otherwise.

And he had to admit, she was beautiful when she was angry.

4

His Wife was beautiful, he thought, as he watched her from the kitchen window. She stood in her garden, gently touching the fragile leaves of a delicate flower he didn't know the name of. She was a child of nature, so in tune with the universe, so unlike him, yet they had been together so long, been through so much.

Sensing his eyes on her, she paused and looked at him, almost shy and self-conscious that he had been studying her. He waved to her in reassurance. Even though she stood at the foot of the long garden, he could see she was smiling.

"Enjoying the weather?" he called to her somewhat superfluously, his voice almost lost in the wind.

She looked almost embarrassed, caught in her moment of privacy.

"Yes................"

He only heard the first word, the wind carrying only the gentle tone of her voice. Why did she choose him? Perhaps because he had an ageless wisdom about him, bought by his experiences and hard times, but also by virtue of an inbuilt intensity and awareness, and a brilliant intuition which he didn't listen to nearly enough for his own good.

These thoughts wearied him, and he sighed as he walked away from the window. Despite his great gifts, life had somehow always been an uphill struggle for him, he was an outsider, a misfit. He had wanted the best for his Wife and children, but seemed unable to provide it for them. With his lack of practicality and shortage of experience and formal education, no one had ever been willing to give him a chance to prove his worth in the World. The years had rolled by, and he had missed the boat. All he had was a mediocre position as a clerk in an office, a job any fool could do.

By this time in his life, the dark forces had gathered against him, and when his bank offered him a chance to apply for a large overdraft, much larger than his salary justified, he made a fatal decision to go for it. He so badly wanted to provide his Wife with something nice in her life for a change, instead of the struggles and deprivation that had attended so much of her life, even before he had met her. Her childhood traumas had been something he was able to help her with emotionally, but her need for social respectability and quiet security matched his own, suffering as they both were from a lack of self-esteem, and the temptation of the overdraft beckoning was too much to bear.

Finally, he filled in the forms giving the information he thought they would like rather than the whole truth. He said he owned his house outright when it was in fact, mortgaged to the hilt; he overvalued the property by 50%; he gave his occupation as 'Manager' instead of 'Clerk'; he stated his income was four times greater than it was in reality.

Some weeks later, the bank telephoned him.

"Your application has been accepted," said the Manager, sounding like a benevolent Father Christmas.

"Thank you," he said, stammering and hesitant,

trying to take on the implications of a new beginning. There was a moment of euphoria, a feeling of sudden success after such gloom.

The first few months were an uplifting time, a time to suddenly enjoy the fruits of life, new clothes, a car, a holiday. His Wife was smiling again, she knew little about the reason for the change in their fortunes, accepting his explanation of a promotion and increase in earning power, which had prompted the bank to extend the gold hand of substantial credit towards him.

"We're becoming rich!" she said, her eyes sparkling and happy.
These were good days.

At first, it had all gone well, so well in fact that further banks contacted him and offered him similar facilities as a response to their competitor's success. Within a few months, he had built up a considerable overdraft facility. He found he had a real talent for convincing bank managers and institutions to accept his applications readily, he somehow knew what these institutions wanted to hear, wanted to see. Even at personal interviews, when they proved necessary, he charmed the gullible managers without any difficulty whatsoever, and to him, the lies were white rather than black. After all, he was paying the money back, wasn't he?

Soon, it had all gone so well that they were able to buy a new house, the house of his Wife's dreams, with a beautiful garden, a six-bedroom Georgian house in the best part of Town. Life gained a cosy domesticity and peacefulness they had never previously known.

"I've never been happier," she said wistfully one day, looking at him in admiration, the architect of their fortunes. There seemed so much money available that he felt able to give up his employment, the very thought of performing such a menial task seemed now to be beneath him in any case; they felt akin to the rich and successful. Their immediate neighbour was a famous Cabinet Minister, the other residents of this exclusive address were eminent professional people, retired Lords and Ladies, up and coming *nouveau riche*. Days were spent on shopping expeditions buying goods that they mostly did not need and usually never used. At nights, he would stroll to the Village pub to dream a while away, making impossible plans, while at home, his Wife happily fussed around the house she was so proud of.

These were the rainbow days, but they were an illusion, for the house was built on cards, not bricks.

5

"Let's pull him in," said the Chief, moving decisively away from the video screen and the figure flitting through the dark streets depicted there.

Susan was startled.

"But I thought you said that we didn't want to let them know that we were on to them?"

The Chief smiled at her warmly. It was true that he had opposed Susan's early requests to move against the system. He realised that it must seem to Susan as if he was almost opposing everything she said for the sake of it.

"I still don't want to alert them Susan, and I didn't disagree with your ideas at all. It's just that we have to let events keep pace with us, not the other way round. What we'll do is keep it low key, pull this little cretin in quietly, as if it was merely routine. Lowlifes like him expect to be pulled, and it will come as no surprise to his paymasters either". He smiled at her again, hoping to reassure her insecurities, and was rewarded with the warm look he saw in her eyes.

Susan nodded towards McKay who muttered into his mobile phone. As they watched like quiet voyeurs as the figure of the petty thief almost laughably stood in the queue for the ATM machine, every few seconds or so looking over his shoulder anxiously, telegraphing the fact that he was up to no good.

Only a few moments later, as the man hastily withdrew the money from the machine, a look of panic crossed his pallid features as a police car swung into view and blocked off his exit path. The man tried to run up an alleyway nearby, but as he did so, a policeman exited there right in front of him. They had thought of that too. The man was unceremoniously bundled into the white panda by the business-like officers.

Susan and the Chief hurried away from the video nasty to liaise with the police car at Theobolds Road police station in Holborn. Almost like children whose game has gone well, they laughed and joked, playfully pushing and shoving each other as they made their way into the lift to the ground floor.

The man was waiting in the interview room, his face frightened but surly. He had seen the inside of a room like this many times. They already knew that his name was James West, a name that made them smile, for 'Jim' was easily translated into 'Jimbo', the police slang word for every little petty thief on the street.

Susan was first to speak.

"Well, well, what do we have here?"

She smiled, but her eyes looked at Jimbo as if he was stuck to the bottom of her shoe. He stared back at her insolently, his bravado fooling no one but himself.

"What have you got to say for yourself son?" she said patronisingly.

Jimbo stared at her under hooded lids, saying nothing, his face filled with tension. He knew he was in for it, but he was no 'grass'.

Susan looked sideways at the Chief. He shook

his head ever so slightly. Susan nodded just as subtly, and they both left the room saying nothing more.

Outside, they compared notes.

"We won't get anything out of him" said the Chief in a matter-of-fact voice.

"I know," said Susan, "I didn't expect to. What I'm really interested in is what he had on him".

"That's right," said the Chief. They were both on the same wavelength. Together they made for the custody Sergeant's desk.

"Hello Bill" said Susan, smiling at the Sergeant. He looked up, and his scowling face broke into a boyish grin.

"Hello Darlin'!" he said, his voice too loud, "How's you?"

"Fine Bill" said Susan, her face a study of method acting, "Jim West – did he have anything interesting on him?"

The desk Sergeant turned to a pile of objects at the side of his desk and handed them to Susan.

"Just some credit cards, a little bit of cash, some dope, and a mobile phone" he said, disinterested. It was all routine stuff.

Susan's eyes gleamed as she glanced through the cards. She took the phone and handed the small package of dope back to the Sergeant.

"OK if we sign for these Bill?" she said, waving the phone and the credit cards in her left hand.

"Sure, no problem" said the Sergeant, reaching for the forms of release.

Moments later, they were back in the car, heading for the office again. Despite the noninterview with Jimbo, they were not disappointed. The cards were a precious lead, and the phone might yield something too.

"We can read the transcripts of Jimbo's interrogation later," said the Chief distractedly to no one in particular. He knew that Susan was of the same mind in any case.

"Yes," said Susan, her mind also far away. She suddenly realised that she was tired, they both were, it had been a long day. She looked at the Chief fondly.

"Shall we call it a wrap for today?" she said with a feeble smile.

The Chief reached over and squeezed her hand.

"Yes, why not?" he said wearily, "We can put a trace on the stuff before we leave, and tomorrow we should learn something more".

Susan smiled at him, warmly this time.

"Shall we have a swift visit to the pub?" she said.

"Good idea" said the Chief, feeling some of the tension coming out on him now.

It had indeed been a long day, and they were only beginning at the beginning.

6

It was raining, and it was time to leave the house. So many of their dreams had been trampled into the dust in this place, yet they were heartbroken to be leaving, his Wife was especially shattered.

"It wasn't real," she said sadly, tears streaming down her face.
She had known only insecurity all her life, and it added to his own sense of anguish that he had only contributed further to her despair.

Bereft of furniture, the rooms stood silent, already a ghost of a place, the central heating closed down till the winter that would follow winter, the garden left to grow uncared for till the summer that followed summer.

It was still pouring when they arrived at their new abode, a rather scruffy terraced house in a poor part of Town, a far cry from the heights they had once risen to. Step by step the furniture arrived, miles too much of it for this much smaller house, the already threadbare carpets trampled with mud as the weather outside grew worse, seeming almost a comment on the condition they now found themselves in. As the last piece of furniture entered the house, the lights failed, plunging their new World into unexpected darkness, this final small event feeling almost too much to bear.

Later that night, in the drab brown-coloured bedroom, they lay emotionally exhausted in each other's arms, sharing tears for their lost dreams.

7

The trail seemed to lead initially nowhere. The names on the cards were of people who didn't seem to exist, their addresses bogus, their details false. Susan and the Chief were unfazed. They had expected no less, and it did, nevertheless, give them confirmation of how the system was being set up, through dummy accounts and addresses. As for Jimbo's mobile phone, it was a stolen one, naturally, and most of the numbers called from it were equally dubious but untraceable.

The really interesting moment came when the phone suddenly rang. The Chief was surprised, but it didn't stop him reacting. Raising his eyebrows conspiratorially, he looked at Susan with her mouth hanging open, picked up the phone and pressed a digit.

"Yeah?" he grunted, rather than spoke the word.

"Leo" said the voice on the other end, just as obscured and gruff.

"What's the score?" the voice asked with anger and irritation.

"You tell me," said the Chief, not knowing what else to say. There was a sudden click as the phone went dead. The Chief flicked through the buttons on the phone, tracing the number. Unsurprisingly, no number had been transmitted. Susan was already calling the line provider to trace the call.

"Leo?" she said, her face perplexed, "Is it Leo calling, or is that Jimbo's codename?"

"My guess is that Leo was calling, though that might not even be his name, as you say," said the

27

Chief thoughtfully.

"What a shame we couldn't record it, and play it over the loudspeakers," said Susan wistfully, regretting the difficulty of recording from a mobile phone.

The Chief nodded.

"There was something though" he said, "Another voice in the background, a deeper, darker voice".

"What was it saying?" said Susan, lighting up, interested.

The Chief looked puzzled.

"The background was noisy, an office or something. It was difficult to hear clearly. It was something like 'pot meal' or 'hot wheel' – it doesn't seem to make sense to me at the moment".

Susan looked hard at him.

"Could it be 'hotmail'?" she said.

"It could be – but that still doesn't mean anything to me," said the Chief, looking at Susan for inspiration.

"Hotmail is a site on the Internet that people can use to send e-mail. More to the point, people can use codenames or aliases through hotmail," she said.

The Chief perked up immediately.

"Now that is interesting!" he said, enthusiastically.

"I'll get straight on to it!" said Susan, as their eyes met and held each other for a few seconds before she looked away.

8

The break up had been swift and ruthless. The Official Receiver had moved against their bank accounts and properties and already he had spent more time at the bleak offices in Atlantic House, Holborn than he could have thought possible. It was such a shabby business, bankruptcy. The bank managers who had been so cavalier in lending him the money lost their smile very quickly when they realised he would have trouble paying them back.

"We demand that you pay us immediately!" said the indignant voice on the phone, the tone threatening and outraged. It was only one of many such calls. They became afraid to answer the phone, or open the mail, but the callers at the door were the worst. To his undying shame, he almost retreated into his shell, leaving his Wife to face the wrath of the debt collectors.

"Is he in?" the aggressive voice demanded, as he hid in the bathroom upstairs.

"No" said his Wife in a quiet tearful little voice.

"He's really dropped you in it, hasn't he?" said the man, feeling unusual sympathy for the defenceless woman facing him, but harassing her nevertheless.

"You tell him we'll be back," he said in a menacing voice.

"Yes."

The quavering voice of his Wife stirred his shame and remorse for the situation he had placed her in. Once again, he had let her down.

His troubles had all begun when one of the banks

realised that his exposure was much greater than they thought, a link was made - an illegal link ironically, for customer confidentiality is supposed to be absolute. In reality, banks talk freely to each other, and once the penny dropped in one, the rest knew within days. Although he was technically solvent on paper, most of his apparent wealth was in property. It was a simple matter for the banks and the Official Receiver to down-value the property and make him technically bankrupt as a form of punishment for being too clever and too devious into the bargain. Banks never like to see their own flaws exposed, and their vengeance is total.

At first, he was shattered and repentant, feeling that he had indeed acted badly, and that he should do all he could to rectify the position.
Week after week, month after month, he worked with the administrators of his estate to clear up the mess. But his attitude changed one day in the Courts of Justice.

He was waiting to be called to the dock for his public examination, when he saw a man arrive in handcuffs, obviously brought to the court against his will. The Judge frowned at the man sternly. It seemed as if he would have the book thrown at him.

"You are John Alfred Simpson, are you not?" said the Judge, in imperious tones.

The man managed to look reasonably humble and contrite.
"Yes, your honour," he said, head bowed.

The Judge frowned again.

"Simpson, despite many communications and orders from this court, you have failed to appear in the matter of your bankruptcy – is that correct?"

The man looked humble all over again.

"Yes, your honour."

The Judge leaned forward in his seat.

"Are you now prepared to co-operate fully with this enquiry?"

"Yes, your honour," the man repeated, sounding very much like a broken record.

It seemed that Simpson was in deep trouble, but to the astonishment of the other man, the Judge smiled.

"Very well" he said, leaning back in his seat, his expression one of relief.

The other man was flabbergasted and deflated. Despite his full co-operation and willingness to do all that was asked and more, he had been treated with contempt and tongue-lashed at every opportunity. Yet here was Simpson, who had flaunted the orders of the court at every turn, and yet was now being treated with kindness and consideration. He suddenly felt like a fool, and he realised that he had not been any the better off by helping his tormentors.

It was a terrible moment of revelation. He knew then that he had been wrong to subject his Family to this agony without even putting up a fight. These officials were people of stone, indifferent to the human dramas being played out, everyone was the same, nothing he could do would make any difference to them. Thus began his true education.

His first step was to divert attention from his true address. It wouldn't save the house, but it would buy time and save many precious artefacts. From then on, in all official correspondence and dealings, he put forward a 'dummy' address, one of the properties he still had access to. In this house he placed a few cheap articles of furniture, so that when the official from the bankruptcy offices came to run an inventory, there was nothing of note to see. The real assets lay at his own home address.

Among these assets he still had some bankcards and accounts which hadn't been seized or noticed by the Official Receiver. He drew all the cash from these accounts and opened another from a completely safe address, unconnected in any way to his past. There wasn't a great deal of money there, but it was enough for a basis of a new beginning. He began to make plans to buy another house using the little cash he had along with a mortgage in a false name, which also coincided with a relative of his Wife's, so that if the worst came to the worst, the ambiguity would save him.

Supplying false income details, he acquired the mortgage, and deliberately targeted an empty house, for time was of the essence.

Within a few months, the sale and purchase were complete, and though their grief seemed inconsolable, they at least had a roof over their head. Better still, by signing as unemployed, he was able to draw weekly benefit to cover very basic expenses. Then, giving the name on the mortgage as his landlord, he applied for housing benefit which exceeded the amount he actually paid in mortgage by quite a considerable sum, thereby guaranteeing himself a reasonable income while he decided what to do next.

Although he had taken steps that were decidedly illegal, he did not at this stage harbour thoughts of a life of crime. He knew he would be forever tainted by the events that had befallen his Family, he still harboured illusions about society and forgiveness and acceptance. He hoped that somehow he would be able to turn things around, find some kind of place, some form of endorsement, a *raison d'être*, a way back into society. It would be some time yet before this last illusion was well and truly shattered.

9

The proprietors of Hotmail had no illusions about their customers. Though most of them were bona fide, genuine people who merely wanted to protect their ultimate identities from the hazards of the Internet, some were sleazy, and even sinister, the alias provided by Hotmail designed to hide to their abuse of the facilities readily available.

The forms these abuses took were many. Some customers sought to obscure the fact that they subscribed to the vast array of hardcore pornography. Some used the opportunity to abuse others by e-mail; others were tax-avoidance punters, whose activities were none the less easily monitored by the Inland Revenue, as they would find out at a later date. The list went on and on. Abuse was common. Thus, Hotmail was not surprised when Susan contacted them about Leo.

"Let's see," said the bespectacled specialist as Susan looked over his shoulder at the computer screen. He typed in leo@hotmail.com to his 'search customer' base. The screen leapt into life with myriad messages and information – Leo was live! Susan glanced at the top lines on the screen.

From: aries@sitemail.com

To: leo@hotmail.com

Message: *'The sun has risen in the east'*; and the next message below -

From: leo@hotmail.com

To: aries@sitemail.com

Message: *'the sun has set in the west'*.

"So there we are," said the operator, satisfied.

Susan patronisingly patted him on the shoulder.

"Well done," she said, "Now can you trace back where Leo came from in the first place?"

The operator nodded thoughtfully.

"Sure, no problem," he said, turning to his desk again. Moments later, there it was, Leo's home base, www.parker.maiden.co.uk.

Susan smiled triumphantly.

"Can you give me a print-out on all that?" she said briskly.

"Can do," said the operator, efficiently setting up the printout. In a few moments, he handed Susan a bundle of papers.

"Terrific!" she said, "Thanks a million".

"Any time," said the operator, deftly sweeping her legs into his glance as she walked away.

"Not a bad looker," he muttered, wishing her skirt was shorter.

Susan's mind was already out of the place, her voice on the phone to Maiden Internet.

"Maiden Internet. Lorraine speaking, how can I help?" the pleasant voice purred.

Susan was formal but friendly, giving her security code before requesting Leo's details.

"Hold on please," said Lorraine, suddenly motivated and serious. A few minutes later, she was back, rhyming off the facts and figures to Susan, who grinned with delight. It was almost too easy, she thought as she dialled through to the Chief.

"Hello Susan," he said, recognising her signal.

"Chief, no joy on the phone trace, but all the same, I've got Leo," said Susan excitedly, "The Hotmail trail led to Amco trust Ltd, money lenders of dubious reputation".

"I know Amco," said the Chief, "That's Fred Parker's place".

Susan butted in.

"Parker? Yes, that fits; the e-mail address has 'parker' in it".

"We're definitely on to something all right," said the Chief, his enthusiasm obvious even over the intermittent radio signal of the mobile phone. Susan was going through a dead phone zone; the signal was breaking up more and more. She just had time to hear a few more words before the signal cut off.

"...ell...done......Sus...n..."

She almost blushed, pleased and embarrassed at the same time.

10

Perhaps if the situation had not deteriorated in the way it did, he would not have taken his subsequent path. Then again, he had proved that under certain circumstances his personality disorder would still assert itself, and lead him to a life of crime in any case, the easy way out, on the face of it at least. As things stood immediately following the bankruptcy, a period of calm came over their lives again, albeit cloaked in the gloom of their lost past.

Nevertheless, he was never to be the same again, and neither was his relationship with his Wife. She had lost that trust in him and his abilities, despite all his efforts and relative success in what was after all a remarkable recovery. It was all to no avail. His aura of invincibility had been broken as far as she was concerned, and though she still felt duty and love for him, she was also resentful and hurt, feeling betrayed by the failed promise of their Marriage and expectations. Correspondingly, though on the surface things seemed unchanged, she now kept at an emotional distance from him.

He was more difficult to live with too. He would spend every day scheming and worrying, a virtual machine, human feelings put to one side in the quest for an upward path once again. He saw that as the only way to find some kind of material salvation or justification for his existence. He failed to see that he was chasing away the most precious thing in his life - a loving relationship with his soul mate.

Perhaps if events had not conspired against them, they might have made it through these darkest of times, bloodied but intact. But the public examination of bankruptcy changed all that, for it revealed his acts of dishonesty over his original applications for credit, and his case was referred to the fraud squad.

"You are in jeopardy!" said the red-faced circuit judge to the man in the dock, as the Official Received and the trustees of his estate looked on disinterestedly. He walked from the court, feeling already condemned, sentenced, at the gallows of his life.

This was shattering news, but worse was to come. The next morning, almost at dawn, there was a commotion outside. As they awoke in fright, a tremendous crashing sound signalled that their door was flying off its hinges.

"Jack – you take the fucking stairs!" said a voice, loud and aggressive amid the grunting and cursing sounds from many others, a melee of chaos and confusion. Without ceremony, the bedroom door suddenly opened, and a Detective Sergeant wearing a white coat, almost like a parody of *Maigret,* entered the room. Brazenly, he gazed at the woman who was trying to hide her nakedness.

"Police," he said, stating the obvious. "Get dressed – now!"
Almost reluctantly, he left the room, but they heard his voice, deliberately loud, speaking to his subordinates.

"Tim – watch out for those back windows."

Shivering with fear, they dressed, their minds racing.

Moments later, the questioning began. As his

Wife sat quietly crying to herself, the Detective-Sergeant, whose name was Hammond, interrogated him endlessly about matters that he had thought were part of the ugly past. Now, in the shape of this human bulldog, they were well and truly resurrected and barking their head off at him. With all the paperwork in their hands, it was an open and shut case, there was little he could say in response. Like many people, he had thought of fraud as *real* criminal activity, stealing from old people, robbing computer systems of thousands, Estate agents conning customers, solicitors robbing client accounts. For most people, exaggerating their income on a mortgage or loan application is not fraud, but the facts are that it is. Fraud is misrepresentation and pecuniary advantage by deception, not just the obvious and lurid examples seen every week in the *News of the World.*

Unfortunately, naivety is not an excuse for criminal behaviour, and he was charged to appear in Crown Court with all the attendant baggage that goes with it.

"I look around me, I see luxury," said Hammond, his personal outrage building up his satisfaction in nailing this nasty crime to the floor. He looked at the woman, who was still quietly crying, her face contorted with misery and disbelief.

"You've made a mess, and you'll just have to wipe your mouths," said Hammond, the nearest he could get to showing sympathy.

They carted him off to the cells, where he spent a miserable few hours, not knowing that this was his future, this drab cold place of heartlessness and despair, a place where human warmth was a thing of memory.

Luckily for him, his brother-in-law was able to provide bail, and free him for the time being, at least until his trial. Till then, life once again took on a nightmare quality. Coming so soon after the awful events of just a few months ago, it began to seem to both of them that suicide was the only option. As the days went by however, they realised they were still somehow surviving, even if every day was a painful one, and they resolved to see it all through as best they could.

The signs from the solicitor were encouraging. He seemed to think that a custodial sentence was extremely unlikely, given all the circumstances in mitigation, which gave a light of hope, but somehow the big black cloud which had hovered over them for a year now was still there, tangible as ever.

The days were just dates on the calendar now; life had lost any resemblance to the world of pleasure and laughter, of security and well being.

How long could they exist like this?

It wasn't long before they had Parker and Amco under surveillance. In no time at all, they established that a network of petty villains was operating under the auspices of Amco. Using mobile phones as their communications, and cryptic messages from 'Leo', a series of instructions was going out to these Jimbo's on an almost hourly basis.

"It works like this," said the Chief, as he and Susan sat facing the rest of the team, "From Susan's investigations and what we could squeeze out of Jimbo, we can see a pattern. Parker's cronies are given collection points for the cards, cheque books etc, the message is by mobile phone, the codename Leo is followed by 'Go'. When the stuff is successfully gathered, the phone call is made in reverse using the same words. The next stage is getting the cash. Again, Parker expects to hear within the hour from the Jimbo that the cash has been collected. A phone call is made – 'Leo, sorted', confirming collection. Jimbo passes the cash onto yet another of his kind, and this time, the money is paid into a dodgy account to be siphoned off at leisure".

"But how does Parker get the stuff in the first place?" asked McKay. The Chief turned to Susan.

"I traced the Internet messages involving Leo," she said, "The other party is called 'Aries'……….," she paused, as a ripple of laughter went round the room.

Susan smiled.

"Yes, very 60's, astrology and all that," she said, anxious to get on with the facts, "The messages between Aries and Leo make it clear that Parker – alias Leo – is just a fall guy, ultimately. Parker is just a small time hoodlum with a merry band of men whose business is mainly loan-sharking, but they're game for anything local that makes money".

"At other people's expense," said McKay, who had run into Parker before in his travels.

"Of course," said Susan wryly.

"Any leads on Aries?" said McKay, frowning.

"We cracked his alias the same way," said Susan, "Through Hotmail, we've nailed him as Alexander Hall, of Forum House, Wirral Road, Liverpool. His phone line gave him away, and as we speak, Tony Simmonds and some of the team are down there, pulling him now".

Right on cue, her phone rang, making the team laugh spontaneously.

"Hello Tony!" one of them shouted out.

"Is that you dear?" said another, taking the Mick out of Susan.

She tried not to laugh.

"Yes?" she said, knowing it was Tony, but not daring to say so, after all the Mickey-taking.

"No go, I'm afraid," said Simmonds, sounding breathless, "The bird has flown the nest. The place is a run-down industrial estate, the target is a unit in there, and it's been wiped out, clean, gone, nothing here at all but a mess of wires and a broken computer terminal".

Tony sounded as disappointed as Susan. Nevertheless, she put a brave face on it.

"OK Tony, don't worry, these things happen. Chummy is probably using a laptop by now. See if you can find out from the owners of the estate the who's and why's of it all".

"Will do," said Simmonds, signing off.

The team sat silently, the joking suddenly stopped. They didn't like setbacks.

"What now?" said McKay, his face earnest.

"We carry on as planned," said the Chief, breaking in confidently, dispersing the atmosphere of gloom, "We round up Parker and all the associates we can......"

"But Guv," said McKay, interrupting the Chief in full flight, "It can't possibly be just down to Parker and that tin-pot bunch, it surely goes much wider than that, for God's sake!"

The Chief looked at the Scotsman patiently.

"I know that too, Dave," he said patiently. "If you'd let me finish, what I was about to say, was that from there, we can piece together how this thing works on a grander scale. I'll bet that Parker's little operation is a sample version of what we can expect throughout the whole rotten apple".

McKay groaned, clutching his hand to his face at his faux pas. He felt a little silly now, and the team responded with fits of laughter.

"You can't win them all Dave," said the Chief, his face full of mischief.

"OK Guv, banged to rights," said McKay sheepishly, as the team broke into laughter again at his discomfort.

12

The morning began with an unaccustomed thunderous sound that seemed to shake the whole building. As his mind struggled to consciousness, the nightmare returned. He was a prisoner.

A single stark light bulb protruding from the grimy ceiling suddenly came to life, causing his companions in the cell to curse and mutter darkly about 'screws' with a few adjectives thrown in.

"Got some burn, mate?" growled one of his cellmates, a black man who hadn't shaved in a long time, his fingernails black and ragged.

"No" he said, daring not to say "Sorry". He instinctively knew that it would be suicide to show weakness in this place of jackals. He turned his head away to avoid seeing the third man squat over a pot to pass the piece of dope he had stashed there from a visit earlier that day.

Outside, in the corridors of this dismal place, he could hear a horde of feet trampling their way down the winding stairs to collect their breakfast, a football crowd noise of epic proportions echoing in the high ceiling of cell block C.

The noise suddenly magnified as the heavy steel door of the cell was thrown open and a voice full of authoritative menace barked "Slop out!" Stirring themselves, the three men pulled together their shabby clothes and seizing their buckets of disgusting excrement and urine, they headed along the landing towards the 'slop-out' sinks, wading through a virtual river of urine to get there. The smell was unbelievable, almost a physical thing in the air, and to the uninitiated such as himself, it lent a sense of disbelief to the unreality already being experienced. Wasn't this Britain? Great Britain? This surely was the kind of conditions and treatment one expected in a tin-pot Republic, not a so-called civilised Country? And yet the proof was there before the eyes, nose, and ears.

"Fucking watch it!" One man's voice leapt out from the general melee as slop from another man's bucket inadvertently splashed on his legs. The two men glared at each other, but the menacing figure of a warder stood suddenly behind them, a massive truncheon in one hand. He stood there for a moment, hitting the truncheon against the palm of his other hand, daring the two men to go further.

"Get on with it!" he said, his voice a mixture of authority and disgust. Disgruntled, the two men looked away from each other, and concentrated once more on the job in hand.

As the wretched figures splashed their foul muck down the

overflowing sinks, a few brave souls attempted the use of the
barely useable toilets, where in almost full visibility, they strained and passed as best they could while hundreds of eyes fell upon them, some waiting impatiently for their own turn at this ugly treadmill.

Shuddering at such a sight, he decided to forego the pleasure and call of nature for now at least.

"You there! Move on – move on, you fucking idiot!"

Dimly, he realised that the officer with the wild eyes was glaring at him. Shivering inwardly with horror, he quickly lowered his eyes, and emptied his disgusting mess on top of the other muck in the sink.

The ghastly ritual of slop-out over, he headed back to the cell, where he and his unsolicited companions collected their battered blue plastic plates and utensils which were hand-me-downs from previous occupants, scarred with the remnants of yesterday's battles.

Down and down the repeated series of metal staircases they went, enduring the curses and insults from the Prison Officers who stood like Gestapo as they passed. Finally, they reached the weary wooden tables that held their first meal of the day, a greasy slice of bacon with a sickly egg thrown in disarray upon a rock-hard slice of fried bread. Somehow, even the colours of the food were wrong, as if nothing in this place had anything to do with nature.

"Give us that, you thieving bastard!" A fight had started at the queue, as the pale-faced young man made grab at the plate of the man next to him, who had presumably stolen his breakfast.

"You slag!" he roared, thumping the other man, who went down on the floor, the food splashing all over the other men nearby. A whistle sounded, and a thunderous herd of prison officers charged into the passageway, knocking down all who stood in their path. With fierce faces and hateful eyes, they bore down quickly upon the pale-faced man, kicking him to the floor, stamping on him, wildly cursing and shouting, as if in some tribal ritual.

Meanwhile, other officers herded the rest of the men back to their cells. Only the lucky ones were able to retrieve some breakfast before being rounded up. He wasn't one of them, but he had no appetite for the grim-looking food in any case.

Back in the cell, the clamour outside gradually died down, punctuated by a series of loud bangs as the doors were forcibly thrown shut, giving meaning to the term 'Banged up'.

Trying to ignore the chomping and slurping animal sounds from his cellmates, his bewildered mind tried to retrace the steps of yesterday, a day to live in his personal infamy, sent to jail.

Southwark is a cold and ugly place at the best of times, he thought. A place where everything seems old and grey, dog shit lines the streets, people in shabby clothes with weary faces patrol the avenues languidly, as if there is no purpose to anything anymore.

There, in that unwelcoming part of the City, they have built a modern Courthouse to disguise their medieval ways, and by the circumstances and motivations which guided and misled him, he found himself there of all places, he who wished to find respectability above all else.

"Five years" the Judge had said, his icy eyes betraying no hint of humanity or warmth as he delivered the words of darkness to the silent and subdued figure in the dock. Stunned, they had led him away down to the cells, his brain spinning, his thoughts of his Wife and children, their pain, their terror at this outcome.

Right up until this day, his solicitor had constantly reassured him that a custodial sentence was out of the question.

"You will not lose your liberty" were the solicitor's last words to him, but somehow he still had gone there in terror, for his own instincts were telling him something different, that the world was going to be changed for him forever from this day.

He had hoped it was paranoia, nothing else, but his instincts had not been deceiving him, here he was, on his way to prison for five years.

All that day he had spent in Southwark, till finally he was taken with the rest of the days catch, and put on a bus for Brixton, that famous dark citadel of iniquity. In the bus were a motley crew, with a large contingent of the black population. Some of them who were obviously experienced in these matters covered up their sorrows with a mixture of curses and bravado.

"Lifed off!" yelled a colourful Rasta man, grinning madly as if it was a badge of honour instead of a death sentence.

"Result!" shouted another, obviously relieved that his sentence was not more than he expected.

Among these vociferous few were dotted a cross-section of humanity, the old, the young, the middle-aged, of all creeds and classes, handcuffed to the rails of the bus in random selection, stuck with each other.

As the bus passed through the Elephant and Castle, it seemed incongruous to see people strolling along the bright lights of the shopping mall, browsing for their Christmas presents with only a few weeks left. To him, it seemed like sights and sounds from another world, a world that was now firmly closed to him.

Tears filled his eyes as he thought of his Wife waiting alone at home. By now she must know his fate, and she must feel more alone now than she had ever felt before. Her past had been unhappy, and he had always set out to chase her unhappiness away, but the strong desire to do that had in fact ended with him presenting her with yet more unhappiness.

Now, as he once more took in his new surroundings, a wrenching fist of despair gripped his heart as he realised that all this had set in motion events that time could never reverse.

13

"So this is Alexander Hall," said Susan, fascinated, as she studied a passport photograph.

"Hardly," said the Chief, his expression cynical, "This passport is out of the 'Day of the Jackals' manual for a start," he said, deflating her somewhat. Even without checking the facts, he was right, she decided, disgusted with own naivety.

"True," she said, looking at the face with new eyes. It showed a rather full-faced man who looked like a foreigner, someone with ethnic origins, a white East European perhaps. But who was 'Alexander Hall'?

Simmonds had uncovered links to a UK bank, and from there, the trail vanished via the bank account and fake passport into an offshore conundrum, companies and trusts and obscure banks which would take ages, if ever, to unravel. It was a dead end, temporary or otherwise.

Similarly, though Parker alias Leo, had been successfully apprehended, his operations closed down, Parker could tell them little more than they already knew. Parker knew he was in deep, and would have happily spilled any beans he could, but his only real substantive contact was with Aries, alias Alexander Hall.

The Chief and Susan sat at the same desk, just staring wearily in silence at each other.

"Where do we go from here?" Susan asked finally, breaking the long silence, "It's all going in a circle leading right back to where we started," she said, slumping into her chair.

The Chief smiled, and placed his hand on top of hers comfortingly.

"Don't be disheartened," he said, "We must expect these obstacles, you should know that. Remember the Markham investigation?"

Susan brightened.

"We thought we'd never see an end to that one," she said, smiling nostalgically at the memory of the case involving large sums of money and a missing MP.

"We turned him up in the end though, didn't we?" said the Chief, gently easing her momentary lapse into depression away.

"Yes we did," she said, sitting up again, her tension easing away.

"You see," he said, in a positive, fatherly voice, "The circle might seem closed for now, but all we have to do to widen the circle, widen the search, and we'll eventually find what we're looking for".

Susan looked at him with admiration.

"I'm lucky to have you around" she said, reaching forward and kissing him lightly on the cheek.

The Chief said nothing, though he noticed she had tears in her eyes as she left the room.

14

He was one year into his sentence when he received the letter he had dreaded.

"This is a difficult letter to write", the words said, "but I have to tell you that our Marriage is ended. I have met someone else, so please do not try and contact the children or I, for we are trying to begin a new life away from all this trouble. I know despite the way things have turned out, you did your utmost for us, and I know you will not be happy with this news, but in time, you will realise that it is the best for all of us. I am sorry to break this news to you in such difficult circumstances, but I'm sure you understand that were was no easy way. Do take care of yourself. In time, you will begin life again, and you must do so positively, if you can......"

He couldn't read anymore, his eyes were full of tears, a knot in his stomach, his throat dry. He could hardly believe the awfulness of the news. His Wife had met someone else! Someone who could offer her the security and laughter that she had never felt sure of with him, she was beginning a new life. Not only was their Marriage over, she asked him to not contact her again, as she was moving away, for the sake of the children too, she argued, they must be protected from what had happened to their Father, it must not blight their life!

Shattered inside, suicidal thoughts filled his mind. He looked again at the bottom of the page.

"Goodbye" was all it said. Almost reluctantly, he looked again at the details in the letter, his mind numb, a sense of unreality dulling his pain.

His Wife had not visited nor written to him for two months, despite his agonising letters. Now she was confessing that she had never read those letters, for she already knew where her future lay, and it was no longer to be with him, she had already begun divorce proceedings.

Though his instincts had warned him this was possible, it was still a shattering blow.

For the first few weeks he drifted aimlessly, numb with shock and disbelief, waking each morning with this new horror to face, and in the situation he was, unable to discuss it with anyone nor find any way of erasing the pain, even temporarily.

They had been through so much together, now he was never to see her again. Worse still, she now loved someone else, a shadowy figure he knew nothing of. His sense of identity had been so wrapped up in her and their children that with prison as an environment as well, he now felt that he had no identity at all, that he didn't really exist as a person. He prayed each night to not wake up the next morning.

And yet, the pain wouldn't go away. Each day would begin with the thunderous noise and the clinging smell of urine and worse, though he had become as accustomed to that as anyone can after a while. But to wake each day and remind himself that his Wife and Family were lost to him brought him emotionally to his knees, thoughts of suicide were a daily part of the diet.

Yet, by the very nature of this place he found himself in, he could show none of this, for any sign of weakness in those grim places is the first step to being a victim of the parasites and vermin who are vigilantly seeking such signs. Like true jackals, they prefer a soft target, an easy prey whose bones they can lick clean.

Knowing this only too well, he kept himself to himself. Luckily enough, he now was totally alone in this tiny space, and he walked around and around, normal on the outside, but crippled and deformed inside, the pain and rejection and loneliness driving him almost insane. It was so difficult to absorb. The woman he had loved for so long, the love of his life, she was gone forever. If she had died that would have been bad enough, but no, she was alive and living with someone else, another man was bringing up his children, it was as if he was the one who was dead, who had no place in this World.

For another three years, the pain still crushed him, it always would when he thought of her, for the rest of his life she would haunt him, not just her, the woman herself, but all she represented, their home, their children, their family life. But now, in tandem with this pain, there was a new obsession, almost rising as a defence mechanism in response to the need to find a purpose to live, an excuse to carry on.

His thoughts began to turn to bitterness against the forces that had sent him here, notwithstanding his own part in his downfall. All around him he could see injustice, and for the first time in his life, he understood that the establishment is about protection and appearance and expediency, never justice, just law, randomly distributed.

This callous disregard for humanity fired in him a

determination to rock the boat, to seek revenge, as well as demanding what seemed to him now was his rightful place at the table. He excused his new level of immorality by saying to himself that he owed nothing to society, and he had nothing to lose by opposing it.

Whatever frauds he had committed, they had been committed at first in innocence, then later in desperation, they were not calculating nor were they criminally motivated. His reward for full co-operation with the authorities had been 5 years of his life taken away, where others, luckier and more evil than he had received practically nothing at all. The blatant unfairness of it all was too much for his already despairing mind, and it tipped him over the edge.

He could have gone all the way, but for an incident in the exercise yard one day. For some reason unknown to him, he had made an enemy. Black Jock was gunning for him, every time they ran into each other on the landing, Black Jock would have a go at him, threatening dire consequences if he didn't hand over his 'burn' – prison slang for tobacco – immediately. Black Jock, a huge intimidating, loud individual, did this with all likely targets on the landing. Being a classic bully, he picked on those whom he decided were weak, or frightened people.

"Right, you little shit. Are you ready to cough up?" he said menacingly, his broad Glaswegian accent an ugly scar on the English language.

He knew that Black Jock had picked on him because he was quiet and unassuming, but Black

Jock was about to find out he had made a mistake. Quietness does not always equal timidity.

"Piss off, you ugly bastard!" he said, his voice full of venom, " or I'll shove those rotten teeth of yours down your throat and out your arsehole!" That said, knowing the eyes of the warders were looking elsewhere, he smashed Black Jock in the face, knocking him back against the rail of the landing.

Black Jock was hurt more by the shock than the punch, and dazed, he slouched away, a glare of hatred in his eyes. But Jock was not one to take up a challenge. Like all bullies, he preferred an easy target. Nevertheless, he made up his mind to get revenge, for the landing was alight with the story of Black Jock's rebuff, and his male pride and credibility had been badly stung.

It happened in the yard. Circle after circle, the squalid crowds turned, then there was a sudden commotion. Black Jock and one of his sycophants leapt forward towards him, razored brushes in hand, ready to slash his face.

"You're for it, you Nonse!" Black Jock shouted in triumph.

Suddenly, a stranger, an older man, jumped between the two attackers before they could reach their target.

"No you don't!" he said, his voice of a man of action. Grabbing the heads of both men at once, the grey-haired man banged their heads together so hard that there was an audible crack, which echoed like the shot of a gun round the yard.

As the two men fell unconscious to the ground,

the warders, late as ever when there was real action, strolled over gently, took the two men away, and another two of their number quietly took the grey-haired man by the arms, and led him inside. The whole thing was softly-softly, so as to not disturb the uneasy equilibrium of the tense crowd in the yard. One wrong move could end in riot and disaster, and no one knew that better than the warders, who had seen it happen often enough.

As the grey-haired man was being led away, the man he had saved looked at him, almost in wonder. A stranger had saved him at his own expense. Who was this man? As they led him off to the block, the two men looked each other in the eye.

An unspoken bond was created that day. Now he may have made only one friend in this friendless place, but his new-found friendship was the kind that everyone cherishes, a once in a lifetime meeting of chance. Over the coming months, they quietly got to know one another, being careful not to advertise the fact, for both men were cautious and private by nature.

Luckily enough, there was an empty bunk in his cell, and he prevailed upon the grey-haired man to request a move there, using the other man in the cell as a diversionary excuse to avoid connecting each other. Although there was still a third man in the cell, the man slept most of the day, and they could talk, albeit in whispered tones.

The older man listened sadly as he heard of his new friend's heartaches, especially the recent loss of his Wife, his soul mate.

As, in turn, the other man learned about his grey-haired friend's terrible journey, he realised that here was a person whose troubles and heartache easily exceeded his own. Feeling guilty, his own series of complaints seemed trivial next to his friend's. All his life, he had confided so little to anyone, but this man was different. In the trenches of despair, they had forged a friendship and a bond for life.

Now, they began to share their pain, their thoughts of what kind of future could possibly await them when they finally left these halls of anguish. The younger man's bitterness and hatred of society began to manifest itself in words, for now that he had someone who was interested in what he thought and felt, someone who listened to what he said with sympathy and understanding.

One dark night in the cell, in one of those rare moments of sharing, yet again, his friend sat in silence as the other man's pain forced itself into the familiar words of anger.

"So they thought what I did was fraud, did they? I'll show them what fraud *really* is!" he said over and over out loud, seething inside as the ghostly lights out in the prison yard shone through the bars of his cell, and the lonely howls and cries from the wounded prisoners echoed throughout the long night.

He knew he had one ally he could count on, and with his friend's help, he began to make his plans with a vengeance.

In their efforts to widen the circle, the Chief and his team were comparing notes.

"As I see it," said the Chief, "We have two alternative ways of monitoring the fraud. Both of them rely on Susan, who is the real computer and ATM expert. Using her knowledge of banking systems, and tying it into unusual activity, we should be able to spot pockets of withdrawals, and from there physically follow where and how the money is dispersed, more or less typical fraud spadework".

Walker snorted aloud.

"Bloody big spadework!" he remarked, in some indignation.

McKay glared at him.

"OK, there's a lot to cover," said the Chief, "But we can do it, and we will do it – if anybody here wants out, they only have to say so. If you think the job's too big for you, then get out now, before you get in the way of those who want to do it".

He looked round the room, his eyes deliberately not fastening on Walker till last. Walker sat there sullenly, looking at his feet, saying nothing.

After a few moments of silence, McKay spoke.

"We're with you all right, Guv," he said quietly, still glaring fiercely at Walker. He would have words with him later, he thought.

The Chief eased off, his voice calm again.

"Good," he said, finality in his voice, "As I was saying, the first element in our work is good old-fashioned surveillance, based on the information that Susan can supply about dubious accounts and activity. The second is the Internet link itself, and I'll let Susan tell you about that".

The Chief sat down, nodding respectfully to Susan, who was dressed in a prim and very official-looking blue suit. The Chief noted with pleasure the flash of white petticoat and beautiful thighs as Susan uncrossed her legs next to him.

"As you know," she said, "The real link between Parker and Hall was e-mail on the Internet. We have a full list of all the communications between them. Given that they used the names Leo and Aries, I thought it might be reasonable to see if there were any other star signs similarly in use. I didn't really expect to find a great deal, for I thought that the people we were dealing with here were perhaps too sophisticated to repeat the same operation every time, but I was wrong. I found every star sign in use, and they were all linked to Aries, alias Alexander Hall".

Susan paused to take a sip of water.

"For instance, there's one here," she said, holding up a piece of paper before reading from it aloud –

"From: aries@sitemail.com

To: libra@hotmail.com

Message: '*you take the high road*' – I'll let you guess what the reply was from Libra," said Susan, smiling as the team chorused at her in unison. As soon as the laughter died down, she became serious again.

"The point is, these messages tally with the kind of traffic we saw between Aries and Leo. They also match up with the other star signs identified – a definite and very clear pattern, wouldn't you say?" Susan looked quizzically at the team.

"That's his first real big mistake," muttered McKay out loud.

Susan smiled at him, then continued.

"Yes, I was pleased to be wrong on this occasion Dave. By the way, Alexander Hall is *still* current, still linking messages with Taurus, Sagittarius, Scorpio, Pisces, and the rest of the gang. He operates now from offshore, but we still think we can put a trace on him eventually. We're trying anyway, it just takes longer, that's all. The point is, we can watch the traffic this way too, as most of the e-mail should link to addresses we can centre in on as soon as they're identified".

Susan motioned to the Chief that she was finished. He gave her a friendly but business-like smile as she sat down, revealing more of her thighs than she would have liked, but pleasing him in the process.

"Thanks Susan," he said appreciatively for more reason than one, "OK team, I'll keep you briefed fully as we go on, but for now, you all have your tasks, you know what to do, Good luck".

With that, the Chief folded his papers and sat down, as the team began to disperse and break into a babble of conversation. Susan was still sitting there, fussing with unnecessarily with her files. He noticed her discomfort.

"What is it Susan?" he asked, as the room emptied, leaving them alone.

She looked at him almost nervously.

"Look Chief," she said, "Forgive me for bringing this up. I don't know how to say it, but I've noticed you looking at me in a certain way, and it's making me uncomfortable".

He squirmed in his seat, surprised by her candour.

"I'm sorry if I've made you feel uncomfortable. It's just that you're a very beautiful woman, and I don't mean just your looks," he said awkwardly and almost shy, though he still looked her straight in the eyes as he spoke.

She looked at the ground, blushing, but then she pulled herself together, and faced him, her features hard, her mouth tight and determined.

"I don't need all this – you don't need all this," she said, as gently as she could in the circumstances. "You're a happily married man, and we work together – two terribly wrong combinations in one package".

"I don't know about happily-married," he said wearily, "But I take your point, you don't need the hassle. I didn't mean it that way, it's just that I appreciate you, and all that you are".

Susan smiled sadly at him, her eyes haunted.

"I just want to get on with my job," she said, gripping her hands together so tightly that the knuckles were showing white.

"I understand – point taken," said the Chief, resignation in his voice, "Don't let it upset you, we can still work together, I won't sexually harass you anymore".

Susan could see how embarrassed he was. She wrung her hands again, torn between silence and truth.

"I've only just got over a difficult relationship," she explained, biting her lip at the confession, "I've only just managed to close the door on it".

He placed one finger gently on her lips.

"Enough said," he almost whispered to her. He picked up his papers and walked from the room.

As he headed for his car, he thought of Susan, sitting there alone in that room, thinking God knows what of him. Then he thought of Jane, waiting at home alone too, as she had been so many times in their life together. What on earth was he thinking of? Was lusting after another woman the answer to his discontent? Was it Jane's fault he was unfulfilled? Of course not!

He decided he must behave himself in future, fantasy or not, it was dangerous stuff. Nevertheless, as his car roared off impatiently into the night, a thought sprang involuntarily into his mind.

'As one door closes, another opens'.

It was indeed a cold night. He shivered, and drove to Jane and the warm comforts of home as fast as he could.

16

The weather was turning warmer now, not
clement as such, but the storms of the winter months
were largely over. As the bus turned off from the
desolate road into Ford open prison, he wearily
assessed his new home. As expected, the reception
area, the public face of the prison system was the
best part to be seen, a reasonably modern brick
building with impeccably clean and tidy rooms, neat
tables, and comfortable chairs, the public face.

Inside the perimeter however, it was a different
story. The bleak huts and drab buildings even in
themselves belied the ghastly interior where cracked
and weary walls housed the dust-filled beds which
had seen so many, so very many occupants, couched
so many woes in their dusty faded green garments.

The stained toilets and tired baths streaked with
black where the porcelain had long gone stood in
silent mockery to public perceptions of cleanliness
and order, all was appearance to the public, the
visitors, for the inmates who had no name, no status,
no humanity, it did not matter. The outer perception
of TV's in every room was belied by the solitary
television set which stood high on the wall of a
bleak concrete building where the phantom pictures
and inaudible sound echoed ghostly through the
deserted wooden chairs.

These were lessons he took in well. winter after
winter and summer after summer he strode the
lonely perimeter road during the light and the dark
hours while the wind howled and moaned, and the
cold Winter rain poured mercilessly upon him, the

heat of the Sun burned his emancipated body, but still he did not feel either, nor did he care. His soul was dead, but his spirit was not broken, for he had a purpose.

Yet another winter and summer came, and still he slogged along these paths, keeping himself to himself, making no friends, but at the same time cultivating a few useful contacts for future reference.

It had been so long. His Family was almost a distant memory, a dream to him now, an impossible possibility. It was almost as if someone else had been married to his Wife, not him, not this creature of stone whose face was so implacably set against the World and himself. He had become an automaton, a person without feelings, a person without real hope, a danger to everyone including his own soul.

Yet another winter came, and as he stood one particular dark night on the perimeter road listening to the wind howling like a wild beast, and watching the warm glowing lights of the reception area in the distance, real life so near, yet so closed to him, he realised how far he had come from the person he once was. He had reached a new plateau, he saw that he was experiencing the meaning of ultimate loneliness. Finally, with yet another long and desperate summer behind him, one autumn he was free.

17

"There's something bothering me," said the Chief, frowning at Susan, who was preoccupied at her computer.

"Yes?" she said, her mind only half listening.

"It's this business of star signs as codenames," he said. The Chief was talking aloud to himself as much as anyone.

Susan stopped what she was doing, and swivelled around in her chair to face the Chief.

"What about the codenames?" she said, interested now.

"How many are there?" asked the Chief, his eyes still distant.

"What – codenames?" said Susan, sounding puzzled.

The Chief sprang into focus, sitting upright in his seat, no longer slouching.

"No, star signs. How many star signs are there?" he said, almost impatient with her.

"Twelve, I think". Susan frowned and thought for a moment, "Yes, definitely twelve,"

The Chief shook his head decisively.

"That's not enough," he said, "Even what we've seen so far – a series of group frauds bound together by an overseeing body – must involve more than twelve criminal gangs. And don't forget, we may only be seeing the tip of the iceberg."

Susan suddenly looked serious.

"You're right," she said, why didn't I notice that before?"

He smiled at her, almost sadly.

"It's not your fault, we were supposed to believe that twelve was the limit. It was a useful diversion to our friend, he's playing games with us. He knows that we would stumble on to that fact eventually, but it's like a fence, it's a preconception that delays and obscures our free thinking." The Chief was nodding his head, almost in admiration at his quarry's ingenuity.

"So that whole Internet game was just to deceive us?" said Susan, unsure of anything now.

"No, not quite," said the Chief, "It was still the method of communication between them, but it does warn us that we make assumptions at our peril. The real clue that made me think about it was, why did they use Aries – itself a star sign – as the central contact? Surely it would have been sensible to use a tangential image, like the sun, for instance."

"Yes, that would have left all twelve star signs free for use," said Susan. "So, I suppose that we have to assume different codenames are being used on the Internet. And the central communication points must be different too, for there's nothing else linked to Aries, as far as I can see. The trouble is, without a clue to go on, and the web being so vast, it's like looking for a needle in a haystack."

The Chief frowned again.

"Well, let's try not to assume anything here. The Internet might not be used in this way again – anything's possible. Let's keep an open mind if we can."

Susan looked deflated.

"So all that work was just a red herring," she said, dejectedly.

"No, of course not," said the Chief, "How can you say that? What you discovered on the Internet gave us our first real insight into how much of this fraud is operating. It also gave us our first successes in what's bound to be a long investigation."

He looked at her, his eyes warm and admiring.

"You're doing a great job," he said, sincerely.

"Do you really think so?" Susan sounded almost like a little girl being praised by her Daddy.

"Of course!" the Chief said, emphatically, "You – and all of the team – have made a good start, but don't forget there's a long way to go."

Susan came back to earth with a bump.

"We're only beginning at the beginning," she said, sounding Churchillian.

18

The system had begun simply enough. His first step was to create a new identity, or rather a series of identities. He scoured the electoral rolls in a chosen area, and found a number of names, each listed as belonging to a respectable address over a number of years previously. But they had the added attraction of having left that address before October when the electoral roll was due to be taken again. This left him free to use this name directly from the same address by simply adding it to the electoral roll himself. In some cases, where he deemed it advisable or desirable, he then transplanted these names onto new addresses that were in fact, empty houses.

From there, he applied for bank accounts in these names, having the mail redirected to an accommodation address which he himself controlled, citing his 'names' as mere customers, each with 'dummy' addresses and listed payments by cash or postal order for the services given. This supplied the necessary alibi should anything go wrong at this stage. When required to produce documents proving identity and home ownership, it was a simple matter to superimpose such details on an original document, sending merely a photocopy to the bank concerned.

He could, in some cases, even produce original documents by writing to companies concerned directly from these addresses. Even supplying driver licences and NHS cards was not a problem, either directly himself or via the numerous dubious contacts he had made in recent years.

As his friend was still trapped in Welling prison, with another few months to serve, he had to do most of the legwork himself. Nevertheless, they would be re-united again soon. For now, they kept in touch by hidden messages. This was an essential contact, for having been in prison so much longer, his friend could supply many useful sources.

Their bond remained as strong as ever, for they shared a zealous enthusiasm to pay society back, but also, they wished to gain power. They both knew from their observations of life at both ends of the scale, that power emanates from money, and they intended to gain both as soon as possible.

Occasionally, he would appear in person at a bank, producing all relevant documents and thereby gaining a precious account, but for the most part, he found that it could mainly be done by post, thereby saving themselves from identification problems should anything go wrong with the application.

Within a few weeks, there existed a series of bank accounts and identities that were ready to seek credit from the gullible financial institutions that relied on such business. Each institution was tested and vetted by a series of applications that each contained trial answers to the maze of questions that were part of the procedure adopted by each company. These questions attempted to give the impression that every facet of the applicant's life was being scrutinised, but they were, in effect, a smokescreen, designed to disguise the fact that the institutions could check hardly anything about an individual at all.

Only the simple statement of electoral roll and any other information supplied from the individual's past involvement with the institutions themselves could in reality be checked. Other than by checking that the phone numbers given on these applications were genuine, there was actually little that the security systems of these institutions could achieve. Credit scoring could only work if the applicant was telling the truth, it was a game of bluff.

The trouble was, such systems were an open book to someone like him, but still, he did his homework, and checked the facts that were actually being monitored by a game of pocket battleship. Slowly, application by application, he built up a picture of the systems he was operating against. Now he was ready to do battle in earnest.

Having found suitable addresses and applicants, and applied in their names, all he had then to do was retrieve the mail that would carry not only replies, but hopefully cheques, cards, and all necessary data to operate them. This was a fairly simple task.

First of all, he had the mail forwarded from each address to his own office. The only way he was visible was at the headquarters, an office in a rundown business estate he ran an accommodation address facility. Among the genuine customers were sprinkled his own 'customers', names and addresses of people who didn't exist. As far as any investigating authority was concerned, he was forwarding the mail for these 'customers' to a series of addresses. Usually, it was a group of flats within a communal front door where any number of people had access to the mail, and the transient nature of its occupants were such that pinning any one person down to anything was virtually impossible. He kept diligent records to support this hypothesis should it ever prove necessary to invoke a suitable alibi.

In reality of course, he opened the mail himself, placing cheques etc. into the appropriate accounts, accepting cards and PIN numbers to enable them to draw cash from these accounts on a daily and weekly basis. He did this by using ATM machines that had the advantage of keeping them incognito. It was a lot of work, but whatever the work involved, it was proving to be very profitable.

Keeping one identity free from all this activity, the plan included the opening of an offshore account using the false name, giving it a business identity. Using another series of names that were also free of fraudulent credit activity, they deposited small sums of cash in each one on a weekly basis, finally filtering the money out to the offshore account on a gradual and steady scale, so as not to attract undue attention.

From small acorns............within six months of the system being up and running, its income was already in excess of £500,000. With this cash in hand, it was time to use this money to upgrade the system, add sophistication, extend the network.

He received a major boost to his morale, when news came to him of his friend's release from Welling after so many lost years. He was sad not to meet his friend at the gate, but given the plans they had made, they both knew it would be extremely unwise to be seen together at any time.

Through his friend and Lieutenant – they

jokingly referred to each other as Commander and Lieutenant – and his many contacts from that sad place of lost humanity, meetings were set up with key criminal personnel in every major city or town, putting a proposal to them which was hard to resist.

One such meeting was in the Midlands. Through a mutual acquaintance, the Lieutenant arranged to meet a local villain called Fraser, whose normal operations included prostitution and extortion. The pre-requisite for this small-time hoodlum, was that he was the local leading light of the gangsters, and led a fairly large, if ramshackle operation, which included many petty thieves and street operators.

The two men met in a local pub. Fraser eyed his new contact suspiciously. The other man seemed at ease, confident but not pushy. Stepping carefully, the Lieutenant outlined the job he wanted Fraser to do.

"We have some business for you," he said, knowing that Fraser was not one to turn an opportunity of making money away. Fraser tried to look nonchalant, arrogantly taking a sip of his beer before speaking.

"Yeah?" he said, trying to sound bored.

"Here's the proposition," said the Lieutenant, ignoring any pretence of formality. "We have a method of raking in money through credit applications that needs a lot of legwork. We need an outfit like yours to collect the cash. Obviously, there's a percentage for you – a generous percentage."

The Lieutenant paused, waiting for the other man's reaction.

Fraser paused again, interested, but trying not to show it. He was fooling himself, not the other man, but the Lieutenant said nothing.

"How much cash are we talking about here?" said Fraser, finally.

"Six figures a week for an opener," said the Lieutenant, noting with glee the flicker of shock that passed across Fraser's eyes.

"What's in it for me?" he said, his greedy eyes glinting.

"As I said, a generous percentage. We can talk about that once you see the details and agree in general," said the Lieutenant. "I'm sure we can come to an arrangement that suits us both."

Fraser licked his greasy lips. He liked the idea of free collection, and perhaps he could rip off a percentage on top. To his surprise, the other man seemed to read his mind.

The Lieutenant himself knew it was time to inject some steel.

"We don't have to trust each other," he said, "We know the exact figures from the forms we fill in, and we also will know what's taken by seeing the balance of the accounts, so you can't say your receipts are less. On the other hand, you're the one who collects the cash, so We can't cut back your percentage without you knowing it." The Lieutenant smiled, knowing he had marked Fraser's card.

Fraser was thinking as fast as his brain was capable of.

"How do we know where and when to get this cash?" he said, betraying his eagerness.

"We contact each other by computer – you have computers in your office, don't you?" said the Lieutenant, knowing that they did from his background research into Fraser's organisation, if that word could be used loosely.

Fraser nodded.

"You mean e-mail?" he said, puffing with pride at his display of intellectual prowess.

"Yes, that's right, e-mail," said the Lieutenant, feigning surprise to feed Fraser's ego. "We'll give you a name and a password, and an e-mail address to contact. From that, you'll be given all the details you need to run this thing."

"What about your password?" said Fraser, still suspicious.

"Our password will be Aries," said the Lieutenant, "And yours will be Scorpio. Look out for a message from Aries in your e-mail. When you get that, we can set the ball rolling. All the details you need will come from that."

Fraser nodded, his mind still ticking over greedily.

"Do we have a deal?" said the Lieutenant, knowing the answer already. He knew that Fraser would never turn down the chance of easy money. He also knew that Fraser would ensure none of the small-time con men in his charge ripped off the system. He was ruthless as well as greedy, and his reputation for violent revenge would frighten the hardest heart. That was a necessary part of the deal.

Fraser licked his lips again.

"Sure," he said, not wishing to seem too eager. "We'll give it a go – but if you try to do us in any way, we'll get to you, mark my words." His eyes glistened, cold like a rattlesnake.

The Lieutenant was cool and relaxed in his reply.

"That cuts both ways," he said, his voice quiet but firm. Then, his voice became soft and conciliatory. "There's plenty for both of us. As long as we both behave, neither of us has anything to worry about. If anybody plays silly buggers, they're only killing the goose that laid the golden egg, aren't they?"

Fraser nodded dumbly, his male pride swollen by his threat. The deal was on.

None of the local villains who were contacted refused, for the prize was too good to be true, a flow of money which would benefit everyone involved. It was not in the interest of anyone to 'rip off' the system, for that would mean that the flow of money would immediately stop. Besides, the local villains had their own form of discipline that involved reprisals no one cared to contemplate.

In each City and Town, a series of 'cells' operated, each one completely independent in its operation, except that all the paper work, all the correspondence was forwarded on via the 'dummy' accommodation addresses to another accommodation address in London, where it was swiftly and efficiently dealt with.

All over each City and Town, a series of 'operatives' swept up and down the high streets, hoovering up money from cash machines, depositing it in accounts whose details had been previously supplied.

It was a thriving business. The system paid the 'controller' of each area, the controller paid his 'staff', everyone was happy.

By now the system could afford a safer luxury, the actual ownership of previously empty houses, along with the adoption of the names held by the last electoral roll register. As an added bonus, these 'names' claimed unemployment benefit, the operatives acting on instructions of identity, then housing benefit, always in excess of the due mortgage, making a tidy profit just in passing.

There were occasionally problems with the operatives, but the local bosses ran each cell on a ruthless basis, and minions were punished beyond the pale in retribution, thus discouraging similar minded minions from making the same mistake.

This then was the structure of the 'cells', when he learned that first the strand of a cell had been seized, then a cell itself, he simply closed down all operations. The moves against the system came as no surprise to him, it was inevitable, as he had guessed. In both cases, another cell was opened in the same area within weeks, replacing the lost income and satisfying the local bosses hunger.

The despair he himself felt inside would not be so easily satisfied.

19

The Chief had decided to go along with Susan's
wishes. For one thing, he had a soft spot for her, for
another, he had nowhere else to go. The only
information he could seize upon was the very
visible sight of local tow-rags running amok with
cash cards in the high street.

It was Susan who had identified some of these
bogus accounts, her keen eye spotting anomalies on
first one account, then with her experience of that,
more and more of these accounts which just did not
stand up to scrutiny. A basic weakness in their
system was identified as being the occupation
question. In these bogus accounts, occupation was
inevitably an accommodation address with a non-
existent employer. A quick run through *Kompass*
and other company information logs would show
the genuine from the false.

It was a more practical route into the workings of
the system, and it was a useful alternative to the
Internet connections, especially at this moment
when the trail was all but lost. The trouble was, her
eyes could not be everywhere. There were just too
many applications to be personally vetted in this
way, she was only scratching at the surface.
Nevertheless, it did give clues as to how this system
was operating, and it would certainly lead to those
who were operating it, at least on street level.

From the vast computers at headquarters, they
had for weeks now been monitoring several of these
bogus accounts, and they even had video pictures of
those who were withdrawing the cash. In typically

thorough fashion, they even had monitored the paying in system, where it was happening, where it was going to.

It was time for a test case. Finally submitting to Susan's pleas for action, the Chief decided to move in. One particular operative was targeted, and just as he withdrew £250 from a machine in the Town centre, he was swooped upon from all sides, taken before he knew what had hit him.

They were not particularly surprised when the interview revealed him as a known petty thief and drug pusher whose intelligence was at a low level.

"Can you state your name and address for the tape please," said Susan in her cold authoritative voice.

"I ain't tellin' you nuffin" said the operative, sniffling defiantly.

"Well, I'll tell you then, shall I?" said Susan, a sparkle of triumph in her blue eyes.

"You're Winston Thomas, you come from Hackney, and we know you already as a petty criminal and drug supplier".

"So if you know all that, why ask me?" said the operative, clearly rattled.

"You don't seem to know what you're involved with here Winston" said this bossy woman who was pushing him around gleefully, "This is not just the usual petty stuff that you've become accustomed to, we are talking millions here, big time".

At the sound of the word millions, Winston's black face nearly turned white. Money was something he did understand, could relate to.

"What d'ya mean?" he said, his certainty

suddenly vanished.

"I mean that you are going to go down for a very long time, my son, unless you can give, and give now!" said his female nemesis.

Despite his familiarity with the police, the operative soon cracked when these big guns came into play, and he was made aware that he was the sole spokesman at this time. He 'sang like a bird'.

Disappointingly though, he could only tell what he knew. His boss instructed him to collect the cash and pay it into the designated account, he knew no more. He didn't even know the name of his boss, he was just an underground figure 'you didn't disobey' if you valued your life. According to the operative, he knew his boss simply by the name 'Scorpio'.

One dark night, he had been accosted by 'Scorpio' and his 'associates' in a long black car, and a proposition was put to him which he couldn't refuse. Besides, the money sounded good, money for old rope. He knew enough about gangsters to realise that crossing Scorpio would not be a good idea, he had heard the same through the grapevine.

He said he didn't know anything about the accommodation address which was linked to the bogus applications, and though it was obvious he was an inveterate liar, the Chief and his assistant believed him, they could see he was desperate to reduce if possible the looming prison sentence.

The Chief and Susan compared notes afterwards, a trifle disappointed that their seizure had so far revealed so little.

"What do you think we should do now?" asked Susan, her eyes for once docile to his gaze, perhaps feeling guilty that she had pushed so hard for an arrest only to yield such modest results thus far.

"I think we have to consider taking the accommodation address" the Chief said with a serious face, pretending that he hadn't noticed her sudden acquiescence to his authority. Suddenly she was doubtful, the roles reversed.

"It seems too easy, do you really think they won't be prepared?" she said, almost hesitantly.

"They may well be" said the Chief, "But having taken their man out, we have little choice, we've played our hand in any case".

Inwardly he winced at what seemed a clumsy dig at the relative barren return in response to her calls for action, but she took no offence.

"You're right" she said, "Having gone this far, we must act, there's no choice, is there?" she added, almost wistfully, looking at the Chief eye to eye. Right at that moment, they both got it. Nothing was said, but the hooks of love tied their anchor on the spot.

Flustered, Susan averted her eyes, and fussed with her papers, trying to deny to herself and to him what had happened, she was confused, wretched, a little girl again.

He was stunned, numb, the feeling catching him unawares. He knew what he had seen, but was it his imagination? He looked pointedly at her. No, she was primly and efficiently organising her papers, he must be wrong. As he stared at her, she turned, looked at him, and blushed. He knew then he wasn't wrong. It had happened. They had fallen in love.

Somehow though, neither could manage to raise

the subject, and they both rather artificially began to talk business, plan the raid on the accommodation address without ever referring to the feelings that had flashed between them. The sub-text of the matter was that even without a proven link to the accommodation address, they decided to raid it anyway.

At office opening time, they burst into the shabby premises on a poor industrial estate and found a quiet man, seemingly surprised by the commotion. Though perturbed at first, he calmly produced all his files and books and left them to sift through, seemingly undisturbed. The books tallied perfectly, his bank account showed no unusual transactions. Satisfied as they could be, they dismissed the man from their minds as any part of this operation. The only way forward now was to check each address that he sent mail to, and that would be a time-consuming business.

Weeks later, they had identified the dubious addresses, but there was no one to be seized there, only a series of empty flats and houses, yielding nothing but the identity of the name attached there.

Taking the logical steps backward, the team traced first the linked 'dumping' accounts, then the offshore accounts to which they were attached. With the co-operation of the off shore authorities, they assembled the details of the beneficial owners of these companies. Inevitably, they were transparently false names linked to a series of accommodation addresses that again led nowhere. Someone seemed to be playing games with them, but who?"

"So who's the brains behind all this?" said the

Chief, thinking aloud.

"Well, it's certainly not Winston!" said Susan with a wry smile.

"And how does the operation work?" the wheels were churning in the Chief's mind.

"As we've seen, the accommodation address stands up, yet there must be a point of collection - can it really be the bogus addresses themselves? Isn't that too obvious? The cover is certainly there, so many people of a transient nature move in and out from week to week".

Frowning deeply, Susan pursued her own thoughts.

"The only real way is to keep track of each person who comes in and out and catch them in the act". As she spoke, the Chief noticed how her eyes softened as she looked directly at him.

"Either that or leave them alone and follow the mail trail" he said, half of his mind on her ("God, what great legs!" he thought, as a glimpse of soft white thigh became tantalisingly visible beneath her rather formal secretarial skirt).

"The Post Office would help us on that one" Susan said, trying to ignore his lustful stare.

"Yes, but where would it lead? That's the question" said the Chief, serious now, business as usual.

"Well it has to be one or the other," said Susan, reverting to her more customary 'bossy' role.

In the end they decided to try the 'trailing' method first, if only to eliminate it from their enquiries. Their first target was a man called Danny, a ne'er do well petty thief who had ducked and dived all his miserable life, and who was now one of the 'operatives' working the system for all it was worth. On one day alone, they watched and monitored his transactions as he withdrew no less than £2,500 from various cash machines across the City. Then he visited a stream of banks, depositing amounts of no more than £500 in each one. Following all this activity, he went back to the squat where he lived, and which was totally unconnected to the addresses linked via the fraudulent transactions he had just made. Nevertheless, they watched him night and day, but at no time did he visit any of the fraudulent addresses. They decided to postpone Danny's demise till another time.

Next, they targeted a number of the fraudulent addresses themselves. Watching and photographing all occupants as they came and went, and surveying their every move throughout every day, they came to the conclusion that no-one was living there who was part of the system, they were all quite innocent, at least on the face of it. That left the accommodations addresses.

The Post Office had confirmed details of the forwarding arrangements that were in place, and as expected, these details showed that in each case of fraudulent addresses, the mail was being sent to a particular accommodation address in the City, calling itself
F.M.S. (Fast Mail Services).

A raid on F.M.S. proved futile. As before, the books tallied perfectly. It was hardly the fault of the proprietor - a meek man with impeccable credentials - that some of his customers were dubious to say the

84

least. Yet the mail he sent on was being received - how was this possible? Their surveillance had revealed nothing. The only answer was to indeed follow the mail itself.

With the co-operation of the Post Office, they arranged that a stringent check would be kept on the flow of mail to the examples they chose of fraudulent addresses. Mail sent out from financial institutions to their 'dubious' clients was marked with a special pen whose markings showed themselves only under ultra-violet light. This would prove once and for all what was happening to the mail.

Decoy mail was sent out, and for weeks afterwards, they monitored its every movement, through the dummy address, to the accommodation address, then to the stipulated forwarding address where it landed on the shabby carpet. To the enormous disappointment of the Task Force, no one collected it. Weeks later, it was still lying there on the dank hallway of the weary house.

"I don't understand it," said Susan, shaking her head in exasperation, "How can they run a system where no-one collects the mail?"

"It's simple" said the Chief wearily, "He's on to us, he's sussed it even before we set it up".

They were both beginning to realise what they were up against.

20

He knew now that the game was beginning to
play for higher stakes. He also knew that this meant
'the big guns' would be called in against him, and
the arrest of Winston proved that. The instant
Winston hit the panda car, the word spread like
wildfire until it reached him, and he swiftly had
given out instructions to all concerned. The
proprietor of the accommodation address was
warned to expect visitors, and the occupants of all
connected addresses were quickly sent packing.

None of this was unexpected, he had always
realised it would be a game of cat and mouse, dog
and hare. The trick was staying one step ahead if he
could. Looking at it logically, he realised that the
connected offshore accounts also had to sacrificed,
although there was of course time to empty all
relevant bank accounts without any danger to
anyone operating them.

What would be his enemy's next move? Marked
mail would be the next option he guessed, and
throughout his whole system he instructed all
operatives in his accommodations addresses to
install a system for checking marks that would only
be seen in ultra-violet light, an obvious move, he
thought. All such mail could be sacrificed, most of
it being largely irrelevant in the short term. After
all, the organisation which sought his capture and
the closure of the system could not possibly at this
stage have a finger on the entire system, they would
only have footholds in strands of it, nothing more.
By watching the marked mail, he was himself being

given a barometer as to how well the opposition was following on his heels, and from where he was standing, he was still showing them a clean pair of heels thus far.

Also, as fast as cells were identified, new ones were being opened, so the flow of money was still increasing rapidly, despite the inroads into parts of the system. The trouble was, as he realised and expected, his would-be nemesis, the organisation and its leader, now had a quickly expanding blueprint of how the system was operating. Only a few vital clues were needed to complete the jigsaw. When that was done, it would only be a matter of time before the system as it presently stood became obsolete. Forecasting the demise of his own system caused him no heartaches, it was all part of the pattern to him. In any case, he had other plans.

21

"It's like trying to fill a bucket with a hole in it" said Susan, as she wryly watched the screens flicker endlessly with yet more fraudulent transactions which had been tracked down. And of course, yet more dubious 'customers' such as Jimbo out there, wandering among the ATM's late at night, like cash-hungry jackals.

It was true. As fast as they closed down a series of operations, others flickered to life, and the difficulty was, as both Susan and the Chief realised, these fraudulent transactions were only the ones which they were aware of. They knew enough about their quarry by now to safely say that they were chasing a constantly disappearing pair of heels.

"There's something we're missing," said the Chief, more to himself than anyone, knowing that he was stating the obvious as far as Susan was concerned.

"Something at the centre of this, something crucial......" his voice tailed off as his thoughts struggled for form.

"Yes, but what is it?" Susan said, her voice irritated with more than a hint of frustration.

"Let's see," said the Chief, reliving yet again a familiar scenario to both of them, "It begins with fake applications from 'dummy' addresses, the mail is routed through accommodation addresses back to these 'dummy' addresses where the cards and accounts are picked up and dealt with. The money is then drawn from ATM's by a series of what we might call 'dupes' who are paid a virtual pittance for being 'up-front' as it were."

"Yes" said Susan, chiming in. "And the 'dupes' are controlled by local *Mafiosi* whom it seems, are also paid for their services."

"Absolutely" said the Chief, stroking his chin in agreement as he warmed to the empathy between the two of them, always an asset when they were nothing more than professional colleagues, but now heightened by the tangible sexual chemistry which bound them silently together.

Trying to maintain a serious air, he looked at Susan only obliquely as he added

"There's no doubt in my mind that someone is controlling the whole thing, none of those local villains, as nasty as they can be, are capable of such grand designs".

"So the money is fed back into 'dummy' accounts, and from there to offshore accounts and then translated to cash." said Susan, so engrossed in the details that she was *almost* unaware of the tingling sensation inside her every time she felt him look her way.

"And presumably from there into another account, probably somewhere offshore again" said the Chief, also maintaining a false kind of composure as best he could.

Shifting his seat backwards as he slid his long legs over his desk, he began to backtrack through the sequences he and Susan had just outlined.

"Somewhere in among all that is the central link that will crack this egg for us" he said, "Now let's see, as we've said before, the mail is the key".

"Yes" said Susan, leaping in brusquely, "But

we've followed the mail to accommodation addresses and from there to the 'dummy' addresses, and we've found no-one who's picked it up. The only people we seem able to lay our hands on are at the bottom end of the scale".

"In every sense" said the Chief, grinning at her, breaking the tension a little. Susan's laugh was tinged with the edge of cynicism that came so naturally to her.

"It's as if we're being fed this fodder, just to keep the wolves happy, so to speak" she said, a hint of self-mockery in her voice.

"Well in a sense I suppose we are" said the Chief, serious now, "But the point is, would the mail - an important item in this chain - be allowed into the hands of such people anyway? Surely it would have to be trusted to someone a little higher up the scale?"

"Yes, but who? And How?" said Susan, perplexed. His own mind was ticking over.

"Someone with good office skills, an appreciation of the value of paper, wouldn't you say?" He looked at her quizzically, a light beginning to break inside his head.

"Like someone who would run an........." She was about to say 'office', but her voice tailed off as she realised the import of her own words and began to catch the thread of his thoughts. They looked at one another.

"Exactly" he said "An accommodation address". Susan was still trying not to clutch at straws.

"But we raided several" she said, "We found nothing, not a thing!"

"They were as clean as a whistle" admitted the Chief, "Or at least, they *seemed* as clean as a whistle, but the pea in the whistle is cracked. Imagine this scenario - the mail is forwarded to the accommodation address, which is, in every other respect run as a legitimate business, the difference being that the mail which is for specific non-existent customers is *never sent* to the addresses shown in the books".

"That can't be true," said Susan, her face full suddenly full of doubt. "We've seen mail for these non-existent customers arrive at the 'dummy' addresses, but no-one's picked it up".

"Yes" said the Chief, still sure of his ground, "But what if the mail for these non-existent customers is vetted first, the relatively unimportant mail sent through to the 'dummy' addresses, and only the relevant important mail is kept back?"

"Then it's sent to a pre-arranged hidden address where it's dealt with at leisure," said Susan, trying to put herself in the shoes of the opposition. A frown crossed her lovely face. Excited, but still unsure, she had yet more objections to raise.

"But we even marked mail - mail which *should* have been important in that way - mail which we knew was part of the fraud, and even that mail actually *did* go to those 'dummy' addresses, yet no-one collected it".

"There's a simple answer to that too" said the Chief, his face grim, his jaw clenched. "Our friend anticipated our move before we made it". Susan's own jaw dropped open despite herself.

"You mean he..."

"Or she?" interjected the Chief, teasing her now. Susan smiled, but tried to maintain a business-like composure despite his flippancy.   "As I was saying before I was rudely interrupted" she said with a smirk, "He - or She! - was waiting for our marked envelopes, and let them pass through for that reason?".

"Yes" said the Chief, sure of his ground now. "I'll place a bet that when we next visit those accommodation bureaux we'll find ultra-violet scanning equipment".

"All of that's very well" said Susan, back to her business-like best. "But if these people are involved, how do we prove it? How do we catch them out? There's no law against having ultra-violet scanning equipment".

"No, but there *is* a law against keeping false accounts and being part of massive fraud" said the Chief, his voice suddenly liberated from doubt, "As for catching them out, we let the next batch of 'dodgy' mail we identify go through unmarked, but we note the fact that it - or at least the meaty parts of it - doesn't arrive at its 'dummy' address..........".

Susan cut in and finished the sentence for him.

"And we follow it through to its actual address.........".

It was the Chief's turn to cut in on Susan.

"With the co-operation of the Post Office".

"Yes" said Susan, her eyes wide with enthusiasm and new hope, "We seize all mail which has passed through the accommodation address and go through it with a fine toothcomb".

"At the same time, we follow 'Chummy' and see

what journeys he takes after work" said the Chief, his eyes lighting on Susan, the woman, rather than just his professional colleague.

"And what goodies he carries with him" added Susan, slightly blushing at the Chief's appreciative stare.

Both elated by what they recognised as a way forward after so long in the doldrums, without thinking into what they were doing, they found themselves in each other's arms in celebration. For a moment they hugged and laughed without restraint. Once consciousness set in however, there was a moment's awkward silence. They looked at each other, almost backing away from the momentary embrace, but before Susan willed herself to move, the Chief took his arms from round her body and placed his hands almost paternally on the sides of her face. Frozen there, they looked at each other, the bond between them open and naked. Finally, with an audible sigh he bent his face forward to her trembling lips and kissed her soft mouth gently till time and the World ceased to function in that very still room.

22

It was a cold grey morning, and they sat in an unmarked car parked in a world-weary business estate watching the activities surrounding the battered building that housed their quarry. 'Mailseal' was the uninspired name of this accommodation agency, and its proprietor, a bespectacled balding man of 58 years, had entered the premises anonymously at 9am. They were already waiting for him.

Alerted by the Post Office that the mail containing cheques, application forms, and bank account bric-a-brac was on its way into the premises that very morning, they had quickly swung into action. It would have been easy for them to delegate such a task to their subordinates, but in the light of the possible importance of the outcome, the Chief and Susan had both unanimously decided to deal with the uncomfortable 'stake-out' themselves. That way there was no one else to blame if it went wrong.

The down side was the extreme discomfort of sitting in a car all day, with little prospect of any real action. The difficulty was, they couldn't risk waiting till the end of scheduled office hours, for the man could leave at any time.

They already knew his name - or at least, who he was supposed to be - they realised that nothing could be taken at face value when dealing with a fraud of this size and scope. He called himself 'Thomas Marks', and they also knew where he lived, the name of his Wife, and had already scanned the details of his bank accounts and phone calls. Needless to say, there was nothing untoward to be seen in all that.

The down side was the discomfort of the car; the compensation was the company. It was tempting in this first glow of their romance to use the opportunity to mercilessly 'snog' in the car, but both were too professional for that. Nevertheless, the air was thick was sexual tension without a move being made or a word said on the subject. He couldn't help noticing how lovely her legs looked stretched out so visibly near yet so far from him. And as for her low neckline..........

Stirring uncomfortably in his seat and getting hot under the collar for other reasons, the Chief tried to focus on the job in hand.

"Well, the mail's gone in now, I'd love to see through those walls".

Susan nervously fidgeted for some of the same reasons as the Chief, nodding sadly at his words

"Well, I suppose we'll know soon enough" she said, as philosophically as she could. Part of her mind was struggling not to think about the way his lips had melted on hers.......... The Chief broke into her wandering thoughts once more.

"I've seen a lot of crooks in my time, but I would have bet on this man being 'straight' until now".

"That's probably why he was chosen for the job" said Susan, her inbuilt cynicism about human nature showing itself.

Several sandwiches later, as the Sun crossed the sky and began to vanish, the lights of the weary buildings began to flicker on. The bodies of the car's two occupants were inwardly crying out for mercy. In their earlier days as fraud combatants, they had both done their time on surveillance, but that was some years ago, and they had all but forgotten the joys of sitting in one place for a day or more.

It was only 4pm, but their still world was jarred into action when Thomas Marks walked into sight from the drab entrance, holding his tired raincoat over one arm, and carrying a black office bag in his other hand. As Marks wandered out of sight round the corner of the office block, the two of them suddenly forgot their aches and pains, and even their proximity to each other - the chase was on!

Softly softly they followed the diminutive figure of Marks through the fading light of the streets. Oblivious to their interest, the subject of their enquiry paused only once, to place some letters in a postbox. Time would show that these letters were the irrelevant mail, which would find its way to the dummy addresses.

Finally, Marks reached his destination, a crowded public bar, of all places. There was no other alternative, both the Chief and Susan followed on, acting for all the World like two lovers on a night out, which in a way they were.

Impatiently, the two pursuers awaited developments - was this just a false alarm? Thirty minutes later, Marks was joined at the bar by a well-dressed young man, they made an incongruous pair standing there together, completely socially mis-cast, the young man for all the World, a 'yuppie', the old man giving every outer appearance of 'suburbanite', and 'Dad's Army' with it.

However, to the gratification of the Chief and Susan, Marks eventually reached into his bag and produced a package, which he passed on to the young man. Within moments of this happening, the young man vacated the premises, and leaving their full glasses behind them, Susan and the Chief followed on.

Jumping into a BMW, the young man roared off into the night, but Susan, in the driving seat of their Mercedes, was a match for the young upstart. Within moments she had fastened on his tail, and hung on to him like a leach.

Through streets and streets of crowded neon they sped, amidst lines of traffic that thankfully disguised their pursuit, till finally, with one final rev of the engine, the BMW skidded to a halt outside a block of flats in a fashionable part of Town. With barely a glance, the young man slammed the car door and hurried into the flats, not noticing the dark car that slid into position near his own.

It had been a long day. The Chief decided it was time for the surveillance to be taken over by his subordinates, nothing was likely to happen for some time, he concluded. Susan drove him home to his Wife, and he kissed her lingering and long outside his own doorstep, which she took as a sign of his commitment to her, though unspoken.

It was several days later when the young man made his move. They now knew him as Tony Wilson, a stockbroker in the very respectable firm of Harding and Grieve, nothing in his previous record showed up as devious or criminal. He was a single man, aged 25, or previous good character - what on earth was he doing associating with people who could get him jailed for a very long time? Shaking his head, the Chief puzzled over this and other conundrums. But seeing Tony leave his premises for the first time since they had followed him, they were eagerly awaiting the next move. Unfortunately, it proved to be a red herring, Tony merely went to his girlfriends, and did what all red-bloodied males do at a time like that, which was very nice for him, no doubt, but very tiresome for the surveillance team, including Susan and the Chief to supervise over.

Days later, nothing had happened other than that, and Susan was once again pushing for action, a trawling expedition to see what could be salvaged from days and weeks of wasted surveillance.

Partly against his better judgement, the Chief agreed, and the next morning, around 6am, Tony was rudely awakened by a posse which charged suddenly into his flat and his bedroom, finding him bleary-eyed and naked, blinking into the sudden light.

Without further ceremony, he was hauled off to the local police station, and dumped in a cell to await interrogation. In fact, he was deliberately left to stew as long as possible, for both the Chief and Susan knew that progress now relied on 'cracking' Tony.

It was unspoken between them that Tony was yet another cog in the wheel, rather than an essential item. Still, he definitely was further up the ladder. He was obviously well-educated, intelligent, upwardly-mobile, though a bit too upwardly-mobile for their liking.

Finally they brought Tony to an interview room, a sparse place with harsh lights and an unwelcome ambience about it. The tape in the machine flickered ominously as they began their questioning.

"Would you care to tell us your part in this fraud?" said Susan coldly, her very official voice being ideal for conveying distaste as well as authority.

"I don't know what you're talking about" said Tony, but his bottom lip quivered as he spoke, and his brow was beaded with sweat.

"I'm talking about accommodation addresses which pass on dubious mail to dubious sources" said Susan, "I'm talking about Thomas Marks, who we know runs an illegal operation, and we know that you are his contact". Tony's sweat glands worked even harder after that one.

"I don't know anything" said Tony, visibly wilting now, "I swear I don't!"

"Well Tony", said Susan, letting the suspect know that she knew who he was, "I think we have you banged to rights. In your flat we have the mail which Thomas Marks passed on to you. We ourselves observed you picking it up, so be a good boy, don't try and insult our intelligence".

Tony looked at Susan desperately, his earlier bravado quickly washing away.

"I only collect the mail and pass it on, I don't even know what it is or what it's for" said Tony, a note of desperation in his voice now.

His face quiet and calm, but with an assertive

tone to his speech, the Chief chimed in.

"Unfortunately Tony, you are about to take the rap for a fraud which so far amounts to something over 100 million pounds". He let that figure sink in, as Tony visibly shrunk.

Before Tony could respond, Susan again grabbed the initiative.

"Your only chance is to help us Tony, otherwise you're gone for a very long time". To their surprise, on Susan's words, Tony suddenly burst into tears, his schoolboy bravado completely burst by reality.

"I didn't know what I was getting into" he blurted, tears streaming down his contorted face, "It was only a way of making money on the side, I didn't ask questions, I didn't know what was involved, I thought it was only minor league" he said, somewhat unconvincingly, but with great desperation.

"No Tony", said the Chief gravely, "This is major league, this is big time". Then he added for effect "And the outcome is big-time for you too".

With that, Tony nearly collapsed with fright, his whole life vanishing in front of his eyes. In truth, he had no chance of avoiding a prison sentence anyway, but Susan was happy to dangle whatever carrots she could to draw him into her web.

Taking a compassionate line, she spoke gently.

"Tony, I know you've been used. It can only help if you tell us all you know".

At this seeming olive branch, Tony looked as Susan through soaked eyelids, almost pathetically.

"Can you help me?"

Susan kept a straight face and looked as

sympathetic as she could,

"We'll see what we can do. But first, you have to help us, it's the only way Tony".

She used his name softly, deliberately, making him feel cared for in his time of need.

Moments later, he couldn't say enough. The trouble was, he really didn't know very much. His instructions had come from a man whose name he didn't know, he only had a phone number, which he rang once when it was time to liaise and hand over the mail. Nevertheless, as Susan and the Chief realised, he represented the next step up the ladder, and using Tony's desperation, they urged him to set up a meeting with his next in line, the man who collected the mail from him.

Tony rang the number - the number that they had checked out and found to be a mobile phone linked to a name and address, which were no doubt false. He was due to meet the man in the mainline railway station at 9pm the following evening.

Susan and the Chief began to allow themselves to feel optimistic.

It seemed at last they were getting closer to the truth.

23

A busy railway station in the heart of the City. A pale-faced young man waits anxiously, his fate seeming to him dependent on the next few minutes. Gazing at his watch over and over, Tony's white face reflected his fears. Would his contact turn up? Tony knew that if he didn't, his own chances of years in a dungeon were certain.

Actually, they were anyway, he just was naive enough to let himself be used in the vain hope that he could be somehow saved from the fate that was already set for him. In reality, Susan and the Chief could do little to help Tony, his fate was sealed, but they were happy to feed him illusion so that he would be a willing tool in the next stage of their attack on the fraud which had dominated their lives for this past year.

Tony felt a hand on his shoulder and visibly jumped. It was his contact. In a mixture of relief and terror, Tony spoke nervously.

"I thought you weren't coming".

The man was urbane, polished, a cut above Tony in social status. Already his antennae were become unhappy with the demeanour of Tony, anyone with sensitivity could see that Tony was too strung-out, too on edge to be natural. It could mean betrayal. He looked around the station nervously. All seemed normal.

Surrounding him were the deliberately non-nondescript figures of the team's 'hard men'. However, the Chief had decided beforehand that surveillance was the best option here - let the man go, but follow him relentlessly till he led the team to the centre of the fraud. So it was with some relief that the contact took the package offered by Tony and vanished into the crowd with the team's best officers in hot pursuit, albeit with great subtlety. For Tony, there was a trip back to the cells, and the temporary illusion that he had helped himself avoid a hefty prison sentence.

As they expected, the man had nothing more to offer them for that day at least. They followed him as he drove his gleaming Daimler to an elegant Town house in a fashionable area. A swift check revealed that the man's name was James Jeffrey Morgan, a City analyst with a salary of some £50k p.a. Greed was an amazing vice, thought the Chief, as he wondered aloud to Susan - what on earth made someone as successful as Morgan get involved in a gunpowder plot like this?

Susan smiled, almost amused at the Chief's relative innocence in such matters.

"It does prove that we must be near the top of the tree" she said, more interested in their progress than the foibles of human nature.

"Could be," said the Chief, "Let's wait and see where we go from here".

It had been another long day, and the success of the surveillance thus far had kept the adrenaline flowing. Now though, they were both suddenly aware of how tired they were. It was time to go to bed, but not necessarily to sleep. They looked at each other, the question in his eyes unspoken.

"Yes" said Susan, her emotions conquering her fears, "It is time". His face suddenly soft, his eyes moist, the Chief took Susan in his arms and kissed her passionately. She wrapped her arms around his neck and gave herself to him, body and soul.

They drove for a while through the drizzling rain and glowing street lights till they came upon a wayside Inn, a smart but anonymous motel. The room service meal was excellent, but the night was long and memorable for other reasons.

24

The morning light was shining into the room when his mobile phone suddenly burst into life. Struggling to wake, the Chief reached for the ringing noise that filled his head almost as much as the champagne from the night before. *The night before*. As he clutched the phone, he looked at the lady lying beside him, stirring now, the duvet cover slipping back to reveal her naked breasts. Smiling softly to himself, he finally connected the phone and focused on the Scottish voice at the other end. It was McKay, his team leader.

"Guv, we're on the move," said McKay.

"Where are you heading?" asked the Chief, his head suddenly beginning to clear. From the sheets beside him came a sleepy female voice.

"Is it on then?"

On the other end of the phone, McKay, recognising the voice, hesitated before replying. So the guys were right – the Chief and Bryde were at it.....

"It's London, it seems Guv" said McKay, "We're steaming down the M1 through Watford, but I'll keep you posted".

"I'm on my way," said the Chief, already rising from bed, revealing his nakedness to Susan, who despite herself, giggled nervously, a sound not unnoticed by McKay.

"Just wait till I tell the lads," he thought, but kept his voice as indifferent as he could when he answered, "Right Guv".

One long lingering naked kiss and several minutes later, Susan and the Chief were on their way to liaise with the team as they pursued their quarry.

Luckily enough, the day was bright and cold, rather than the drizzle and haziness of the night before, so the Daimler's progress could be easily monitored. Before too long, just as the Daimler reached the outskirts of London, the Chief's car pulled in tandem with the team, thanks to McKay's precise directions. In the thick traffic, there was nothing odd about a series of cars tailing each other through the increasingly busy lanes and streets reaching into the heart of London.

Within sight of Tower Bridge, the Daimler swung into an expensive car park, and one car from the team was delegated to follow, the rest stopped and waited around the streets outside. The radio crackled as McKay and his men followed Morgan from his car to the busy streets below.

"He's out of the car park Guv, I'd say he's headed for the bridge itself" said McKay, his voice tough and brusque, but flowing with the excitement of the moment.

"Is he carrying anything?" asked the Chief anxiously. The radio crackled again.

"Yes Guv" said that gravel voice, "He's got a black briefcase, one of those soft ones you carry under your arm, more like an attaché case I suppose".

"Good" said the Chief with some release of tension. "Keep on him. We'll be with you in a moment".

Susan handed out Swift instructions to the rest of the waiting cars. Everyone else in the team was to follow McKay on foot, spreading out on the other side of the road from Morgan, some walking swiftly beyond him so that they could then approach his path from the opposite direction.

The bridge that day was bristling with tourists and working people, but it was also bristling with McKay and the team's best officers as well as the Chief and Susan, who were determined as ever to be in on the act.

There were so many people milling around James as he strolled languidly across the bridge that it was impossible to tell who would be the contact. Suddenly it happened. To their surprise, a slim elegant man who looked extremely unlike a crook scooped the attaché case surreptitiously from James as he passed him and moved on without the two ever having eye contact.

McKay's voice crackled again over the airwaves.

"What's the score Guv? Do we take them or leave them on spec?"

"Take them!" said the Chief decisively as Susan nodded her agreement.

Hardly had this exchange taken place when a seemingly anonymous crowd of people leapt upon both men, bundling them to the ground before they had time to even register surprise. As their prey hit the deck, the members of the team were like a pack of wolves, the adrenaline in their own bodies pumping, making them shout and swear aggressively at the two men, when it was plain there was little they could do in response in any case. As innocent onlookers gasped and gaped, the men were whisked off in an unmarked car which immediately headed for Holborn police station in Theobolds Road, adjoining the offices of the Fraud Squad in Richbell Place.

For all the fame of this police station, its inner demeanour was bare and drab, its walls sprayed with tired and ugly graffiti and worse. Many a lost miscreant had passed through these doors. It looked as if a decent cleaner would not be seen dead in the place, and the latest inmates looked decidedly a pair of square cogs in round holes.

James Jeffrey Morgan they already knew all about. The second captive was an aristocratic looking man, and when he finally was allowed to speak, it was with a cut glass accent, expressing indignation at this treatment thus far.

Singularly unimpressed with this show of social snobbery even in the face of blatant fraud, McKay's voice cut across him like a whip.

"This is how we treat criminals, and whatever class you consider yourself, you are now equal with the lowest," he said, his contempt clear and unequivocal, the words delivered with that special edge of venom which a Glaswegian delivers best.

Driven now to silence, in a matter of moments the man found himself pushed into a dank and dark cell, his mind a jumble of questions and answers which were not pleasant to contemplate.

For several hours, he lay on the blue plastic bed, adjusting to his new surroundings, to the new life he undoubtedly would now face, for unlike Tony, he was not stupid nor a coward, but he was a realist, and knew that there was little he could do to avoid his fate.

Much much later, the door suddenly opened, and without comment or ceremony he found himself, as he had expected, delivered to an interview room, a place devoid of human warmth or comfort, just a bleak overhead light and stark table and chairs, cold and aluminium.

After a short time, a woman and a man came in. The woman was very handsome, he thought, though her features were somewhat cold and unfriendly, very formal he judged. She stared at him blankly, almost as if he were a specimen in a glass case. The man was sharp-featured, studied, almost a caricature of Sherlock Holmes, he thought, almost laughing to himself at the absurdity of the situation. But it was no laughing matter, as he well knew.

"We know who you are," said the woman coldly, regarding him with disdain, "You are Piers Tremain, a supposedly respectable businessman. Well, your respectability ends here" she said dismissively.

The man was less formal, more matter of fact, analytical.

"Piers, you are up the creek without a paddle. Are you going to co-operate? It's your only chance", he said, somewhat conciliatory in tone.

Piers laughed without humour in his voice.

"Not that old chestnut, surely!" he said, mustering up as much disdain as he could, "You and I both know there's nothing you can do to help me now, so what's the point?"

The woman again fixed him with her cobra stare.

"The point is Chummy, you can kiss goodbye to life for a very long time. Your only hope is to gain a little credibility with the Judge by helping us clear this whole thing up once and for all".

"By helping you, I'll help myself you mean," said Piers, smiling mockingly, " How gullible do you think I am? I somehow don't think so, do you?" He said forcefully.

The man interjected, a note of conciliation still in his voice.

"Of course we can't prevent your appearance in Court and the outcome of a sentence against you, but you and I both know at the same time that your only hope of some reduction in that sentence is to help us as much as you can. All we can then do is to make that known to the Judge, and that we can certainly do. It's true it won't stop you going away, but it will in all probability reduce the time you are away. And don't forget we are talking about a fraud here that amounts to at least 100 million".

The mention of money always did the trick, he thought, for criminals as well as Judges. Nothing upset them more than the mention of large sums of money. People were expendable, but money came first to the good and the bad, as well as the ugly.

Piers however, was not that naive. He well knew what the sums of money were, and he merely asked for a Solicitor, thereby ending his interview for the time being at least.

25

The interview with James was considerably more rewarding than their first encounter with Piers. James was clearly still in shock, a person who had enjoyed the rewards of his ill-gotten gains, but who had never truly focused on what the penalties for capture would be.

His mind was reeling with thoughts of his Wife, his Family, his respectability, position...........

Into these feverish thoughts, the cold voice of Susan punched through.

"Well my Son, you're in a fine mess, aren't you?" she said, standing there with her hands on her hips, completely in charge. The Chief sat quietly, enigmatically, letting his own presence and obvious authority speak for itself.

Susan was pacing up and down now, like a tiger patrolling its cage.

"The question now is - are you going to co-operate, or are you going to be awkward, which is it to be?" she said, like a much-feared schoolmarm, scolding her errant pupils.

Bottom lip quivering, James spoke in a tremulous voice.

"If I tell you all I know, will it go easier on me?"

Seizing on his words, Susan dived in like a bird of prey.

"Of course it will!" she said, being economical with the truth.

"Tell us all you know and we'll have a word - mind you, mess us around by telling us a lot of piffle and we'll see you off completely!" she said, her beautiful face strong and angry as she spoke, frightening the life out of James. The Chief had not yet said a word. Now he eased in gently.

"James, tell us about your contacts, who they are, how you contact them - tell us all you know about this situation you've found yourself in".

To their amazement, James reeled off something in the order of a hundred names of the people he collected from. The figures were staggering, they had thought of James as a mere cog in the wheel, but when they added up, it seemed to Susan and the Chief that they had indeed taken a very large bite out of the fraud, much larger than they would have imagined.

James had not a great deal more to tell, but when he had finished giving the details of his contacts, an immediate operation was launched to find and arrest as many names on the list as possible. James was put to work trawling through photographs of villains he could put faces to, as names were often likely to be an alias rather than the real thing.

The numbers would seem frightening to an outsider, but to the team, it was all the lines they expected - a host of middlemen, office managers, local crime gangs, along with some thousands of petty crooks on the streets delving into the insides of the ATM's. All of this meant a logistics nightmare in terms of pursuits, arrests, and confinement, but on the plus side, as far as the team were concerned, it meant a major inroad into the destruction of the 'sting'.

They now could visualise what they thought of as the size of the thing. If James could yield such results, what keys did Piers hold?

"He won't talk," said Susan, "I know his type. His arrogance is holding him up, we won't get anything out of him". The Chief shifted uneasily in his chair.

"The trouble is, by going for broke and arresting these two now, especially Lord Muck here, we've rather burned our bridges. I know you're basically right, yet to get further with this, we have to nail him down, and there's only one way".

Susan's lovely face took on an expression of dismay.

"Oh no!" she said, pushing her body away from the desk where she had been leaning, "You can't mean you're actually going to make a deal with that creep! Surely not!"

As the Chief opened his mouth to speak, she jumped in again.

"We can't let him get away with this!"

"I know it goes against the grain," said the Chief, anxious not to upset her more than he could help, "But can you think of any other way? If we just send him down, we have to begin all over again with the rest of it. Do you want to do that?" "No, of course not" said Susan, pouting a little, "But at least now we have the knowledge of how it works, we can use that to our advantage".

"It is true we know *something* of how it works, and it would help, but how long will it take that way?" said the Chief, "But I'll lay a pound to penny that Tremain knows *exactly* how it works. And we both know that if he could be induced to sing, Tremain could shut this thing down for us in

113

one fell swoop - but we have to act fast, before our friend can adjust himself - or herself - to what's happened here today".

Grinning now at his familiar teasing, despite her frustrations, Susan took on the implications of what he had said.

"You mean you don't think Tremain is the one?" she said, unsure of where she stood on the matter herself.

"No, he isn't" said the Chief. "Stop and think about it - the figures add up, but he was too readily up for grabs, too expendable".

"Isn't that just his natural arrogance?" said Susan, still seeing the formidable Piers as the possible brains behind the fraud.

"I would put him down as second in command myself" said the Chief, "For me, there's got to be someone standing outside, watching over the whole thing without getting his own hands dirtied by the troops".

"It does make sense," said Susan, softening now, respecting his cool detachment that worked so well against her fiery sense of combat.

"We're nearly there," said the Chief, putting his hand gently on her arm, "What does it matter that we give Tremain a lifeline? The exchange is the complete collapse of this fraud, and that's the important thing here, isn't it?"

"I suppose you're right," said Susan, putting her hand on top of his, "I just hate to see a toad like Tremain get the last laugh".

"He'll hardly do that" said the Chief, "He'll be living in fear for the rest of his life, he'll never see his friends or his social haunts again, he'll be a wanted man from now on. The only difference is that he won't be wanted by us, and which of those options is the worst?" Susan's face became more tranquil as she realised for herself the wisdom of his words. Either way, Tremain was finished.

Still, when Piers was hauled in to the interview room once more, Susan found it difficult not to be riled by his smooth demeanour, his lack of remorse, his amused and detached sense of superiority, ironic in the circumstances of supposed jailer and jailed.

"I won't mess about with you Tremain," said the Chief coldly, "I have a proposition for you. Tell us all you know, and we will give you immunity from prosecution. You'll be a Crown witness. Of course, it means that you'll have to be under protection, for your own safety, as much as anything else, and we'll expect to know everything you know, or the deal will be off."

"You call it protection – I call it prison," said Piers, his sneering face turned serious for once.

Piers was not averse to the concept of a deal, he was a realistic man. He had, in the idle hours since his arrest postulated to himself that such a deal might be on the cards. He had already pondered the questions such a deal raised for him personally. He too realised that his life as he had known it was over from the moment he was seized on Tower Bridge.

Nevertheless, he still registered surprise when the sharp-faced man with the hawk eyes put the plan forward without any preliminary 'warm-up'. Tremain's eyes narrowed as he took in the man properly for the first time. He began to realise that he had underestimated this man, he was indeed a formidable opponent, and a man of sensible pragmatism. As Tremain knew, a lesser man would have taken him uphill and down dale through many exhaustive and time-wasting interviews before even contemplating such a deal. He knew at this moment too that this man had not underestimated him.

Noting the woman's studied disdain, he perfectly understood the chemistry between the two, and her intense dislike of him, but he was wise enough not to smile at the woman's discomfort, except perhaps inwardly, while the plan was put to him in measured tones by the restrained but unusually alert man. Discarding his usual outer flippancy, Tremain listened with care.

"If you think protection means prison, perhaps you should try the real thing. There is a big difference, believe me," said the Chief, his tone earnest, convincing.

Piers thought for a moment. The deal, such as it was, amounted to a witness protection programme. True, he would never go to jail, but he would exist in a prison of the mind, and even his physical surroundings would be decided by others, and subject to change for the rest of his life. As well as that, there was the always-obvious threat of reprisals. He would be, after all, be sending thousands of very disgruntled people to jail for a very long time. Worse still, he would have to face each one of them in court, and it would take years and years for his debt to his captors to be expunged. And when their use for him was over, what special steps would they take to protect him then?

Piers knew all of this, but he had no choice, it was the only way.

"I'm agreed in principle," he said, his voice containing a note of surrender, "But I'll need my Solicitor to go through it with you."

The Chief shrugged. He knew he had him.

"Fine," he said, in a voice of indifference.

As they left the room, Piers was already writing to his Solicitor, instructing him to negotiate the legal cover for his actions and well being. Sighing deeply, he signed the letter with a flourish, and resigned himself to whatever fate held.

26

The conference room was crowded, and a buzz of expectation filled the air. On the platform, the Chief and Susan sat with heads of operations in teams from all over the Country. As the Chief rose to his feet, the murmur slowly died until the great room was filled with silence, a pregnant pause.

"Ladies and Gentlemen, Colleagues" began the Chief, "As you know, we have successfully taken hold of this fraud and shaken it by scruff of the neck". At these words, a great cheer like a football scrum roared through the crowd, the enjoyment of the fruits of many months hard slogging work, the fruits of a sensed victory.

Waving his hands towards the crowd to bring quiet to the room again, the Chief went on.

"Yes, it's a moment to savour, but it's not a time for complacency, we still have much to do before we can say we've killed the beast"

He turned to the board behind him, turning over the first page of a large printed document full of coloured numbers and boxes.

Grasping a pointer, the Chief turned again to his audience.

"Thanks to the efforts of you all, we have as you know, many people in custody, some mere minions, some major players, many more at this very moment being hunted, and caught they will be" he punctuated the last few words aggressively, whacking the palm of his hand with the stick as he spoke.

"You also know that we have in custody one of

the really big fish in this very nasty pool, a gentlemen - if I can use that word in its lavatorial sense - named Piers Tremain". There was a ripple of laughter and scorn which carried contempt for the vivid contrast of criminality and class embodied in the aristocratic figure of Tremain, now highlighted on the monitor screen high above the stage.

Playing his somewhat theatrical role to the full, the Chief grinned amiably at the image of Tremain, then the audience, sharing with them the ritual disrobing of their quarry.

"Now then", he said, waving his stick around like a musical baton, "We have a picture of how exactly how this system works, and what it consists of".

Pointing to the first box at the head of the page, the Chief said, "Here we have the operative, the bottom of the scale. For the sake of identification, we call this representative sample 'Jimbo'.......".

Laughter again filled the room as everyone in that place had at some time or another arrested a 'Jimbo' many times over. To emphasise the point, an obviously mocked up identikit 'photofit' of a representative 'Jimbo' appeared on the huge screen, it's Neanderthal features and gormless expression a composite of every street cretin they had all run across at one time or another.

The Chief paused, grinning, enjoying himself.

"Now Jimbo scouts the machines, picking up his goodies, and depositing them in a series of banks - all false identities of course. From there, the cash goes to a series of offshore accounts, and from there, it's converted to cash again and vanishes".

Moving to the next box adjacent to 'Jimbo', the

Chief went on.

"Our friend 'Jimbo' gets his orders from these nice people, the local gangsters who run the show for the masterminds of this operation. Then, moving down to the next box below, all the material the gang needs comes indirectly from the local accommodation address, run usually by elderly gentlemen who have fallen on hard times and have nothing better to do. The mail - or at least the filtered parts which are relevant - are passed through by courier to the local agent, then from there to the area agent, and from there to our friend Tremain".

As he spoke, the Chief shifted his pointer through a series of boxes, each illustrating the individuals concerned.

Pointing to the 'Mafioso' connection, the box at the very top of the page, the Chief said "These nasty creatures were recruited presumably by the person we shall call 'x' - the nasty mastermind behind this whole unwholesome scheme - but all subsequent dealings were through the supervision of Tremain. Via his instructions, they were fed their credit cards, bank withdrawal cards etc by their local controllers. These so-called local controllers vetted the mail they received, delivering the cards for the ATM's to the gang leaders, delivering on the what you might call 'new' business - the forms that had to be completed etc".

Then, turning to the next page, the Chief, his eyes glinting cold and grey, spoke solemnly.

"Now we come to the serious bit. The money involved, the strategics, the resources, the people in this vast fraud".

"Colleagues, Piers Tremain, the main controller, handled no less than 20 area controllers, each area controller himself dealt with 5 local controllers from five accommodation addresses, five local gangs, and roughly 200 local operatives".

An audible gasp filled the room as the numbers sunk in.

"Yes colleagues" said the Chief, his voice grave, his manner serious, "20 area controllers; 100 local controllers; 100 accommodation addresses; one hundred local gang leaders; 1,000 local operatives, some 1220 people involved, a kind of record in itself". Really, it's networking fraud - a sort of avaricious *Amway*".

Letting that sink in, the Chief slowly turned another page, then turned back to address his audience.

"It worked as follows:- each accommodation address took on board no less than ten false identities which lasted approximately a three month cycle in terms of cash yielded. The month after these initial ten identities were taken on, another ten would be installed. Keep that cycle going, and you arrive at one hundred identities per annum. Now we come to the cash involved. Dealing with it as 100 units per accommodation address - For each operative - even £100 a week would equal £1,000, equals £50k per annum; for the office manager - £20k p.a.; for the local controller - £20k p.a.; for the area controller - £10k p.a. [a mere fifth of what he receives p.a.]; for the big man, Tremain himself - £10k p.a. - but from each unit! A cool million per annum for our fine feathered friend! So, to summarise, each accommodation address had 100 false identities, each identity yielding some £60k per annum, that is, £6m p.a. per accommodation address. As you've seen, costs for each 100 identities amount to some £200k p.a., so profit for *each* accommodation address was £5.8m p.a.!".

The crowd gasped as the figures sunk in. Nodding his head as he turned the next page, the Chief spoke quietly, solemnly.

"Yes, I know. We next have to visualise what this means overall".

Pausing while he turned the page, the Chief could feel the tension in the room, as his colleagues debated the implications in hushed tones. Finally, the Chief resumed, pointing to a series of highlighted figures on the page.

"What this means in terms of hard cash is - A total income of £600m per annum; the fraud has been running for some two years, therefore gross income equals some £1.2b. Subtract from that costs as follows - local gangs at £140k p.a. times 100 equals £14m p.a., or £28m gross; mind you, out of that the gangs had to pay their Jimbos, and though we have no idea what the exact figure would be, it would have to be something at least in the region of £5k p.a. per Jimbo, in other words a thousand Jimbos equals £5m p.a., i.e. £10m gross. 100 office managers at £20k p.a. comes to £2m p.a., £4m gross. 100 local controllers, the same figures again; 5 Area controllers at £50k each p.a. equalling £250k p.a., £500k gross; and finally, Tremain himself at a price of £1m p.a., £2m gross. A sum total of costs colleagues, amounting to £20m p.a., £40m gross; all

of this leaving a cool net profit for the fraud of
£5.8b p.a., £11.6b gross so far".

An excited hubbub of noise had spread through
the hall, and the Chief stood in silence, letting the
overheated audience get it out of their system. For
minutes he stood there quietly and patiently, till
finally the noise subsided and he was ready to
address the delegation again.

"As you know, at the outset of this operation, we
had in mind a fraud somewhere around £100m.
What we have ended up with so far is a figure at
least 100 times that". He paused again, looking
gravely at the assembled teams, the people who had
seen this through from its beginnings to its present
state of unravelling. He spoke to them sincerely, a
hint of emotion beginning to break through in his
voice.

"Colleagues, the fraud we have uncovered
together is the one of the most complex any of us
have ever faced. It is nothing less than an assault on
the very way we live our lives. The inroads we have
made into the discovery and dismantling of this
audacious crime are a triumph, your triumph, a
tribute to your professionalism, a vindication of the
skills you - we - have acquired together".

The Chief paused, the silence absolute, the
atmosphere of tension as well as pride in their
performance hanging almost visibly in the air. The
Chief's voice was calm again, it was time to sound a
professional note of warning.

"Our work so far in this case has indeed been
remarkable, and remarkably successful too, but it
would be wrong to assume that we are there, most

emphatically, we are not. We still have much to do. All of us now know the names, the faces, and most of all the method, but all of these villains, large and small have to be nipped in their nasty little buds and tucked away where they can do no more harm".

Staring forcefully at the audience to ensure that they had got the message, the Chief had one final thing to say.

"As for the fraud itself, we still have to be vigilant against complacency. Even if we arrest everyone connected thus far, what's to stop our enemy from digging up yet more hirelings and carrying on? After all, we may have caught some big fish - Tremain is the prime example - but the man - or woman! - himself............"

A ripple of laughter interrupted him, and out of the corner of his eye, he could see Susan smiling and blushing slightly at their private joke being aired in public.

The hall was quiet again, and he continued.

"As I was saying, the *person* who is ultimately responsible for this mayhem is still out there with some £11b in his pocket. That can buy an awful lot of Jimbos or Bimbos, or anything else you care to name. But of course, if he tries it again, we'll be ready for him. It would take a long time now for him to regroup from nowhere, and we now know the way he works. If at any time he shows his hand, we'll clobber him, sooner rather than later".

The Chief turned the next page on his charts, then looked at the audience again.

"Of course, what would be best and safest of all deterrents is to nail the bastard, strangle him at birth before he fathers yet another Son. Unfortunately, we have very little to go on. Even our old friend Tremain knows very little, but if this so-called mastermind raises his head above the parapet, we'll be ready".

Already the crowd of his colleagues, sensing that the end of the conference was near, began to gather their papers and shuffle restlessly, men of action happier on their feet than their backsides.

The Chief was ready to let them go, there was now little he could add.

"Colleagues, you have a lot of work to do, so I'll belt up quickly now. There are faces to find, people out there who need clobbering, nasty little vipers who need to be stepped on if we are to shut the shop up on this latest epidemic, this disease which is the product of a warped mind".

The Chief paused theatrically, his eyes sweeping across the whole room, linking himself to every person in the place.   "Colleagues, as I said, you have work to do. Now go and do it!"

A burst of enthusiastic applause swept the huge room, and then there was only the noise of raised voices, scraping chairs, rustling papers, and tramping feet, as the delegates to the conference fought their way to the exit doors.

The Chief himself turned to Susan, sharing a smile and a few words, her look of pride and love washing over him as they left the stage.

As they came out of the main hall into the foyer, McKay was waiting for them, his face ashen. Knowing it was unusual to see his old friend and colleague disturbed in this way, the Chief spoke to him gently.

"What is it Dave? What's wrong?" McKay was so visibly upset he almost stumbled over every word.

"Guv, it's *still* happening. It's happening again, as bad as ever - *worse* even".

McKay, a strong and pragmatic man seemed somewhat unnerved. The Chief himself couldn't believe what he was hearing. Standing just behind him, Susan's own face registered shock.

"Do you mean the frauds are still carrying on?" she said incredulously. Looking sheepish and little battle-fatigued, McKay nodded averting his eyes.

"The computers are going crazy Guv, the screens are absolutely filled with dodgy transactions".

They rushed over to the operations room to study what was happening. It was true. It was as if they had done nothing to combat the fraud, the banks were leaking money at an enormous rate. Suddenly angry, the Chief grabbed his jacket and rushed for the door, Susan closely behind.

"Where are you going?" she said, unsure of her ground. The Chief was for once in danger of losing his famous composure.

"I want a word with that Pratt Tremain. He owes us an explanation. If he's sold us a puppy............".

He paused there, not sure of controlling his temper. This should never have been possible, he thought to himself, his brain racing. If they had truly cracked the fraud, although it was always possible for it to be resurrected in some way, it should have been impossible for it to continue unabated. The Chief's recent elation was now well and truly crushed. He thought of the bombastic statements he had made at conference - how foolish they now seemed! If only he could turn the clock back an hour or two, he thought wistfully. His thoughts once again hardened as he thought of Tremain. He couldn't wait to get his hands on him.

A sleepy Tremain was roused from his bed in the safe house and bundled into a car, burly detectives surrounding him. An hour later, he sat in the interview room, indignant at this latest rough treatment, when he was supposed to be wrapped in cotton wool.

He saw the Chief and Susan enter, and knew straight away it was trouble. His mind tried to focus on what could be wrong; it was no good, there was nothing he could think of.

"Tremain" said the Chief, looking nowhere near as friendly as he once did.

"You've sold us a pup. You gave us the story, and it stinks!"

Piers was genuinely surprised.

"I don't have any idea what you mean," he said in his best aloof voice. Susan cut in.

"Don't bother with all that crap" she said, her voice an icy steel.

"You undertook to give us all you had, and you didn't, did you?".

Piers was genuinely indignant now.

"Oh yes I did!" he said, "Now if this is some kind of ploy to take away the rights I gained from these disclosures and the succour I gave you, then my Solicitor will have to be called to address this very

great wrong you are trying to impose upon me".
They knew him as an indignant and haughty man,
but his act, if it was one, seemed convincing.

The Chief, still breathing hard, but a little calmer
now was next to speak.

"Tell me then Tremain" he said, in as measured a
voice as he could muster, "If you gave us all you
knew, why is the thing still running as big as ever?
Can you tell me that?"

Piers looked at them both, an understanding
flickering behind his bright eyes.

"Wait a minute" he said, "Just hold on there! I
didn't at any time say that all *I* knew covered the
whole of the system. I *did* give you all *I* knew, and
the results are plain to see, your relative success
speaks for itself - you've positively *basted* in it! - all
at my behest - I can do no more!".

Piers looked at them, his eyes askance, his
attitude critical, patronising. A light was dawning
behind his eyes. He paused. He looked at them with
incredulity.

"You mean you actually thought you had finished
the whole thing because you had *me*? Very
flattering, I'm sure, but you have miscalculated, my
dear jailers. I did give you all *I* could - the fault for
what you made of it all is entirely yours - what more
do you want from me now?"

Even Tremain was finding the pressurised
situation getting to him.

"I can see now that you just didn't ask *all* the
right questions" said Piers, comprehending the flaw
in their approach, "You were always determined to
make me feel that you both knew much more than

you *actually* did, and this is the down side of such pretence!"

Piers sat back in his chair, his arms folded, his cold eyes glinting with more than a hint of amusement and triumph.

Susan was feeling frightened all of a sudden. Forgetting her usual disdain for Piers, she looked at him almost like a little girl, speaking haltingly.

"Are you saying that you only covered part of this, not the whole? But the sums involved.........." . Her voice tailed off, the thought too great to take in. The Chief carried on for her.

"The sums involved are *already* massive, what size of a so-called system can we be talking about here?"

"As I've said, your own pre-conceived ideas have shot you down" said Piers, not without a little scorn in his voice.

"I thought you knew I was only *one* Controller, one of several".

"How many?" said the Chief.

Piers' reply was instant.

"Three".

Three! The Chief felt suddenly sick. Susan's face was ashen as they both took on board what that one word signified. That meant *three times* the figures already known! Piers could see how shocked the other two suddenly felt. He almost felt sorry for them himself.

"There was something else I've been meaning to tell you" he said, almost in consolation. The Chief looked up, his mind struggling to leave his thoughts behind.

"Yes, what's that?"

"It's about my contact - the man himself," said Piers. Wearily the Chief looked at him, his voice suddenly tired.

"You said he always wore a hat and dark glasses, you never had a good look at his face, you knew nothing about him, you said".

"That's true" said Piers, "That is absolutely correct, but I do remember something, I remember his name, when I was speaking on the phone to him, I heard someone in the background speak his name and he involuntarily responded to the voice, so I know it must be true".

"And what was it?" said Susan, suddenly alert.

"It was Alan," said Piers.

"His name was Alan".

27

The news from the Midlands was not good.
Marks had been arrested, as had Tony, the local
controller. Before he could be stopped, James too
had walked into the trap, and had taken with him
Piers Tremain, a major catch for the authorities. As
well as these leading figures, there was the
possibility of the associated capture a thousand
operatives, as well as a nearly a hundred
Accommodation Bureaux Managers and their Local
controllers, then there were four more Area
Controllers - all were now in severe danger.
However, none of this was a complete surprise to
him. He had always known this day would come,
the thing he could not tell was who would fall. He
did not personally know any of these people, though
he knew them by name.

He was not even sorry for them, only slightly sad
to see the beautiful system he had set up begin to
decay, as all things must.

All these minions, both lofty and small, were
themselves dispensable, he had always known they
would not survive, despite the reassuring tones
passed on to them about their future. It was always
necessary in War of any kind to motivate the troops,
even though their only real purpose was to die for
the cause if necessary.

He somehow doubted that Piers would die for the
cause. He had learned enough about him to know
that he would barter whatever information he had
for any chance of leniency in his own case. This
much he knew about Piers, and he had planned

accordingly. Having said that, there was nothing he could do to save the thousands who would suffer if Piers talked, which he guessed he would. All he could do was wind down the relative operation contacts and tell them it was every man for themselves.

The system had begun its first stages of disintegration, but there was still much to savour. This after all, was only one region, not the whole system. A great deal of money had changed hands, and more would still flow through the breaches. Neither he nor the system he had created was ready to call it a day. Despite the apparent setbacks, as far as he was concerned, it was all going to plan. His enemies would feel they had begun a fight back, that they had won a great victory, but as far as he was concerned, they were still pawns in his game, and there was much to play for.

As he sat in his place of solitude, drinking a glass of *Asti*, he afforded himself a bitter smile, devoid of human warmth. The game goes on, he thought. His enemy was no doubt savouring a moment of triumph, yet victory was still his, not theirs. But why did he feel so dissatisfied, so incomplete?

28

The rain splattered against the window of his office, ten floors up in a City skyscraper. Lost in his own thoughts for a moment, the Chief abstractly watched the pattern of the beads of water as they rippled across the dark glass. Beyond the window, it was a grey and hazy morning. Far below, the red buses, black taxis, and assorted cars, obscured by the rain, wound their way through the City, the noise below reduced to total silence by the double-glazing and the distance. A host of umbrellas seemed to scurry like termites, threading their way through the almost stationary traffic.

With a heavy sigh, the Chief turned at last to face the rest of his team, sitting there silently, watching him, their faces almost as long as the desk. They knew how he felt. The gloom lay heavy in the air.

Susan nervously played with a pencil, glancing furtively at the Chief every so often, wishing she could say a word of comfort, put her arms around him, *anything.* He glanced at her and smiled, his eyes tired but full of warmth for her.

"Well lads - and lassie" he said, nodding in Susan's direction, "It seems we did get egg on our faces. But let's not lose sight of the fact that we have made a major breakthrough. Even if we haven't closed it down as we rather naively hoped, we have dealt it a massive blow, and as Susan has correctly stated, we now know exactly the system it operates under. If we do our work properly from here on in, we still should achieve a total meltdown".

"Aye Guv" said McKay, his rough voice coming from a deep weary well inside himself, "But we all know how long it took to shut down what we have so far – a year! Now we have twice as much to do - how many more years does that mean, and by the time we crack it, will the Banks be closed down in the High Street? Won't the Country be skint?"

A worried murmur of conversation sprang up briefly among the team.

"That's unnecessarily pessimistic," said Susan, her sharp voice cutting through the babble of noise, "It took us a year because we began from scratch, and had to work without a thing on the blackboard. Now with what we know we should be able to crack the other 'arms' of this in a fraction of that time".

McKay's assistant, a thin bespectacled man called Raymond Walker chimed in.

"Saying that, you have to assume that the fraud won't be altered in those other 'arms', as you call them. They've played us like a violin up to now, why should they conform to your expectations all of a sudden?"

From the noise that sprang up, it seemed that quite a few of the team agreed with Walker. Listening quietly, the Chief could see that the team's faith in its own abilities had been severely dented by recent events. He stood up from his chair to attempt to regain control, to emphasise the points he wanted to make.

"Look everybody, you know I'm as down as anyone else about what happened - I take the blame for it, I was fed a line, and I fell for it, as I was meant to". A stream of protest washed around him.

"No Guv" said McKay, his gruff accent biting hard, "We're not having that, are we lads?"

He looked around the table as every voice agreed with him.

"If there is a failure here, it belongs to all of us. We are a team, right?"

"Yes!" shouted the others, Susan standing and banging the table, caught up by the moment.

"Dave's right Chief" she said, "We stand or fall together, and speaking for myself, I'm damned if this thing is going to beat us!".

"Nor me!" barked McKay, as the voices of the rest of the team sang like an echo to his words.

All of a sudden there was a fire and commitment in the team again, the atmosphere was charged with determination and even enthusiasm, their tails were up, their will to win reignited.

The Chief just stood there, looking at them proudly, nodding with quiet satisfaction as he did so.

"Right" he finally said, "Let's get down to it".

The voices around him stilled, the hush expectant.

"First, we have to understand why it went wrong for us, at least in perception. As I've already said, let's not lose sight of the fact that we did everything right, we closed down a hellofa operation, even with the fact that it's only part of a whole, it was a real big bite we took, was it not?"

He paused, letting the reminder of a victory gained set it.

"What went wrong beyond that is purely to do with perception" he said. "In a way we were set up - well, we *definitely* were. We were fed a string of

135

images about the operation of the fraud - *local* operatives; *local* gangs; *local* Office Managers; *local* controllers - this series of images were ones which we, as methodical people ourselves, could entirely relate to. Do you see the point?"

The Chief paused, looking up to see if his explanations were taking root. Satisfied, he continued, his voice becoming more earnest, more passionate with conviction as he went on.

"Right, a series of images. Now we've got to *local* controller; *Area* controller - then what comes next? Yes, we followed the Area Controller, and he led us to - *CONTROLLER..* We were put on the bus and when it reached *that* point, as indeed we were meant to, we thought we had arrived at our destination".

A mutter of understanding spread through the team. "Yes" said the Chief, nodding gravely as he spoke through clenched teeth. "The crucial missing word is *REGIONAL*".

The buzz of conversation around the desk almost contained a grudging respect for the enemy they were trying to destroy. The Chief, sensing the mood, took up the theme.

"No, we're not dealing with a nonentity here, are we? But let's not forget that crooks are by nature devious, twisted, nasty-minded little vermin, and a clever crook - even a *brilliant* crook - **is STILL a crook!**"

These last few words were belted out, the Chief's voice roaring like a cheerleader.

A roar of approval greeted him. The enthusiasm for the cause was now vigorously renewed, everyone in that room was now champing at the bit to be on the hunt. The Chief allowed himself a quiet smile of satisfaction. Confidence was totally restored.

"Yes, we are getting a good idea now of what exactly it is we're up against" said the Chief, a grim tone to his words, "But two can play that game, can they not? Like anyone else, our friend can't help but show his natural characteristics. It's obvious that he is a born organiser, almost neurotically neat, labels for everything - that gives us a clue. One thing follows the other. According to Tremain, there are two other Controllers - in other words, two more complete installations of this particular fraud at work. Knowing now the kind of mind we're dealing with here, I put it to you that Tremain was fed that piece of information deliberately for *our* benefit. He wasn't lying - he was programmed. Think about it - we have seen clear evidence all around us of a very meticulous - albeit ugly - mind at work here. Why should someone be fed a line like that? Even someone as obviously high in the scheme of things like Tremain? Surely such information, if true, would be priceless to us? Why give it away for nothing? The answer of course is that 'three' is a red herring".

"But if that's true, how do we know what we *are* dealing with" said Walker, an uneasy feeling of doubt now surrounding the team.

The Chief spoke swiftly, not wishing to lose the momentum of enthusiasm so easily.

"From here on in, we go by the evidence of our own eyes and instincts, not our enemy's. We identify where the action is taking place, and we follow it through to the same level as we did with Tremain, except we do it *Region to Region*, almost like a sample check".

"But Guv" said McKay, "We'd just be groping in the dark, chasing shadows, putting the lights out on individual 'arms', as you call them, but not knowing how many 'arms' this beast has".

"Not really accurate" said the Chief quickly, "We can roughly guess what we're dealing with by the state of activity left. It might not cover *everything* that's happening - it definitely won't - but given the size that each 'arm' would tend to be, we can get a very clear idea of the approximate size of the total fraud and quickly snuff it out, 'arm' by 'arm' if necessary".

"That's right!" said Susan enthusiastically, "And more to the point, we have a methodology of dealing with each network we find. We *can* snuff it out".

Looking at her with appreciation for her brains and toughness as well as her beauty, the Chief repeated her words to emphasise the point.

"Yes we can snuff it out, and quickly too, as I've said.........".

Before he could quite finish his point, Walker stepped in again, a doubt still in his mind.

"Guv, can you really be sure that Tremain - and the team as well - *was* fed a dummy? What if there really *were* only three Controllers? That leaves two somewhere in the Country, but where? Doesn't that make the two harder to find, if that's the case?".

"No," said the Chief, looking hard at Walker with

138

some impatience in his voice. "No, three *isn't* the figure. For a start, we know that the roots of Tremain's branch began in the Midlands. The reason for the final contacts being in London are clear to me - to make us think that Tremain's area was the south Midlands and the South. That would leave the North Midlands and the North as the second 'region', then Scotland as the third. That's what we were *meant* to think, but it doesn't stand up if you think about it. For a start, if Tremain's region was cleared out as it's supposed to be, why are we still getting tremendous activity in the Midlands and the South?"

He looked questioningly at his colleagues, but they only listened quietly to what he had to say. "It seems obvious to me that the so-called 'regions' are divided differently to what we were meant to believe". McKay's deep gravel barked through the room once more.

"Guv, how many 'regions' would you say there were?"

"Five" said the Chief, "As far as I can guess anyway". A gasp of disbelief filled the air. A worried Walker was the first to find his voice again.

"But Guv, we remember the figures - surely another year or two of what we've seen multiplied by five would cause havoc!"

An excited murmur cut Walker off before he could say more. The Chief stood again, his movement sending the team into silence again.

"Yes, but we're going to see to it that this particular video nasty is not going to run another year or two!"

Another chorus of approval swept over him as he sat down again.

Susan was the next to speak.

"Can we define those regions with any certainty?" she asked, her voice calm and businesslike.

"Yes, I think we can," said the Chief, welcoming her ultimate professionalism and dedication as well as looking appreciatively down her blouse.

"Region 1 - Scotland and the North; Region 2 - the West Midlands; Region 3 - the East Midland's - Tremain's Region, by the way; Region 4 - the Southeast; Region 5 - the Southwest".

His eyes hardened.

"And don't forget we are now talking about a gross fraud of something in the region of £6b" he added.

He looked at the team pointedly, letting that penny drop.

"I think that's a fair summary," he said, drumming his fingers on the desk and scratching his head. It had been a long week.

"The activity we can monitor, combined with the known likely size of each possible Region, gives us what I think is quite an accurate picture of where we are with this," he added, sure of his ground.

McKay's mouth was hanging open.

"We've got a bloody awful load of work to do," he said, almost thinking aloud rather than talking to anyone in particular.

"Yes we have" said the Chief, "And we already know how to do it. We split the teams into four, each takes a proposed 'Region', identifies the operatives and gangs, links it to an office manager, let him take us to Local Controller, then to Area Controller, then to *Regional* Controller, even if that's our title rather than theirs. Then we clobber the lot - hard".

"Guv, isn't there a case for following through on surveillance beyond the 'Regional' Controller?" asked McKay, "Surely we want to cut this out at its source. Wouldn't that save us a hell of a lot of time?" "No, I don't believe it would" said the Chief, his face suddenly serious, "Dave, I can see your logic, I'd love to follow it through like that, but I just can't accept the contact to the man himself being that simple. I think he's cynical to the point of seeing everyone - even the Tremains of this World - as expendable to the cause. According to Tremain himself, he simply handed the stuff over to a courier when he was told to, and that in itself had no apparent pattern to it. What that tells me is that the courier was just a paid minion, expendable as always, and knowing as I do - as we now do - who we're dealing with here, there would definitely be substantial contingency plans to cover anything that happened beyond Tremain. That's not to say we can't crack it, but my guess is that if and when we nab him it will take extreme stealth and planning, or possibly a breakthrough by paper trail or computer or some kind of link like that, some connection he - the man himself - hasn't accounted for. I think we could follow the Regionals and the couriers forever and a day, and he would still slip out of our hands. Besides, on the purely practical front, we can't let this fraud run and run and grow and grow while we try to catch *him* out - we just don't have the time. We've already seen the sums involved, and we know what's in store for us if we don't nip this in the bud smartish. No, we go for *total closedown.* If we can't be sure of cutting the head off directly, then the best we can do is to leave the head without a body. We already have the method of doing that, and more to the point, we *know* it works. When all five 'Regions' - or more, if necessary - are closed, *then* we examine ways of dealing with this Alexander - if that really is his name - the germ who's caused this disease".

The Chief stood again.

"Time to get to work" was all he said.

Outside, caught in the inclement weather and the grey haze of a winter afternoon, the crowds were hurrying home. The day was growing dark now, lights were beginning to appear in the vanishing buildings as the room emptied and lay still again, only the sound of the rain on the window remained.

29

The system was a regimented structure, but part
of his brilliance was the ability to recognise when to
let go the neurosis, to admit the necessity for
throwing an unexpected spanner in the works. He
had fed Tremain and the others with logical labels,
as was his own instinct, but on a sudden impulse
and burst of creativity, he had resisted labelling
Tremain and his equivalents in the manner the
system itself cried out for. In a moment of
revelation, such as he was subject to, he realised
instantly the inference that would be drawn from
such a scenario. Yes, they would think that any
controller they captured was one of his kind.

Going on from there, it was a simple matter to
conceive feeding such controllers with information
as they were likely to divulge when under caught
and under pressure, as they would undoubtedly be
sooner or later, whether they realised it or not. By
feeding these false figures to the controllers, he
planned on squeezing at least another year out of the
system before the howling wolves tracked it down
and devoured it whole. If, he reasoned, his pursuers
were looking in the wrong places, making the
wrong plans, then he and the system would have
more time to clean up. Already a cool £5.8b lay in
his domain, even after costs of £200m. Another year
should fetch a further £2.32b.

The light was fading in the garden. Standing there
at the window, he gazed across the marbled patio
and beyond to where the elegant trees swayed in the
gentle breeze. His mind went back to another time

when she strolled in such a garden, her long blonde hair tugged by the autumn wind, her delicate fingers touching her beloved flowers more gently than a butterfly's wings.

Tears filled his eyes, remembering. He cursed himself, turning from the window and the darkness of the evening garden glowing in the arc lights. Why must he continually fill his head with old ghosts?

She was gone, gone forever, it was as if it had never been, never happened at all. The things he dreamt of almost every feverish night were the stuff of nightmares, of things that could never be. Such days of happiness were closed to him, closed forever. He could make untold millions, billions, but he could never buy her love again, could never see her face again, she now belonged to someone else. He had been all but forgotten, as if he never existed.

His long involuntary sigh echoed through the huge and elaborately decorated room, a room that despite itself was filled with pain and silence.

30

The effect of the Chief's strategy was immediate and dramatic. Using the same methods which had trapped Marks, Tony, and Piers Tremain, within two months they had surveillance on four crucial area controllers of the system. Each area controller was deliberately targeted at a point somewhat central to the theoretical 'regions' proposed by the Chief. To prove his theory, each area controller would sooner or later make contact with his own completely separate (regional) controller. If this happened, it would show that there were at least four more 'arms' of the system at work. If abnormal fraudulent activity carried on after the elimination of these 'arms', then it would seem to prove the existence of yet more.

Prior to the awaited swoop on the area controllers and their contacts, the team held a strategy meeting to ensure that no stone was left unturned, and more to the point, to try and avoid egg landing on their faces again as in the Tremain debacle.

Turning to each section leader of the team, the Chief briefly summarised the situation they now found themselves in.

"Well lads" he said, confidant and business-like, "We seem to have identified the area controllers we want, or at least, a representative sample of them, each one hopefully linked directly to a separate strand of activity".

As he finished speaking, he looked at Susan, signalling that she, as the co-co-ordinator of the four teams, should take over from here.

Unsmiling and stern, Susan was determined to play down her love life to the team, having grown aware that everyone knew about the Chief and herself.

"Using what we learned from the seizure of Tremain and his underlings, we began by targeting the street operatives, the fodder used by the local gangs to mint the machines; from there, we linked them to the gangs themselves, and pin-pointed the accommodation addresses which were used in the scam. Following four of these to their local contact was fairly routine, and the link was also made from local to area, not without some difficulty this time - cautiousness had set in, no doubt as a consequence of our earlier action against their counterparts".

Susan paused, shuffling through the mound of papers in front of her.

"Although we all know roughly the state of play, perhaps it would be a good idea for each section leader to give an appraisal of how things stand right at this moment". Glancing up, straight-faced, she singled out McKay first.

"Dave, can we open with you?"

The grizzly Scot nodded distractedly as he ran through the details of his team's work so far.

"As you say Susan, it was a fairly simple task to put surveillance on the accommodation address, the local controller, then the area controller. All this of course, thanks to you for sifting out the right contacts among the flotsam and jetsam in the first place. The state of play at the moment is that we're waiting for a move by the area controller. What I propose is.........."

Susan butted in before McKay could finish.

"Hold on Dave, we'll get to that afterwards when we've heard from everyone else". She turned in her seat and directed her attention to Walker.

"Ray, you've got the South West - what's the situation there?"

Walker, a thin serious young man who felt distinctly uncomfortable working with a female boss shifted uneasily in his chair and avoided eye contact with Susan.

"We're in an almost identical situation to Dave," he said, nodding respectfully at his superior officer in the team, "We followed the chain through to area level, and it's a matter now of playing a waiting game. Everything's in position and ready to go".

He wanted to say more, but he had already seen McKay cut off in his prime, and was wary of sharing the same fate, especially in the hands of Susan. From the cold look she gave him as he finished, he guessed that the feeling was mutual, but it was hard to tell with Susan, she was always so cold and informal anyway - except when was lying under the Chief, he thought uncharitably, stealing a glimpse at her curvaceous figure, wondering briefly what she was like in bed.

But Susan had already moved on. Simmonds and Taylor gave identical up-dates, the whole thing was in place, just waiting, waiting. Susan could sense their impatience, their anxiety for questions as yet unanswered.

Looking at the Chief as formally as she could manage, Susan passed the chair over to him.

"Chief, as far as evidence goes, we have masses

of e-mail linking the gangs to the activity on the street, and the instructions from above, so we can move as we want at street level. We know for sure that everything from this level down is nickable, even if we still don't know how much we can reel in from here. So everything's in place, I'll leave you to tell us what you want done from here on in".

The Chief smiled a small wry smile at her. How frustrating that they had to play out this charade when everyone in the room knew that they were sleeping together.

"Thank you Susan, thank you lads" he said, clenching his hands, slouching forward across the desk as he spoke, "You've all done well to get as far as this so quickly, and now it's imperative we move decisively in all directions. Walker, Simmonds, Taylor - when the contact is made with the controller, jump on them all with hob-nail boots - haul them in, then begin the trawl for all the arteries which flow from your controller - all the areas, the locals, the offices, the gangs, the Jimbo's, etc etc - and don't forget that behind all this human rubbish is a pile of paperwork and money - accounts, offshore, cards, and most of all - cash. Get hold of some of it if you can, otherwise it's all gone walk-a-bye for good. I'm sad to say that it's unlikely you will be able to get hold of any - we didn't last time after all - but we have to follow all the trails, we can't make any assumptions. Remember what happened last time - we got stuffed!".

Seeing the question on McKay's face, the Chief turned to him next.

"Dave, I singled you out because through your

particular network, I want to have a crack at seeing if we can reach the man himself - 'Alan', if that really is his name".

The brusque Scot's face broke into an unusual smile.

"Thanks Guv" was all he said, his pleasure obvious. The Chief addressed him again.

"What I suggest we do is when it comes down to the contact between area and your controller, we don't seize him, we watch him. For this reason, I'm afraid your team will have to be the last one to move in any case. It will probably mean your investigation going on for a while after the others have hopefully closed everything else down - OK?".

More than happy with the news, McKay grinned like a little boy who had just been told he could go out to play.

"Right" said the Chief, determination and steel in his voice. "Let's close the buggers down".

31

Within two months, three whole strands of system operation were seized and shut down. The scale of arrests and seizures were an awesome mass of operational detail and sheer hard work. In Bristol, Newcastle, and Glasgow, startled shoppers were amazed to witness scenes of major arrests before their very eyes as controllers and their area contacts were knocked unceremoniously to the ground, and whisked off with great efficiency in cars with screaming sirens in a matter of moments. Although these very public arrests were merely the high-profile tip of the iceberg, they established in the public mind a sense that something dramatic was taking place all over the Country, and for the first time since the fraud crisis had begun, details began to emerge into the light of TV day. Scenes of the dramatic arrests in Glasgow were filmed by a tourist with a camcorder, and shown on 'The News at Ten' and many other important programmes. Unknown to the viewers and the broadcasters, among this footage could be seen the Chief and Susan, as well as the members of the Scottish team who had planned the arrests.

However, as questions began to be asked, and media pressure steadily built, the powers that be, through the offices of Farquhar-Brown, the APACS Director-General, prevailed upon the Chief to give a press conference.

In the brightly-lit press room of APACS were crowded a phalanx of TV and press cameras, as well as a noisy host of reporters, all awaiting the entrance of the Chief and the various connected parties, mainly represented by Farquhar-Brown himself.

The buzz of conversation rose and fell quickly as the Chief entered the room with Farquhar-Brown and the APACS PR guru, a rather dapper middle aged man called Wesley Sykes.

Sykes was the first to speak, his voice only just heard through the frenzy of clicking camera and jostling for position among the reporters. In the background, the technical staff adjusted the microphones to compensate for the din.

"Gentlemen, we have called this press conference to clarify the situation regarding the recent series of arrests and your subsequent interest in them" said Sykes, stating the very obvious.

"Can I introduce you to Mr Farquhar-Brown, the Director-General of APACS".

With that, Sykes sat back in his chair, leaving the cameras to swoop on Farquhar-Brown. No stranger to the mass media, Farquhar-Brown was completely unfazed by the battery of questions and flashing lights. Smiling his diplomat's smile, he cut through the confusing babble of reporter's questions with a statement of his own.

"For some time now, we have been monitoring unusually high fraudulent activity in the banking sector, with particular regard to fraudulent identities involved in the misuse of credit facilities. We became concerned primarily because we realised at an early stage that this activity was being orchestrated by a particular source. Through use of the Internet and mobile phone network, contacts and instructions were handed out on an organised basis, spreading a web of deceit and fraud of unprecedented proportions. Obviously, we could not allow this to go unchallenged, and to that end, an expert team has been working to eradicate this subversive attempt to undermine the banking system. I'm very pleased to say that we have had some success in our endeavours, hence the series of arrests which you have witnessed for yourselves in recent days".

Hardly had he paused for breath than Farquhar-Brown was met with a deluge of questions. He smiled patiently, his public face perfectly groomed for such a situation.

"Gentlemen, I'm sure you have many questions to ask, but they would be better directed at our Chief of Operations rather than myself". Smiling smoothly, Farquhar-Brown introduced the Chief sitting on his left. Every camera in the place was now clicking furiously, in millions of homes throughout the Country the Chief's lean features appeared on the TV screen, his words calm and authoritative.

"Michael Johnson, ITN" said the bespectacled reporter, his mild manner belying his determination to be first.

"Do you know who is orchestrating this fraud? Is it the work of a crime syndicate?".

"No, we don't know exactly who is behind this" said the Chief, "But I personally believe we are dealing with one individual rather than a crime syndicate as such".

"You mean he's a sort of criminal Mastermind?" said Johnson, already visualising a catchy quote for the headlines.

"Well, that's a bit emotive" said the Chief, unwilling to confer any hero status on his sworn enemy, "It was a very complex fraud, but fraudsters of all kind fall in the end, and this one is no different".

"Does that mean you're on his trail?" asked the man from 'The Sun' newspaper.

"When are you going to nick him then ?" he added cheekily, clearly irritating Farquhar-Brown whose nose twitched with distaste.

Before the Chief could answer, Nicholas Winter, a BBC reporter chimed in.

"Can you tell us how much money was involved?"

"Something in the order of £10b" said the Chief, causing another flurry of flashing lights and gasps of astonishment. Out the corner of his eye, the Chief could see Farquhar-Brown giving him and old fashioned glance. He realised that the establishment would have preferred to put a cosmetic glow on events, the truth could hurt, and he had blotted his copy book in Farquhar-Brown's eyes.

"And have you recovered any of this money?" asked Johnson, cool and professional.

"Not as yet" said the Chief, somewhat reluctantly, as it seemed to imply failure, "But it's early days".

At the mention of missing money, Vic Greaves, the man from 'The Sun' leapt in.

"You mean to say that this geezer's ran off with ten billion quid and you haven't even got a sniff of him?"

Greaves smirked gleefully. As far as he was concerned, he had heard enough.

Imagining the awful headlines the next day, Sykes interjected, trying his best to deflect such thoughts.

"Really Gentlemen, as the Chief of Operations has just stated, investigations and arrests are at a very early stage, so it's far too premature to be discussing the possible outcome at this point in time. I think the appropriate phrase is 'Watch this space'..........".

He wasn't allowed to finish his words, as Vic Greaves from 'the Sun' finished it for him.

"Yeah, we're watching it all right - the space is where the Mastermind and the money were - you've blown it, haven't you", he said, voice sneering triumphantly. All around him, cameras and tape recorders flashed and clicked in a sudden frenzy. Despite any further attempts by the panel to deal with questions sensibly, the tone of the media coverage was set. Millions were missing, and a 'Mastermind' with it - they had the headlines they wanted.

Reading his newspaper the next day, the Chief was not particularly phased by the focus on the missing money and the man with it. The PR problem was a headache to the likes of Farquhar-Brown and the people he represented, but it was of no great interest to himself, other than the fact that it could lead to undue pressure on him eventually.

For the meantime though, he was more concerned about the state of his investigation. He was pleased with the way it had gone thus far. With the benefit of their earlier experiences, closing down these current 'arms' of the massive system had been conducted in a manner which was more professional by far than the closing of the first 'arm' of the fraud.

What was different too about these arrests compared to the arrests which closed the earlier operation was that a much more thorough surveillance had taken place. Each area controller had been allowed to make all his local contacts; each controller had been allowed to make his area contacts, the arrest only taking place when all other contacts were known. It was far more in depth than the original 'trial run' had been capable of.

Step by step, the Scottish region, the West Midlands region, and the South East region were closed down with ruthless speed and efficiency.

There was only one more matter to deal with now, and time was of the essence since the media were hot on the trail, and the prey would be even more on the alert than ever.

The last strand or 'arm' of the fraud as known had also been under massive surveillance. All the gangs, operatives, local and area controllers had now been identified, as had the controller himself. Now it was a matter of waiting for him to make the vital final link.

Weeks had gone by without action, and the team was becoming nervous. All important team members were now seconded to McKay's team as the operation had reached a critical phase. The other snag was that although every known contact and participant
was under surveillance awaiting developments before their arrest, nothing could be done until the drama had played its final card. The cost was, of course, horrendous, and worse still, every week that went by meant more money out of the banks and

into the giant system. It was galling to say the least, but until the controller made a move, there was nothing they could do but sit on their hands and stew.

It had seemed just another boring day with endless cups of coffee and tired conversation when the radio suddenly crackled with McKay.

"Guv, it's go" he said, taciturn as ever.

Instantly the adrenaline was flowing as the team including the Chief and Susan assembled themselves at the point of surveillance, a large house in the best part of Southampton, where the controller, Martin Boswell lived in some style.

As Boswell cruised through the busy streets in his Lexus luxury car, a series of anonymous vehicles took turns at following him while others waited equally anonymously at pick-up points along the way.

The radio crackled again.

"Guv, he's just gone into *Farnham Securities* - it looks like a deposit box job" said McKay gruffly.

Driving at some distance behind the convoy, the Chief betrayed his own anxieties.

"Keep back, let him do what he's got to do, don't interfere" he said. At the other end of the radio, McKay looked at the radio in his hand with disgust, then glanced at his assistant.

"Do I look stupid?" he thought, bristling with indignity, "Right" he said, in place of saying nothing at all. Perhaps the Chief was just hyped up. Shortly afterwards, Boswell came out of the building again, and this time the Chief was wise enough to leave McKay to organise things his way. McKay turned his attention to Walker.

"Ray, you take half of the lads and keep an eye on Boswell. The rest of us will stay here and watch things this end".

"Sure Boss" said Walker, hurriedly getting on Boswell's tail as he roared off back towards his house, it seemed, though everyone involved in this investigation had by now learned to take nothing for granted.

The Chief's voice crackled in McKay's handset.

"Dave, can you get in there and find out what the score is - what has he left etc? Also, arrange a signal with the Manager in there so that we'll know for sure if and when we've got a bite".

Slightly irritated at the interference in what to him seemed obvious procedure anyway, McKay just barked "Right!" into the radio and signed off without further comment.

Immediately he headed into the luxuriant foyer of *Farnham Securities*, where he was met by a rather pompous receptionist.

"Can I help you?" she said, looking at the rather drab figure of McKay with cool disdain.

"I want to see the Manager - immediately!" barked McKay without ceremony. The Secretary's aloof demeanour was dented by McKay's ID card, and without further delay, she nervously contacted the Manager to appraise him of the situation. Within moments, a thin Mediterranean looking man with a sallow face rushed into the foyer, smiling unconvincingly at his visitors, extending his hand to

McKay.

"Hello. I'm Mark Webster, how can I help?"
McKay shook his hand without enthusiasm, and
explained what he wanted. Clearly nervous, the
Manager took McKay through to the deposit boxes
and with two silver keys, he opened the box which
Boswell had used only moments before.

Inside was a bulky package of envelopes. A cursory
glance showed that they contained mainly
application forms and correspondence made out to a
variety of names. It was just as McKay had
expected.   Putting the package back in place,
McKay turned to the Manager who was fidgeting
nervously, trying to imagine what to tell his
superiors, McKay quickly gave him his instructions.
 "What I want you to do is signal us by telephone as
soon as someone calls to take away the contents of
that box. We'll be waiting outside. Do you
understand?"
 McKay's voice was at its stern best.

"Yes, of course" said the Manager, his voice dry
with tension.

They did not have long to wait. A motorbike courier
pulled up outside and soon after he entered the
building, the phone rang. It was Mark Webster.
"He's emptying the box now" he said in a shaky
voice. "He'll be leaving any minute now. He's
wearing a.......".

McKay interrupted him brusquely.

 "Yes we know. Thank you for your help".
He switched the hapless Manager off before he
could clutter the airwaves any longer. Quickly he
called the Chief.

"Guv, it's a go" was all he said.

"Right" said the Chief, "I'll be with you any moment now".

Just as the Chief pulled into sight, the courier was roaring off in his revved-up motorbike, overdoing the throttle manipulations in a reckless urge to show his doubtful macho tendencies. With some subtlety, gained by years of practice, the team slid in behind the would-be Barry Sheen, following him through winding streets without giving away themselves away.

Given the choice, none of the team would have opted for following a motorcycle, for one thing, they were fast and mobile, for another, there was always the chance of them disappearing down a particularly narrow pedestrian walkway where a car couldn't go.

Nevertheless, they stuck to their task, and if necessary, they had the 'flying eye' of a helicopter should it be required as a backup.

Eventually, the cyclist came to rest at a modest house in the suburbs of the Town. As the team drifted around the house, the rider vanished inside, only to reappear just a few minutes later. The Chief despatched some of the team to follow the rider, while himself, Susan, and McKay & company stayed on watch over the house.

While the main team sat on their hands, waiting with growing impatience, Walker and the rest of the team pursued the courier at a safe distance while he took a leisurely cruise out of Town and into the countryside.

For miles upon miles they followed him, the day

growing darker now, his figure on the saddle becoming vague, obscure. They were all tired. It had been a long day. Soon, the rider pulled into a council estate and adjacent to some lock-up garages. Whistling casually to himself as the team watched with myriad eyes, he produced a set of keys and opened up one of the lock ups, then swiftly deposited his bike in there. It was easy to see why he needed the security, thought Walker. One look around the estate could tell anyone that anything with wheels that wasn't supervised was going to be wheel-less come the morning.

They followed him up the decrepit stairways and turd-filled passages till he reached a crummy door, its paint long gone, disgusting splashes of God-knows what covering its pathetic exterior.

Walker called the Chief.

"Guv, our friend is to ground. It's a run-down council estate - it looks like he's settling down for the night. He's wandering around swigging a beer and he'd down to his string vest".

"Just hang on there till I give the signal Ray" said the Chief, but as he spoke, a courier suddenly arrived at the house he was watching. The Chief hurriedly signed off.

"Ray, something's occurring here - we'll keep you posted". The Chief clicked off the signal from Walker, and turned to Susan and McKay, nodding their understanding. Switching on his transmitter again, the Chief addressed the rest of the team who surrounded the house.

"OK, when this joker comes out, we split again - Dave and his team stay here with Susan and myself, the rest go with Simmonds after the courier".

An echo of voices acknowledged the Chief's command, and they sat quietly in wait for the next move, their minds suddenly alert.

They didn't have long to wait. Moments later, the courier emerged and set off at a cracking pace, followed by Simmonds and his team. Sometime later, they came to rest at a smart cottage deep in a rural setting. Again, the rider vanished into the house, only to emerge within a few minutes. It was becoming like a game of cat and mouse. As he roared off once more, the team was once again split. Liaising with the Chief, and with his agreement, Simmonds took charge of the team who remained with the house, while Taylor and the rest followed the rider on his mysterious journey.

Back at the first house, now that the Chief and his team had heard from Simmonds about the latest movements, anxiety was beginning to set in.

"How long can this go on?" said McKay, his doubts echoing those of the Chief himself. The Chief shrugged, knowing that nothing he could say would be relevant or helpful.

"What do we do now?" asked Susan, her lovely eyes half-closed with exhaustion.

"First, we wait" said the Chief, though he knew everyone in the team had really put up with enough for one day, "Give it a few more hours" he said, aware of what he was asking of them.

Time passed. Darkness had come, and with it, the urge to sleep. All of the team were struggling to keep awake, something had to give. The radio suddenly sprang to life, making them all jump. It was Taylor, who had followed the second courier.

"Guv - the courier has been at rest for half an hour, but nothing else has happened". The Chief wasn't in the mood for pleasantries. "What kind of place has the courier stopped at?" he snapped with irritation in his voice. He wanted to know what new problems he faced.

"It's a hotel - a very up market hotel about five miles outside Rustington" said Taylor. It had been a long night for him too.

It was midnight now, and the Chief decided enough was enough. He addressed Taylor first of all.

"Get into the hotel, grab the courier and anyone else in his vicinity. Go through the guest list and check everyone out - and I mean *everyone* - don't let anyone - and I mean *anyone*, staff included - don't let them leave the premises till the check is complete. Is that understood?"

"Yes Guv" said Taylor, glad of the action, secretly excited by the prospects offered by the hotel - definitely not the kind of place a courier could afford. Perhaps glory could be his tonight, thought Taylor.

Meantime, back at the town house, the Chief had made contact with Simmonds, who was still outside the house in the country, waiting for the word to go in. The Chief didn't mince words.

"Simmonds, get in there *now*. Grab the occupants and the package - don't let anyone give you the slip".

"Don't worry Guv," said Simmonds confidently, "No-one is going anywhere without us on their

162

backs".

The Chief switched his transmitter over to general transmission. "OK everybody" he said, "It's a go, I repeat - it's a go".

With his words, a last rush of adrenaline coursed through the limbs of the tired watchers as they sprang suddenly into decisive action.

Outside the council flat of the first courier were stationed Walker and his team, and in very short order they charged the decrepit door and knocked it to smithereens. Inside, a very shocked courier was slouching on the filthy bed, dressed in only his string vest and grubby underpants. He had been smoking a joint and listening to heavy metal. Before he could move he was pushed with no great finesse onto the floor, his face stuck like glue to the ancient decrepit carpet.

Meantime, miles back along the road, the occupants of 43, King Henry Avenue were asleep in bed when the door crashed spectacularly open. The elderly couple in bed were clearly distressed and shocked when The Chief, Susan and McKay suddenly occupied their bedroom.

In the house in the country, the two young homosexual occupants were rudely awakened by a host of cars outside, then a sudden commotion at their door. Without warning, the fashionable door flew off its hinges, blasted to one side like a piece of matchwood. Lights everywhere came on, and there was the sound of men swearing and shouting, pandemonium was breaking out. Simmonds and his men were breaking in. The two young men clung to each other in fright, one of them breaking down.

In a quiet country lane, the majestic hotel, which had been settling down for the night, was suddenly besieged as if by the *SAS*. Lights and unusual noise intermingled with raised and unfamiliar voices, filling the long corridors, while the elegant foyer was a scene of chaos as Taylor and his men took command of all operations and movement. Meantime, standing in the town house among the belated protests of innocence from the elderly bespectacled man and the wails of woe from his roller-haired Wife, the Chief was trying to make sense of all that he had heard and seen that night. As he stood there distracted, stroking his chin, allowing his mind to wander among the debris of the evening, the radio suddenly crackled to life. It was Simmonds at the country house.

"Guv, we're in, but as we blagged the house, we had another visitor, another courier. When he saw us giving it what for, he tried to make a run for it, but we nabbed him. Just thought you'd want to know".

The Chief felt suddenly sick. He got the picture now. It had already been a long day, but the questions were just beginning.

32

The search of the house in the Town proved entirely negative as regards new information. Other than the surveillance that had confirmed the delivery of the package, there was nothing there whatsoever to connect the people who lived in the house to the fraud that they found themselves caught up in.

As for the first courier - only the surveillance of the deposit box and the houses could link him fairly and squarely to the fraud. In both cases, the only proof was surveillance, nothing else of value had been discovered. The interviews could possibly yield more fruit, provided there was any more to be had. The Chief thought it unlikely.

The second courier had been caught in his underpants at the hotel, but he was alone, and he had nothing incriminating in his possession. Every guest and member of staff at the hotel was thoroughly checked out, but no one there seemed of dubious origin or identity, though checks would necessarily continue for some time.

It was in the second house, the house in the country, that Simmonds and his team found the package that the couriers had collected and despatched.

"Why was it still there?" asked Susan, rhetorically. "Obviously to lead us on a wild goose chase" said the Chief with some bitterness in his voice. He cursed himself for not being more vigilant and aware. He should have realised that it had been too easy to think he could pin his opponent down by normal standards of surveillance. Once again he had been unnecessarily complacent, he thought.

Piece by piece, his interviews with the house occupants and the couriers revealed the safety measures for what they were - a remarkable series of precautions - so excessive as to be paranoid - precautions designed to minimise the possibility of capture. From the separate accounts of the couriers and the occupants of the houses, the Chief slowly pieced together what those safety measures were.

It was a sober meeting the morning afterwards in the cold light of another day. To most of them it felt like the *same* day. Some of the team had been up all night interviewing the couriers and occupants. The Chief and Susan had not been to bed, not even to sleep.

They were both annoyed and frustrated, and not just because of the sufferings of their rationed love lives. It was true to say that the team now had the success of closing down the system which had opposed them, but their main target - the big fish - had effortlessly slipped away with the money.

With bleary eyes, the Chief addressed the team assembled together in the high-rise office building. Talking as if from a great weariness, the Chief tried to describe the events of the last few days.

"How did he avoid us?" he said, his eyes sad, his voice tired but defiant, "It worked like this - courier one picks up from the deposit box. He takes the package to a designated house. He leaves, and goes straight to his own home. When he gets there, after a pre-determined interval, he calls a number by mobile phone and says one word - 'Safe'. The person who gets the call is the second courier. Neither knows anything about the other, all they have is a telephone number each and the signal. If the second courier had not received the signal, he would not have set out. But having received the signal, the second courier collects the package from the house and delivers it to house number two. He then sets off for a very plush night in a five star hotel, all at company expense, and all for our benefit, the point obviously being that we are meant to think our Mr Big is staying there".

A muttering began among the team as they began to get the point.

"Yes" said the Chief, the expression on his face serious, "The package *remains* at the second house, which is what we would expect, but because of the hotel, we are faced with a double bluff - is our man - the man himself - in the house or in the hotel? Meantime, the courier in the hotel rings a phone number and says that word again - 'Safe'. On that signal, another courier - a third - calls at the house. As it happens, by the time this happened, we had played our cards in any case, but knowing what we know now, had we waited a bit longer it wouldn't have made the slightest bit of difference. For this third courier was another red herring, a decoy. Not only is *he* a decoy, but any numbers of couriers can call at that second house, and any one of these can leave empty handed. Each courier receives a signal - 'Safe' - and this is the instruction which tells him to set out to pick up a *possible* package, and he doesn't know until he reaches the house if he will receive the package or not. If he doesn't, his instructions are to then proceed to his home, and after a time transmit the word 'Safe' to the next courier whose phone number he has. Needless to say, all the phone contact numbers are licensed to non-existent customers, nor do any of the numbers held by these phones link to anything remotely like an actual person or address - a dead end there" said the Chief, knowing no-one in this room was surprised by that news.

After a sip of ice water, the Chief continued.

"Somewhere along this chain - it can be at any point - a courier is selected to *actually* collect the package, and the house occupants are informed of this by the one word over their phone - 'Safe'. As soon as they hear that word, the holders of the package know that they must give it to the next courier who calls. The courier who gets the package has a previous instruction that tells him what route to set out on, and what to look out for. Before each job, each courier is given a new instruction like this, each one different, individual, so that there are at any time a variety of options for the gang to operate under".

Susan could not resist butting in.

"Then this selected courier is met somewhere along that route, and delivers the package which is then driven some distance, then changed over at least once more before reaching its final destination".

The Chief looked at her appreciatively.

"Yes" he said wearily, "From what we've gleaned from our three couriers - regulars with 'the firm' - it would seem likely that very soon after it was delivered to men in a car, a helicopter took the package on its final lap of the journey".

He sighed, and looked up at the tired faces of his team.

"It also seems that once the 'active' courier is on his way with the package, his progress is monitored by helicopter as well, and presumably at the same time, the traffic behind the courier is analysed for safety".

"The idea of the earlier couriers is, as I've said, to make a series of decoy runs, hopefully with the pursuers in tow - and that's precisely what happened to us, my friends!" said the Chief, a rueful grimace crossing his strained features.

His face still tense, he looked at the team meaningfully.

"In other words lads, once again we were handed a donkey, and we fell for it, or at least, I did".

Nodding sadly in acknowledgement, the Chief continued.

"OK, we failed so far in our attempt to get the man himself, but we have - I think I can say - successfully closed down a very major fraud - no mean achievement, and there's still a lot of investigations going on, they might yet yield something significant".

No one in the room believed that, least of all the Chief himself, but he somehow couldn't leave it on a negative note with so much having been achieved by himself and the team.

"Three couriers and four house occupants were arrested last night," said the Chief, "As well as the final controller. That means our attempts to shut the fraud down have been entirely successful".

"Cheers!" he said, lifting a glass of ice water as a tribute to his friends and colleagues. With a great shout, they did the same.

There was still much work for the team to do. The exciting stuff seemed to be over, but there was still all the legwork to do, all the checking on papers trails and closing of fraudulent accounts, as well as the pursuit and arrest of hundreds, even thousands of individuals who had become embroiled in this enormous fraud. There was the hunt for the 'Mastermind', and of course, the cash, all £5 ½ b of it.

As for the Chief himself, although he was sorry to not have captured his prey at this time, his thoughts were mainly on the coming evening, and a date with Susan. It promised to be very interesting indeed.

33

From a Sun-drenched balcony he watched the waves breaking on the shore. It made him think again about the course his life had taken. How different it had all turned out! What had happened to that rather idealistic young man who hoped to be an accepted and even celebrated citizen? Looking back sadly, he realised that he could barely recognise his own self, he had become someone else, someone else who was almost the exact opposite of everything he had stood for, he had become a complete negative of the man he had once been.

Irritated by his inner thoughts, he realised that they were being fuelled by the unexpected collapse of his system. In just three months it had vanished under the ocean. It was supposed to stand up for another year at least.

He realised that his false signals had not been successful, they had not bought him the time he had planned for. His respect for his opponent had grudgingly grown in these last few weeks too, though he also recognised his own arrogance had a part to play. Had he been less secure in his own ability to outfox his opponent, he could easily have made plans to re-create the system as it stood, confusing the opposition, and thereby gaining the time and cash he had originally planned for.
As it was, thousands were under arrest or being hunted, and the system was in tatters, the flow of money ceased. The ill will created by the sacrifice of these thousands of employee's would be

considerable. He knew that it would be difficult to secure the co-operation of crime syndicates from here on in.

Even now though, there was much to do. There were still foolishly loyal, though expendable minions who were at this very moment feverishly collecting cash linked to offshore accounts that were in severe danger of closure and loss of valuable deposits. By the very nature of the essentially cash transactions, necessary to disguise the trail, the job was a massive one. Luckily, it was a job that had been constantly in hand since the beginning of the system just over two years before, so the task was well on its way to completion. The equally daunting task of putting the cash back into the banking system as 'clean' money was also well in hand, so at least the income which the system had generated was completely safe for the foreseeable future. Still, the sudden disintegration of the system was a warning to him that forces out there - more than likely one person - were formidable too. He could now begin to imagine something of what his opponent was like. Perhaps, he thought, it was good that the system linked to that opponent was now defunct. At least the battle had ended evenly, he decided. His opponent had achieved the total closure of the system a year or so before it was scheduled to end. As for himself, he still had his freedom, and he had something else too -he had the cash.

34

Another evening in Finsbury square. Once again, the rich cigar smoke filled the huge conference room. The elegant table was lined once more with the great and the good. At the head of the table, Farquhar-Brown was making his report to the committee.

"Gentlemen" said Farquhar-Brown, his cultured voice booming richly in the chandeliers, "I am pleased to report that the unusual level of fraudulent activity has ceased. There have been some thousands of arrests, and I can categorically state that this particular fraud is at an end". With a smile of self-satisfaction, he paused, which gave enough time for Lord Sefton to intervene.

"So the fraud is closed down - congratulations are due - but what about the proceeds? Where is the money?" he asked in a voice of indignation. Murmurs of agreement rippled around the long table.

Farquhar-Brown was at his urbane best.

"Gentlemen, as we speak, investigators are still following the paper trail through a maze of accounts. We must await the outcome of their deliberations".

Speaking from the far end of the table, the squat and rather ugly Chairman of Coutts, Bankers to the Queen spoke with accusation in his voice.

"You say that there have been thousands of arrests - but tell me, do any of these arrests include the ringleader of this gang?".

Farquhar-Brown smiled benignly, his face a

perfect mask.

"We certainly have many of the key players - the top five players in fact, as well as almost everyone from there down. Some are in custody at this very moment, others are being sought - enquiries are continuing apace". Farquhar-Brown smiled again, hoping this would suffice.

Another High Street Bank Chairman, Lord Wetherby was next to speak.

"You're avoiding Lord Sefton's question - have you or have you not got the so-called 'Mastermind' of this operation behind bars?"

Farquhar-Brown wriggled uncomfortably, not particularly willing to admit anything negative.

"It is true that we do not at this moment of time have the perpetrator of this fraud behind bars, but we are on his trail - we know his name, for instance, and it's only a matter of time before we close the case. The main thing is, the threat to the banking system has been removed".

Mutterings of discontent spread among those at the table.

"As long as you have someone like that at large, there will continue to be a threat" said Sir James Telfer, the Chairman of Yorkshire Bank.

Farquhar-Brown smiled his oily smile again, his best reassuring
tones in operation.

"Rest assured Gentlemen, we will leave no stone unturned till we find the person who is responsible for our misfortunes".

Grunts and noises of vague satisfaction came from the assembled hordes as they settled happily back into their vintage port and cigars.

Once again he was summoned to the great marble and glass halls of Finsbury Square. In the reception area of the Director-General's office he waited patiently, familiar with such routines.

"Ah, there you are!" beamed the Director-General, stepping grandly from his office with a weak handshake, "Come on in!".

The Chief shifted uneasily in his chair, not particularly comfortable with the pomp and ceremony that seemed to him to have no real practical purpose other than to pamper the occupants of such offices.

Smiling a Cheshire cat smile, Farquhar-Brown professed an amiable stance.

"Well well, I think we can say that it was a task carried out with distinction".

He waited in vain for the Chief to say something, a comment perhaps, but the Chief remained quiet. He felt he knew what was coming, he had been here before.

Farquhar-Brown pretended not to notice the Chief's indifference to his charm.
"I must say you deserve every praise for the work you did in closing down this veritable attack on our institutions". Again he waited for a response, but there was none.   Farquhar-Brown decided to get down to brass tacks.

"You have performed a valuable task, and now it's over, it's time to return to normal duties".

The Chief had expected this, but still felt impelled to protest.

"The job *isn't* done" he said, his voice brimming with stubborn determination, "We haven't succeeded in identifying nor capturing the person whose scheme this really was. OK, we've closed down operations thus far, but what's to stop this person - if he wants to - starting all over again with a slightly or even drastically altered system? I really must insist we finish the job and track this person down, otherwise it will come back to haunt us, mark my words".

Farquhar-Brown was tired of diplomacy. After all, he was now dealing with a mere subordinate, not a Captain of Industry.

"You will cease all operations in this matter as from today," he said, his voice petulant and now devoid of diplomacy, "You will return to your normal duties, as will everyone else on the team that was assembled for this purpose. The local fraud investigators and police can now take over the reins and tie up any loose ends that there may be". Farquhar-Brown looked pointedly at the Chief.

"Is that clear?" he said unambiguously.

"Yes" said the Chief reluctantly, knowing there was no way out, "But when this comes back with a vengeance, don't say I didn't tell you so".

With great force, the Chief threw his pile of papers on the Director-General's desk and walked out of the room before Farquhar-Brown could say another word.

Alone in his office, the Director-General muttered to himself in indignation.

"Stupid man! Why doesn't he understand?" he said to no one but himself.

Outside the Chief was stamping along Finsbury Square, trying to control his temper and his contempt for Farquhar-Brown. It wasn't all over by any means, he thought.

It had only just begun.

PART TWO

EQUITY & INVESTMENT

1

The storms of spring were ending; the sky began to take a more cheerful aspect, days were warmer, the sun smiled on the crowds who once more filled the City parks.

Among this melee of voyeurs and lovers, the Chief and Susan sat on a park bench, enjoying a lunchtime sandwich together. The days of the last major fraud seemed almost forgotten now along with the rainy season just gone. Even though it had only been a matter of months since they last worked together, both of them had worked on many individual projects that gave a sense of distance to it all.

Like most professionals, they did not give a great deal of thought to a task which had been successfully completed and which was now behind them. If they thought of it at all, it was to remember how and when they fell in love.

The early days of their romance with all its attendant rose- coloured view was now being tempered with the realities of their relationship coming home to roost. For the Chief, life at home with his Wife and Family had become intolerable. On the face of it, his Wife had no proof and no reason to point a finger at anything specific, but as all women do when their man is not really with them, she *knew*.

The attention he was suddenly paying to his appearance was a giveaway in any event, partners who suddenly change a lifetime's habits are giving out a warning sign, and the Chief's Wife was not one to miss the significance. Therefore the pressure was on the Chief to conform or lose his marriage, the choice was his. In reality, he felt committed to Susan, so the choice should have been a simple one. However, in the tradition of men the World over, he was undecided, hesitant. The thought of giving up all he had worked for and beginning at the beginning again, especially at his age was a daunting prospect.

Yet he loved Susan, the trouble was, did he love her enough? It was the classic pincer movement in the war of the sexes. Susan, as a single and independent person, was becoming more and more exasperated at the stalemate she found herself in, and the strains were beginning to tell on both of them.

Still, there were the times when all that was forgotten in the heat of passion, and with the sun shining over the rooftops once more, it seemed a sign that all was well with the world, and somehow everything would work out for them too.

As the Chief fought his way through a pastrami sandwich, a strip of the spicy meat lay suspended from his mouth. Both his hands were full, so in between muffled fits of laughter, he frantically chewed the other end of the pastrami in a desperate but somehow vain attempt to swallow it whole and save his messy embarrassment. Susan was in fits of giggles herself as she saw her usually somewhat stiff and formal boyfriend lose all his composure over the pastrami, which was slapping his face in the tongue-wrestling match he had to indulge in. "Hang on!" she yelled between gales of laughter.

Her own hands were full, so Susan dipped her head down beneath the Chief, and took the swinging end of the pastrami into her mouth, both of them working their way through it until their lips were almost touching. At that moment, they looked deep into each other's eyes, and the laughter stopped, time was suddenly suspended.

They were about to kiss when their reverie was disrupted by the sound of a mobile phone. The Chief sighed sadly, the spell broken as he reached for the insistent telephone.

"Yes" he said through a mouthful of sandwich, his eyes and mind still on Susan.

"Can you come up to the office as soon as possible?" said the instantly recognisable voice of Farquhar-Brown at APACS, "There's something I must discuss with you," he added, brisk and businesslike, no pleasantries to offer.

The Chief frowned.

"I've got rather a lot on right now - will next week sometime be all right?"

"No" said Farquhar-Brown, his voice the rigid and unyielding instrument of bureaucracy, "I'm afraid it can't wait that long - come tomorrow at two".

The line went dead.

"What is it?" said Susan, catching the gist of the conversation but nothing more.

"I don't know," said the Chief, a thoughtful expression on his face. He looked at Susan.

"But I can have a good guess" he said.

They stared at each other in silent understanding. Just then, the sun was suddenly lost behind a cloud, and there was a slight chill in the breeze that had

unexpectedly appeared. summer wasn't yet in its
stride as they hurried from the park.

2

It had been so long since he had last walked the streets of London. Hurriedly, he pulled the collar of his coat round his neck as the filtered rays of a weak insipid sun struggled against the elements of a cool spring day. It was a day which would seem reasonably mild to anyone accustomed to the weather at this time of year, but for someone like him who had grown used to an altogether more agreeable climate, it seemed positively chilly. Shivering slightly, he turned to hail a cab that was wandering amiably along Pall Mall.

"Where to, Guvnor'?" said the gruff cabbie in a disinterested voice.

"Piccadilly Circus - *The American Express club*" was the reply, the voice equally impersonal, distant.

They sat in silence as the cab bumbled along through the heaving traffic, until finally it reached the club, its outer aspect a self-conscious attempt to create an impression of 10, Downing Street. As the cab trundled off, its driver cheered somewhat by a £5 tip,

He entered the club, welcoming the blast of warm air that immediately greeted him.

He made his way past the flickering screens that connected some of the club members to the Stock Exchange. Then, he by-passed the convivial lounge, and took the small flight of stairs which led to the library, a fairly small but very presentable room with a cheery view of the street below. A fake log fire smouldered gently, and other than its gentle crackling, the ticking of a grandfather clock was the only discernible sound.

As intended, the room had only one occupant, his Lieutenant, his friend. Right back from the days of prison, as they made their plans for the future, they had assigned themselves the roles of Lieutenant and Commander. It was tongue-in-cheek and affectionate, but it was also a fair reflection of the roles each man played in the organisation of the system.

As his friend walked in, the grey-haired man's chiselled features broke into a boyish grin, and the clipped precision of his every movement pointed to a man of great personal discipline and physical prowess, an ex-soldier perhaps. The expensive suit he wore could not conceal his wiry build and athletic movements. He rose like a prowling cat from the large leather chair.

They both smiled warmly, and embraced each other like brothers, as always scorning a formal handshake. They had been through so much together; their friendship had survived into the reality that was life beyond the cell doors. Each thought of the other as the only person they could trust in this World, but even then, they both retained reservations, time and history had taught them never to take anything for granted.

The visitor took off his coat and warmed his hands at the fire for a moment.

"Where have we got to now?" he asked his Lieutenant, the initial pleasantries over. The older man reached for his black briefcase and shuffled through some papers, bunching them together and handing them over.

"Somewhere along the way" the Lieutenant said, unconsciously quoting Nat King Cole, which caused his companion to mockingly raise a questioning eyebrow. The Lieutenant laughed, and suddenly broke into the line of the song, his companion joining in. They grinned at each other like little boys in the middle of a game.

"First things first - Shall we have some drinks?" said the Lieutenant rhetorically. He picked up a nearby phone.

"Two Jack Daniels' and Lemonade please, ice and no lemon in both cases" he said briskly, then turned back to his companion.

Crouching in conspiratorial fashion, the two men bunched their heads together, studying the reams of paper strewn across the highly polished table.

"As you can see," said the Lieutenant, "We're now approaching an approximate spread of the whole Country - a thin cover, mind you, but one which touches every corner, albeit slightly at this stage".

He pointed to a map awash with various colours. The Commander studied it closely, his eyes narrowing in concentration.

"What's the exposure?" he said, his hand casting a shadow across the Counties on the map.

"Roughly speaking, 10,000 at the moment - it's a constantly fluctuating situation as you know," said the Lieutenant, a master of his brief, "Giving an exact figure is not really possible as it changes from moment to moment, but that's just about where we stand at this precise time".

"Cost?" was the next question. The Lieutenant was equal to that as well.

"Initial outlay in the region of £120m; gross value obtained £800m; £680m in debt exposure" he said, his voice giving no hint of emotion, as if he was delivering mere numbers from a page, not juggling in massive amounts of cash.

Listening quietly to his Lieutenant, the Commander nodded in satisfaction.

"And what about........." He began, but just then, a young lady in a smart blue business suit walked in carrying the drinks on a silver tray.

"Good afternoon Gentlemen" she said, her voice a perfect mixture of business and pleasure, "Shall I leave these here?" she asked, looking questioningly at a small table close to where the open briefcase lay.

"Yes please," said the Lieutenant as he hurried across to close his briefcase. The two men waited in careful silence as the young blonde woman unhurriedly arranged their drinks, confidently pouring half of the lemonade bottles into each glass, stirring the mixture in thoroughly. Finally, she obtained the Lieutenant's signature and with a last warm smile, she left the men alone again.

He finally could complete his sentence.

".....And what about associated matters?"

"10,000 at average £100 per week equals £1m per week; projected outcome in the region of £62.4m per annum. Running costs as follows - 100 administrators at £25k pa each, £2.5m; area co-ordinators at £50k pa each, £5m; Regional co-ordinators at £100k pa each, £500k; no cost for operatives, as they keep social benefits of £50- £80 per week for themselves - total costs of £8m. This amounts to a gross profit of £54.4m in the first year". The Lieutenant paused for a moment to let his words sink in. His friend was preoccupied, thinking about the implications.

Finally, he smiled a grim smile of satisfaction. The second phase really had begun.

They met in the street and each did not know nor recognise the other, though they were sworn adversaries. One man felt a warm breeze ruffle his thinning hair and took comfort from it, but to the other man, the wind carried a chill he did not welcome.

It was in Haymarket, just south of Piccadilly Circus. One man was walking from the American Express club, the other to a hastily arranged meeting in the offices of Chase de Vere, celebrated brokers to the great and not necessarily good.

The street was strangely quiet for a late London afternoon, as if fate had decreed the scene must be properly set for such an auspicious occasion, but anticlimax had a part to play too, and the men passed each other without ceremony or comment.

The Chief hardly noticed the shadowy figure who slipped past him, though he smiled to himself when he saw the man shiver, his unseasonably tanned skin betraying the fact that he was an occasional visitor to these shores.

The Chief did not give the man another thought as he reached the junction at the bottom end of Haymarket and crossed straight over to the extravagant and well-appointed offices of Chase de Vere.

As the Chief disappeared into the building, the other man hailed a taxi, and headed for the Grosvenor Hotel in Park Lane, where he could look forward to some fine food, drink, and most of all warmth.

Meantime, inside the offices of the venerable brokers, the Chief was being shown into the main boardroom where there was already a gathering of important officials, including Farquhar-Brown. Presiding on this occasion was Neville Whitewood, the Chairman of the Council of Mortgage Lenders.

The meeting had already been in session for some time, when the Chairman introduced the Chief. The Chief was ushered to a seat next to Farquhar-Brown, and sat in silence as the Chairman finished his introduction.

"...............So Gentlemen, we believe he has particular expertise and experience of problems which relate to this matter. Let us hear what we has to say".

The Chairman looked towards the Chief meaningfully, then sat down, the room expectant and hushed, the assembled officials subdued and silent, an atmosphere of concern hovering over the table.

The Chief rose to his feet almost languidly, but his eyes were hard and concentrated, his voice though soft, expressed confidence and competence. He knew the officials need reassurance. They did not want to hear negatives or ambiguities, and he knew better than to tell the unvarnished truth. And on this occasion especially, the truth was not good. "As you know" said the Chief, his eyes seeking out every face around the table, "We have a situation here which is causing concern. Housing benefit fraud has reached unprecedented proportions. On the face of it, this should be none of our concern, but we also fear that much of this 'new' fraud so to speak - as opposed to fraud which is always there with us in any case - is linked to the mortgages we have unwittingly granted. In other words, we are unwilling accomplices. I can confirm to you that I believe this to be true. The connections in the methods of the fraud are plain to see, but I can also add one further thought, the thought which Mr Farquhar-Brown and I share - we believe that we are dealing with the same people who orchestrated the great credit fraud of some two years ago".

An uneasy murmur sprang up throughout the room. The Chief allowed the voices to subside, then continued.

"Yes Gentlemen, this is the thought which has brought us to your table through the good offices of the Chairman, who now shares our views. Another associate who shares this view is John Saunders, the Head of the fraud unit at the Benefits agency".

The Chief paused here to introduce a mournful looking gentleman sitting immediately across the table from him. Saunders looked round the table, acknowledging the curious stares of his new colleagues.

The Chief took a sip from a glass of water, then continued.

"John and I will be in constant touch with each other during this investigation".

The Chief looked round the table, letting the silence do his work for him for a moment. Finally, he spoke again.

"Another thing I should add. When I say that we are dealing with the same people, I mean that the same forces are being used against us, and no doubt many of the same personnel. However, in my opinion we are dealing principally with the warped plans of <u>one</u> individual, the same individual who was the so-called 'Mastermind' the newspapers referred to at the time. You probably also know that although his fraud was detected and closed down, he himself has not been apprehended, hence the problem we now encounter".

The Chief could read the next question in everyone's eyes.

"What to do about it? First we monitor it, then we analyse its strengths, its weaknesses, and when we have a clear view of how it operates and whom it operates through and from, we place our foot above this nasty little toad, and stamp it out".

The Chief's words carried authority and conviction, which comforted the assembled officials, as they were meant to do. He himself knew it would not be that simple. His adversary was a cunning and skilled operator; he knew that from his previous experience. At the same time, the Chief relished the chance of another crack at getting his opponent behind bars as soon as possible.   Another benefit of this new wave of excessive fraudulent activity was that Farquhar-Brown had to some extent been neutered and by-passed, being left sheepishly aware that time had shown the Chief had been right, and he, the great and celebrated Director-General, had been shown to be hopelessly wrong. For the time being at least, Farquhar-Brown would keep a low profile in this case, giving the Chief some breathing space to make some headway.

The Chief frowned to himself as these thoughts

crossed his mind. There was a great deal of work to do. He knew more than anyone that it might not be anything like as simple as portrayed to the insecure delegates.

One thing he knew for certain was whose head would be on the block if he failed.

4

It wasn't difficult to find her. Given his vast resources and resourcefulness, he had the details in front of him within days of his decision to have her traced. She was living in Hemel Hempstead just outside London, and she was living with a man, she was unmarried.

Along with the file on his desk, there were photographs, bittersweet memories of the past. Seeing her face was like a ghost come to life, it haunted him as he stared at her, his heart gripped by a red hand, the emotional pain intense. To see his children grown older and yet so recognisable was almost too much to bear. To think that he was a stranger to them crippled him inside. Yet he had to look, he had to open that box.

Some days later, he travelled to England, picked up a rental car from Hertz, and drove to Hemel Hempstead. For some hours he sat parked nearby the pleasant but modest suburban house where his family lived. Eventually, she emerged, smiling and happy, the children in tow. He felt his heart almost stop, his throat went suddenly dry. He watched her shuffling the children into her ancient car, and studied her legs, her figure, her face, until she vanished into the car and drove off. He didn't follow.

Night came, and he was still sitting there, his brow wet with perspiration from the tension and the trauma. He turned on the car engine, and when the temperature reached the appropriate point, feeling suddenly cold inside, he switched on the heater, but the trouble was, the cold was inside him.

Then she came back, and unloaded the children. A man was with her, the man she lived with. He couldn't hate him, but he wished he hadn't seen him, it was as if he had been replaced in every way. It made him feel that he, her husband, the children's father, had never been alive. His eyes filled with tears as he contemplated the alternative life he could have had but for the events that had overtaken them. He turned on the car engine, but not to warm himself this time. He slipped the car into gear and drove away, into the night.

5

"What would you like for Supper?" his Wife asked, her voice disguising the tension between them. The Chief looked up from his papers, squinting over his glasses at his Wife.

"Some cheese on toast would be fine thank you". He always had cheese on toast, so the conversation was somewhat superfluous, but the rituals had to be observed.

They both knew the marriage was in trouble. He had grown more and more distant from her, his relationship with Susan had taken precedence, he was a virtual stranger to her, and because of his guilt, he treated her even more off-handed, even more as a mere servant.

She also knew this, but tolerated it, for the alternative was disaster and chaos, the end of everything she knew. She even knew about Susan. A so-called 'friend' had told her long ago of the affair, but she did not dare raise the subject with her husband, for it might mean that he would confirm the worst, and her world would end.

So they played out this charade, acting 'normally', but actually, nothing was normal at all. The Chief's thoughts were all with Susan. He knew he had to do something about it, for Susan wouldn't wait forever, she was an action girl, she expected decisions, decisive decisions from the man she looked up to. He wasn't sure he could deliver. There was so much to lose, all his hard-earned material gains could go up in smoke, and all for the sake of a bit of skirt. The trouble was, he loved her, that couldn't be dismissed by appeals to his logic or practicality. He didn't want to lose her, and he most certainly would if he didn't leave his Wife and soon. He felt trapped and alone in his dilemma.

"Would you like some tea as well?" The dispassionate voice of his Wife broke through his deliberations.

"Yes Dear, if you don't mind," he said, a creature of habit in his responses as well as his preferences. He gazed absent-mindedly at the TV screen, not really taking in the cheap American sit-com that was wafting across the screen like a cheap commercial.

"Shall we go to Shirley's on Sunday?" said his Wife as she swept in with a supper tray.

"If you like Dear," said the Chief, trying to put some false enthusiasm into his voice, "Give them a ring," he said encouragingly, not really enthusiastic at all.

"All right then," said his Wife, mollified, but not fooled by his limpid acceptance, "I'll do that," she said, her voice indifferent, automatic.

"Fine," he said, watching the inane TV screen as if it was the most important thing in the World.

6

Farquhar-Brown was at his most indignant self. His childish face pouted with rage as he confronted the Chief, pacing the room like an angry Schoolmaster.

"Weeks have gone by, and no results!" he howled, his voice rising to a feminine shriek, "Now we find that the situation is even worse than we could have forecast - property galore is being taken over by dark forces" he wailed, his voice rising in tones full of self-pity.

The Chief remained calm, having heard it all before.

"That's not quite true," he said, as gently as he could, "We are aware of the activity, and we are monitoring it. We are merely waiting our chance to do something specific about it. As for 'property galore', we are aware that there is a concerted effort to buy across the land, but it is on the face of it at least, entirely legal. The only thing we have is the dubious method of financing the mortgages through fraudulent housing benefit claims - that's our only hold at the moment," said the Chief, pausing to allow the somewhat apoplectic figure of Farquhar-Brown to calm down, sit down, *anything*.

The restlessness filled the room.

"The thing is," said the Chief, shifting uneasily in his chair, "To pull this off, we're talking here about a superior organisation, such as we encountered in the credit scam, which if you think about it, makes perfect sense".

He looked at Farquhar-Brown, who was suddenly

still and silent. For a moment that seemed eternity, the two men looked into each other's eyes. Farquhar-Brown was the first to speak.

"This is beginning to get out of hand," he said. The Chief nodded gravely.

"Yes" he said, "But I'm afraid it will get worse before it gets better".

7

"Where are we with it now?" he asked his Lieutenant, as they sat on the veranda overlooking the bay. He sipped quietly at a Jack Daniels, half his mind on Hemel Hempstead. His grey-haired companion put down his glass, and flipped through a series of papers, which would have no meaning to anyone other than him.

"We've reached our initial target of 20,000 properties" said the Lieutenant briskly, "To get there, we've set up 200 small property companies, each with a 'front' man operating from a virtual dummy address. Each company controls around 100 houses, and each property has usually one tenant each - bogus tenants, of course. The deal is that we keep the housing benefit, the 'tenant' gets the social security payment to keep him happy, all in return for us setting up the identity, and using him/her merely as a body to attend when necessary. Each so-called 'applicant' can collect benefit for himself, and if applicable, his so-called family, without deduction from us. Each 'applicant' can claim, on average, up to ten times in a false name - he/ she can earn something like £500-£800 a week".

The other man smiled.

"And how many so-called 'applicants' do we have?" he said, somewhat sardonically.

The grey-haired Lieutenant fumbled through the papers, although he already knew the answer.

"Around ten in each company, adding up to about 2,000 in total so far," he said. "Some have 'families', some have 'partners', others are alone, but in general terms 2,000 is the figure".

"Yes, and with that exposure, they take all the risks," said the other man, smiling with satisfaction. Of course he knew exactly what the situation was without being told, but they both acknowledged the value of a regular review and the old adage of 'two heads are better than one'.

The grey-haired man grinned back, old soldiers sharing a trench.

"The beauty of it is, none of these people have a clue as to where all this is coming from".

"Nor do they care" said the other man, "As long as they get enough to help them fix".

With that last comment, his face grew hard, his mouth pulled tight, his bitterness against society showing itself. For a moment he stared into space, his mind elsewhere, then he visibly pulled himself back to the present.

"What about the income?" he asked.

"20,000 tenants at approximately £100 per week each equals £2m per week equals around £100m per annum" said the lieutenant, reeling the numbers off almost like a machine, "What next?" he asked. "Do we carry on as we are?"

The man looked at him silently for a moment.

"Yes" he finally said, "For now at least, we carry on as we are".

"Another 20,000 it is then" said his grey-haired companion with some satisfaction in his voice. He liked a long campaign almost as much as he liked the sound of gunfire.

8

As quickly as the second phase was being set up, it was being attacked. In another room in another place, the enemies of the system gathered with determined purpose. Around the flickering computer screen, Saunders, Susan, and the Chief stood watching, their faces tense and obsessed. They knew they were on to something.

"See!" said the Chief, pointing to the answer provided by their robotic friend. The question had been relatively simple – 'in a given area, list how many claimants have the same landlord?'

Susan bit her lip with tension and excitement.

"97 claimants have the same landlord," she said, stating the obvious, knowing no one was really listening to her.

Saunders was next to speak. A cautious man, he instinctively reacted against the excitement of the moment.

"Yes, but all this means is that these tenants *do* have the same landlord. I agree it's a rather large amount of claimants relatively, but it doesn't actually prove anything, especially if the landlords are legitimate".

"True" said the Chief, "And the landlords *are*, in my opinion, likely to *seem* legitimate, but what about the tenants?"

He paused, letting his words sink in, his eyes begging the question.

Susan got it immediately.

"Yes!" she said, suddenly animated, "We monitor the tenants, look into their background, find out just how genuine they are".

The Chief smiled at her warmly.

"You see, the problem until now has been that we know the likely vehicle. It's not too difficult to guess that a property company would have to be set up, in my opinion, knowing who we're dealing with, it's likely to be a *series* of property companies, area to area, just as before. The problem I think we'll face is that these companies are likely to be, on the face of it at least, legitimate. They'd only have to supply a basic deposit to buy a property. With commercial mortgages easy to obtain as long as you have the cash deposit, there would be no questions asked. The difficulty then is that these companies are not doing anything wrong, so how can we clamp down on them?"

As the Chief paused for breath, Susan stepped in.

"But if all the tenants housed by such a company prove to be non-existent or fraudulent.........." She paused, letting the Chief finish the sentence for her.

"Then we clobber them hard!" said the Chief with relish.

"So we look into the tenants who are connected to these companies," said Saunders. The others had forgotten for a moment or two that he was there at all. Shaken from his reverie, the Chief nodded his head thoughtfully.

"And my bet is that we won't have to look very long or far" he said with a deadly certainty.

9

James Germaine was doing very nicely thank you. In his smart office situated just off the Strand, he had just signed another happy investor to his bond-washing/gilt savings plan. His company - or rather, the company he was associated with (he could hardly set aside the largesse of his fellow directors who had financed the set-up of the plan) - Germaine Rouse, was now one of the most talked-about and bold investing strategies in the Country, if not yet beyond. Even that proviso was to be soon addressed.

From modest beginnings, the company had grown into a mammoth organisation, which now controlled investor's funds of some £500m. Most of that money was already held and controlled by his partners in the Isle of Man, where Germaine Rouse had installed a sister company, Germaine Rouse (IOM) Ltd.

James Germaine sighed happily as he contemplated the traffic through his smoked glass window. The business had done very well for him personally too, he reflected. He now had all the things in life he'd always craved - a large mansion in Surrey, a chauffeur driven Rolls Royce, a premium personal account with Coutts. All this, and a young and adoring new Wife who had suddenly found him to be a charming and charismatic man who just happened to also be a millionaire. Life could be very sweet, he thought to himself. He had every confidence in Albert Rouse and his associate, Pierre Arroneux.

These men had changed his life. Before they arrived
with their proposals, he had a society name, good
breeding, City connections, but he had no money,
not since his Father had lost all his wealth through a
series of disastrous ventures and poor investments.
Befuddled by drink and debauchery, and
severely depressed by
the state of his life, James' Father had died
penniless and alone in a squalid flat in Battersea.
James was only 12 at the time, away at boarding
school, and he learned of his Father's death in the
same moment he was asked to leave the school
because of unpaid fees.

That disgrace had stayed with him, and though
his many rich society friends had helped find him
various jobs and kept him in their circle, he had
always carried that feeling of poverty and of being
patronised with him. He had survived, but the scars
were always there, and life had been a struggle.

Until that day he was introduced to Albert
Rouse. Apparently a friend had recommended him
as the 'front' man for a new investment company
which would set the World alight. It was an
opportunity James could hardly refuse, and he had
in any case, warmed to Albert Rouse, finding him
charming, but modest and quiet, not a brash man at
all. To James' eye, Albert Rouse looked and acted
like a man who had been in the forces, a soldier
perhaps.

With his upright stance and clipped regimented
style, he seemed to be very self-disciplined, or used
to discipline, and his grey hair made him seem
rather distinguished.

10

It was a bright summer day when the Chief and Susan moved in together. The idyllic weather seemed a good omen for their future, Susan was happy and ecstatic, all she had dreamed of for so long seemed to be coming true. Wrapped up in the warmth of her own happiness, Susan did not seem to notice that the Chief was quiet and introspective. Perhaps she had dismissed his quietness as preoccupation with work.

Yet work was actually going well. Within a month they had succeeded in identifying and closing down at least nine property companies, and were in the process of seizing nearly 18,000 properties which had participated in housing benefit fraud. Not only that, the rate of increase of closing down property companies was accelerating all the time, it was now running at a rate of 5 now, 7 next week, and that ratio would improve week by week.

But as Susan had shrewdly pointed out, as fast as they were closing them, new companies were springing up. All they could do was speed up the ratio of closures till it overtook the new companies rate by a considerable factor.

On this, their first night together in their own house, these thoughts still walked the hallways all through the night when the waves of lovemaking had crashed and roared then ebbed away.
It seemed a long time till morning, and neither had slept much, especially the Chief, his mind awash with personal as well as professional problems.
Both of them remained fairly quiet over breakfast,

and afterwards they drove to the office, closed in their own thoughts, Susan's decidedly more rosy than the Chief's.

Susan, thinking that he was worrying about work, tried to cheer him up.

"All we need to do is to speed things up, get quicker results, and we'll have him" she said.

The Chief hadn't been thinking about 'him' at all, but warmed to the theme anyway, glad of some respite from his worries and guilt.

"Yes, we'll stop him again this time, but will we catch him?" said the Chief, "He's like an animal we're trying to net. We know the area he's moving in, but we also know how good he is at moving on to pastures new. If we don't catch him in this terrain, he'll move into seemingly legitimate business, making it even more difficult for us to pin him down. I say 'seemingly', for the die is cast now, he won't be able to play it straight for long, it's not his nature. When he raises his head again, we'll be waiting".

"And we just might get him this time" said Susan reassuringly. The

Chief smiled at her weakly, but did not say out loud what his own opinions on that were.

"What kind of person do you think he is?" asked Susan, knowing that the Chief welcomed the chance to talk about 'him'.

"He's essentially quite neat, neurotically so" said the Chief, absorbed in his analysis, forgetting his pain for a few moments. "Every so often he remembers to throw a spanner in the works, but he feels a great need to conform - he could have been a very valuable member of society, but he feels rejected, resentful. He's like a naughty child who craps in the corner to annoy his parents. Essentially he's a creature of the system you and I embrace, but he's gone wrong, fallen off the rails with a vengeance".

Susan looked at him, her eyes sad and thoughtful. "You mean he's quite like you really, only you've remained on the side of the good guys?" Her lovely face took on its usual demeanour of toughness.

"But reasons or not, he's still one of the bad guys, isn't he? We still have to eliminate him without fear or favour - or do we make excuses for everyone from Maxwell to Hitler?"

Unsmiling, the Chief fixed his eyes on her, his expression serious. "There but for the grace of God" he said.

11

Billy Rawlings had 'made it big' in the pop music World. All over the planet, people of every creed and colour sang along to his songs. Now, from his humble beginnings in a council housing estate in East Dulwich, he was living in a mansion in Hertfordshire, his every whim and fantasy indulged. He welcomed his role as victor with the spoils of his campaign.

The trouble was, deep down he was still a simple lad from a council estate. True, he had a natural talent for music and for composing the bland tunes and simple lyrics which appealed so much to his peers. He appealed to them because he was like them, he thought like them, they related to him and what he said. Not that he was unique by any means. Out there in the countryside there were thousands like him, every bit as talented or more so. But Billy Rawlings was the one who had the luck as well as the talent, though such ironies passed him by, he quite naturally assumed it was his God-given talent alone which had elevated him above his contemporaries.

Billy had a problem, which most people would welcome with open arms - he had a lot of money, and didn't quite know what to do with it. Having bought the big house, the series of classic cars etc etc, there seemed nothing else to do, and yet this money kept piling up. He had his accountant nagging him to invest it, but Billy didn't know how, and didn't trust anyone including his accountant. The answer came when a friend of his, a star of a well-loved TV soap, suggested meeting Pierre Arroneaux.

Billy had already heard the name. Everyone knew that Arroneaux had become the darling of the fast set. Gregarious and personable, yet able to mix arrogance with humility, Arroneaux was well known at all the fashionable clubs and events. A roll call of his clients consisted of the very rich and famous from movie stars and pop stars to best-selling authors and artists, to tennis players and golfers, to racing drivers and blue-bloods - anyone who was rich and better still, famous, could be part of the Arroneaux club.

He took their money and undertook to make it grow in a big way, though he was always vague about the mechanics of actually making the money grow. The clients were content to receive their monthly statements showing a considerable rise in their already vast fortunes. Through word of mouth and by sheer force of personality, Arroneaux was almost a law unto himself. To be considered as one of his clients was to be *in*.

And so it was that the famous Billy Rawlings met the famous Pierre Arroneaux. At the Grosvenor House Hotel in Park Lane, London, they met over an expensive lunch - which Pierre subsequently charged against his Billy Rawlings client account. Billy was no fool, but Pierre's mixture of confidence, sophistication, and sheer bravado carried the day as it always did. Obviously rich himself, Pierre had the good fortune to not seem as if he cared whether Billy wanted to be a client of his or not. It was an irresistible mixture.

Following the meeting, Billy went off, whistling one of his favourite 'cheeky chappie' melodies, happy that his finances would be in good hands from now on.

Billy was really whistling in the dark, for he would not have been quite so happy had he known who Pierre Arroneaux really was.

12

It was mid-summer, but the sun declined the invitation to come out. A rather cool breeze ruffled his thinning hair as he shivered across the street and into the American Express club.

"Why was it always so damn cold in England?" he muttered to himself as he felt the last draught biting his heels before the door closed behind him.

There was more than the weather irritating him. He knew that something must be wrong when his Lieutenant had summoned him so unexpectedly from the summer residence. He hurried upstairs to the library, where his Lieutenant was waiting with a Jack Daniels to warm him up.

They greeted each other in the customary fashion, patting each other on the back like brothers before settling down to business.

"So what's the score?" he said, looking at his companion quizzically.

The grey-haired man pulled a face.

"Disintegration is moving faster than we expected" he said, shuffling through a sheaf of papers, "We've now reached the stage where the rate of disintegration is at a factor of plus ten per week and rising".

"Do you mean ten houses?" asked the other man, more in hope than anything else.

"Ten companies" said the Lieutenant brusquely, "That makes 90 companies closed down so far".

"In other words, around 90,000 houses seized by the courts," said the other man, his face stern, his mouth a thin line.

"At this rate, I estimate total closure within two weeks" said the lieutenant, not prepared to soften the blow. The other man sat silent for a moment, considering the ramifications.

"What about pulling out and selling what we have left?" he asked, almost pleadingly.

"No time" said his companion. "They'll be gone within two weeks as I said".

They looked at each other in silence.

"Well that's it then," the man said finally, "We've no choice - they're gone, and that's it".

The Lieutenant was not a man for crying over spilt milk.

"The lost deposits I calculate come to around £3.24m. Lost equity I estimate at £2.16m, total losses, £6m. Income up till now I put at £66m, gives a total profit of £60m from the venture".

The other man finally smiled.

"Not bad" he said, comforting himself, though he knew his expectations had been much higher.

The grey-haired man looked at him, eyebrows raised. Seeing the unspoken question, the other man broke the silence.

"Now we move on to the next phase" he said, "It's much sooner than we anticipated, and to be honest, on this occasion we've been outflanked by our enemies, but we still have a lot to do".

For a moment he stared at his friend in silence.

"We've been down in the bottom end of the market, dealing with the dead men for long enough. It's time to move onwards and upwards," he finally said.

The Lieutenant looked at him knowingly.

"You mean our plans for the Internet?" he said, the

question in his eyes.

"Yes," said the other man, his face determined, "The battle is lost, but the War goes on."

The grey-haired man smiled. He liked the analogy.

13

As they stood and watching the flickering screens, the team, augmented by Saunders could not help but show delight in the progress they were making. 136 companies closed thus far - it was a tremendous feat of investigation as well as logistics.

"How many arrests do we have now?" said Saunders, for once almost smiling.

"Nearly 10,000" said Susan, her voice full of triumph and elation.

"And another 4,000 on the run" reminded the Chief, "As well as that, we have seizure orders on 136,000 houses which these companies owned, which means some of the lost money will be recovered".

"Minus the mortgages of course" said Saunders primly, irritating everyone else who were well aware of the nuts and bolts of the situation. Ignoring the tension that had sprung up, the Chief brought everyone's mind back to business.

"And their rate of growth I judge to be around plus 2 per week - they won't be able to keep this up!" he said, unable to disguise his feeling of victory.

Susan smiled, seeing him come alive again pleased her.

"At this rate, we'll have them closed down within weeks!" she said, touching his arm as she spoke.

"That's what you think!" said another voice, the voice of the gruff Scotsman McKay.

"Look at this!" He said, pointing at the screen.

The room was plunged into sudden silence as everyone stared at the screen in stunned disbelief.

"It's gone blank!" said someone, though everyone could see the same image.

"It's over," said the Chief. "There's no more left to close".

The silence gave way to hysterical cheering and backslapping as the team celebrated their triumph. Even Saunders accepted Susan's kiss on the cheek with a nervous smile and flushed cheeks.

The Chief and Susan found themselves face to face among the melee. He looked at her, remembering his guilty thoughts about his Wife, and thinking of what he had put her through.

"I love you," he finally said. Her eyes filled with tears.

"I love you too," she said, and their tender embrace turned into a passionate kiss, which caused everyone around them to cheer and shout "For he's a jolly good fellow!"

The sound of wine bottles opening was like an honorary burst of canon fire as the couple finally stopped kissing and accepted the embrace of the crowd.

Among this moment of triumph the Chief reminded himself that they had won a battle, not the War. He was naturally unaware of the irony attached to these thoughts.

PART THREE

SAVINGS & INVESTMENTS

1

The by-election at Burnham Green was unexceptional in most respects; the death of a sitting candidate, the election of the incumbent party - Labour - the usual motley crew of protesters, raving loony, and 'spoilers'; but among these ill-assorted bedfellows, a new kind of candidate caught the eye. Though ostensibly Tory, Jonathan Charles had fought the campaign on issues such as total integration into Europe and changes in tax laws which verged on complete abolition as a future goal.

These issues being raised had come as a surprise to Tory Central office in Smith Square. The candidate had been selected to fight the seat because not only did he have impeccable credentials as an ex-councillor and son of Eton, he was simply by a mile the most charismatic of the potential candidates available, he had seemed an obvious choice. At his selection interviews he had given no hint of such policies, only blandness and 'the party line' had emerged at that time.

Now however, to the dismay of the hierarchy, these controversial subjects were hitting the street at an alarming rate. The street was bad enough, but in this age of multimedia, the TV cameras were only too glad to seize on every juicy word, especially as the utterances seemed so far away from official Tory policy.

Mutterings from Downing Street to Smith Square began to rumble the jungle telegraph until they reached Burnham Green, but to no avail.

"Have you spoken to him?" asked Simon Reece-Morris, Principal Secretary to the Party Chairman, William Craddock.

"Yes," said the man on the other end of the line, his voice uneasy. John Bolton, the local party Chairman, felt intimidated by the big guns of Central Office leaning on him. Increasingly anxious, he tried to explain. "I've spoken to him several times on the phone, and had him in here personally. He's very charming and polite, but the bottom line is that he's basically told us to get lost".

Reece-Morris was about to hit the roof. It was a delicate time for the Party, and here was this new upstart dictating terms, not toeing the Party line.

"Tell the little shit that we want to see him as soon as this election is over!" Without waiting for a reply, he banged down the phone.

Bolton stared at the phone in his hand, the distant dialling tone ringing on incongruously as if he didn't know what to do next. It was all very well for Reece-Morris to hand down ultimatums, thought Bolton. He knew he had tried everything from threats to entreaties to Jonathan Charles' better nature, all to no avail.

The candidate seemed impervious to such blandishments and veiled threats. For one thing, for a new candidate on the political trail, Jonathan Charles seemed to have a substantial machine working on his behalf, completely independent of the Tory party itself.   Hence Bolton and the local party machine were somewhat bemused and taken aback when they were virtually side-lined by a squad of well organised, well-heeled executives, whose sole purpose was to get the candidate elected as near as damn it at least. Money seemed to be no object. Television time, radio time, and mountains of advertising for the candidate plastered the burgh. Jonathan Charles was *the* name on everyone's lips.

Understandably, the Labour candidate, Tom Green, was among those who were most perplexed. After all, this should have been a safe seat, and here he was being fought by someone who, in some ways, seemed further left than him, and that was saying something. It was like getting ready to face your opponent, only to find he was standing behind you all the time.

Green found that not only was Jonathan Charles an unusual candidate, he was an unusual person. Challenging him to a debate, getting him there, and trying to pin him down was like trying to get your hands on soap beneath the bath water. Cool as a cucumber, Charles would effortlessly deflect attacks as if they had never happened. The aggressive questioner was always left looking flat-footed and more to the point, unethical. Charles had a manner that was impossible to ruffle, a kind of wisdom emanated from him. Whether this wisdom was justified or not, the perception of the audience was all that mattered, and the answer from them seemed to be that Jonathan Charles was a breath of fresh air, a welcome new face, but to the expected beneficiary of the by-election, Jonathan Charles was a definite threat.

In the event, Green need not have worried. At the last election Labour had won this seat with a majority of 25,543, and though the gap was narrowed considerably, it was not enough. On the day in question, Green was elected with a majority of 3,221.

From the point of view of both Labour and Tory, this was a shocking result. This early into a new Parliament, and following their massive election victory, Labour should have expected to hold this seat with great comfort. To lose such a majority was a source of major concern, one that the national newspapers seized on with glee.

On the other hand, the Tory's also had a problem. The policies which Jonathan Charles had advocated, and his blatant refusal to toe the party line had obviously meant his head would be on the block from the list of future candidates. Yet not only had he reduced the majority in a safe Labour seat by 22,000, he obviously had charisma by the bucket load, and more to the point, he had clout.

Money had been poured into his campaign such as had never been seen before for a new candidate - for any candidate, for that matter.

Surprised as he was at the result of the Burnham Green election, Reece-Morris was still determined to have his say with Jonathan Charles. A crisis meeting was held at Smith Square, and the candidate himself was invited to attend The intention was to give him a grilling, drag him over the coals at the very least, but as the local officials had found to their own cost, Jonathan Charles was no ordinary candidate.

He sat down in the chair, directly facing the inquisition as if it was the most natural thing in the world, seeming oblivious to the hostile atmosphere in the room. Reece-Morris sat beside Craddock, whose stern expression was akin to Stalin getting out of bed on the wrong side. He glared at the candidate. It was the first time they had met.

"Mr Charles, you have deliberately misled the Party. At your selection, you gave an undertaking that you would follow Party policy and the manifesto. Since then, all your pronouncements have blatantly gone against that line, despite instructions being handed down on a regular basis. You chose to ignore those instructions. Do you have an explanation?"

Craddock continued to glare, his face contorted with indignation. At his side, Reece-Morris had a smug but subtle smile of satisfaction on his face.

"I disagree that I have failed to honour my undertaking to the Party," said Jonathan Charles, his calm unruffled manner irritating Reece-Morris more by the minute. "The undertaking I gave was to act in the Party's best interests. I believe I have carried that out to the full. As well as that, I have placed all my energy and resources at the disposal of the Party, and I don't think anyone can point a finger and say I have lacked commitment to the cause".

He paused to let his words sink in.

"Obviously, there are differences in style and even content on occasion. Within the bounds of Party policy, and within reason, is it wrong to express one's own opinions as a thinking, feeling, human being? Presumably, I was chosen because I am an individual rather than an automaton, yet I am criticised for bringing colour to my campaign".

"Colour is all very well, Mr Charles, but content is another matter. Your views on integration go far beyond Party policy, indeed they oppose it," said Craddock, his voice mellowing as he warmed to Jonathan, much to the irritation of Reece-Morris. "Furthermore, some of your other ideas are, at the very least, controversial. Do you expect us to endorse them, to change the Party line just for one candidate?"

Jonathan smiled reassuringly, creating a subtle empathy with Craddock that was already undermining the other man's resolve.

"Mr Craddock, of course I accept that the Party is greater than any individual, certainly greater than this particular candidate, whose contribution is at an early stage. I, unlike yourself, have the luxury of not being committed to the collective responsibility of being in the shadow cabinet. That means I can express myself in a wider context, though I admit that sometimes allusions and ideas have rather overreached themselves at times. Were I to ever achieve the responsibility of high office, I, like yourself, would be duty bound to restrain my flow of ideas in the public domain, and this I would readily do".

Craddock looked at Jonathan searchingly, the tension easing in his face.

"And you would give us such an undertaking? You would state categorically that the Party is your first concern?"

"Of course," said Jonathan, no longer smiling, suddenly serious.

Reece-Morris could hardly contain himself.

"That's all very well, Mr Charles," he said, his expression haughty, "But that's not how it seems from where we're standing. Your public pronouncements were nothing less than a statement of intent that goes well beyond the remit of the Party".

"I think Mr Charles has already dealt with that question," said Craddock, much to the fury of Reece-Morris, who immediately fell into a sullen brooding silence. Craddock had been fooled by the man's smooth demeanour, he thought, quietly fuming as he sat there impotently.

"May I comment further?" said Jonathan, hurriedly trying to smooth the ruffled waters of Reece-Morris in his sullen silence.

"Please do," said Craddock, noticeably relaxed.

"I understand the concerns expressed by Mr Reece-Morris and yourself," he said in conciliatory fashion, "But in any by-election, and indeed, especially when banished to opposition, the idea is to win, or at least, maximise the vote. Sometimes, in doing so, you have to focus on particular concerns, even to the point of magnification. This can, as in this instance, put a strain on Central Office and the manifesto. I regret that, but I had no option other than to remain single-minded in the election itself. To stop and listen to voices from the wings, as it were, however correct, however well intended, would be to lose the central drive of my campaign. In further defence of my stance, I would point to the result itself. The gain was significant, was it not? Had I reached Parliament, the Party would have had another seat, a valuable seat for its own purposes. To me, the greater good applies, the ends justify the means in this case".

"But Mr Charles, you did not win the seat, despite your liberties with our manifesto". Reece-Morris was obviously still riled.

Jonathan leaned forward, his face earnest again.

"Mr Reece-Morris, Mr Craddock. I give you my word that on being selected for a seat that is even a moderate prospect, I can deliver for you and the Party an outstanding result. I have placed all my resources at the Party's disposal thus far, and this I intend to do again, but this time, if selected, I intend to win!"

At these last few words, Jonathan's voice hardened in determination.

Craddock gave a small smile of acceptance.

"Thank you, Mr Charles, for coming to see us. We shall indeed take your comments on board when we consider reselection. We will let you know our decision in due course".

The two men shook hands, both warming to the other. Reece-Morris reluctantly shook hands with Jonathan before he left, his face betraying his frustration with the way the meeting had gone. Jonathan left the meeting satisfied with his performance. He knew he had dealt with the attempted buffeting with a style that amounted to contemptuous ease. He knew that the power brokers of Smith Square realised that he must be given a reasonably safe seat. His power was too impressive to resist, despite his controversial views. Reece-Morris could not be won over, but he was not the centre of power, Craddock was the key. Jonathan knew that Craddock would now attempt to rationalise his approach to the extreme views expressed at Burnham Green. He would tell himself that perhaps these could be reasoned with, smoothed out, contained within the Party machine.

Jonathan Charles and his financial backers had other ideas.

2

Jane was 'playing up'. The Chief was a most unhappy man. As he sat in the cramped bedroom of the tiny flat he now shared with Susan - there was practically nowhere else to hide with his own thoughts - he pondered wearily over the events surrounding the break up of his marriage. Here he was, living with a very beautiful and intelligent woman whose sexual attraction had delivered its promises in triplicate. He loved Susan deeply, yet why did he still feel love and heartache over Jane?

True, Jane was also a beautiful and intelligent woman, but he could clearly see that after twenty-four years together, they had drifted apart in many ways. The coming of Susan had opened his eyes to what fulfilment was again, and his marriage to Jane had been for a long time in a state of apathy at best.

Susan appeared in the bedroom doorway, her face perplexed. "What are you doing sitting through here?" she asked. The Chief smiled ruefully at her, in a somewhat artificial manner.

"Now Darling, you know I can't stand those American TV sitcoms you watch - nothing personal, but no thanks".

Unsure of exactly what his response was hiding, Susan smiled sadly, and went back to the frantic sounds of her soap opera.
The Chief returned in his mind to his own soap opera. His last conversation with Jane was fraught to say the least. Though her eyes were red rimmed, they looked at him coldly, almost as if he was a specimen spiked spider in a glass case. Her words

227

were full of venom, her financial and settlement
demands were becoming ever more impossible and
unrealistic. It was obvious she just wanted to crucify
him for leaving her, for loving someone else.

The easy thing to do would be to fight back, to try
and hate his Wife as she seemed to hate him, he
thought. Yet he couldn't do it. There was the guilt,
of course, there were the children too, but he knew
it was more than these things. He still felt love for
her. But how could that be when he loved Susan?
He had no sexual desire to be with his Wife, and he
had found complete sexual satisfaction beyond his
wildest dreams in his relationship with Susan. It was
as if he had become two persons, one who required
the love of the soul mate he was bonded to, the
other requiring the sexual love which his soul mate
somehow was not able to provide him with.

He had split up with his Wife, but in the process, it
appeared as if he had also split up himself, and
neither self seemed able to exist as a whole person.
As his anguished mind peered through the quandary
of his own scattered emotions, the aggravating
sounds of the frantic TV filtered through from the
next room.

He knew that there would be no sleep for him again
that night.

3

In his life he had known moments of happiness, but only in these flickering instants had his life amounted to anything, there was no thread of happiness running through his years. Now, as night fell and he sat alone in dark luxurious room of his substantial house overlooking the bay, he was only too painfully aware of where he stood in the scheme of things. For today, he had met with his Wife.

Sitting here now, immersed in his pain, he admitted to himself that he should never have arranged the meeting, no good could possibly come of it, but his regular clandestine visits to the place where she lived had gnawed at his insides till he succumbed to temptation.

Through his contacts, he had arranged for his Wife's bank manager to ask to see her about her account. However, when she called at the bank she was shown into a private room and asked to wait. After a few moments, a man walked in whom she did not at first recognise.

"Hello Edith" he said, and she instantly recognised that voice, her face turning ashen white, her eyes wide and disbelieving.

"It's you" was all she could stammer.

When she had composed herself, she studied him as he spoke. He seemed old, weary, his eyes were lined with torment, he was.......different, different to the man she remembered so well.

"How are you Edith?" he said, the question containing far more meaning than the words alone conveyed.

"I'm fine" she said, her face hardening as she

looked at him questioningly, "But why have you done this? Why are you here? Why the pretence?" He smiled sadly.

"Would you have met me if I had asked?"

They stared at each other in silence, both knowing the answer to that question.

"How did you find me?" she said, knowing as she spoke that her question was pointless. She knew better than anyone, how resourceful he could be. He smiled ruefully, knowing that no detailed nor specific answer was necessary.

"You know me," he said, a bitter thought crossing his face as he spoke.

"But the bank manager........." she said, realising what connections her former husband must have accumulated. A dark thought came to her.

"What are you involved in?" she said, her instincts warning her that all was not well with him.

"It won't surprise you to know that I have contacts," he said, looking at her quizzically, "I've made progress since I last saw you". It sounded almost like a childish boast. She looked at him sternly, her face severe again.

"Have you?" she said.

He knew what she meant and quickly changed the subject.

"How are the children?" he asked, feeling his eyes welling up with tears despite himself. It was so wonderful, and yet so painful to see her, to talk to her. He longed to reach out and hold her hand, but although the understanding and bond between them was still somehow tangible, there was an invisible barrier which he knew he could never cross.

"The children are fine, not so much children now, they've grown up since you've been gone" she said, a sadness in her eyes. She looked at him gently.
"They don't remember you" she said, knowing how that would hurt him, but feeling that it must be said.
"I know," was all he could mutter, his voice cracking, his face contorting in an effort not to show what he was feeling inside, as if he could hide it from her, of all people.
She reached out and put her hand on his. He almost recoiled with the shock of her touch, the touch of a ghost.
"It has to be this way," she said, looking at him sadly, "There's no other way, you know that, don't you?"
He looked at her, his mind disagreeing, but knowing that she was talking about her own feelings, not his. He said nothing, and they stared at each other silently for an eternity.
She stood up, looking down at him as he sat there.
"Please don't contact me again," she said, "It's not good for either of us, and the children are content as they are - I know you're not selfish, and I know you'll remember that what I've said is true".
He sat there, numb, saying nothing.
"It's for the best," she said firmly, staring hard at him to make sure he got the point.
"One more thing" she said, her hand on his shoulder now, "Don't go too far, will you?"
"You know what I mean," she added forcefully.
They both knew what she meant.
       He tried to hold her with his eyes, feeling her slip away, vanishing forever. His heart was

gripped inside with a red glove.

"Take care of yourself" was all he could manage to say. She looked at him with eyes that were almost guilty for her present happiness, a happiness she knew he could never achieve, whatever else.

"You too" she said, looking at him sadly, and then she was gone.

4

Billy Rawlings was strolling round beside his indoor swimming pool, a large cocktail glass in one hand, his financial statement from Pierre Arroneaux in the other. Billy was very pleased with himself indeed. Not only was his recording and film career making him millions, his investments were doubling, tripling his wealth.

"Monica, listen to this" he said, feeling the need to share his exuberance with someone. His rather sycophantic girlfriend responded as expected.

"Oh Billy, tell me, tell me!" she gasped, her fulsome cleavage heaving towards him, giving him an eyeful he was already quite bored with. Almost oblivious to anything Monica said or did, Billy used her as an excuse to speak about himself. She was his temporary audience.

"These investments off shore are reaping fantastic dividends" said Billy, his voice excited and echoing through the high halls of his rather gauche and gaudy mansion.

"The UK investments brought in 10-15% in the last year - which is good in its own right - but the offshore stuff fetched me a cool 58%! What do you make of that?" he asked, stopping his monologue, looking at Monica as if for the first time.

"Wonderful Billy, just wonderful!" she fawned, brazenly allowing one breast to fall nakedly from her skimpy bra.

God she could be irritating, though Billy, aware of her vacant expression as well as her exposed breast, which looked slightly ridiculous out there on its own.

Somehow sensing that Billy required more of a response from her, Monica temporarily saved the situation by her next big thought.

"Why don't you put more of your money into offshore investments Honey?" she said, recovering her composure as well as her lost boob, her face adopting a serious expression.

Billy looked at her gravely, the fun gone out of it for him. An audience that didn't understand was almost as bad as an audience that hated you, he thought. But she was right in what she said, he concluded. Perhaps she wasn't always as dumb as she looked.

"Yeah" said Billy, "That's exactly what I intend to do. I'll call Pierre over tomorrow", he said, quietly contemplating.

"Will I like him?" said Monica.

"Yeah, I'm sure you will," said Billy, smiling to himself. One thing for sure, Pierre would like Monica - he liked them with curves, no inhibitions, and no brains. Most of all, he liked to rough them up a bit. Maybe Monica could stay awhile after all, thought Billy. At least till tomorrow, then Pierre could take over the reins. They could ride off into the sunset together. The cow and the cowpuncher. The thought made Billy laugh out loud. He liked the thought of Pierre being saddled with his trade-ins.

For one thing, he thought, Pierre was a bit too smug and smart by half. Billy was glad of the profits Pierre was making for him and his friends, he was glad to spread the word about this financial

Messiah, but at the same time, he decided that no-one, especially a smart-assed foreigner was going to be his guru forever and a day. He would use him, use his knowledge. Then, when he deemed the time was right, he would pull completely out, leaving Pierre high and dry, just as he would do to Monica tomorrow. She had been enjoyable for a while, but now she had served her purpose, outlived her usefulness, and Monica and Pierre could both get screwed in more ways than one.

Unknown to Billy, he was the one who was really being screwed.

5

The phone rang on Jim Barton's desk. Slightly irritated, Jim stopped working on his latest piece for *The Times* 'Insight' team, grabbed the phone and growled.

"Yes?"

The male voice on the other end of the line seemed unfazed by Jim's brusque manner - the caller was Tom Parkins from Cazenove, the up-market City brokers.

"Jim, it's Tom here - I've been looking at this Germaine Rouse business as you asked me to - I can't for the life of me see how they can justify the returns they claim, it's just not feasible".

"Do you know what you're saying to me?" said Jim, incredulous and interested now.

"Of course I do," said Tom, "But the returns they forecast aren't just a little way off achievable, they're miles out unless someone is carrying a loss".

"And we both know who that someone is, don't we" said Jim, his voice suddenly serious.

"Well" said Tom, "They're not running the whole show for charity, are they?"

Jim smiled cynically to himself.

"Only their own" he said.

Jim said his goodbye and thank you to Parkins, and sat at his desk, excited and nervous at the same time. For months now, he had been monitoring Germaine Rouse and its activities, like all good reporters, he could smell a rat, and despite little headway with the investigation, he had persevered. True, there was still no tangible evidence, but he had noted James Germaine's steady accumulation of the usual trappings of megalomania. There was the large yacht, the personal jetliner, the acquisitions into unrelated areas like property, brewing, vineyards in France and the like, none of which he should have been able to earn from his admittedly large income alone.

It was also true to say that none of the records of Germaine Rouse's accounts were alarming in any way, and the accountants - the very respectable firms of accountants - had so far given them a completely clean bill of health. Thus far too, there were no complaints from the investors, who seemed content with their ever- escalating returns. But Jim Barton had seen all of these things happen before, and in his opinion it would all end in tears for the individual investors, as usual.

He gathered up the papers he had put together on the Germaine Rouse case, and hurried to his Editor, Fred Harrison, who in his turn, was slightly irritated when Jim burst in on him. Irritation went with the job, no one took it personally, not till the sparks began flying anyway.

"What is it?" snapped Fred, his mind already losing the thread of what he had been doing. Impatiently, he shuffled the papers in his hand as he focused on Jim.

"Fred, it's the Germaine Rouse business. I've just had a call from Tom Parkins - the City broker who we asked to look again at the returns for investors - to put it bluntly, he says 'No Way', it can't be done".

Fred looked hard at him for a moment. The silence

seemed an eternity, thought Jim. Finally Fred made his decision.

"We go with it" he said, "Take Cliff, Alice and John, and get to work on it big time".

Jim grinned all over his face.

"Thanks Boss" he said turning to go.

"Don't thank me" said Fred, "Just get it right - OK?".

Jim, still grinning, nodded and rushed off to assemble his team. There was a lot of work to do, and no time to lose.

6

The flickering screens of the rows and rows of computer monitors were frantic with activity; this in itself was nothing unusual, but the level of cash withdrawals had caused at least one computer operator to gasp with astonishment. Johnny Stein was sharper than most, and when he saw the waves of activity, he didn't hesitate. Within moments, his Controller was by his side.

"What is it Johnny?" she asked, gazing anxiously over his shoulder.

"These cash transactions taking place - they're way above the norm for this time section" said Johnny, running the program back so his controller could see what he'd observed. He didn't really have to. The screens were still alive with the same level of activity.

Denise, his controller, patted Johnny appreciatively on the shoulder.

"Good on you Johnny" she muttered, though her voice was already looking ahead to the unwelcome task of phoning her Director of operations. Denise knew that it wasn't the best of times to do it. The Director was a social animal, probably preening himself at some function or other, but she knew there was no choice, the situation was too serious for that, and she had to, above all else, protect her own back.

As expected, Michael Renton, the Director was irritated and snapped at her. In the background, multimedia music was playing, almost lost in the hubbub of an assortment of voices, screaming, laughing, talking, shouting.

"Yes - what is it now!" Renton snarled, distracted from his attempts to grab the pretty blonde Wife of another guest.

"We've noticed an usually high level of cash withdrawal facilities Sir," said Denise humbly, "What do you want us to do?"

There was silence for a moment as the exasperated Director realised that he couldn't in all conscience avoid this one.

"I'll deal with it," he said reluctantly, and with great irritation. "I'll send someone down," he finally said, slamming the phone to end the conversation without politeness or formality. At the other end, Denise, looked for a moment at the dormant phone, muttered a few silent curses and went back to her position.

A short time later, a visitor arrived at the computer room. He was a tough-featured veteran of such situations, who was used to being called out at all times and in a great hurry to boot.

"My name's McKay" he said, shaking Denise's hand brusquely.

It didn't take McKay long to evaluate the situation. Grim-faced, he stepped to the side of the vast room and dialled a number on his mobile phone.

"Yes?" a voice answered.

"Chief, it's Dave" said McKay, "I've had a call out, and I'm afraid it's bad news."

"I know what you're going to say Dave," said the Chief before McKay could complete his summary.

McKay was not surprised. He knew well enough by now, how sharp his boss was.

"Yes Chief, you're right," he said. "It's started again"

7

It was a sad day, one of the saddest of his life. It was the day he left love behind, the day he left Susan, for always through the glimpses of supreme happiness he had experienced in the last few months, he had been haunted by Jane's face. Step by step the guilt had grown until he could bear it no longer. Something had to give, and it was their love.

This last morning in their bedroom had been one of the most traumatic days he could recall. He didn't have to say anything, Susan could sense his dilemma as he paced the room from the very early hours. She looked at him sadly, but there was fear in her eyes.

"You're bewildered, aren't you?" she said, in pity as much as accusation. He couldn't frame a reply. He felt lost, frightened, alone. The unfamiliarity of what was now his life was closing in on him, and much as he loved Susan, the darkness was overtaking him, the fear was overshadowing the love.

Susan was a strong woman, she'd often said to him "If you ever want to go, then go - I'm not the type to cling to your legs". She realised at this moment she was stronger emotionally than he was, and she loved him enough to hand him the gun that would finish them both.

"You want to get out of this, and it seems you're waiting for me to release you," she said, her voice and her eyes hard and cold, the hurt showing through. He looked at her sadly, guilt written on his face, his own weakness feeding on itself.

"But I love you" was all he could stammer. Susan looked at him, her mouth a thin line of pain. "Not enough, it seems," she said with finality.

Susan suddenly leapt from the bed, and began furiously packing her cases.

"What are you doing?" he said, stating the obvious.

"You won't make a move - though you want to - so I will save you the trouble" she said angrily.

He never offered a response, for he knew that she was telling the truth, he did want 'out', he did want the pressure taken off, he did want to return to all that was familiar, all that was safe and comfortable. And yet, he loved her. His torment kept him silent, the two opposing forces inside him counteracting against each other. How could this be possible? His mind was reeling with pain and confusion, he could hardly think at all, his feelings were in a mess, all over the place. Here was the woman he loved, and yet part of him was glad she was 'letting him off the hook' - what on earth was going on inside his mind? His heart lurched with despair as he could see no easy solution to this crisis of identity. It seemed as if his personality, his whole being was now split into two people, the man who loved Susan, and the man who lived with Jane and the children as husband and father. Which one was he, the person who stood here drenched in his own confusion?

Susan had finished packing, yet now she had, she did not know quite what to do. Part of her still hoped he would come to his senses, tell her it was all her imagination, it was all just a bad dream. Instead, he stood there like a lemon, saying nothing, obviously stunned and incoherent, immobile, doing nothing to stop her. Tears filled her eyes as a devastating thought came to her.

"I suppose it was just the sex," she said, her voice quivering with shame and emotion. It was his turn to feel shame and guilt, and he looked askance at her, not yet daring to look her in the eyes.

"Oh no" was all he could say, his voice unconvincing and limp. His heart ached to hold her, tell her that she was so wrong. How could it be just the sex?

The love they had shared was special, it was he who was at fault, not Susan nor the love between them. Perhaps he was just too old for the dramatic change which was necessary to bring them together, he thought. Another thought occurred to him, and before he could stop himself, he said aloud to Susan.

"The trouble is, we have no history together".

As the words came out, he realised that it was the wrong thing to say at that moment. To compare the time he had shared with Susan to the past he had shared with Jane, seemed, he realised, crassly insensitive to Susan's feelings, especially at the very moment when their own brief history was coming to an abrupt end.

Susan burst into tears, and struggled out the door with her case. He stood there, not stopping her, not helping her, even when she returned for case after case, lamp after lamp, carrier bag upon carrier bag. He just stood there. Watching. Thinking how cruel and callous he was, rooted to the spot by a torrent of conflicting emotions.

He heard the roar of the engine, and stirred himself

sufficiently to watch her car race off at great speed. A sense of unreality overwhelmed him as he looked around the room they had shared for such a brief flickering time.

He saw that she had left behind the ring he had given her as a token of their love. His eyes could barely see it glisten through the tears that filled his eyes, but there it lay, a final comment, lying on the mantle above the fireplace. Almost in desperation, he cast his eyes to the ceiling, then back to the room. Somehow he moved himself, his automatic legs miraculously taking him to the bedside cabinet where lay the letters he had written to her, thousands of words of love, now obsolete and empty.

Knowing he must, he began to pack his own meagre possessions. It was time to leave this place, which had once been a place of love. Now it held only devastating memories, and mountains of grief to climb in an effort to live again.

He locked the door and drove away to whatever the future held.

8

The lights were burning late in the offices of APACS. Once more the smoke from rich Havana cigars drifted like clouds through the crystal chandeliers of the ornate boardroom. In the chair for the meeting was Farquhar-Brown, who called the meeting to order.

As the hubbub died down, the Chief, who had only just arrived as usual, glanced hurriedly around the table. To his right, a few places down, he could see Lord Wetherby. Sitting at the left-hand side of Farquhar-Brown was John Sanders, Head of Fraud at the Benefits agency. Turning to his left, two places along, Sir James Telfer of Yorkshire Bank gave him a cursory nod. Immediately opposite the Chief was Wesley Sykes, the APACS PR guru. Through a haze of smoke, the Chief had a brief glimpse of Lord Sefton, and many, many more men who were famous among the banking and financial community.

"Gentlemen" said Farquhar-Brown as the room became finally silent, "I have called this meeting to discuss our present difficulties with fraud, in particular, fraud in the mortgage and housing benefit areas................"

As the Director-General's voice droned on, the Chief found his mind drifting away to the traumatic events of his recent life. His homecoming to Jane, though fraught with difficulties at first, had now settled into a comfortable routine, at least as far as Jane and outward appearances were concerned. The Chief himself was deeply troubled and unhappy. At night he would wake, gasping and sweating, his dreams full of Susan and that last goodbye. She haunted him in his lonely hours, and worse still, he now had to see her every day in the course of his work, yet they could not talk nor look at each other except in those moments when duty demanded it. The strain was telling on them both, and he knew it couldn't go on as it was, something had to give. The trouble was, he still loved her, and though he was grateful to see the general sense his life made again, it was also obvious to him that life with Jane could never be as it once was, the old days were truly gone forever.

He was caught between two women and two lives. One life held all his future and capital investments, not to mention the security he drew from Jane's mere presence, and yet he had another life now, one in which there was only Susan, who held his heart, his emotional commitment, but with whom he shared nothing else. They had no history, no past, no possessions - they had only each other, and now, they didn't even have that.

Yet the Chief knew that something tangible remained - his love was undiminished, and the anguish of their enforced silence and separation was tearing him apart. At first, he could see from looking at Susan what she was feeling inside. She was pale, drawn, haunted. It had obviously affected her deeply too. But Susan was a woman of great strength and determination, and as the weeks had gone by, she seemed to have shrugged off the depression and trauma, she was beginning to laugh again, though to the Chief's chagrin, her laughter was reserved for everyone else but him.

"..........and we are resolved to deal with this matter thoroughly and professionally........." Farquhar-Brown was still making all the right noises.

The Chief sighed wearily. It was all very well for the Director-General to promise everything to the multitudes, it wasn't Farquhar-Brown who would have to deliver. He pulled his mind away from Susan, and thought of the problems he was having in dealing with this fraud. Perhaps he wasn't in the right frame of mind, he thought, but it did seem that events were slipping away from him. He should more accurately say "frauds" he thought, for there were now two clear revivals of the systematic attacks on credit and housing benefit which had seemed vanquished not so long ago.

To have the frauds to deal with all over again was bad enough, but the fact was that the frauds were being operated under considerably altered procedures, albeit with some of the same characteristics. As the Chief well knew, this meant starting the investigations from scratch, and time was on the enemy's side, not his, despite Farquhar-Brown's positive statements (and expectations).

The Chief's mind returned to the present. The Director-General was winding down his soothing speech. Within a few moments, he had invited comments round the table, and as usual, most of the familiar faces had their say - Lord Sefton, Sir James Telfer, Lord Wetherby et al, most of their comments showing barely hidden anxiety and insecurity about holding on to their own wealth and position. It was the usual mutterings and grumblings. The Chief

248

sighed again. Though he rose to his feet next, and gave all the familiar assurances within a report so vague as to almost negligible, his heart wasn't really in it, and he finally sat down to a flat reaction, the atmosphere dull, a feeling of stillness in the air. As Farquhar-Brown introduced John Sanders, he gave the Chief an odd stare, his eyes questioning. The Chief realised that if he didn't get his act together soon, his head would roll, despite his commendable record thus far.

It was late. As the meeting finally closed, the Chief hurried from the boardroom before Farquhar-Brown could accost him. As it was, the Director-General was trapped with Neville Whitewood and Wesley Sykes, giving the Chief the opportunity to slip away, though he could feel the Director-General's eyes on his back as he hurried from the room to his waiting car.

Listlessly, he drove through the neon streets and into the countryside, his mind numb, his thought processes dulled by his anguish over Susan. Life seemed so pointless without her, he thought. Yet when he had lived with her, he was restless and unhappy - why? That question had hurt more than any other since Susan and had parted. He sighed deeply again. His life seemed to have become a bridge of sighs, he thought, as his car cruised quietly into his dark driveway.

Jane was already in bed. He poured himself a stiff drink, and sat down on the couch, stretching his legs out wearily. Languidly, he switched on the TV, but kept the 'mute' button on, his eyes not really taking in the frantic images crossing the screen.

What now? His thoughts desperately tried to move on from Susan, Susan, Susan.

Forcing himself, he opened his brief case, and sifted through his papers, aware that he had to begin to focus on the job in hand, otherwise everything would fall, his whole life such as it was, without Susan. Farquhar-Brown was waiting in the wings with an axe should he falter.

He looked at his notes on the credit fraud. Since it had sprung up again, they had tried to dismantle the fraud using the same methods as before, but it hadn't worked. The accounts that they had managed to identify as bogus had been targeted as before, and linked to accommodation addresses, but so far, it had proved impossible to find any flaw or dubious contact within the accommodation addresses. Sipping at his drink, his mind managed to make the next logical move. There was only one answer - the accommodation addresses were genuine. The system had been changed. It should have been obvious, he realised. But for his preoccupation with Susan, he wouldn't have taken this long to 'fall in'. Cursing himself, he poured another drink, and tried to visualise what was going on.

If the accommodation addresses were actually genuine, then it must mean that the houses used for the fraud were not being sidelined as before, but were actually being used for collection purposes. The Chief already knew from enquiries with the Post Office that there was no mail being forwarded from the houses the fraud was centred on. So, he thought, the next step is to target each house. As he said it to himself, he immediately realised the problem. If the fraud was as widespread as before, then it would mean a slow and painstaking process, for *each* bogus account must be completely individual!

"Yes" he said out loud, "But the system itself *must* contain centralisation in it *somewhere* along the pipeline - what we have to do is follow just one strand until it becomes multiple".

It was no good, he was getting tired, his mind was clouding over. He began to drift into sleep as the half-sat, half-laid on the couch. His weary soul permitted him one slight smile before he gave in to unconsciousness.

"I'm definitely on to something" was his last thought.

His restless dreams though, were all of Susan.

9

The television cameras recorded the moment; it was in the early hours of a rainy Wednesday morning that the diminutive local official found his one minute of fame. As the eyes of the Nation watched and listened, a white-faced, bespectacled Alf Rogers nervously and self-consciously delivered the verdict of the polls.

"As Returning Officer for the district of Langton in the region of Humberside, I hereby declare that the electorate of Langton have cast their votes as follows - William Knowles...... [at this point the breathless voice of the TV commentator interpolated "Labour"]........ 11,431 [audience cheers]........; David Hepplethwaite...... ["Liberal"].........4,657 [cheers/laughter/howls of derision].........; Lord David Sutch...........["Monster Raving Loony"]...........879 [ironic cheers/laughter]............; Jonathan Charles...... ["Conservative"]........ 17, 468.......[howls of delight/screams of dismay].........". The next candidate's name was all but obliterated by the melee following the mention of Jonathan Charles, but Alf struggled gamely on to be heard through the ensuing din, nevertheless, the TV commentator's voice was the first to be heard.........["Independent"]...........Alf's voice returned to the airwaves......... "244 [laughter/abuse].............; Winifred Oku......["Black Workers for Freedom Party"].........29 [a handful of cheers]...............I therefore declare that the said Jonathan Charles is hereby elected as Member of Parliament for

2

Langton and District"..........[triumphant cheers/dismayed howls of frustration].............

By any standards, it was a sensational victory for Jonathan Charles. The TV studios were ablaze with light and excitement. Pundit after pundit analysed the result, and its implications. On the BBC, Sir Roger Drake was interviewing the Chancellor, Adam Clayton in a 'Panorama' special.

"Chancellor, what do you make of this result?" he asked mischievously, a twinkle in his eye.
The rather pompous Clayton pulled a face, showing his dismay.

"Well, it's obviously a freak result" he said, his mouth pouting almost in a sulk, "Come the General Election, this will be reversed, and we'll have the seat back".

The Chancellor was about to continue, but Sir Roger was not famous as 'the Grand Master' for nothing. Before Clayton could say another word, Sir Roger was back at him.

"But Chancellor, surely this should have fairly easy to hold this seat. After all, we're supposed to be in a period of Labour ascendancy. As well as that, you've been making *all* kinds of remarks about the extremist nature of Mr Charles himself - not even a *mainstream* Tory, according to your lot, yet he's given you a bloody nose, here, hasn't he?"
The Chancellor gave Sir Roger a cold stare, then countered.
"Mr Drake........."
"*Sir Roger*, if you don't mind" interjected the crusty interviewer.
"I apologise - *Sir Roger*," said Clayton, now clearly

irritated, but trying not to show it, "Sir Roger, you know as well as I do that in mid-Parliament, the Government of the day always suffers a reaction from its own supporters. It's a reminder that we must be vigilant, not be complacent. These by-elections inevitably produce the kind of freak result we've seen tonight. When this sort of thing happens, all the clichés come out of the woodwork from you and your colleagues. We all sit here and talk the thing up hill and down dale, yet we all know equally well that the likelihood - certainty, I'd say - is that we will reverse this result come the election".

Sir Roger decided to move on.

"Very well Chancellor, but what have you got to say now about the Labour party's comments regarding Mr Jonathan Charles himself? Hasn't he proved you wrong on that score as well?"

"That can't be so," said Clayton, his Donnish face haughty and disapproving, "As I've said, the result here isn't based on policies, it's based on voter and supporter reaction against the sitting Government, nothing more. As for Mr Charles himself, I think you'll find that not many Conservatives within his own party would approve of his agenda. He represents an extreme point of view which, but for his funding - which he has yet to explain, by the way - I suggest to you without that funding, his vote would have been akin to the Monster Raving Loonies".

Sir Roger smiled. He enjoyed it when his opponents were rattled.

"But Chancellor, are you saying that the voters - and, as you've said by implication, your own

254

supporters are so unintelligent, so easily led, that it only takes superior funding - questionable or otherwise - to convince them to vote from someone whom you describe as an extremist?"

Adam Clayton was becoming annoyed now.

"It is very damaging for someone in a responsible position like yourself to misrepresent what I am trying to say".....

"I am not misrepresenting you, I am quoting back to you what you said, and drawing the obvious conclusion from it" said Sir Roger, waving his papers at Clayton, as always prepared to swap blows with his opponent.

Before the Chancellor could say more, Sir Roger deftly switched the angle of the controversy, therefore leaving his controversial comments naked for the viewers to digest.

"But while we're on that subject, Chancellor - you say that Jonathan Charles has not explained his funding - what do you mean by that?"

Clayton recognised that he had been outmanoeuvred, but realised he had no option but to follow the agenda set by Sir Roger.

"I mean that vast sums of money have been poured into supporting Mr Charles - unprecedented advertising, a support team working with him which would be the envy of a Presidential campaign in the United States - all this, yet it bears no resemblance to his declared expenses".

Sir Roger fastened his eyes narrowly on Clayton.

"Are you saying that Mr Charles is guilty of corruption?"

Clayton was not about to fall for that one, as Sir

Roger well knew.

"No, of course not" blustered the Chancellor, uncomfortable, but determined, "What I am saying is that clarification is needed, questions have been asked by myself and others, but no answers are forthcoming".

Sir Roger's producer signalled to him that the interview was over. "Well, we shall hopefully have the answer to that and other questions in the near future. Perhaps we will have the opportunity to talk to Mr Jonathan Charles ourselves, in due course. Meantime, thank you Chancellor, for taking the time to talk to us here at the BBC. We shall leave you, the viewers with the images of the evening in Langton - back now to the Municipal Hall in Langton, where I understand Jonathan Charles is making his acceptance speech".

"....................for too long Britain has been allowed to sink beneath the weight of its own history........." Jonathan Charles was at the microphone, his deep baritone easily rising above the chorus of catcalls and abuse being hurled at him from the floor of the Municipal Hall. Beneath the great lights, a sea of bodies heaved and howled, the victors and the vanquished mingling unhappily.

On the platform behind Jonathan Charles, the motley crew of candidates stood variously happily and gloomily, depending on their expectations. Standing awkwardly with his crestfallen Wife, who knew what diatribes she would have to listen to for the next twenty years, the Labour candidate, William Knowles, was bitter and silent, his mouth a gash, his eyes black with resentment and fear. He knew that this result spelled the end of his political career as far as the big league was concerned. It should have been an easy seat to hold, he knew that, and he also knew that the selection board at Walworth Road would now sideline him as 'a loser', for the days of 'comrades' were gone, now that a 'New Labour' party aspired to so much that was American.

To the right of William Knowles, David Hepplethwaite, the Liberal Democrat candidate was quietly pleased. He wasn't expected to win anyway, and for his first attempt at a Liberal seat, he'd not done too badly, increasing his party's vote since the election. He could be sure of a safer seat to fight for next time. The other minority candidates mainly stood laughing and smiling, especially Lord Sutch - they were only in it for the beer, or a laugh at least, only Winifred Oku, of the 'Black Workers for Freedom Party' stood there scowling, her wildly unrealistic expectations having come home to roost. As for Jonathan Charles himself, it was a triumphant night, yet he did not seem unduly elated. It was, after all, no more than he expected as his right, the reward for his talents, his power. Beside him stood Elsbeth, his beautiful (and obligatory) Wife. As she stood watching and listening to her husband with a suitably proud smile on her lovely face, she knew that this was only the beginning of a long adventure. She knew Jonathan Charles well enough to recognise that fact clearly enough. Jonathan was winding down his speech.

"........For too long, we have been rendered impotent, silent - now, thanks to you, the voters of

Langton with your sense of vision, your courage - thanks to you, my brothers, my sisters and I are no longer silent - we have a voice - and mark my words, WE INTEND TO USE IT!".

As Jonathan Charles turned away from the microphone, the Municipal Hall erupted in a crescendo of noise, the cheers obliterating the negative sounds of the opposition.

Back in Smith Square, the watching Conservatives were not as overjoyed with their remarkable victory as might have been expected.

The malign influence of Reece-Morris had prevailed somewhat. Loathe to grant Jonathan Charles a completely safe seat, he had managed to push Craddock far enough to draft Jonathan Charles into what was at best a very tight squeeze, the likeliest predicted outcome having been a narrow Labour victory. The inescapable logic of Reece-Morris that had swayed the more magnanimous instincts of Craddock had been simple - if Jonathan Charles was as good as he and his considerable support team were supposed to be, then they could prove it by taking a marginal seat rather than a safe one. Well, much to their chagrin and mixed feelings, Jonathan Charles had taken on their challenge and bested them. These Tory Grandees may to some extent have become party dinosaurs over the years, but there was nothing wrong with their political antennae. Craddock and Reece-Morris should have been celebrating a fantastic result for the Conservative Party, but as they watched the TV images, they remained quiet and uneasy.

They could smell trouble - and they were right.

10

It was an awkward situation. They sat across the table from one another each knowing that communication was unavoidable, part of the territory, yet neither wanted to be the first to speak.

Susan's throat seemed to her to have a lump of cotton wool in it, but she steeled herself and forced the words out despite her reluctance - someone had to take the initiative.

"Shall we begin?" was all she could manage to say, but at least the dark spell was broken. The Chief self-consciously coughed, feeling rather clumsy and stupid.

"Yes", he stammered, shuffling the papers on his case for the sake of doing something with his hands.

The ice cracked, Susan closed her mind to the person she was talking to, and assumed her usual professionalism.

"The credit scam is definitely playing a different tune somehow," she said, purposefully leafing through her own set of papers in a green file, "We've identified a number of bogus accounts, and successfully tied them to accommodation addresses as per the last scam. But so far, surveillance and investigation has revealed nothing - no progress at all. To all intents and purposes, the accommodation addresses are standing up clean as a whistle".

"Perhaps we're looking in the wrong direction" said the Chief, his face thoughtful, "It would be typical of our quarry to elude us by changing the system - and yet, and yet........"

the Chief hesitated, formulating his thoughts, his mind for a moment drifting away from the lovely vision of Susan.

"...........and yet..........our friend wouldn't change the system, he would only modify it" said the Chief, almost triumphantly.

"Are you sure?" said Susan, looking doubtful.

"Yes I am" said the Chief, his chisel jaw set at its most stubborn, "I've lived with this particular villain for a long time - I have a good idea how his mind works, and he's basically too neat and neurotic to completely revamp a system of working. What he would typically do is shuffle the cards in some way rather than scrap and rebuild".

Susan looked at him quizzically.

"So we have to do some lateral thinking" she said, averting her eyes as he turned to look into them. Her eyes flashed, her mind grinding through the gears. "What if the accommodation addresses *are* genuine?" she said. "What if the addresses given are the places where the mail is collected?"

"Yes of course" said the Chief, "We have been rather complacent, haven't we? We *assumed* that the system would work as before, and linked into the accommodation addresses, but 'it ain't necessarily so', is it?"Susan just smiled uncomfortably, still aware who she was talking to. The Chief stared at her for a moment, preoccupied, then shook himself awake.

"Right. First thing is to check if the mail is being forwarded - contact the post office - very remiss of us, we should have automatically done that anyway".

Susan nodded abstractedly. The Chief continued, almost oblivious to his subconscious feelings for Susan.

"That's right" he said, "But what's done - or rather is not done - has come and gone. Let's check these addresses, follow who collects the mail, see where it gets us. My guess is it will pay dividends".

Susan nodded, unable to answer verbally, her conscious mind back on the problems at hand. She switched the subject, kept her mind going.

"What about the Housing Benefit side of things?" she asked, her voice strained, her manner stilted, self-conscious.

The Chief looked at her gravely, as if she was saying the most important thing in the Universe.

"My guess is that we're looking at purchases and 'dodgy' tenants who are not linked to the same places. That's one lesson our friend has learned from our successful closure of the previous system".

"So how do we catch up with him?" said Susan, trying to stick to the chosen agenda. The Chief looked thoughtful.

"There must a common denominator somewhere," he said, "We know that the place isn't common to a group, and we know that the Landlord isn't, so what does that leave?"

"One thing we can be sure of. The so-called 'tenants' are *not* genuine".

Susan's eyes flashed.

"You mean they are not bona fide citizens of the UK?" she said. The Chief got the point immediately.

"Yes! Of course! We check any suspect names

against NHS records at Stockport, and crosscheck them with National Insurance records at Newcastle," he said, almost triumphantly.

Susan looked at him obliquely.

"Then we target the address and follow the mail trail till it gets us somewhere".

They looked at each other in silence for a few moments. They both knew they were a good team.

"I miss you," the Chief finally said.

"No you don't" said Susan, her mouth a bitter gash, "You miss the sex".

The Chief looked hurt, his expression twisted with pain.

"I want to be with you," he said finally. "What *you* want is an affair," said Susan, sweeping up her papers and vanishing from the room, leaving the Chief in his own silence.

As he sat there alone, his mind reeling, after a while, the insistent ringing of the phone finally came to the Chief's attention.

"Yes" he said abstractedly. It was Farquhar-Brown.

"I'd like you to meet and talk with James Barton" he said, "Mr Barton is leading 'The Times' 'Insight' team. They have unearthed some material which you may find interesting".

The Chief could hardly raise the enthusiasm, but responded as best he could.

"Of course" he said, "When would you like us to meet?" Farquhar-Brown mentally noted the indifference in the Chief's voice, and marked him down another notch in his appraisal.

"I've taken the liberty of giving Mr Barton your phone number, and he will contact you in due course," said the Director-General, his voice now colder and more official than ever.

The Chief was past caring. So yet another PR exercise has to be conducted he thought. Who was this James Barton anyway? Some do-gooder reporter who wanted to make a name for himself *a la* Woodward/Bernstein?

However, when he did meet Barton, a week or so later at a fashionable restaurant in Hyde Park, he realised that he had badly underestimated him. As the Chief approached the assigned table, he saw a tall, dark-haired man of about 35 sitting there. Alert to the Chief's arrival, Barton rose to his feet.

"James Barton?" the Chief asked rhetorically. The handsome reporter smiled disarmingly.

"Jim" he said, extending his hand for the Chief to shake.

Within a short time of meeting him, the Chief realised that Jim was an earnest, obsessive kind of person, the kind of person who would tread through hell and shit backwards to get where he wanted to be, to find what he wanted to find. He had found out a fair amount, as the Chief was about to discover.

"Have you heard of Germaine Rouse?" said Jim.

"Of course" replied the Chief, "They're investment managers, aren't they? - And top division if I hear correctly".

Burton looked at him, his mouth tightening.

"Top division they may be, but up to skulduggery they certainly are".

Jim quickly appraised the Chief of Tom Parkin's review of the figures, and set it in conjunction with the planes, the yacht, the vineyards, the seemingly unconnected and wild investments, which were more the mark of a dilettante than a sensible investment manager. The Chief pulled a face.

"And where have we heard all this before?" he said.

"Exactly" said Jim, on the same wavelength, "It's the latest in a long line, isn't it......". The Chief interrupted.

".......And they all end the same way.........". Jim finished the sentence for him.

".......the investors get stuffed".

They looked at each other in silence for a moment.

"So what have you got?" said the Chief, interested now. Jim leaned forward, conspiratorially.

"I've followed the paper trail, and the ultimate holding company is 'Goldcrest Ltd', an offshore company - Isle of Man, in fact. The Chief was impressed.

"How did you manage that?" he said, knowing the difficulties of sailing through the rough waters of trailing anything offshore. Jim smiled warmly.

"We have our contacts" was all he was prepared to add.

"OK" said the Chief, "You've found a trail which I presume is also the path where the money's been siphoned off - is that right?"

"Correct" said Jim, "And the figures are terrifying".

"As I would expect" said the Chief, "But surely this is the territory of the DTI, not APACS, and more to the point, me. So where's the connection?"

Jim was fumbling in his brief case, and after a moment he pulled out a sheaf of headed papers.

"You're right" he said, "When I had enough

evidence to be going on with, I figured it was time to blow a whistle in the direction of the DTI.......".
"........Who as usual, are slow on the uptake," interrupted the Chief, making Jim smile again.
"True, they are on most things" said Jim, but I was lucky - the official I contacted was no mug, and when I pointed out one or two things, he must have recognised something relevant, and rang the Director-General at APACS straight away".
The Chief was puzzled now.
"So what did you show the DTI?" Jim handed over the papers he was holding, "I showed him these," he said solemnly.
Despite himself, the Chief showed his surprise.
"The bank statements of Goldcrest Limited with the Bank of Scotland, Isle of Man - how did you get hold of these?"
The Chief looked at Jim, becoming more impressed with this unassuming reporter by the minute.
"I have a friend of a friend of a friend who works there," said Jim, like any good reporter, keeping his sources close to his chest.
Looking at the sums involved, the Chief whistled through his teeth.
"As we expected, a lotta lotta dough is sifting out of investor's pockets - but I still don't see how I connect directly to this". Jim took the papers back from the Chief, leafing through them.
"We have to go further back for that - these statements cover about four years - look at these entries here". Jim pointed to the relevant page.
"See? A very high number of cash deposits on a regular basis - and note the time scale - what does

that remind you of?"

Jim waited, looking at the Chief. He didn't have long to wait.

"Bloody hell Jim! - these have to be deposits linked to the biggest credit scam in history!".

Jim smiled, nodding his head.

"Exactly - what we need now to confirm that completely is knowledge of where these credit deposits were made".

"That means going through official channels to the Manx authorities" said the Chief, aware of the problems that presented.

"And that's where you come in" said Jim, knowing he had taken his sources as far as they could lead him thus far.

"I'll get right on it," said the Chief, rising from the table, anxious to get started. Almost apologetically, Jim held him back by the arm for a moment.

"Just one thing" he said, "I want to be in on this - I want to know where it leads, I can even be of help - you've seen that".

The Chief looked at him seriously.

"You have a right to that Jim. I promise you're 'in', and we'll keep in touch with each other all the way, but there is a condition."

"What's that? - name it" said Jim, the grin disappearing from his face. The Chief looked at him sternly.

"Nothing to be printed without *my* involvement and giving the go-ahead to print - OK?"

"Fine with me" said Jim, grinning again, and reaching out to shake the Chief's hand. The two men smiled at each other warmly, both knowing their meeting was a good omen for a fruitful partnership.

Pleased and excited, they both headed off with fresh enthusiasm to uncover the mysteries of Germaine Rouse and its criminal connections

11

The room itself was business-like and bare, bureaucratic rather than ceremonial, but it still had the sombre trappings of all Courts of Justice. The Judge's robes still carried that aura of the days of hanging, the Royal crest instantly reminding everyone present that the laws of the state, the sheer almost visible power invested in this room was centred on the human presence of the Judge.

The power itself was no longer the substance of life and death, but the verdict of the Court still had the awesome ability to change lives forever, to create or destroy, albeit in a more subtle (though sometimes worse) sense than the grim days of corporal punishment.

The Judge glared sternly over his spectacles.

"Ladies and Gentlemen of the Jury - have you reached a verdict?"

The foreman of the Jury, a thin-faced man with a fiercely determined expression of honesty on his face, stood up solemnly.

"Yes, your Honour," he declared proudly.

Judge John Brooks stared hard at the figure in the dock, then turned his attention back to the foreman.

"Do you, the Jury, find the defendant guilty or not guilty?" he said.

"Guilty" said the foreman, his words causing the man in the dock to visibly wilt.

The Clerk of the Court handed the verdict to the Judge.

Judge Brooks milked the moment, letting the heavy

silence fall and oppress the Court. Finally he signalled that he would hear the submissions from Counsel. The usual rituals were then performed, with first the prosecution explaining why in their opinion White should receive the maximum punishment, then the defence followed, arguing as many mitigating factors as possible. The Judge listened patiently, knowing as the barristers did that he had already made up his mind what the sentence should be before they uttered a word. The ritual had to be complied with.

At last, silence fell. The Judge stared at the defendant with cold hard eyes.

"Terence White, you have been found guilty of conspiracy to defraud. The sums of money involved are frankly staggering, and your participation was not minor. Your learned Counsel pleads that you are of previously good character, but that does not mitigate your transparent dishonesty...............".

As the Judge spoke, the Detective Sergeant smiled at McKay who was sitting next to him in the public gallery. They really had him nailed, the smile said. The Judge was coming to the expected coup-de-grace.

"............Terence White, the sentence of this court is that you be imprisoned for a term of three years.........."

The policeman gasped. McKay was incredulous - three years? Surely this was a travesty! Involvement in a major - a very major fraud - surely seven to ten? They listened in shock to the Judge - worse was to come.

"............but the Court will suspend this sentence. If

however you commit further crimes during the suspension of this sentence, then the term of this sentence will be carried out in full, and you will have to serve this time in addition to any new punishment which the Court sees fit to decree".
McKay and the Detective Sergeant were aghast. What on earth had happened to justice?

12

The Chief was also less than amused by the report brought to him by McKay. That very morning, he had another meeting with Jim Barton, who had promised to look into the matter further on his behalf. Jim had sombre news.

"Listen to this," said Jim, his face serious and animated at the same time, "Danny Wilkinson - six months; James West - Jimbo to you - community service; David Marks - suspended sentence - and that's only to name a few. Altogether I found something like five hundred or so cases where an unexpected leniency was shown to people indicted and implicated in the credit and housing scams".

The Chief was frowning now.

"What about the common factor - the Judges? Was there any corollary there?"

"Yes, quite definitely" said Jim, becoming even more animated, "Out of this sample of five hundred, the same six Judges were sitting".

They both looked at each other, the importance of what they were suggesting silencing them for a moment. The Chief was first to speak.

"Jim, did you find any who had the opposite result?"

"That's the strange thing," said Jim, looking puzzled, "There was also a cluster of people who received what you might think of as severe sentences. One man – Jeffrey John Morgan - who received eight years despite having little 'previous'; Winston Thomas, six years; another 'local controller' received twelve years; an accommodation manager who received ten; a Regional controller who got fifteen - the list is just as long as the list who were treated leniently. It seems to be all extremes, either one thing or the other".

The Chief grimaced.

"And to make matters worse, the same six Judges presided again". Jim nodded his head solemnly.

"But how did you know?" he asked. The Chief smiled grimly.

"Obviously there's a carrot and stick system operating here. If you stay loyal, you will be 'looked after', if you don't, if you talk to the authorities or misbehave in any way, you will be punished.....................".

The Chief paused, seeing Jim's face go ashen white.

"What is it?" he asked.

"What you've said has just connected something I was concerned about" said Jim, his eyes reflecting a new level of fear, "During my investigations, I found that several key players had died in mysterious circumstances - in some cases, they were obviously executed, though the murders remain unsolved. For instance, James Jeffrey Morgan, killed in a prison riot at Strangeways; Martin Boswell, killed by a hit and run drive while awaiting trial".

This was even worse than the Chief had anticipated. The crime wave he was struggling against had reached a new dimension.

13

It became increasingly clear a sinister element had begun to publicly emerge. Up to now, these brigands had almost a Robin Hood status, robbing the banks, the institutions, who were no friends of the populous, and for whom there was no sympathy but that from the establishment itself. But when the beatings, the tortures, and the murders began, it was plain to see that the forces at work were taking on the characteristics and behaviour of the Mafia.

A somewhat dubious 'loyalty' ethos was at work - if you betrayed the system, harsh punishment would fall upon you, from 'fit-up's to beatings, to personal disaster and ultimately death as a final punishment and supreme deterrent to others who would otherwise weaken in their resolve. If you remained loyal despite the threats and promises from the authorities, then you would be 'one of us' - protected, apparently invulnerable, and the system had the resources and the contacts to enforce either option.

Sitting remotely in his offshore paradise, he did not necessarily disapprove of this ethos, but he did violently oppose the degree. News of the deaths had filtered back to him slowly, and as soon as he heard, he was devastated, for he was at heart a religious believer, and knew that his soul had received a mortal blow.

His morals were at the very least ambivalent, but he had lines of conduct, which he never wanted to cross. Now, as the architect of this system, he was, like the leading members of the third Reich, completely implicated in these crimes against humanity and God, even if he himself had not dirtied his hands directly. He paced the floor restlessly, waiting for the man who had directed such operations, his Lieutenant to arrive and explain himself.

It was several hours later when the Lieutenant arrived. He marched in, knowing instinctively that all was not well. This time there were no hugs of welcome, as he expected. His friend's face was a mask of anger and accusation. What on earth was wrong? The Lieutenant poured himself a drink. He sat down wearily, took a sip, then looked at his friend and commanding officer.

"Spit it out" he finally said.

"Murder!" was the only word his companion spat at him. Several times he said it, his voice lashing the air like a whip.

"Murder! - that's what we're here to talk about! Who gave you the authority to play God?" he said, staring at his lieutenant as if he had crawled out from under a stone. The Lieutenant stayed calm, sitting quietly sipping his drink. He had seen his friend's wrath many times before, he knew the complicated and tortured soul who laboured beneath the mask. First he let the tight silence stand. Then he looked at his friend gravely and said in a quiet voice.

"You did". The other man exploded again.

"I did not fucking give you authority to kill anyone!" he said, shouting, almost demented, an element of despair behind his anger, "I agreed we should have an enforcement system; I agreed the levels; I did **not** condone killing".

The Lieutenant took another sip of his drink, then sat the glass down gently.

"Look" he said, "OK, you did not specifically agree that our enemies should be executed - [at this word being uttered, the other man visibly flinched] - neither did you specify what those punishments should be, you left both decisions to me. What I decided to do is my responsibility, not yours".

The other man was more in despair than anger now, he knew that nothing could be done to raise Lazarus from the dead, nothing could save his own soul.

"I'm completely implicated, don't you see? To say that it's none of my responsibility isn't good enough - this is my system, my war with authority...........".

The Lieutenant interrupted him, his voice containing steel.

"Unlike you, I *have* been in a War" he said, standing up to emphasise his point, "Let me tell you that in a War there are no half measures - everyone has to know where they are, there can be no holding back - maximum violence must be generated to achieve objectives".

The man was quieter now, though his eyes were still wild and red. Knowing his friend as he did, even in his anger and despair he could see that because of all the hurts and injustices he had suffered, his friend had lost some of his scruples along the way, more than he himself had.

This was not to say that his friend was at heart an immoral or uncaring person. The Lieutenant himself would have been shocked to hear himself described in that way, but he had let himself become embroiled in a 'them and us' mentality. His formative experience as a serving soldier had helped to propagate his view of *actually* being a lieutenant even now, a soldier at War with his enemy.

Now, his undirected actions had caused an almost unthinkable breach with his best friend. Standing there in silence now, the Lieutenant thought of the warmth and brilliance of his friend, and all they had achieved together, all that they had been through to reach this moment in time, to stand here together in this silent room, so highly charged with emotions, memories, and regrets.

His friend looked at him sadly. He put his arm out, touching his companion's shoulder. The anger dissipated, replaced by a weary acceptance and grief.

"My friend, this is meant to be a war of *minds*, not a war of physical violence - the killings must stop - do you understand me? The killings **must** stop!" His voice rose several decibels in volume as the last words tumbled out.

The two old friends looked at each other sadly, one's eyes were filled with tears, the other's with understanding and compassion.

He said the words once more, his voice a pained whisper.

"The killings must stop". The Lieutenant bit his lip. The other man stepped back.

"What is it?" he said, anxiety in his voice. The Lieutenant looked at him, his eyes reluctant to meet the gaze of the other man.

"There already is a contract out" the grey-haired man said. Then, seeing the question in his friend's eyes, he added "No - it's too late to stop now". He looked at his watch, and looked at his friend, shaking his head.

The man's eyes filled with tears again, but he said nothing. He walked to the dark window and stood staring silently out at the night.

The Lieutenant quietly gathered up his papers and left.

14

The House was noisy, excitable, a clamour of voices competed with each other for Madame Speaker's attention. The lady herself was adept at ignoring the considerable noise such egos made to bring attention to themselves, and had already made her mind up to call upon one of the new arrivals in the House to make their maiden speech.

"Mr Jonathan Charles" she intoned decisively, then sat down with a flourish that brooked no opposition. In any case, the cheers rang out from the Tory side of the House to welcome the new MP to his seat while at the same time reminding the Labour side who exactly had won the by-election. Jonathan Charles rose, soaking up the electric atmosphere, the air of expectancy, which greeted his every utterance – his reputation had preceded him. He was wise enough to realise that this was a tricky moment, he had to strike a fine balance between making an impression, without seeming too immodest or over-confident.

Although he had given some thought to his approach to the House, and had a rough idea of what he wanted to say, he had deliberately not composed a set speech of any kind. H realised it was best to gauge the mood of the House from moment to moment rather than relying on an expertly constructed text. What would be lost in careful consideration would be easily compensated for by hopefully being in tune with the expectant crowd of curious faces before him.

He began slowly, his voice suitably humble and

studiously apprehensive, seeming a little nervous, though he was nothing of the sort.

"Madame Speaker, I thank you and honourable members for allowing me this opportunity to address the House for the first time. My thanks also go to my constituents who have placed their trust in me to represent them in this Parliament. I am humbled and grateful for that trust invested in me, and I pray that I will be able to justify their faith by pursuing all that is in their interest to the best of my endeavours".

As he spoke, Jonathan made a point of addressing not just the whole panorama of the House, but each individual within his sight, momentarily maintaining eye to eye contact, all the while concentrating on displaying an expression which contained strength, humility, and friendliness in equal measure.

"If I am asked to define my defining principle as a Member of Parliament beyond the obvious one of representing my constituents to the best of my ability, then I would have to state clearly and categorically that I wish to see Britain truly integrated within the European Community.........".

Jonathan had to pause here, for the house immediately burst into a storm of protests versus cheers of support. Madame Speaker rose indignantly, causing Jonathan Charles to sit down as required by the house rules.

"Order! Order in the house!" said Madame Speaker, her voice full of contrived outrage. "Honourable members must allow Mr Charles to speak!"

The house gradually and reluctantly quietened, though murmurs of discontent still grumbled in the distance. Jonathan attempted to look as apologetic as possible, but stuck firmly to his speech.

"Thank you Madame Speaker" he said, bowing graciously towards her, "I do realise of course that this is a subject that has caused honourable members great anguish, and it is with great reluctance that I raise the subject so soon following my election to the house. However, I feel that it would have been disingenuous of me had I not informed honourable members of my position in this matter at the outset. I presume that every honourable member is entitled to his or her own views in this great Parliament of ours. We may disagree a little at times..........(a ripple of ironic laughter rang through the house)........., but the idea surely Madame Speaker, is that our very disagreements form the stuff of democracy, forged in a flame of high passion which can and should cover every possible point of view in its journey to the truth".

Cries of "Hear hear!" and "Well said!" followed Jonathan Charles to his seat, even his bitter opponents conceding that it was a fine maiden speech.

Jonathan was quietly pleased, though he ensured that his countenance gave no hint of smug complacency. He had been accepted as one with the house, but in his own quiet way he had still nailed his colours to the mast.

15

Judge John Brooks did not know it, but he was now a marked man. Following a meeting the Chief and Farquhar-Brown had requested with the Home Secretary, the Judge's bank accounts and personal documents were being quietly scrutinised by accountants from the Serious Fraud Office. The SFO had come up with some interesting facts. Though Judge Brooks had been a successful barrister before his appointment to the bench, his lifestyle now surpassed anything he should have been capable of.

Not that he was the only Judge or Senior Official under investigation. At least five of his fellow Judges were among those whose affairs were being simultaneously investigated. It was now time to collate these investigations, and the Chief scheduled a meeting of his team as well as an emergency meeting with Farquhar-Brown which would ultimately lead to another major meeting of the APACS committee.

First though, the Chief had to compare notes with Jim Barton, not just from the point of view of honour, but because Jim held the keys to parts of the enquiry which the Chief was not familiar with. Only by putting their two keys together could they see the whole picture thus far.

They met at a mutually discreet office that belonged to neither of them, an anonymous place in a nondescript government building.

As the Chief laid out the papers containing the results of the accountant's investigations into the

Judges and Senior officials, Jim whistled self-consciously. As an investigative reporter he was used to seeing massive sums of money vanishing into greedy men's hands, but this was on a scale he had never before witnessed. He looked at the Chief incredulously.

"So what you're saying is that any one of these people is a multimillionaire several times over".

"Yes" said the Chief solemnly, "Judge Brooks for instance has a portfolio of shares and a string of his own investment companies – offshore of course. And these are only the ones we can identify. As you know, not all of the jurisdictions are willing to co-operate. Even so, there are planes, boats, properties etc – you name it, they've got it".

"All the usual, in other words" said Jim, his mouth a bitter gash, "The point is though, can we prove a link to organised crime?" he said, sounding doubtful.

The Chief hesitated, biting his lip thoughtfully.

"Well there is one interesting factor. All the initial payments have come from a series of offshore companies whose jurisdiction is difficult for us to crack, but it is clear that around half a dozen companies have funded all these individuals in their pursuit of wealth".

Jim was impressed.

"So there is a common link, even if it's difficult to prove a criminal connection – do you have a list of these companies for me to look at?"

"Sure" said the Chief, reaching for a loose sheet of paper lying on the desk and handing it to Jim.

"Oh my God!" said Jim, turning white, his face

aghast. "I recognise one of these names from the Germaine Rouse investigation".

"Which one is that?" said the Chief, rushing round to stand looking over Jim's shoulder at the paper. Jim pointed almost nervously at the page.

"This one – Lazarus Investments Inc. – it's one of the cash black holes where investor's money vanishes".

The Chief was becoming animated, sensing progress in sight. "Now if we could find the ultimate holding company..............". He paused, seeing the look on Jim's face.

"I already do," said Jim.

"It's Goldcrest".

16

Alone in his modern castle, he restlessly wandered round the high-level perimeter road he had constructed so long ago. It gave him an overview of the sea at the front, and at the back, the wild countryside, a desolate but beautiful place where he could feel free of human contact.

Here at night though, it was also a lonely place where the wind moaned softly like a wounded creature. Stopping for a moment, he watched the distant lights of the isolated dwelling places that flickered spasmodically among the shifting trees. How he missed her at times like this!

Then there was his system, his reason for living. Always mindful of high-tech, it had now gone full tilt into the world of the Internet and high finance. The days of the high-scale but small-time credit scams was gone, the last phase had begun. Yet even all of this had gone sour, his mortal soul was in danger of everlasting damnation, for he was still soulful enough to realise that we are all here on earth for a purpose. His ambiguity on the subject had allowed him to rationalise his behaviour by feeling he was righting a great wrong, but he also realised that he was one of the lost ones, one of those who could not fit into the world of men.

Part of his rationale was to tell himself that he either had to fight for survival or die, but now he had crossed the Rubicon. He may not have pulled the trigger directly, but as the architect of the crimes, he was ultimately responsible, and he knew better than anyone what the price would have to be.

Bad enough that he had lost all that was once dear to him. He had known since she had gone that life could never have meaning for him again, but to lose his immortal soul as well.....................

Tears came momentarily to his eyes as self-pity and despair got the better of him. Then, tightening his mouth, he steeled himself against his weakness and forced his mind away from thoughts of her.

All meaning was now gone, he told himself. All that was left was the system. Shivering in the cool evening breeze, he turned his steps back toward the house, his mouth a bitter gash, his face a haunted mask.

17

"I don't understand this," said Susan, her beautiful face tight and perplexed as she viewed the series of screens stretching as far as the eye could see. The Chief came over to stand beside her, catching the delicate fragrance of her subtle perfume as he leaned close to her face.

"What is it?" he said, studying the screens with interest.

Susan, self-conscious of his closeness, pulled herself ever so slightly away.

"Look" she said with (she hoped) professional detachment, pointing at the screen in front of her, " Activity in withdrawals has almost completely dried up – as far as I can tell, these are all genuine transactions we are seeing now".

"As far as we can tell" cautioned the Chief, but he could see that Susan must be right. Even the volume of overall transactions was down massively and was dying even more moment by moment.

"What do you think it means?" said Susan in an almost frightened little girl's voice. The Chief 's face hardened.

"Well, it's certainly nothing we've done" he said, "It's true we've been making inroads into it, but we had still a long way to go to close it down".

Susan looked at him for a moment, puzzled.

"Then why is it closing itself down?" she asked, at a loss to understand, "Does this mean that it's over?"

"I'm afraid it's bad news rather than good," said the Chief, "It means that our friend is ready to move in to where the real money is".

They looked at each other without expression, the situation too serious for even thoughts of each other.

18

Gregor Bowen was also a worried man. The flamboyant MP for Caithness was unusually serious for one of the most colourful characters in the House of commons. Through his long-time friend, the Chancellor of the Exchequer, Gregor had managed to arrange a meeting with the Prime Minister.

It was late in the evening at Downing Street when Gregor was admitted into the Prime Minister's chambers. The Prime Minister welcomed him warmly enough, but Gregor could see the tiredness in his eyes. Being Prime Minister was a tough job these days, thought Gregor, though he knew well enough that almost every MP in the house would give his eyeteeth for a crack at it.

"Gregor, how good to see you" said the Prime Minister, switching on the charm that was part of his image and trademark.

"And you Prime Minister" said Gregor, his unusual seriousness not going unnoticed.

"What's the problem?" asked the PM, as they both sat down in the smart but uncomfortable chairs.

"It's the Integrationists," said Gregor, his face betraying his anxiety once more.

The PM almost relaxed. "That old chestnut", he thought. The recent spate of by-elections had indeed produced a motley crew of individuals with cranky ideas and wild concepts of Britain vanishing as a nation, all its history vacuumed into the wider history of Europe, the land itself becoming no more than an outpost at the edge of Northern France.

"Come on Gregor" said the PM almost scornfully, "that rag-tag bunch are troublemakers, but their views would never gain currency"

Gregor frowned, annoyed that he could be so easily patronised. He had thought the PM would know he was no fool, even if he often acted like one.

"You underestimate Jonathan Charles at your peril" said the older man, his eccentric white hair covering the deep frowns on his forehead. The PM realised he had upset the old man, and inwardly cursed his own tiredness, blunting his usually sharp sensibilities.

"I know what you mean Gregor," he said soothingly, trying now not to seem too patronising, "Jonathan Charles is indeed a formidable opponent." He recalled only too vividly the times in Parliament when his own cabinet ministers had been out-fought and out-thought on their feet by the slippery and cunning Charles.

"He would indeed be a threat if he happened to lead a sensible group, but their views are to say the least, eccentric, and not likely to gain any ground in Parliament or the Country, but I will keep an eye on them, of course. I have been doing that very thing in any case, as you might expect" said the PM, quietly relieved that it was nothing more serious than a warning about something he was already well aware of. He had known for some time all about the 'secret' meetings between Jonathan Charles and his mob of clones.

Gregor was becoming exasperated now, his

natural courtesy being gradually blotted out by his
frustration.

"Prime Minister, will you hear me out!" he
almost shouted, startling the PM at this late hour.
The PM fell silent.

Breathing heavily, his face suddenly red, Gregor
explained.

"Prime Minister, I would not waste your
time by telling you
things you already know. I'm sure you are well
aware of the activities of these people, their
meetings, their secret financial arrangements
and inducements, but I was privy to a meeting
between Charles and two of his cohorts. They
were dining at the Clarence club in a private
room, but I happened to be in the annexe next to
them – I go there for a quiet snifter on my own –
normally speaking, no-one uses the room
adjacent, it was just pure chance I was there. As
soon as I realised who the people were, I knew I
had no choice but to stay there until they left,
trapped, that's what I was".

The PM smiled sympathetically, knowing that
Gregor was trying to explain his inordinate
eavesdropping.

"Go on" he said patiently.

Gregor licked his lips, nervous tension showing
as he recalled the events of that night.

"Most of the talk was what you'd expect,
integration, isolation......"

"The overthrow of the Government" interjected
the PM, his expression a mixture of dislike and
amusement.

The older man stopped and looked at him almost with pity.

"Prime Minister, I don't think you realise the significance of what I'm trying to tell you. These people made it absolutely crystal clear on that night that they are linked to major crime and money laundering on a scale never before witnessed. They're not just interested in overthrowing the Government or even the Country – they intend to destabilise then destroy civilisation as we know it".

The Prime Minister sat in the tense silence, unsure of how to proceed. He knew Gregor as a true eccentric, yet he also knew that he was a shrewd parliamentarian and nobody's fool. Yet could he believe that things were as serious as all that? Was it all just wild talk? Even if it was, the PM reasoned, he would have to take account of it in his dealings with Jonathan Charles.

As he bade farewell to Gregor, with a sincere thanks for the meeting, he decided to ask a few discreet but important questions among the mandarins and the dark forces they controlled.

19

Billy Rawlings had had enough. He had been a star so long that he had grown used to getting his way in everything he did or asked for. Yet Pierre Arroneaux remained elusive despite the efforts of Billy's staff to locate him or get straight answers to straight questions. The biggest question of all was 'where was Billy's money?" It seemed as if Pierre Arroneaux had vanished along with it. It didn't exactly leave Billy on the breadline, but it certainly made a sizeable hole in his once vast pot of gold.

What worried and infuriated Billy was that he was not the only dupe in this financial tangle. Many of his own friends had been sucked in by the charming but elusive Mr. Arroneaux, mainly by Billy's recommendations and introductions, just as he had been introduced himself. They had all been taken for fools, and Billy was not used to looking like a fool.

Still, he would have to get used to it.

20

Not that it was any comfort to Billy and his friends, but they weren't alone in being taken for a ride. The sudden crash of Germaine Rouse amid scandal and controversy had left many innocent investors stranded without a penny to their names. The fall had come so suddenly. One moment, the contented investors were receiving a return far beyond their wildest expectations, then without warning the cheques had dried up without a word of explanation.

As the beleaguered staff at Germaine Rouse tried in vain to deal with the wrath and fury – not to mention panic – of the investors who now swamped the Germaine Rouse offices as well as the switchboard, the newspapers reacted with horror and indignation that such a thing could occur in 'Great' Britain.

Ironically, the person who started the ball rolling in Parliament was none other than Jonathan Charles. Using all his eloquence, he calmly attacked the Government's handling of the Germaine Rouse affair and other related matters.

Striking just the perfect tone of intelligent concern and righteous indignation, Jonathan was in full flood, inflaming the passions of the House.

"Madame Speaker, honourable members, is this any way to regulate and supervise the rights of our citizens? Perhaps there are those among us so mean in spirit as to say that the disappearance of the funds of the famous are simply a matter for gossip and innuendo and nothing more. Does the fact that someone is well known and successful negate the individual's rights to justice and fairness in our society? But, Madame Speaker, even if we could possibly accept that scenario, which I for one could not, then what are we to make of the disappearance of millions of pounds of ordinary investor's money with the collapse of a so-called respectable company such as Germaine Rouse?"

The atmosphere was heating up in the House, and in the gallery, reporters avidly soaked up every detail, noting at the same time the grim expressions on the faces of the Prime Minister and his cabinet as they sat silently listening to Jonathan Charles.

Sensing that the mood of the House was with him, Jonathan continued to crank up the atmosphere of hostility against the front bench and the Government in general.

Using the silences wisely, he looked for moment around the House, at the faces of his colleagues, his opponents, making eye to eye contact with many of them, his face silently asking a question. Finally, he continued.

"Madame Speaker, those of us who care about justice, freedom, the rights to protection which every citizen of this country should expect and enjoy, are at this moment in time filled with sadness and horror that such things could happen today in our Britain. Yes, Madame Speaker, OUR Britain, a place, which, despite our many differences of opinion - sometimes our very fierce differences of opinion – a place which holds all our hopes and aspirations for the future, a place which we can believe in, and more to the point, a place which contains those values dearest and most important to us".

Again Jonathan looked silently almost sadly across the floor of the house, his eyes finally falling directly on the front benches opposite and at last on the Prime Minister himself.

"I find no joy in pointing out these painful truths which we are all aware of" said Jonathan quietly, his voice falling to almost a whisper, causing the house itself to fall into silence, straining to hear his words. Across the nation, people watched these scenes unfolding on their TV screens, on their radios, on the Internet, the whole nation transfixed by the drama.

Jonathan was the master of the moment, but was wise enough to downplay it, too cunning to concede his enemies respite by bringing melodrama and attention to his own performance, knowing that the words themselves, if delivered properly, would deal the fatal blows.

Gripping the silence, Jonathan's voice rose to firmness once more.

"Madame Speaker, it would be bad enough that Germaine Rouse, that Pierre Arroneaux were granted licences by this Government, our Government, which is meant to protect our people, but the fact is, sadly these instances are like drops in the ocean of this Government's incompetence. Crime and fraud are at their highest level ever, the figures and percentages attempting to mask the misery caused to millions of people, to our Institutions, to our very livelihood and well-being. We are seeing unprecedented waves of massive manipulation and greed – one after another, incident upon incident. Credit and housing benefit fraud stand at unprecedented levels; Lloyds; Blue Arrow; Clowes; Guinness; Arroneaux; Germaine Rouse. Whole streets and communities have been sold off for the land to be squandered, ways of life demolished, gone forever, all in the name of crime and corruption – do I have to go on? Must we have litany upon litany of this corruption and mismanagement?"

As Jonathan's voice rose in decibels, so the level of noise in the House increased till things were at a fever pitch. It was time for the coup de grace, and Jonathan was just the man to deliver it.

He looked directly at the Prime Minister again, his voice and his eyes cold and hard.

"You Sir, have presided over a Government which is not just incompetent. It is, in the eyes of not just myself, but my fellow members on BOTH sides of the house, a Government which is almost criminally negligent and lacking in the skill and the will to deal with the crucial issues which affect our people, and to you Sir, I say – GO AND GO NOW!"

The House exploded in uproar as Jonathan sat down, and though the speaker chosen by the PM to answer was the ineffectual Trade Minister, it would not have made any difference who the replying speaker was, the house was in no mood to listen. A vote of confidence was inevitable, realised the Prime Minister. It would be seen by the House as the only chance he had to reassert his authority, and he had little choice but to announce the vote of confidence forthwith. As he set the events in motion, he thought back to his recent meeting with Gregor and realised sadly that he had not listened as hard as he should have.

Questions had been asked, and investigations were under way, but the Prime Minister's political sense was good enough to tell him that his Government was finished, the vote of confidence was certain to be lost, a General Election was inevitable.

PART FOUR

BANKS & TREASURY

1

As Henry Rollinson, the former Prime Minister had known better than anyone, the failure of his Government to win the vote of confidence in the House meant that he was also destined to lose the General Election itself. A mood of change swept the Country, it was a time when extremists could enter the door of democracy on a tidal wave of reaction. The Integrationists – as Jonathan Charles and his merry men were dubbed – were the most significant beneficiaries of this mood of change. Having successfully infiltrated the Tory party to gain credibility, the Integrationists were now ready to fight on their own platform, successfully disassociating themselves from the now discredited Conservative party. Their plans had proved successful, the General Election had favoured them to the detriment of the other main parties. The Integrationists did not control the House of Commons, but their number amounted to almost a third of Members of Parliament in the chamber, and the two main opposition parties were almost similarly split. It called for a consensus Government, but the days of cosy pacts between the main parties had gone. With the Integrationists holding a position of power and influence, they were not about to squander their opportunity by being reasonable.

The likeliest candidate for Prime Minister was Terence Flood, the new Labour party leader – no one would at this stage have tolerated a

Conservative Prime Minister without a clear mandate from the people. Terence – or Terry as he was better known in political and journalistic circles – had a slight difficulty. He had always been vigorously opposed to Jonathan Charles and his policies, and had said so on every suitable occasion, but he realised that he could not form a Government without the Integrationists. Immediately following the General Election, a meeting was somewhat reluctantly arranged with Jonathan Charles.

Flood's elegant Chelsea home was the setting for the encounter. Like two caged animals, they circled each other warily, the small talk fooling no one, least of all the two protagonists and uneasy bedfellows.

Jonathan Charles was not one to beat about the bush.

"What are you prepared to offer?" he suddenly shot across Flood's bows. Slightly startled by the lack of preliminaries, Flood nevertheless quickly regained his composure.

"A place in the Cabinet for yourself and another colleague" said Flood.

"It will be a senior post of course," he added, having seen by Jonathan's face that he was less than impressed.

"I want to be Chancellor," said Jonathan, noting with satisfaction the brief look of dismay that flickered across Flood's red face. Flood was caught in a dilemma – he had promised the job of Chancellor to his campaign manager and not-so-friendly rival Gareth Flint, the former Shadow Minister for Wales. Besides, what Charles was asking for was way beyond anything envisaged by Flood. He had intended to offer the Integrationist Employment, or Health if necessary, not any of the three principal offices of State. Before he could completely recover his composure, Jonathan Charles made his second demand.

"Also, I want two of my senior colleagues in the Cabinet. One is to be Trade Secretary, one is to be Employment secretary". This was too much for Flood.

"I can't possibly sanction that!" he blustered, "My party and the Country would never accept it!"

Jonathan gazed at him fixedly, his expression unmoved.

"Oh yes you will – and so will they" he said calmly but confidently. "That's the deal – take it or leave it".

Before Flood could answer and still his racing thoughts, Jonathan took a sip of his drink, and cut the conversation off.

"Think about it and let me know when you're ready" he said, quickly finishing his drink and leaving Flood standing in pool of indecision.

The door had not even closed before Flood realised there was no alternative but to acquiesce.

Jonathan Charles would be named Chancellor before the week was out.

The Chief was worried. Noticing his discomfort, McKay tried to cheer him up.

"Come on Guv!" he said brusquely, almost embarrassed at showing emotion.

"The credit scam's closed down, housing benefit and social security fraud are back to something like normal levels – what's so bad about that?"

The Chief looked at him wearily.

"Dave, we didn't really close them down – they closed themselves down – what does that tell you? Do you think it means that the syndicate has gone out of business? Do you think that Germaine Rouse, Arroneaux, Blue Arrow, Guinness – all of those and more – are totally unrelated? It's what comes next that worries me – the scale of it has to be colossal".

"But Guv" said McKay earnestly, "There's always been scandals like those, aren't you getting a little paranoid? OK, so there are links with a couple of those, does that mean they're all linked?"

"I'm afraid in this case it does Dave," said the Chief, sitting back in his desk slowly, wearily. "These are all part of a pattern, it fits with my feeling about this man who is running the whole thing………." "The Mastermind, you mean" interrupted McKay. The Chief looked at him sharply.

"I don't like that word – it flatters and elevates someone who is, after all, just a common thief. It's bad enough that the papers build him up, but one of my one as well…………". He tailed off, exasperated, but McKay was having none of it.

"Look Guv" he said, his jaw set determinedly. "When you talk like that, it's obvious you're taking this whole thing personally, him versus you, the battle of the giants – that's bullshit, and you know it! This is just business, just a professional business, that's all!"

For a moment the Chief looked angry, then the fire in his eyes subsided.

"You're right Dave, it is just business, not personal".

The older man looked at him almost sadly.

"Well isn't it time you remembered that?" he said, surprisingly softly for a man with a rough Scottish accent.

The Chief smiled despite himself, and stood up, placing his hand on McKay's shoulder. "Thanks Dave" he said, making the Scotsman squirm and go unusually red in the face.

"Piss off!" said Dave, making them both laugh with relief.

His life had become so dull, so routine, but it
was the only way to be safe, he knew that too.
Nevertheless, it seemed to him a terrible price to
pay for his freedom, if that was the right word. They
had given him a pleasant house – though not up to
his usual standards – and all his worldly needs were
taken care of. There was just this awful boredom, a
feeling of being in limbo, not really alive.

Outside, as the rain fell against his window, he
could see the nearby ocean moving restlessly as
night approached the elegant bungalow at the top of
the cliffs. That feeling of ennui began to engulf him
again, and he sighed unhappily as he ambled
listlessly over to the drinks cabinet for yet another
time too many.

They looked after him like a child. It was a good
metaphor, he thought. Everything he ate and drank
was tested and vetted, every phone call in and out
was heavily censored and scrutinised for safety,
long before a conversation – rare as it was – finally
reached him. When the postman or milkman called,
his keepers kept him well away and out of sight.
Even the whores they brought him were vetted for
cleanliness as well as security, for God's sake! This
last thought made him crash his glass too hard
against the wooden surface, breaking the delicate
crystal. A red sliver of blood mixed with brandy slid
down his hand and dripped steadily onto the floor
while he watched it dumbly.

"Shall I kiss it better?" The woman's voice
startled him. She stood in the doorway, a gorgeous

creature, adorable but intelligent eyes staring at him as he took in her figure, so revealing in her tight-fitting dress. Her hair was long and in waves, dark red, almost auburn, and her smile was shattering in its unassuming beauty.

He lit up immediately, his fears of a useless evening suddenly vanishing.

"They didn't warn me you were coming", he said, feeling not a little silly at being caught out so easily. "Where are they anyway?" he asked, noticing the unusual absence of his minders on such an occasion.

"Don't worry about them – it's me you need to worry about" she said, smiling, holding out her hand formally. "I'm Laura". He opened his mouth to introduce himself, but Laura spoke first, putting a perfumed hand gently across his mouth as she did so.

"Oh, I already know who you are!" she said teasingly. He warmed to the game. "Yes, you know who you think I am, but you don't know who I really am".

She smiled inscrutably, disarmingly. "Oh don't I now?" she said, pulling herself close to him, wrapping her body around his. "We'll see about that" she said, and pressed her very feminine mouth to his, catching him by surprise again.

The scent and feeling of her made his head spin. Laura was not your usual run-of-the-mill whore, he thought. Then again, she seemed to know her business. He felt her hand undo his trousers and before he knew it, she was gripping him, fondling him with both hands, rousing him awake. He began to tear at her clothes, she at his. In moments he was naked, and Laura merely wearing suspenders, stockings, and stiletto shoes as they rolled on the floor, then finally on the bed. God she was wild! He thrilled to her aggressive thrusts. She was controlling the action, using his body, arching it into the positions she desired, placing his manhood into herself here, then there, turning him over, opening him wide to her will, her tongue and mouth entering him till his mind was silently screaming and begging for release.

Not finished by any means, she took him into and beyond her gorgeous lips, deep down into her throat, with consummate ease till he had vanished inside her. Laura's beautiful mouth caressed the full length of him, until she sensed the critical moment coming, then she suddenly pulled away, exposing him once more, leaving him throbbing with tension and ecstasy, a quivering wreck.

Now, before he could protest or comment, she reached by the side of the bed and produced two sets of handcuffs, swiftly chaining his feet and hands to the bedposts. All the while she was caressing his manhood by rubbing her wetness across the length of itself till the essence of her ran down into his secret crevices. He heard a voice moaning softly, and realised it was his own.

Triumphantly, Laura sat across him, and never taking her eyes from him, she placed her womanhood fully on his mouth, his face, drowning him in herself till finally, she slid her body down until her wetness reached him again, drenching him in its sweetness. In sudden sweet surprise, he found himself pushed into her smaller space until his full length was consumed inside her once more. As Laura heaved on him steadily, he could take no more. He heard himself shouting without concern deliriously, and he knew he had reached the point of no return.

It was as his climax exploded inside her that Laura plunged the knife deep into his throat.

4

On the day of the Queen's speech, the
manifesto produced an uproar. There was a bill in
favour of a Federal Europe, ceding all Government
powers to Brussels. There was a bill denying
mortgage lenders the right to repossess; tax havens
were to be protected against tax investigations; even
the Queen found herself delivering a message that
her Government would abolish *her*!

In theory, even as the Prime Minister of a
minority Government, Terry Flood should still have
been able to prevent the most extreme measures of
the manifesto from reaching fruition, but Flood was
a weak man, a man hungry and voracious in terms
of coming to power for himself, but he did not
contain within himself enough ethical belief to bring
strength or belief to bear when it was most needed.

In that respect, Jonathan Charles was the
opposite. His strength and belief had driven through
these controversial measures, and there were more
to come. Within months of his have taken office, he
had devised a bill asking Parliament to devolve all
powers of devaluation of the pound to Brussels.
When the bill was passed, the pound would have to
live within the exchange rate mechanism led by the
Germans and the Deutschemark.

Frantically, moderate members of Parliament
tried to reverse these trends, but they were
outgunned and outnumbered, even though they had
the vast support of the population at large. It was all
too late. The general election had been held, the
Integrationists had been given the power. The

British public had called for change, and change was on the way, though it was not the change they had originally in mind.

5

Jim Barton and the Chief were comparing notes. In the Chief's rather nondescript office in the City, they sat among an ever-growing mound of papers and faxes, piled across the drab desks and even on the vacant chairs.

"How are you getting on with the links to the Goldcrest accounts?" asked Jim.

The Chief glanced at him, pulling a face.

"These things take time Jim – too much time"

Jim gave a wry glance.

"I know exactly what you mean" he said.

"We have the clout in the Isle of Mann, and we will get authority eventually, but it has to go through the appropriate courts, and it's a slow business, even with the pressure on" said the Chief somewhat sadly. He was lost in thought for a moment.

"How about you?" he finally said, turning towards Jim with a quizzical expression.

"Well" said Jim, with a contained look of certainty which told the Chief Jim had something. He sat forward, attentive to Jim's words.

"I followed the paper trail from some other interesting contacts. You know all these property transactions you've been concerned about?" (The Chief nodded impatiently).

"In all these huge transactions, certain names have stood out. In individual councils, the same individuals have railroaded through planning permission, and at other times, demolition of those properties they deemed to be condemned".

The Chief grimaced.

"Condemned is the word" he said "but only condemned to oblivion by greed and corruption".

"That's more like it" said Jim, his eyes cold with bitterness "they have the properties condemned, demolish them, and buy the land up cheap with new planning permission for industrial wastelands".

"Certainly not houses for the people" agreed the Chief.

Jim shuffled the papers in his hand, glancing at a few names and places as he spoke.

"The same names figure prominently in a majority of these transactions, and in turn, they all link to senior officials in central Government".

"That figures" said the Chief " It would have to lead there somewhere, for it would never work on a purely local level – too many obstacles and difficulties without support – criminal support – from on high".

"That's right" said Jim, "But there's more. Every one of these contacts is linked indelibly with the Integrationist party. There are a few isolated cases of officials affiliated to other parties, but speaking purely from the outside, these are usually people with flawed characters and flawed lives who can be 'got at' in my opinion".

"And who gives the ultimate sanction on this activity?" said the Chief, knowing the answer already. Both men spoke the same sentence together.

"The Minister for Trade and Industry".

"An Integrationist, of course" added Jim.

The Chief looked at him gravely.

"Do you know what you're saying Jim?"

"What am I saying?"

Jim wanted the Chief to voice what he himself already knew.

"You're saying that this conspiracy touches to the very heart of Government" said the Chief, his voice almost cracking with tension.

"Yes" said Jim, "It's nothing less than an attempt to destroy the fabric of our civilisation".

"If that's the case" said the Chief, "Then all Integrationists must be suspect and…."

"That includes the Chancellor," said Jim grimly.

"The right honourable Jonathan Charles" said the Chief, aware of the import of his words.

6

How he missed her! Even after all these years of familiar solitude, the loneliness could still bite. He realised that his last contact with Edith had not helped him; it would have been better to leave the memories locked in his heart, for nothing would ever bring her back, he was only torturing himself.

Before he could sink deeper into his melancholy, he saw the lights of the car approaching far down below where he stood on the cool veranda. The evening breeze gently moved the silk curtains, waving them into the spacious and elegant room behind him. Sighing deeply and audibly, he took a sip of his Jack Daniels before he turned back into the room. The drink tasted strangely bitter, he thought, realising at the same time that the bitterness was the taste of his own despair.

A few moments later, the Lieutenant came in and exchanged familiar greetings. The feeling between the two men was once again warm, they had endured too much together to ever harbour long-standing grudges against each other. Nevertheless, the first subject was a tricky one, and the lieutenant cleared his throat before speaking.

"It's done" was all he said. The other man visibly winced, his face a twisted expression of pain, but he said nothing, merely nodding in understanding.

The two men sat down, the lieutenant pouring himself a drink as he relaxed with his bundle of papers.

"So where are we now?" asked the other man.

The Lieutenant took a swift sip of his drink.

"Our diversionary tactics in renewing and prolonging the credit activity are over as agreed. They served their purpose, but as you know, they quickly ran out of steam. Even with the changes we made, the authorities are aware of how the system works in general terms. We expected that, albeit sooner than we intended, but now, all activities related to credit and housing benefit etc have been completely wound down. As we speak, the last of the funds have been siphoned out of the system, and into areas of safety. Property and land purchases have reached saturation point, and the selling has begun. Suitable purchasers from abroad have been identified, and they have instructions to pay the asking price to our specification, that is, to our identified foreign accounts, notably in Switzerland".

"And from there to Liechtenstein?" Said the other man.

"Yes, of course" the Lieutenant replied, brushing the other man's comment aside tersely. "Through our Internet bank, connections are almost fully established. We still have one nut to crack, but he will be dealt with sooner rather than later".

The other man visibly tensed.

"No more deaths!" He insisted, fixing his lieutenant with a steely determined gaze.

The other man grimaced.

"I accept that – I gave my word," he said with a pained expression on his face.

"There will be no more deaths, but I reserve the right to use any and all other methods to bring about our objectives. It is those very objectives you seek even more than I do – is that not true?" he said, his voice strong and challenging, even to his best friend.

The other man softened, knowing the value his companion placed on their friendship, their loyalty to each other.

"Agreed" was all he said, looking at the other man with wisdom and even love.

"And what of the shares? And the currency?" He had returned to his true form.

The Lieutenant smiled at his friend's impatience.

"I was about to come to that, if you'd give me a chance!".

"Sorry" said his friend, "You know what an old woman I am when it comes to detail".

The Lieutenant smiled again, taking no offence at his friend's natural impatience. They knew each other too well for that.

"The shares are proceeding as planned. Of the top twenty UK blue chip shares, we now own the maximum permitted without disclosure in each of them. We are in a perfect position for hostile takeover bids when ready".

The other man nodded grimly.

"That of course, includes the major banks" he said.

"Naturally" said the Lieutenant, aware of his friend's need of reassurance.

"As for the currency situation, we have our man already established as a mainstream player," said the grey-haired lieutenant.

"He is completely in place to begin a run on the pound, with all of its implications, political and otherwise", he continued, pausing only to take another shot of whiskey.

"And what of Jonathan?" asked his friend.

"Jonathan will be Prime Minister before the end of the year" replied the lieutenant.

"Good" said the other man. "But how sure can we be of that? Surely a majority vote for Jonathan cannot exist without the co-operation of some of his opponents?"

"Yes, that's true", said the grey-haired man, "But Jonathan has a great deal of support in any case – or perhaps it's best to say that Rollinson doesn't".

The other man's impatience got the better of him again.

"Can we even be sure it will be Rollinson?" he asked.

The Lieutenant looked at him sombrely.

"Flood will be gone as soon as the shit hits the fan. Rollinson is the Deputy PM – he will be in place only until a proper election of the leader has taken place. Jonathan will be installed not just because of his own support, but because we can guarantee a switch of allegiance at the time of asking".

"The usual way?" said the other man.

"Yes" said the Lieutenant with a tight smile, "The usual way".

"So our plans are taking shape" said his friend, finally sitting back in satisfaction.

The Lieutenant looked at him again, his face a study of stubbornness and certainty.

"Britain will vanish as an entity within a decade of the new Millennium"

With that, both men spontaneously clinked their glasses together and drank to that, before throwing the beautifully-cut glasses into the huge fire As the shattering and shocking sound echoed through the room, they laughed like mad children till the tears ran down their faces.

7

McKay and the Chief had decided to repair to
the pub – it had been a long day.

"What do you want, Guv?" Dave asked in his
gruff way.

"G and T please" said the Chief, straightening
the collar of his jacket as he looked around.
Suddenly, he saw her enter the saloon bar next door.
It was Susan, and she was hanging on to Walker's
arm! Walker, of all people! What on earth was she
thinking of?

McKay had just ordered the drinks when he saw
the look on the Chief's face. Turning around and
following his gaze, he saw the reason for the Chief's
discomfort.

"Oh I see" he said, "The cat's out of the bag".

The Chief was thunderstruck.

"You mean you've all known about this? And
no one told me?"

"How could we Chief? We all knew what it
would mean to you. Anyway, just because they're
going out together doesn't mean it's serious, does
it?" Said McKay sheepishly.

The Chief was unconvinced.

"You should have told me Dave" he muttered,
disgruntled.

The Scotsman shrugged.

"Maybe – I did what I thought was best. I
couldn't win either way, and neither could you".
He placed his hand briefly on the Chief's shoulder.

The Chief sighed deeply.

318

"You're right Dave – what could anybody say. I suppose that's it then" he added, resigned to losing Susan for good.

"Let's finish this and get back to the office" said McKay philosophically.

"Yes, we've got work to get on with," said the Chief, grim-faced.

Back at the HQ, Jim Barton was waiting, waving at them excitedly from the end of the long corridor which led to the Chief's office. The Chief quickened his steps, knowing that Jim had something important to tell him. As the two men hurried down the corridor, Simmonds saw them, and rushed out towards them, almost as excited as Jim.

"Chief! Chief!" He shouted, trying to get his attention.

"Not now Simmonds!" said the Chief, turning to McKay who was just behind him.

"Dave, can you deal with this? I must talk to Jim urgently first".

McKay collared the unfortunate Simmonds, leaving the Chief to get to the office unscathed. Jim's face was a mixture of triumph and excitement.

"What is Jim? What have you got?" said the Chief, barely suppressing his eagerness.

Jim turned to the video player at the corner of the room and pressed 'play'.

The screen flickered briefly, then the scene settled to show what looked like the foyer of a bank. A smartly dressed man walked in carrying a brief case. With military precision, he marched up to the

319

reception desk and introduced himself to the young woman sitting there.

"Who is that?" said the Chief, hardly daring to ask.

"That is the man who opened the Goldcrest account" said Jim "and his name is Alan Scott".

"How the hell did you get this Jim?" said the Chief in admiration, "The authorities haven't even reached first base yet!"

"It wasn't strictly ethical for a start, so don't ask!" said Jim, glancing nervously over his shoulder as he spoke. "Let's just say that our newspaper has a large budget when it comes to investigations the editor judges are serious enough to warrant it".

"Alan Scott" said the Chief, running the video again and again, staring at the tall grey-haired man with fierce interest. "Could he be the one?" he mused.

Jim looked at him, suddenly serious.

"Well, if it isn't him – the one – then he's certainly someone who's very close to the action".

"I wonder if it's worth running this one past Piers Tremain?" Said the Chief, "He may just recognise him from this video".

At that moment, McKay walked in, just in time to hear the Chief's words.

"I'm afraid it's too late for that Guv" he said gravely, "Tremain is dead – they got to him after all".

The Chief's jaw dropped open in shock.

"He was in a safe house – a supposedly safe house – what the hell happened?".

McKay's expression grew darker.

"Not a pretty sight. A girl was obviously involved. He was covered in his own blood and semen. Naked and chained to the bed with a knife in his throat and his private parts missing".

The men shuddered visibly.

"What about his minders?" said the Chief, his brain running away ahead of itself, "How did she – they – get around them?"

McKay grimaced again.

"The same Guv. They found the two men trussed up and castrated in the same way. Obviously a hard working woman".

"Any clues?" said the Chief, more in reaction than hope.

McKay pulled a face. "Well, we have her DNA, that's for sure. Other than that, not a one that we can see so far Guv, though we're still working on it" he said, hesitating briefly, wondering what else could be said in a delicate manner. "It's a very messy business" was all he could manage.

The Chief turned again to the video that had run on to show Mr Alan Scott walking towards the camera. As he passed below it, Scott looked up straight into the eye of the camera, almost as if he was confronting and mocking the men in the room that sat staring in silence at his image.

"Well Mr Scott" said the Chief, breaking the tense silence, "You have a lot of questions to answer when the time is right".

He reached over and switched the video off, plunging Alan Scott into darkness once more.

8

The House was in uproar. The Historic building had seen many a verbal battle of epic proportions, but this debate neared the top of the list, it was like anarchy. Hardly any speaker could be heard, and the sitting had already been suspended once, yet it had made practically no difference to the hostility and rancour, spreading like wildfire among the Honourable members.

The most recent time Parliament had witnessed such scenes was the passing of the bill that denied mortgage holders the right of possession over their properties. The bill had predictably caused the lenders to severely restrict any lending, which of course meant that no one except the very rich could now buy a property. Unscrupulous mortgagees now also took full advantage, and mortgage arrears were rising swiftly and sharply.

All of that only increased the fury of the opposition benches, and as if the flames needed fuel poured upon them, this bill involved the thorniest subject of all – Europe. The pound was to be linked inexorably to the ERM, with all of the implications therein. The proposal was to tie the pound to the Deutschemark, a task that was, to most experts, beyond the capability of the ailing pound. Without devaluation as an option, many members of Parliament and experts fore saw a run on the pound that would be the ruin of Britain. However, both Flood and Rollinson had, at various times, given 'concrete' assurances that the pound would never be devalued. They were in a political trap of their own making, and it weakened any opposition they could give to the Integrationists.

Jonathan Charles, being Chancellor of the Exchequer, was the man in the firing line, but he was well equipped to deal with the wild scenes and feeding frenzy of those who opposed his plans. He knew he had the backing, if only just – and for foul as well as fair reasons – of the majority of the House, so he could afford to amuse himself by castigating his opponents with his rapier wit.

"You Sir, are an abomination as a Chancellor!" screamed out a Conservative MP, his face red with anger.

Charles smiled, calm amid the storm.

"The honourable member can, if he wishes, describe me as an abomination and a Chancellor – that may be two things he can ascribe to me, one of which I do not necessarily agree with". The majority of the House chortled with mirth, while many continued to scream abuse and agreement with the previous speaker.

Jonathan's voice rose ten decibels, gaining the momentary attention of the House.

"However!" he said, his voice ringing above the melee, "I in turn can only use one of those words to fairly describe the honourable member, and that word is not 'Chancellor'!"

Jonathan sat down as the House exploded in a mixture of admiration and hate. He was the coolest man in the chamber. Jonathan knew that despite the fuss, the passing of the bill was a foregone conclusion.

The fate of the pound was sealed.

9

Margeles was the new man on the block. Yes, his name had been known in financial circles for many years, but people in the know were agog at how this moderately wealthy Armenian who had seemed merely a bit player in the financial markets of the World had transformed himself into *the* supreme manipulator of events. The sheer power of his wealth was what impressed the World most, after all, only someone with incredible resources could shape events as Margeles did, changing administrations, threatening Governments very existence.

His rise had not been slow and steady, it was meteoric. Only the previous year, he had been anonymous, just another financial punter playing the currency game, switching constantly from currency to currency to make a deal here, shade a deal there. Then suddenly, his power and influence blossomed. Many unkindly said that he was too stupid to be so influential in his own right, he was a puppet of a powerful man who wanted to remain anonymous. Some touted the Sultan of Brunei, one of the richest men in the World, as the Machiavellian operator behind Margeles, a not unreasonable scenario when one considered the Armenian's background in shipping and shady Eastern commerce.

Whatever the truth of the background, it had to be conceded that Margeles was a force to be reckoned with. Only the year before, Governments

324

of the third world had succumbed to his manipulations, which in itself had caused countries of every colour and creed to sit up and take notice. For as everyone knew, the downside of the fully connected economies of the World was that events affecting any one Country, however small, impacted on every other Country, even reaching the relatively rich of the West.

Margeles had been known in financial circles for some time, and his rise as a major player had been noted and reported in every financial journal. Yet the first time most people in the street heard his name was when the part he had played in the devaluation of the Spanish Lire hit the headlines. People were bemused and astonished that one man could cause Governments to change direction and even fall. It seemed somehow obscene, and the ordinary man and woman shivered at the cold draught of insecurity that seemed to threaten the money in their own pockets.

As Margeles began to publicly threaten the pound, quietly an MI5 investigation was set in motion. What it uncovered immediately was a series of trust funds administered by Margeles, presumably for his own ends. Whatever the funds were for was not known. Even MI5 could not penetrate the deepest secrets of the world's hidden trust funds, they could merely point to their name and existence and surmise. The Chief had, by way of routine, been sent these musings, but it seemed remote to him, a world of paranoid politics with little connection to his current investigation. He filed the papers away till another time.

Margeles, the private man inside all these images, was unconcerned by other people's fears or insecurities, or even their future. He was essentially a weak and greedy man, almost a caricature of what people superficially perceived about him. His vanity and pompous demeanour made him an easy target for those who wanted to use him for their own ends. They had needed a financial player who was familiar, yet relatively anonymous. They also needed someone who was corruptible, and Margeles certainly fitted the bill in that respect. He had no scruples whatsoever, his only purpose in life was to increase his own wealth and position of power in the eyes of others. Even his own family, his Wife, his children, were mere baubles in his would-be Empire.

Those who controlled him understood very well his character, or lack of it. They indulged him like a child, let him play with limousines, planes, boats, casinos, they even encouraged his ludicrous purchase of a prestigious Kensington department store, much to the wrath of an equally childish rival who had his own cold greedy eyes on the same agenda.

All these trifles were indulgences that the controllers of Margeles could well afford. They were considered simply as expenses in a wider game, and each indulgence granted meant that Margeles was further in their debt and control.

Margeles liked his life style. Margeles wanted it to continue for as long as life.

Margeles presented a rich and pampered face to the public, his ridiculous ego loving every sweet minute of his gaudy elevation.

Margeles did as he was told.

10

Once again the lights were burning late in the offices of APACS in Finsbury Square. At the long table were the familiar faces of the great and the good, or at least, those that had coveted and finally achieved positions of power in the financial institutions. Lord Sefton was there, Lord Wetherby, Sir James Telfer of Yorkshire Bank – all the same indignant and proud faces graced the table with the bad humour and the collective ignorance that comes with the unopposed arrogance of power.

Heading the meeting as usual was Farquhar-Brown, the APACS Director-General. At his side sat the oily –skinned figure of Wesley Sykes, his public relations Chief, who had seen a brandy and port too many these past years, and whose concentration was not as it should be, suffering as he was from the onset of gout.

The Chief was another uneasy guest, standing out like a sore thumb in his modest suit and unaffected demeanour. He noted with distaste the proud and pompous features of his fellow guests, and knew only too well what the meeting was for – self preservation of the dinosaurs.

Farquhar-Brown had barely called the meeting to order when Sir James Telfer rudely interrupted him.

"Never mind all this waffle – what are you going to do about this situation? It is intolerable that the Government can be allowed to prevent us realising our securities in the face of outrageous debt and negation of responsibilities!"

"Hear! Hear!" The voice of Lord Sefton rose above the melee, intermingled with the gruff mutterings of those of his ilk.

"The law must surely be obeyed, but a law which is wrong in principal can and indeed, should be opposed" said Farquhar-Brown soothingly, ever the pragmatist. "We will do all in our power to persuade those who hold high office that these policies are doomed to failure. It will become obvious that with the severe restriction of lending policy, pressure will be brought to bear on the Government by those who can no longer purchase a home, and indeed by those who cannot move to another home when they wish to. Gentlemen, I believe that our present policies will yield rich fruit, given time and patience". As he spoke, Farquhar-Brown knew as well as anyone that nearly everyone in the room was not impressed by the concept of neither time nor patience.

He pressed on regardless.

"Nevertheless Gentlemen, there are other pressing matters you wish to raise. I call Sir Thomas Beecham to say a few words."

The portly knight struggled to his feet.

"Thank you Director-General" he said grudgingly, dismissing Farquhar-Brown with a wave of his cigar. "My concern is the rise and rise of the so-called I-Bank, whose presence in the high street is non-existent, and whose interests and concerns are not shared with us. I note that I-Bank are not and have never been represented here in these good offices." Beecham waved his lethargic arm in a circle illustrating the auspices of APACS as if he himself were the architect of its environs.

"This I-Bank [He said the word with the supreme disdain and distaste that only a Jewish boy made good was able to muster] is not only stealing our business away on the Internet, I would also point you to the stealthy way in which it is undermining our very fabric, buying up our shares like thieves in the night. I tell you, they are poised to take over every one of us here, and where will that leave society? What protection will the ordinary consumer have against such greed?"

The irony of his own position totally escaped someone like Sir Thomas Beecham. Only months before, his bank had opened a new war between themselves and their rivals by charging customers for withdrawing their own cash from cash machines, causing the other banks to do the same. All these Captains of financial industry may have shared the one roof at APACS, but in the high street, they were deadly rivals, who would do each other down at the drop of a hat.

Nevertheless, Beecham had touched a nerve. None of those present wished to see anyone of their rivals take their profits and eventually their business away, but to see an outsider muscling in forced them to temporarily unite in their determination and fear.

A mutter of excited conversation sprang up as Beecham sat down. Farquhar-Brown sought to smooth the ruffled feathers.

"Thank you Sir Thomas. I think it safe to say that we share your concern. In the light of these and other associated matters, I have asked my associate here to investigate the background of I-Bank, beyond the simple remit of the Bank of England, which I-Bank have successfully dealt with."

Farquhar-Brown indicated that the Chief should stand and say a few words. The Chief rose, almost reluctantly, but when he spoke, it was with clarity and conviction.

"Thank you Director-General. Gentlemen, I too am suspicious, I have to say, of I-Bank. There are many things which have happened in this Country this past few years which seem unconnected, yet I believe that there is a genuine conspiracy to undermine the very fabric of our society. I believe that I-Bank could – and at this stage, that's all I am able to say – I-Bank could be part of this conspiracy. The signs may not be verifiable at the moment, but they are ominous. I-Bank is indeed buying up shares in every important institution in our Country, and not just in the financial sector either. Every blue chip company seems to be a target. The Government and the monopolies commission are aware of these facts, but while the shares held stand at the maximum permitted, there is little the authorities can do. Even in that respect, another worrying trend is that many of the other shares of these institutions are held by foreign investors in unnamed trusts. There must be a danger that I-Bank and/or their associates are also behind these purchases."

There was an audible gasp around the room as everyone realised that a bad situation had suddenly become worse. The Chief paused to let the worried mumblings ebb away.

"However, we are not totally helpless in all this. There are things we can and will do, and my colleagues and I are working right now to get to the bottom of this."

"About time too" muttered Lord Sefton indignantly, wishing to exercise his power of some minion or other to make himself feel more at home. A mutter of approval and "Hear! Hear!" rippled along the table. The Chief wisely ignored this childish display.

"There is one more thing I have to say" he said gravely, his voice conveying the importance of his concerns. "I cannot emphasis enough that our concerns about I-Bank may or may not be well-founded. We simply cannot say at this point in time. For that reason, I must ask you all to keep this conversation entirely confidential. For one thing, we may be indicting a perfectly legitimate business…….. [there was a chorus of sneering and snorting as the guests voiced disapproval of such a notion]…….and even if our assumptions prove to be correct, the less we can alert our quarry to our intentions, the better."

The last comment at least drew a mutter of agreement as the Chief finally sat down. Having discussed the situation with Farquhar-Brown over the last few weeks, the Chief knew what was about to be said, and crossed his arms expectantly, quizzically looking sideways at Farquhar-Brown as he rose to speak.

The Director-General had foregone his usual bland inscrutable demeanour. His face and his voice conveyed gravity.

"Gentlemen. You have heard my colleague outline the gravity of the situation we may face. This is nothing less than a fundamental attack on all our guiding principles and way of life."

Farquhar-Brown looked round the suddenly silent room.

"I therefore propose that as soon as we have reasonably concrete evidence to confirm our worst fears have been realised, we summon an emergency meeting with the Prime Minister."

A chorus of hushed and sombre voices called out "Agreed", and as the meeting broke up, like mourners departing a funeral, they filed out one by one in silence.

http//www.i-bank.co.uk

The Chief sat staring at his computer screen and the web page in front of him. "Millions of new customers every week!" the banner at the top of the web page screamed. The Chief knew it was a true statement. The bank seemed more concerned with gaining new customers than making money. The interest rates they offered were generous to say the least, and the loan facilities contained facilities of application that totally lacked intrusion (and therefore security). No wonder customers were deserting the high street banks in droves, he thought.

He scrutinised the list of Directors. Not one name stood out that he knew. Then one name seemed to ring a bell. *Calder Hall*. Where had he seen that name before? He reached inside a drawer of his desk, and extracted a sheaf of papers, filed previously then forgotten. Quickly, he flipped through the pages then halted at a name. *Alexander* Hall. Was it a connection, or was it just an innocent coincidence? His eye caught the photograph of Alexander Hall, taken from his passport. Where had he seen that face before?

Perplexed, he pressed the intercom on his desk.
"Yes Chief?" said Susan.
"Susan, have you got a minute? Can we have a look at through your gallery? There's something I want to check up on" He said, trying to ignore the feelings that churned inside whenever he heard her voice.

Susan was ice itself, formality personified.

"That will be fine Chief," she said dispassionately, disappointing him yet again.

He strolled down the corridor to Susan's room, carrying with him the Alexander Hall file.

She didn't look up immediately as he walked on, but eventually turned to face him.

"What have you got?" she said, curious but still studiously detached.

"I know we ran this photo through the gallery at the time," he said, trying to hide his sadness, "But can we run it again? I'm sure I've seen this face before."

Susan shrugged. She knew her own skills at seeking out connections in that line, she doubted a new search would reveal much, unless new information had been entered since. She entered the details in the computer.

'IDENTIFY THIS MAN'.

It was only moments later when the substantial resources of the huge computer system sprang into life on the screen.

They both gasped in amazement. The picture of the man on screen was markedly different to the man whose passport photograph they held. The man in the passport photograph was clean shaven for a start. With the full beard, the glasses, and the extra weight, they would hardly have recognised the man. Nevertheless, once the computer had pointed out the connection, the result was undeniable.

"Axel Margeles," said the Chief, his voice almost a whisper.

'Margeles', the infamous currency speculator whose involvement in the recent run on the pound was causing such anguish in the press! That connection made the Chief raise his eyebrows in triumph and horror at the same time. The discovery showed that Margeles was linked to the bank and to the corrupt system itself.

"Thanks Susan," he said, noting how pleased she was, despite trying to disguise it. He tried to look deep into her eyes, but she lowered her gaze, and turned back to her computer as if preoccupied.

He returned to his office, and turned again to the pages of bank transactions lying on his desk. 'Goldcrest Ltd' said the bold name at the top of each page. Only received that morning after what seemed endless and wasteful haggling in the Isle of Mann courts, the statements had yielded much in the way of concrete information regarding the movements of funds in and out of the shady company.

There was even minute by minute confirmation of sums which he and Susan and the team had personally witnessed being paid in by apprehended members of the credit syndicate scam. If that was not enough, there was a clear connection to the funds used to set up James Germaine and Pierre Arroneaux. Share support was also obvious in the cases of Blue Arrow, Guinness, and other dubious City transactions and take-overs. The only thing there hadn't been evidence for, was a clear link to I-Bank, a crucial missing element if the Chief and Farquhar-Brown were to convince the Prime Minister of their fears. Now, with the link to

Margeles and I-Bank, the connections and the threat was obvious.

There was much digging still to do. However, it was only one day into receipt of the accounts, and the Chief's team was already sifting through the vast bundle of papers, with clear instructions as to what they were looking for. Sitting among the team, working as hard as anyone was Jim Barton, anxious to be in the thick of it.

The Chief handed Jim his information on Alexander Hall, I-Bank, and Margeles. Jim whistled, impressed and interested, then he turned back to rummage among his papers.

"Look at this!" said Jim, handing the Chief a couple of pages. "This money being moved here has got to be the death throes of the old credit and HB squeeze – the sums involved are staggering!"

The Chief had grown used to seeing the mammoth amounts of money bandied about the World's illegitimate systems in their endless search for an ideal laundering environment, but the untold billions vanishing from Goldcrest's accounts were on a level hitherto unknown.

"And where are these funds going?" said Jim, asking a rhetorical question.

"To Switzerland and Liechtenstein, of course" said the Chief.

"But where to ultimately, that is the question" said Jim, sounding vaguely Shakespearean.

"If only we could establish more links with I-Bank, just to be sure of our ground," said the Chief wistfully, somewhat apprehensive about an approach to the Prime Minister without sufficient proof. "These funds are going out in that way and that size for a particular reason, that much is obvious – but where's the link? I can't see it."

Jim looked at him askance. He handed the Chief yet another piece of paper with Jim's childish scrawl across the page.

"Well here's one at least", he said, pointing to the transaction he had underlined, "This transaction can be traced to the account of a gentlemen by the name of - wait for it – Alexander Hall".

"Alias Axel Margeles" said the Chief, becoming animated, "And Margeles, as we know, is a beneficial Director of ....." here, the Chief paused, letting Jim chorus along with him, "I-Bank!".

Both men smiled at each other, but their eyes showed the serious concerns behind the smiles.

Finally, after a short poignant silence, the Chief spoke.

"It will take months at least to get anywhere with the Swiss authorities, and it's probably impossible to ferret anything out of Liechtenstein. The connection with Margeles is all we really have at the moment. Then again, it may be slightly tenuous, but I think we do have enough now to approach the Prime Minister".

Jim, unaware until this point of the deliberations at APACS, was suitably impressed by the name-dropping, and pulled a long face.

"That's fine as it goes," he said, "But who *will* the Prime Minister *be* by the time you contact him?"

The Chief had to concede that it was a good point.

12

Julian Somerfield had been a Conservative MP for more than twenty years now. He had grown used to the ways of the House, using it more as a social club than for any great matters of State. Somerfield had long since forgotten that he was there principally to represent his constituents, such fantasies and illusions as he once had about himself had long since vanished in the smoke-filled brandy haze of his own ego.

A portly gent, with a liking for pretty girls, the younger the better, he was a font of casual corruption and vice which traded in every iota of his currency as a member of Parliament for favours, sexual and otherwise. In that sense, he was already completely corrupted, so it could not be said in absolute truth that he was compromised as such by the events of August first.

As was his wont, he spent the early part of the evening dining at Claridges with a few fawning friends who could indulge his ego without him having the inconvenience of indulging theirs. As the evening progressed, he noticed a beautiful woman sitting on her own at a nearby table. At first he was merely interested, but as the brandies began to take effect, he found himself drifting away from the endless monologues which seemed to so entrance his sycophantic admirers. One by one, his companions sensed his interest in the lady in question, and winking knowingly at each other, they gradually excused themselves from his company until he was at last alone.

Somerfield was not a shy or even subtle man. Thankful to be free of his encumbrances, he waddled over to the lady's table, and asked if he could join her for a drink. To his delight, she smiled graciously and warmly, and in a perfect cut glass accent, she invited him to sit down and take an cognac with her.

As he waffled interminably on, at the same time he noted her exquisite face, her perfect smile, her haunting eyes, her long flowing auburn hair. Laura was her name, he discovered. It was like music, a name like that, he told her, congratulating himself on a fine turn of phrase.

The evening quickly wound down, and with his dreams of lechery scarcely able to contain themselves within his trousers, Somerfield offered Laura a lift home. Of course, he had no intention of taking her home, his intention was to get her to the nearest bed as soon as possible, something that Laura did not seem to encourage, but on the other hand, did not discourage either.

However, Somerfield felt thwarted when Laura insisted on going to her own place rather than his, and he felt his spirits (and much else besides) wilt as his dreams of carnal conquest seemed to vanish. He need not have feared, and soon rallied again when Laura, having reached her apartment in fashionable Mayfair, invited him in for a coffee.

'Coffee' to Somerfield was a metaphor for something else, and his demon dreams were soon at full cock again. Hardly had the pair entered Laura's apartment when he began manhandling her, something she did not apparently protest too much about, though she did make one or two pleas for him to restrain himself as he drew her close to him. His excitement mounted as he felt her large throbbing bosom pressing against his chest and for the first time, her lips parted to allow his tongue to enter, even though she demurely blushed as he did so. He found such virginal qualities so attractive in a woman! All the better to ravish her, he thought, his ambitions struggling to be free from the constraint of his clothes.

After a great deal of huffing and puffing, he had managed to expose Laura's breasts, finding to his awe just how big and well-shaped they were, the delicate nipples standing out from being exposed to the air. Seeing how shy she was, he had done her work for her and exposed himself, placing her hand there on him. He did not mind that she seemed inexperienced in that way, holding him gingerly as if unsure how to proceed. It somehow added to the thrill of capture for him.

His next task was to reach up inside her dress, which he did with some difficulty, Laura seeming trapped in a mixture of desire and uncertainty, one moment holding his hand back from reaching further towards her, the next, allowing him a few more inches of ground. Eventually, with a feeling of great triumph, he had her in his hand, feeling the wetness and softness of her as he reached further and further inside, making her involuntarily groan with shameful pleasure. At the same time, despite herself, Laura was manipulating him in a steady rhythm, causing him some anxiety about staying the course.

A new tack was called for, he decided, suddenly taking his hand from her and pushing her on her knees before him so that her lips almost touched his manhood there and then. Laura hesitated, as if frightened, but he had her by the back of the head, and forced her onto himself, pushing relentlessly till he had entered all the way into her throat. He looked down in satisfaction to see her face buried in his hair, the whole of him inside her, as she gurgled and choked with the first flow of him entering her.

However, his relief was to be short-lived. He had only just begun when she suddenly forced herself away from him, leaving him incomplete and constricted, cut off in mid-flow. He felt an unreasonable anger rising in him, but knew better than to express it there and then. He would make her pay in full for her stupid virgin ways, he thought.

Seeing his disappointment, Laura looked at him with a mixture of guilt and innocence.

"I'm sorry, did I stop too soon?" she asked with a look that said she was anxious to make up for what she had done, or failed to do, her mouth and face still wet with the result of her withdrawal. Somerfield affected a wise humility.

"Not to worry, my dear, it was lovely while it lasted" he said, hoping Laura would take the hint.

"You must let me finish it properly this time" said Laura, descending to take him in her mouth once more. Somerfield stopped her just as her lips reached him.

"No, no, my dear – not that way" said Somerfield soothingly, "If we are to do it, we must do it properly". Laura looked at him, her eyes widening.

"You mean – all the way?" she said, her little voice like a frightened girl, beautiful eyes wide and staring.

"Yes" said Somerfield reassuringly, "It will be all right – trust me".

With that, he took her hand and led her along the corridor to seek the bedroom.

Inside, he turned on a bedside lamp and began to slowly undress her, marvelling all the while at the treasures hidden by her long prim dress. So she was a genuine redhead, he noted, seeing the delicate curls which adorned her womanhood, the sensual curve of her spine as it reached outwards then down to the delicate places hidden within her.

She in turn, shyly undressed him till he was fully naked, his manhood thrusting at her again, eager to fulfil the earlier thwarted promises. Suddenly, Laura stopped, looking at him questioningly, almost tearful.

"What is it?" Somerfield asked, sensing her discomfort.

"You won't hurt me, will you?" said Laura, like a little girl again. Even an insensitive oaf like Somerfield was touched by her fear.

"Of course not" he said reassuringly, touching her face gently, "Why would I do that?"

"I've only been with one other man" Laura said, "and he hurt me dreadfully – he did things to me that I cannot begin to tell you about". With that, she broke down in tears. He felt himself getting irritated again, his hopes beginning to dwindle.

343

"Look!" he said, "Tell me what you don't want me to do, and I won't do it – I promise!" a note of desperation in his voice.

Laura's tears trickled down her face once more. She looked at him, pain on her face.

"It's not what I don't want you to do – you can do anything you like" she said, making his hopes suddenly leap.

"It's just that you have to promise me that you'll lie there and let me do whatever has to be done. I'll do anything you ask, just tell me, but you must promise to let me do it to you, rather than the other way round" said Laura, her voice hesitant but firm at the same time. Somerfield needed no further bidding. It sounded quite exciting, he thought.

"Of course I promise!" he said, sounding a mite too eager. Laura still looked doubtful.

Somerfield looked round the room in desperation. His eyes fell on some silk scarves lying by the dressing table.

"Look!" he said triumphantly, springing over and retrieving the scarves, "You don't have to take my word for it. Tie me up with these! Then you can do what you like without fear!" Laura looked at him hesitantly.

"Are you sure?" she said, in her little girl voice again.

Somerfield knew he was nearly there.

"Of course I'm sure!" he said, as convincingly as he could manage.

He handed Laura the scarves and made for the bed. As he lay on his back, Laura frowned.

"What is it" he said, fear clutching his heart yet again.

"It's just that I'd like you lying face down and across the bed" said Laura, her voice a quiet sulk.

"Face down? " said Somerfield, thinking of the restricted possibilities that entailed.

"Just to begin with" said Laura, almost apologetically.

"Why across the bed?" said Somerfield, puzzled.

Laura smiled a rare smile, touching his heart as well as everything else.

"I can do what I have to better if I can reach you everywhere" she said.

The thought of that melted Somerfield's doubts, and he shrugged, and lay face down across the bed, his podgy bloated body covering much of the elegant bedspread. Laura took the scarves and tied him securely by the hands to the metal frame of the bed. Then she pushed his legs up so that he was in a squatting position with his rear end high in the air. With his manhood dangling incongruously, he looked like a donkey on heat. Laura tied his ankles to the metal frames, pulling his legs wide apart as she could without destabilising his position.

Somerfield was intrigued and excited. It seemed as if it was going to be fun.

"What now?" he said, in eager anticipation, looking round at Laura. To his surprise, Laura was sitting in a chair a few feet away, a negligee now placed over her suspenders and stockings, her stiletto shoe poised in the air as she crossed her legs provocatively. Somerfield sensed something wrong with her. Laura's whole demeanour had changed. She no longer seemed virginal, prim, uncertain. She suddenly looked like a very confident sexually aware woman, and more than that, she was looking at him with an amusement in her eyes, the look of a spider when it sees the fly.

He heard a door opening from the adjoining room. Three men entered! His heart leapt in fear, especially when he saw that the men were all but naked! Without exchanging a word, the men got to work on him. One entered him from the back, going all the way without hesitation, causing a pain he had never experienced before. He would have cried out in agony, but another man was in his mouth, pushing himself as far as was possible inside Somerfield so that it was all the fat MP could do to breath at all. In panic, he felt the third man take him in his mouth and work on him ferociously, his body responding despite his fear and humiliation.

In a very short time, both men inside him began to empty themselves, and to his shame and horror, Somerfield felt himself involuntarily do the same to the third man at that very moment. His mind was a raging sea of torment and insanity, but out the corner of his eye he could see Laura standing close to the mass of bodies heaving at him. She was taking photographs, for God's sake!

Finally, at last he felt the men ease themselves from him, shaming him by drawing their wetness across his face, his body. He was almost too devastated to care by that point. At least they were leaving him to fight again for his breath, as he shuddered at the taste, the feel of them, unable to reach with his hands and wipe away the stains that covered his body, his face, his mouth.

To his horror, he saw the men move toward him again, only this time in a different order. He was able to utter only one cry of despair as they again entered him, one shutting off all sound other than Somerfield's muted choking, and the whole deadly sequel was repeated. Time after time that long night, they abused him, both with themselves and with implements and other items, notably a marrow, which almost split him in two.

All the while, Laura stood there, her long red hair flowing, her womanhood gaping in front of him, mocking him, the endless click of the camera the only sound to interrupt his own body noises which tormented him in his agony.

As yet more flowed inside him in both places, somewhere amidst his anguish of body and mind, Somerfield realised what the photographs meant. They meant that he had been well and truly compromised.

Somerfield may not have appreciated it at the time, but in dealing with Laura, things could have been a lot worse.

13

Something had to give, and it was Terence
Flood. Since the Tuesday before, when the
Governor of the Bank of England, Christopher Lee-
Martin had visited number 10, Flood's position had
become untenable. Lee-Martin had warned the PM
in no uncertain terms that unless Britain withdrew
from the ERM and devalued, the run on the pound
and the attempts to forestall it would render Britain
bankrupt in a matter of months at best.

There was no doubt that Margeles was the major
player in this manipulation. Like J P Morgan, the
legendary American from the beginning of the
century who could bail out or ditch and manipulate
Governments at his will, Margeles, aided by the
instant communications of the computer age was
similarly able, at the end of this century to exert the
same power. It was more subtle than in Morgan's
time, but if anything, it's effect was more numbing,
chilling. Morgan could bankrupt a Country.
Margeles was capable of bankrupting the World.

Despite the MI5 investigation, nothing untoward
could be found. His greed and self interest was
apparent in every machination he had ever made,
but that was a statement of character, not a criminal
offence. Margeles' bank accounts and secret trusts
were known, but, impenetrable, and again, that did
not constitute any wrongdoing, or at least, any
wrongdoing it did constitute could not be seen.

Margeles himself, when interviewed by
television and the press, professed himself to be a
humble financier, denying any part in the troubles

of the Government. And the Government's troubles were, at this moment, very real. Flood could see that if the Country were to survive intact, the pound would have to leave the ERM and be immediately devalued. Most commentators would agree, but unfortunately for the Prime Minister, the most important person in his cabinet second to himself was violently opposed to this proposal. That was of course, the Chancellor.

Jonathan Charles was unmoved by appeals to save the Country and the pound. This after all, had been the reason at the heart of his demand to be Chancellor, so that he could withstand the inevitable requests for withdrawal from the ERM. Each cabinet meeting was at the moment, a war scene, reminiscent of the passing of the bill itself in Parliament. The crucial fact was that the devaluation supporters, including Flood himself, were constantly outvoted by Charles and even by Conservative and Labour members, who, unknown to their colleagues, had more to lose than a concern for Britain and the pound.

In a strong Government, with a cabinet of his own making, a strong Prime Minister would have taken the decision by himself in any case, overruling any dissent. But this was not a cabinet of Flood's making, and in any case, he was not and never could be a strong Prime Minister. Therefore, he prevaricated as long as possible. That is, until the Governor of the Bank of England's meeting. Frustrated by the lack of co-operation from the Chancellor, the Governor had sought to go over his head to the Prime Minister, hardly believing that anyone sensible would put the Country at risk for the sake of mere dogma.

Flood did not care about the Country, but he cared about his good name, and he was also panic-stricken about being the one left holding the baby when the shit hit the fan, so he did the next best thing. He ran from office to leave someone else to find a chair when the music stopped.

That someone was, for now at least, Henry Rollinson, the Deputy PM.

The headlines screamed the news – 'Floods of tears in Downing Street' and similar banners (and worse) appeared in the tabloids. Still, for now, a little bloodletting had whetted the appetites of those who constantly plot to undermine the successful. It had also taken everyone's sights off the main question – how was the thorny question of devaluation and the run on the pound to be tackled? And who was the man to do it?

The MP's, the news moguls, the people themselves would have thought of him as the last person to have as Prime Minister when it came to the question of the pound and leaving the ERM, but Jonathan Charles had other ideas. At the first cabinet meeting of the new executive, he eyed Rollinson's chair with envy and intent.

Just wait, he thought, just wait.

14

The new Prime Minister was too wily a political animal not to know exactly what was going through the mind of Jonathan Charles. If Rollinson was unduly concerned, it never showed, but then, he didn't know the half of it. The PM was about to go on a learning curve.

The meeting took place at Downing Street, arranged by the highest channels in utmost secrecy. The Prime Minister was intrigued by the unusual arrangements – instructions not to discuss the meeting with any members of cabinet or other officials? What on earth was going on, thought Rollinson. All he had been told was that the meeting was a matter of sovereignty and security, a wide ranging but lethal statement which had the Prime Minister agog. Realising that there must be constitutional and secrecy implications, the PM decided to bring internal security at the highest level into the meeting.

Around the table with Rollinson were Farquhar-Brown, the Chief, and Jim Barton, whose inclusion had caused the security chiefs endless anxiety, given his close relationship with Fleet Street. The Chief had however insisted that Jim must be included – citing to Farquhar-Brown and co. what sterling work Jim had carried out. In fact, as the Chief rightly said, without Jim's involvement thus far, there wouldn't be any call for such a meeting. It had to be right and proper to include him.

The Prime Minister called the meeting to order, and introduced those around the table to each other.

Apart from the APACS team and their associates, the Prime Minister introduced Armand Heathcote, the cabinet secretary, Sheila Remington, the head of MI5, and Lyle Patrick, the Attorney General. No other officials, minor or major, were informed or involved, thanks to the diligence of Remington, who quite naturally, was always alert to subversive elements.

The Prime Minister wasted no time on trivial small talk. He could sense this was an ultra-serious business.

"Gentlemen, make your presentation", was all he said, his face a serious unsmiling mask.

Farquhar-Brown rose solemnly and slowly, voice calm and assured, but earnest and concise.

"Prime Minister, we have become aware of a serious threat not only to your Government, but to our whole way of life, indeed our existence on this Island. We asked for this meeting to enable the forces of decency and democracy to act before it is too late."

Farquhar-Brown paused to let his words sink in, then continued.

"We have, as you know, gone through a time of huge financial scandals and great pressure on Government. We believe we can show that all of this is not coincidental. It is nothing less than a concerted and orchestrated attack on our financial and political systems. The intention, we believe, is to undermine Great Britain itself, to bankrupt the Nation, to remove from the World all that is British and consign us to history".

The Prime Minister interrupted.

"It sounds as if you're describing the general activities of the Integrationist party, but at a more extreme level and cynicism than we've seen so far. Is that fair comment?"

Farquhar-Brown stared back at the PM, his face gripped with tension.

"Yes. We believe that the Integrationist party is a central tool in this operation, though the party itself is merely a vehicle for the ambitions and mad desires of an individual or individuals who have the ultimate hand of control".

"You say you have proof of this?" said the Prime Minister, frowning deeply.

"Yes" said Farquhar-Brown gravely, "We can take you through every line and connection, but that may be a task for your staff – your highly-vetted staff – rather than yourself. We can confidently show connections from the highly-publicised credit fraud, through to the housing benefit and social security fraud; from there, we have indisputable links to Germaine Rouse; Guinness; Pierre Arroneaux; Blue Arrow; Maxwell, Lloyds – the list goes on and on, but contains all these familiar names and more."

"These are indeed very serious matters" said the PM, stroking his chin thoughtfully, "But serious though they are – and I for one do not attempt to diminish what is being said here – they cannot be said to strike at the heart of Government and democracy itself, can they?"

"Hear me out, Prime Minister" said Farquhar-Brown calmly, "The funds from these criminal enterprises was siphoned out via Swiss and

Liechtenstein banks and into share purchases of our top twenty blue chip companies".

Seeing the look on the Prime Minister's face, Farquhar-Brown added "Yes, of course that includes our major banks. We also can show links to the internet and I-Bank. As you may know, Prime Minister, I-Bank is poised to swallow up the business of the major banks. What you may not know is that I-Bank is also ready to swallow the banks themselves, thanks to a full shareholding of each bank's portfolio, and this portfolio is only the visible part of the holding. We do know that many more shares of the banks are held by offshore trusts, and our suspicion is that I-Bank also controls these trusts. Through various other trusts, we strongly suspect that I-Bank is the major shareholder in almost every Internet provider. The implications are obvious, are they not?"

Farquhar-Brown paused for effect before delivering the body blow.

"It's hidden in the small print, but we have uncovered the fact that an ultimate senior Director of I-Bank is...............Axel Margeles".

Despite himself, the Prime Minister gasped. Margeles was the major problem confronting the Government at that very moment. His manipulation of the pound, thanks to the currency being chained to the Deutschemark, had swept Flood out of office, and Rollinson in. Rollinson of course knew that he had not only inherited the highest office of State, he had inherited the giant headache that was Margeles.

The Prime Minister was aghast.

"Is Margeles the man behind all this?" he said, obviously shell-shocked.

"No, we don't believe he is" said the Chief, as Farquhar-Brown nodded to him. "Margeles is just a dupe, a convenient front for people who cannot afford to show their own faces."

"Do we have any idea who these people are?" said the PM, feeling a little helpless in the face of all this shocking information.

"We have a name and a photograph," said the Chief, "It's all in the files". He placed his hand over the boxes of evidence they had brought with them.

"Do you believe that the Integrationists are behind all this?" said Rollinson.

"No" said the Chief, "As the Director-General said, the Integrationists are, like Margeles, simply a cover, a blanket organisation funded and constructed to achieve the power to destroy the institutions which they disingenuously say they support".

Farquhar-Brown cut in.

"We do believe, however, Prime Minister, that the leader of the Integrationists is highly involved in all this at every level".

The Prime Minister stared at the Director-General, his face a study of worry and excitement.

"We are talking about the Chancellor of the Exchequer! Are you suggesting we arrest him too?" said Rollinson, his mind reeling with the constitutional implications for all of them.

"No – not quite" said Jim, taking a sidelong look from the Chief as his clue to jump in on the conversation, "For one thing, we don't have conclusive proof. However, given the nature of these accusations and possibilities, it would be extremely unwise to involve the Chancellor, nor indeed any of his close colleagues in such investigations. Forewarned is forearmed, as they say."

Sheila Remington was smiling grimly as she listened to all this.

"Prime Minister, if I can contribute here" she said, her voice bristling with authority.

Rollinson nodded grimly, his thoughts racing ahead. Remington continued.

"If what we are told here is accurate – and we shall, of course, study the evidence for ourselves before making a judgement – then we should - we must – place all suspects - and I do mean ALL suspects - under immediate 24 hour surveillance".

Remington stared at the PM, waiting for an answer that was some time coming.

Finally, Rollinson gave a deep sigh, and agreed.

Remington, a cold, hard, dedicated, driving woman, was still not satisfied. She wanted Rollinson to spell it out.

"And this surveillance is to include the Chancellor himself?"

Rollinson sighed again.

"Yes" he said, in an almost inaudible voice.

Lyle Patrick, the Attorney General coughed as a signal he wanted to intervene. The Prime Minister signed that he should speak.

"Prime Minister, it is indeed highly unusual that a Minister of High Office should be investigated without his knowledge, nor indeed the knowledge of

Parliament itself, and there are constitutional and legal aspects here. However, in my opinion, as you are the holder of the highest office, the office of Prime Minister, you are entitled to override such concerns in the name of the greater good, the survival of the democracy and monarchy itself. You would of course, have to justify such actions openly in Parliament once the investigation has run its course, but beyond that, you must be able to invoke whatever forces are required provided you are acting on behalf of Parliament and the Country, and not in your own self-interest".

"Thank you, Attorney-General" said Rollinson, not necessarily comforted by Patrick's words. He knew where the buck would stop if things went wrong.

Heathcote, the cabinet secretary was next to speak, his cultured voice still managing to sound disinterested, even in the face of these startling revelations.

"Prime Minister, given that all we have heard is based on genuine fact, should we not now re-consider our position with regard to withdrawal from the ERM?"

Rollinson looked at Heathcote almost in fright. He had heard enough shocks for one day. He also knew the political implications of a pull out of the ERM at this stage. The Government was in a no-win situation. If they stayed within the ERM, the pound could collapse completely, and the Country could be bankrupt unless they found a way to halt Margeles. On the other hand, if the Government withdrew – and it was by no means certain that a majority could be achieved in the House – then the Government would be totally discredited, and political survival would be all but impossible.

Rollinson gave a true politicians answer.

"First we must ascertain the value and quality of proof in the matter of these allegations. Then we must investigate the facts using all modern methods available to us. Thirdly, when we have a full picture of the situation, we can make a judgement as to what should be the next step".

It was the cabinet secretary's turn to frown.

"I must remind you Prime Minister, that time is of the essence. You will recall your meeting with the Governor General of the Bank of England only last week".

Rollinson shuffled uneasily.

"I do realise the implications and limits upon our decision-making process" said the PM, showing his irritation with Heathcote. "But we must know what we are dealing with before we know how to deal with it".

At that, the Prime Minister swept from his desk, bidding all goodbye brusquely.

The Chief dutifully handed over all his papers to Remington and the cabinet secretary. As he left 10 Downing Street to walk in a drizzle of rain, he felt a vague sense of anti-climax.

He glanced at Jim, who was silent and unsmiling. He understood Jim's uncharacteristic silence.

All they could do now was wait.

15

Bunton's usual toothy grin had been replaced a scowl of indignation.

"I've been smeared by dirty journalism!" he moaned at the group of reporters with their banks of cameras pointed directly at him. By approaching his troubles with this attitude – right or wrong – Bunton was guaranteeing himself the future hostility of the 'dirty' journalists present in the room.

One of them, the ever-cheeky Vic Reeves from 'the Sun' chirped in.

"From where we're standing, you ain't too clean yourself mate!"

The roar of laughter that followed did not seem amusing to Bunton. This very week, the 'News of the World' had broken the story and pictures of Bunton, sexually cavorting with young under-age girls. The publicity-seeking Bunton, Chairman of *Maiden*, one of Britain's most successful and fairly new companies had suddenly found himself dying by the sword instead of living by it. His exploits in hot air balloons and self-seeking so-called 'mercy missions' had built up a goody-goody image which not many people but Bunton himself actually could stomach. So he was not about to get sympathy from the press or public. His amiable grin appeared regularly on the TV news, promoting his latest antics, or publicising his forays from the music business to airlines, financial services, and of course, the Internet.

He frowned at the journalist's refusal to toe the party line he was advocating. He was a man who was quietly used to getting his own way, and like most megalomaniacs, he could be extremely childish when crossed. He stamped his foot in petulance, and demanded silence. The room came to a grudging halt. The journalists, after all, wanted a story, wanted to hear Bunton hang himself from his own mouth.

"These stories and pictures are completely misleading – I did not attempt nor have sex with these young girls. I am a happily married man, for God's sake!"

This latest comment did nothing to convince the journalists. They had seen too many so-called happily married men similarly protest when confronted by such evidence.

"I have today instructed my solicitor to issue a writ for defamation of character against 'The News of the World' said Bunton. The tough journalists nodded soberly. Well, at least Bunton had put his money where his mouth was. The proof would be in the pudding, and they would have their story either way. An avalanche of reporters heaved from the room at once to catch the next deadline before their bitter rivals and colleagues.

Bunton had no idea who his hidden enemies were. He knew he had plenty, any successful person who had to step on toes and not be squeamish about the feelings of others while on the way up was bound to have the knives out against him.

Another world away from the press reception, the orchestrator of Bunton's misfortunes was reading 'The News of the World' with delight. One more push, and he would have control of the entire

Internet. Bunton had been a difficult nut to crack; for all of the toothy mogul's perceived boyishness, he was a tough enough man in business terms, but it looked like his fall was imminent, leaving his business wide open for take-over.

He smiled a rare smile of satisfaction as he mused on where the system stood. He had them in a classic pincer movement, he decided. Margeles had begun a run on the pound that was gaining a life of its own as other speculators came into play in concert with Margeles. The Government had no choice thus far but to support the pound using the reserves. These reserves were rapidly becoming depleted. The sensible thing to do, as the Governor General of the Bank of England had been urging for weeks, was to leave the ERM and devalue, despite the massive loss of face for the Government. Flood and his supporters in the Government had reluctantly accepted that this was the right course of action, but they were not allowed to take that action because the Chancellor and his motley band of followers would not allow it. This was the dilemma which Rollinson was now faced.

A grim sense of triumph settled over him as he pondered what would happen next. All these years of scheming and dreaming had led to this point. Now something had to give, and it seemed to him that his plans were close to completion.

It looked like the end of democracy in the land of his birth; it looked like the end of Britain itself.

16

Susan was working late, much to Walker's annoyance. He stood behind her fussing and fretting as she worked furiously but methodically at the computer, feeding in data, constantly questioning the ruthlessly efficient machine as if it was one of her minions.

Walker was getting more impatient by the minute.

"Are you coming or not?" he finally asked, his show of patience breaking down.

Susan hardly noticed him, her mind was elsewhere.

"No, you go ahead" she muttered distractedly, her fingers working overtime.

Walker puffed in exasperation and stormed off without her. So much for his great plans for the evening, he thought. Tonight he had intended to nail her, she had promised, now when would it be? He snorted in frustration as he barged into the lift, startling two timid secretaries.

Susan was blissfully unaware of her would-be lover's thoughts. Time after time, she re-submitted the grainy photograph to every databank she could think of. Again and again, she typed the same request into the computer: - 'IDENTIFY THIS PERSON'.

It had been hours now, with no tangible result, but she was a woman obsessed. Apart from anything else, it took her away from her personal problems. She could not shake the emotions of the past somehow, no matter how many times she told herself she had moved on. She was now with another man, but somehow Walker had brought her no peace. Somewhere inside herself was the answer she could not face, so she took her trauma out on the computer, making it pay for the inner turmoil she could not resolve in herself.

Yet again, the search result came back – 'NOT KNOWN'. One more databank, she thought, feeling weariness and disappointment beginning to overtake her. What databank? She pondered the figure in the photograph for a moment, noting his presence, his bearing, then with a lateral thought, she realised there was one obvious candidate she had somehow missed. Using her priority code, she was able to enter the databank she sought without difficulty. Once again, she submitted the photograph; yet once more she asked the same tired question – 'IDENTIFY THIS PERSON'.

She physically flinched as the computer suddenly flashed a series of details in front of her. Her whole body tingled with excitement and a sense of unreality as she studied with awe the face in front of her. It was the man she knew as Scott, except that his name was not Scott, it was something else.

And even more interesting than the photograph was the sad history of the man she had pursued so ruthlessly, so efficiently. That was a story in itself.

She saved the details to disc, and switched off the machine. Sitting there in the darkness, she hardly knew what to feel anymore.

It had been a hard year.

17

The Chief had only time to take a quick gulp of his cold coffee before rushing to his car. He was late for his meeting with Sheila Remington, and that would never do. He recalled the frosty voice that summoned him to her office, and involuntarily shivered with apprehension. At the same time, his anxiety was outweighed by his curiosity. What had Remington uncovered? His driver sped along Whitehall as if he too was anxious to discover these secrets.

Moments later, he was ushered into the plush suite of offices, a far cry from his own drab resources, he dryly noted. Remington did not smile nor make small talk. She did not even offer him a seat, but he took one anyway, indifferent to the air of animosity she somehow engendered. His unease with her attitudes had been replaced by a feeling of relief that he too, did not have to indulge in the usual masks and false camaraderie.

"What do you have?" he asked brusquely, skipping the formalities.

She fixed him sharply with a shark's eye.

"We have analysed your data, and we concurred with your findings" she said, almost reluctantly.

"Consequently, we have monitored those individuals identified by you as central participants in this affair. We have transcripts and photographs of meetings and telephone calls which clearly implicate almost of all those individuals in a conspiracy."

Remington paused to hand over to the Chief a series of photographs and typed manuscript of the details of conversations between Integrationists, financiers, and other major players in this drama. The Chief was impressed, but was not enamoured enough of Remington to say so.

"So we have Margeles and a host of others. We also have the Minister for Trade. What of Jonathan Charles?"

Remington gave him another of her cold fish stares.

"Mr Charles has at the moment remained elusive. He has not met privately with any of the other participants, and none of his known telephone calls have constituted any illegality or improper use of power."

The Chief pulled a face of irritation before Remington continued.

"However, we know that he uses a mobile phone which we do not have account of. Many times a week he drives to a remote place and sits in his car using this phone. We therefore strongly suspect that this is the missing link, but as he uses different cars, often hiring them at the last moment, we have been unable to put a trace on the calls as yet. However, we shall achieve that purpose, and we shall know exactly what Mr Charles' involvement – if any – is, sooner rather than later."

The Chief nodded enigmatically, unwilling to show any warmth to this cold woman, much as he admired her awesome efficiency and intelligence. She wasn't bad looking either, good legs, striking eyes behind the glasses, lovely mouth. The thought sneaked in, and he mentally slapped himself to stop it.

Remington snapped him out of his reverie.

"Have you been doing anything?" she asked, almost scathingly.

"My colleague, Susan Bryde, has discovered exactly who Alan Scott is", he said, noting with satisfaction that even Remington was taken aback. He was almost minded to point out to the bureaucrat that his department could be efficient too, but resisted the temptation. Instead, he handed over to Remington the details on Scott. She studied them with unusual interest in her cold eyes.

Her eyes weren't actually cold when you looked right in them, he decided. In fact, she had great depth and warmth hidden in there somewhere, he noted with fascination and a healthy dose of male hunter instincts lurking in the lower regions.

"Susan – Susan Bryde, my colleague - found him via army records. His name is John Devane, a former serving soldier; indeed, a Lieutenant-Colonel in the SAS, no less." She looked hard at him. She could read as well as him, he could see she was thinking. Unknown to the Chief, she had also decided that he was a typical male chauvinist pig.

The Chief continued as if he hadn't noticed her stare, which he had. He enjoyed her annoyance, warming to the game. He rambled on, unconcerned by her stare of hostility.

"Holder of the MC for gallantry in the Cypriot troubles, as well as Ulster, and decorated and mentioned in despatches no less than six times for undercover actions throughout the hot spots of the

World; then he fell off the rails. Killed a man, served 12 years for manslaughter; his career and life ruined."

"He dealt with the man because he had raped and killed his Wife," said Remington, almost in defence of Devane, irritated by the Chief's cold and to her, selective summary of the facts. She didn't like getting her own medicine, the Chief decided in amusement.

He decided to be brutal with her.

"He cut the man's balls off and stuffed them in his victim's mouth before he topped him," he said, looking her full in the eye.

She did not flinch, though she privately thought that such a thing might do a lot of men, including the Chief, some good.

The Chief got a flash of that one, and smiled inwardly, seeing her animosity surface.

Not overly enamoured of that image himself, he swiftly moved on.

"He actually did serve the full twelve years – for an army man, so used to discipline in the general sense, he just couldn't accept the dictates of the prison warders."

Remington was moved to the defence of Devane again. From her time at the Home Office, she knew all about prison warders and their ways.

"All prisoners are subject to the abuse of power by prison warders, it is a way of life in these places. Devane obviously had too much ridiculous male pride to be subjugated to their will". She looked at the Chief defiantly, knowing he would be surprised at such an anti-establishment view, especially coming from a very senior servant of the Government. He also noted that she had, while defending Devane, managed to impugn men in general.

He could not let her know, but he was surprised and gratified to find some humanity behind that cold façade of hers. He looked at her with new eyes, and being a man, could not omit the equal appraisal of her curves, her full breasts thrusting through the prim blouse despite the formal trappings of disguise. He had another surprise for her.

"Susan also linked Devane to Albert Rouse of Germaine Rouse. They are one and the same person." He said, pleased to note Remington's surprise.

"Are you positive of that?" she said disapprovingly, noting with discomfort and distaste his male interest in her body.

He met her eyes with his own unflinching stare.

"Positive. We have confirmation from James Germaine, among others."

Remington looked at him unsmiling, her mind obviously flicking through the facts.

"We shall find Devane," she finally said. She stood up without ceremony, signalling that the formalities of the meeting were over. Then she shocked him.

"We will leave it there for now and retire to have a drink" she said, not waiting for his acquiescence. He was taken aback, but merely concurred, as if she had said the most natural thing in the World.

It was growing dark when they left the grand building, and by the time they reached the underground car park, it was darker still. They climbed into his car, and she surprised him again. Before he could start the engine, she suddenly grabbed him by the hair and pulled him towards her, kissing him full on the lips, her tongue parting his mouth aggressively, seeking out his throat.

He was startled of course, but not startled enough to stop him responding in full. Her mouth was so soft and delicious, her lips surprisingly full and luscious, as she caressed him with her tongue, her hands roaming all over his body, resting finally on his already responding manhood.

Suddenly, she stopped kissing him. Fixing him with those cold bureaucratic eyes again, she surprised him for the third time that day.

"I can't have full sex with you – I won't tell you why, it's none of your business, but I will give you an oral, if you are agreeable to that". She paused, as if waiting for affirmation.

He felt like sending her a memo, but merely nodded, dumbstruck, and intrigued.

"Very well" she said, and with that, she swiftly revealed him to her sight, and set about her task with an efficiency equal to everything else she did in life.

It had been a memorable meeting, decided the Chief.

18

It was a night of the long knives. The World reacted with shock and horror at the news. Arrests included senior Judges, Council leaders, senior policemen, and even previously eminent Peers, Bishops, and members of Parliament. Among the most prominent people to fall were the Minister for Trade and the Chancellor himself. It was noticeable that most, if not all, were from the Integrationist party.

In the newspapers and television studios of the World, arguments raged about the constitutional issues of whether the Prime Minister had the authority to arrest his own cabinet colleagues and fellow members of the House. The dilemma was perceived – exactly whose democracy was being protected? And yet, was the alternative that nothing should be done?

The Government was in turmoil, the House alternatively worried and outraged. The Prime Minister was due to face the House that same afternoon. He would have some explaining to do. The pound slumped even more drastically, despite the absence of Margeles, whose home for the night was Brixton prison.

At the heart of all this turmoil, but away from the madding crowd were the Chief and his team, surprisingly quiet and subdued for people who had participated in one of the major dramas of the twentieth century.

McKay broke the silence.

"Do you think we can nail the Chancellor?" he said, looking at the Chief with concern.

"Perhaps" said the Chief, thinking of Remington, and that memorable night, "The main problem is that Remington wasn't granted the time to provide the conclusive proof we needed. Time was running out for us, we had to grab all that we could and stop the thing, rather than wait to tie up every loose end."

McKay looked at him, mortified.

"It's a bloody big loose end, Guv!"

The Chief nodded sympathetically.

"I know Dave, but sometimes you can only do what's possible, nothing more. We still might get him on conspiracy, that's the basis of the arrest, and to be fair, not everyone arrested will go the whole way. It's a cleaning and sweeping operation as much as anything. It has to be widespread to stop the rot. It's inevitable that some innocents will be dragged into the mire in the name of the greater good."

"That scum deserves to be swept into the mire" said McKay, his mouth a bitter gash.

Susan put her hand on McKay's arm in comfort. She looked at the Chief, and noticed that he had flushed. He was jealous, she realised. Involuntarily, her heart leapt out to him, but she kept her emotions in check, saying and doing nothing but looking at her shoes.

"What about I-Bank?" said Walker, noting with irritation Susan's reaction.

The Chief could hardly bring himself to speak to Walker at all, but tried to rise above his human feelings and speak like the good bureaucrat he was.

"The Governor of the Bank of England is closing them down as we speak," he said. "Unbeknown to I-Bank, a Bank of England official has been auditing the accounts, and there was more than enough evidence of money laundering and stealing from customers on a grand scale to warrant the closure of the bank, and the arrest of key officials as well".

Susan looked at him with concern.

"What about all the customers? All those ordinary people whose money – whose life savings – are tied up in the bank – what happens to them?"

The Chief shrugged resignedly.

"The usual, I'm afraid. Their deposits are, for the moment at least, gone. I'm sure eventually the forces of order will restore something of their balance, but for now, it's a matter of closing the bank's doors, and the customers are last in the queue".

"It will take years for them to see a penny," said McKay, remembering BCCI and other fiascos. They all knew he was right, but did not like to think too much about the personal disasters they had helped bring down upon ordinary people.

The Chief listened to all this with great discomfort. The greater good had a lot to answer for, he decided.

Just then, Simmonds rushed into the room, waving a fax excitedly.

"What is it Tony?" said the Chief, trying to calm the man down.

"It's Rouse – I mean Devane – we have him!" Simmonds blurted out, hardly able to contain himself, making the others laugh with relief and excitement.

"Well who do you have Tony? Is it Rouse or Scott or Devane? Or somebody else?" said McKay in his usual gruff humour.

The Chief smiled. Privately, he was thinking 'God bless you Sheila'.

"We have all the people he is," he said in cryptic but quiet satisfaction.

19

There was something about the way the Chief had said 'Remington', Susan decided. She had seen that look on his face, a look almost of guilt. Was he having an affair with Remington, that cold fish from MI5? Susan could hardly believe it, but she was surprised at her own jealousy.

It was her own fault, she decided. The Chief had tried many times to win her round again, but she had always rebuffed him, and now, she was with Walker. She decided she must end this tawdry affair, he was a stopgap, she realised, a mere pawn in her game with herself, an attempt to hurt the Chief and herself in the process.

The next day at the office, she sought out the Chief. Susan could be forthright in her actions, though such decisiveness rarely translated itself to her relations with men. Now though, motivated by her fear of losing the Chief to another woman, Susan was determined, and when Susan was determined, not much stood in her way.

Certainly not the Chief. He was sitting in his office rummaging through the papers of the last few days, when Susan walked in purposefully. He looked up in surprise, but only smiled politely when she walked in.

"Hello Susan" he said, hoping his voice did not betray the leap in his heart at seeing her. Susan didn't speak. She moved round the desk before he could twitch, and flinging her arms round his neck, she kissed him with all the love and passion she could muster.

He sat there like a tailor's dummy, his head reeling, his heart pounding, as Susan gave him the full force of her female desires. Then, without a word, she took him by the hand, and led him from the building. He followed mutely, like a child being taken to school.

A short time later, they lay in bed together, the first wave of their physical love fully consummated.

"I love you," she finally said, the first words spoken between them for the two hours since that kiss in the office.

"I love you too," he said, almost embarrassed by the force of their mutual passion and exposure to one another. There was something Susan just had to ask.

"Did you have sex with that Remington woman?" she asked coyly, cringing a little at her display of jealousy, but feeling the need to know the answer.

The Chief chose the Clinton definition of sex.

"No, of course not!" he said, smiling as reassuringly as he could. He decided that discretion was the better part of valour, and attack was the best form of defence.

"In any case" he said, his voice full of mock-indignation, "What about you and Walker?"

Susan blushed and looked at him with her eyes humbled.

"What about him?" she said, not knowing what else to say, hoping the subject would quickly vanish.

The Chief was not about to let his advantage go.

"Did you sleep with him?" he asked in a mixture of masochism and pain.

Despite her feelings of discomfort, Susan was not about to lie, nor would she put a glossy shine on events just to please someone else, not even him.

"Yes" she said, in a little girl voice.

"Oh, I see," said the Chief.

"No you don't!" said Susan, seeing his face fall, "I said 'sleep', not anything else!"

The Chief looked sceptical.

"Why, did you stop him?" he asked, aware that he was making her squirm, but wanting to know more, yet not know more at the same time.

"No, he couldn't manage it" said Susan, blushing furiously again, remembering that night when she had found Devane, and rushed to Walker's place full of excitement and triumph, only to end up drinking too much, and found herself naked in bed with Walker.

"That doesn't surprise me," said the Chief uncharitably. Then another thought occurred to him. He took the scenic route to his question.

"You could have found an alternative if you wanted to."

"I didn't!" said Susan, getting angry now, knowing what he meant.

"You mean you didn't..........."

"Of course not!" said Susan, her voice rising and shaking with emotion, "He only touched me a couple of times, that's all!" she said, almost in tears.

"That's bad enough," said the Chief grimly. They sat in silence for a moment.

"Would you have?" he suddenly asked, torturing her as well as himself again.

"If things had progressed, who knows?" Susan said, calm now, getting tired of the evasion, "But they didn't, so it's purely academic."

"All the way?" he said, getting deeper into it.

Susan looked at him, unsure for a moment.

"Oh, you mean...........yes, no doubt I would have eventually – it's what most women would do for their men, isn't it? Isn't it what you all expect from us?" she said, getting indignant now, tired of his probing and questioning. What good was it all doing?

He remembered Sheila Remington, and suddenly felt ashamed of himself. What right did he have to question her, especially after what he had done? Surely what mattered was that two people who loved each other should be together again, no matter what had occurred during the time of separation. Life was too short for such petty recriminations.

His face softened, he could see the way forward, but his eyes still glittered with mischief.

"So you're still a virgin then?" He said, looking at her quizzically.

Susan looked puzzled.

"Hardly!" she replied cynically, then she saw his wry smile.

"Oh, you mean in *that* way!" she said, her voice cracking with relief that the tension between them was passing.

"Not for long!" she said, and turned out the light

20

John Devane – for it was he, the Lieutenant, Rouse, Alan, and all the other names and aliases he had used throughout the good and the bad years – had, unusually been caught by surprise. Had he known how close the authorities were on his heels, then he of all people would have also known the vast resources that could be brought to bear against him. An expert in survival on many fronts, he would have been better placed than most to avoid capture.

His enemies, though, knew that too, and they had moved swiftly for that reason, even at the risk of losing other vital members of the operation. For they knew John Devane must be close to the true source of power, and they hoped that he, unwittingly or otherwise, would lead them to his ultimate contact.

Devane's moment of capture was seen afterwards by the whole World. It was in a terminal of Heathrow airport, at the height of the air traffic. Luckily for Devane, he was booked on a flight to Canada, which had little to do with any of his more dubious missions. It was meant to be a private moment, a visit to the grave of his Wife, whose family came from Toronto. There was no chance of those plans causing grief to his friend, was his first brief thought as he was seized by the forces of law and Government.

Even then, he had the physical power and knowledge to fiercely resist capture, but he was too sensible for that, knowing resistance would be useless. He knew that in all the circumstances, the powers that be would have ensured that far many more troops were on hand than were ever needed for his capture. He simply shrugged, and went quietly with them, despite the strong-arm tactics of some of the younger men, he used his physical strength and knowledge to prevent them humbling him in public. He held his head high, and walked straight despite the best efforts of the storm troopers to make him do otherwise.

In another part of the World, looking on in despair, John's friend was pleased at least to see him take that deadly walk with pride. He knew that would be important to John, and he sighed with relief, albeit his heart was heavy, his thoughts black with anguish at the plight of his friend.

He had not yet had time to absorb what meaning all this had for his plans, but he could sense easily enough that they lay in ruins. Even with the system intact, the removal of John would have dealt a mortal blow in any case, he knew that. He himself may have been the ultimate brains behind the idea and the strategy, but John had not only provided the logistics and the contacts, he had played a full part in the planning and implementation of how these grand ideas were to come to fruition. It had been a true partnership, and now it had been rent asunder by the very forces he was so violently opposed to.

At this moment however, his main concern was for his friend, the last human being on earth whom he could relate to. Now he also had to plan for his own survival. A future that had always seemed bleak now also contained the possibility of loss of freedom. He had to admit to himself that he felt frightened, not just of what the system would do to him, should he be caught, but fear also of his inner self, of what he might do if pushed to extremes.

As he watched the videotape of John being taken in custody, the World was suddenly a much more empty and unfriendly place.

21

The Chief was also watching TV as Susan burbled around him merrily, making them something to eat. Sipping at his tea, the Chief watched with a jaundiced eye as Bunton, the born-again mogul, proclaimed loud and clear his so-called vindication and acquittal of all accusations against him.

That was not quite true, as the Chief knew. A conspiracy had existed against Bunton's company *Maiden Internet,* and that had indeed taken the heat off the toothy tycoon, but the questions about his involvement with the young girls were not by any means resolved. Still, the forces that be had determined that no further action should be taken against Bunton. *Maiden* was just too big a concern, in all its various wings, and there had been enough flak flying just lately. The downside of all this was that everyone had to suffer the insufferable Bunton bleating his innocence on every channel one turned to. He was good at public relations and selling himself, the Chief said to himself in concession and contempt at the same time.

As for Jonathan Charles, he had met his match in Sheila Remington. Despite the elaborate precautions he had taken, Remington had succeeded in placing a probe in his latest hired car, and his drive to the country to make his surreptitious phone call proved to be pointless in terms of security. Enough was said on line to fully incriminate Charles as part of the conspiracy. Unfortunately, the recorded conversation yielded nothing in the way of clues as to the other party on the end of the line. The phone call was of short duration, the number called was an anonymous mobile, and the person on the other end of the line had taken the precaution of using an electronic voice disguise that was proving impossible for the experts to crack. Still, Jonathan Charles had been well and truly nailed, as had the conspiracy itself.

Provided the Country survived – and that was by no means certain as yet - the usual medals would be handed out. They always were at a time like this, as the Chief knew. They would probably throw him some trinket or other, though Farquhar-Brown would be the one in line for the big prize, despite having done little but appoint the team to their task. That was the way of these things, as everyone involved knew.

Susan walked in with their plates, and he smiled. Life was good, despite his darker thoughts. He had decided to leave Jane for good this time. It was a lousy time to leave her, just before Christmas, but was there ever going to be a good time? It was for the best for both of them. Jane would understand eventually, he hoped they would be friends, but he knew that her bitterness was such that this might never happen. That made him sad, but he had decided that his life and Susan's was important too. He couldn't live on behalf of anyone but himself. He had made his bed, and now he would lie in it. He smiled at that thought, memories of the night before flooding back.

"I love you," he said, smiling at her with his eyes as much as his mouth.

Susan looked surprised.

"Where did that one come from?" she asked, trying not to look too pleased.

"Will you marry me?" he said.

"Are you serious?" asked Susan, nearly dropping the hot plates. She hurriedly put them down on the table, and turned to him, putting her arms around his neck. He repeated the words.

"Will you marry me?"

"Of course I will. It's what I've always wanted, " she said, tears welling up in her eyes. She looked at him, suddenly serious.

"It will have to be a Registry office," she said hesitantly, knowing what a romantic he was.

He smiled. That mischievous twinkle was in his eyes again.

"Well, at least we can truthfully still play 'Here Comes the Bryde'!" he punned at her.

"No, that was last night," said Susan playfully, "and by the way, if that was meant to be the dress rehearsal, you're supposed to kiss the 'Bryde', not blow her head off!"

He suddenly looked concerned and embarrassed at the same time.

"Was it OK?" he asked anxiously.

She reached forward and kissed him gently but fully on the lips, then stood back a little, looking tenderly into his eyes.

"It was beautiful" she said, "I'm glad I'm not a virgin anymore – the trouble is, I'm a novice at it, I need more practice".

"I find that a bit hard to swallow," he said, without thinking about what he was saying.

Susan raised her eyebrows, and both of them burst into laughter.

It was going to be a fantastic Christmas.

22

Wandsworth. The very name of the place struck dread into the heart of those who knew the system well. The vast majority of the British public had no conception of what prison in the twentieth century meant, even in a so-called 'civilised' Country.

Those who had experienced the system were under no such illusions. Not one of the Country's many jails contained vestiges of human dignity, but some were worse than others, and Wandsworth topped the bill. It wasn't just the state of the place. God knows, the place was filthy enough, and the conditions in general would have had the country up in arms had it been dogs who were kept chained up like that, but no one would be upset over people, especially people who were perceived of as 'them'. In any case, it could be said that the conditions were no worse than for a soldier in the Falklands war, nor a coal miner at his place of work; but the real source of the misery and despair was the warders who guarded the place so zealously.

Wandsworth was a stronghold of the Prison Officer's Association, and among this body of men there was the usual profiles of bullies and cowards, who only too readily mistook the power of the state invested in them as their own personal power. Then again, the state itself turned a blind eye to the abuse and

excess peddled in their name. The Home Office was renowned for indifference towards the cruelty and petty behaviour of its officers. The theory was that if people had misbehaved badly, then they should not expect to be treated as human beings.

The trouble with this policy was that it did not teach miscreants and even people who had genuinely made mistakes that crime and lack of social responsibility was not appropriate nor worthwhile behaviour. By glaring example, the prison system showed people even more clearly that what paid most of all was to have power, however it was misused.

Devane was no stranger to these rules. A hard and proud man, he found it difficult to restrain himself with the mean-spirited and downright nasty creatures who were, in theory, his guardians and protectors as well as his warders. In reality, Devane knew from practical experience that he had to take care of himself in Wandsworth, for no one, least of all the cowardly warders, would lift a finger should he be placed in danger.

And danger there was, in abundance. The drug operators, the petty rivalries, the thieves and the brigands were all here in all their glory, ever ready with a flick knife, or a deadly toothbrush fitted with rows of sharp razors that could slash a face to ribbons in a few mad seconds of the exercise parade.

Devane had seen all this before, and dealt with it. Even at his now advanced age, a man of his experience had no problems in dealing with other inmates, though sometimes it took a show of power to demonstrate that he was a force to be reckoned with.

Such an opportunity came his way in the first week of his capture. Devane was in the queue for breakfast, waiting patiently in line as the con men and the dealers sneakily plied their trade. Then, out of the blue, a black man behind Devane suddenly pushed himself in front, glaring at Devane with an arrogant challenge in his eyes, daring him to question the move. Devane knew full well what shirking such a challenge would mean. It would send a signal to every slimy toad in Wandsworth that he, Devane was weak, available to be used, abused. On the other side of the coin, any move against the arrogant asshole would be seized upon by the guards with glee, meaning time added on, and further sanctions including a possible beating. The choice was a limited one.

Devane did not hesitate. In one swift movement, he suddenly had the black man by the neck, and without hesitation, he pushed the man's head full into the metal soup urn that was simmering and bubbling next to them. All hell let loose, the man's desperate muffled screams and kicking filled the air, tables were scattered, hot food spilled everywhere, whistles blew, and warders ran from every crevice in the dark corridors of Wandsworth.

Seconds later, Devane was punched and kicked and grappled to the floor by teams of warders.

"Hold the bastard down!" cried one, his teeth gritted in fury.

"We'll teach you, you filthy scum!" said another scrawny specimen, his spindly fist hitting out bravely at an unprotected target. Boots were flying in, even though Devane was already prostrate and pinned firmly to the ground. As he lay there, absorbing the beating, Devane had no regrets. He had marked everyone's cards, and he was relatively safe now, as safe as anyone could be in these halls of the dead.

"Get him down the block double quick!" shouted out the Chief Officer, standing back with a look of distaste across his cold authoritarian features.

Devane spent a week in the 'block', solitary confinement, chained to the wall with a belt fastened securely to him as if he was a wild animal. He had done no more than defend himself in a system which offered him no protection from exploitation and abuse, but the system's answer to its duties, was to merely inflict its own abuse instead of addressing the issues. Besides, for these beer-bellied brigands in uniforms, it was more fun to be a bigot and a bully. To show human kindness and understanding was the mark of a fool.

Some were worse than others. Devane had known he had made a mistake that first day when he had put forward an application to the landing officer to be given a special diet. The warder's face had immediately broken into outrage, and he poked Devane in the chest, his finger stabbing repeatedly as he spat out his words of hate and venom.

"Special? You want to be special, do you? I'll tell you how special you are, you filthy piece of shit! You'll get what I give you, you fucking scum, you stinking vermin!".

The furious warder took Devane's written application and tore it into shreds, stamping on it again and again like some demented child in a tantrum. Then he stormed off, cursing and kicking at any convict in his way, weaving a path of chaos as he worked his way along the landing.

Devane turned to the convict sweeping the stairs, who had looked on askance at the incident, pretending he wasn't there.

"Who the fuck was that?" said Devane, gesturing with his thumb.

The man looked around uneasily, his pale thin face worried and frightened.

"That was Woodford" he said, then turned hurriedly back to his work, signalling that the conversation was over.

"Was it now" said Devane thoughtfully, knowing that he would cross paths with Woodford again.

It turned out to be sooner than Devane had expected. One day into the punishment at the block, the door suddenly opened , and in walked Woodford, his childish and cruel face twisted with a mixture of satisfaction and excitement at the sight of Devane pinned helplessly to the wall.

"Think you're smart now, do you?" he said to Devane, his face contorted with rage.

"Think you can take the piss on my landing and get away with it, do you?", said Woodford, clenching his fists till they were white. Devane glared at him defiantly, saying nothing.

"You fucking piece of shit!" exclaimed Woodford, suddenly rushing over to where Devane stood helplessly. A flurry of fists thumped into Devane's face, breaking open his mouth, splitting his eyebrows. With relish, Woodford meted out the punishment, ensuring that the huge gold ring he wore on one finger featured prominently in every blow struck, marking Devane again and again.

John felt his head going, he was beginning to lose consciousness. He thought it would never stop, he was helpless, there was nothing he could do but absorb the punishment as best he could. Suddenly, the door suddenly swung open. It was Clark, another warder.

"That's enough!" he said, bounding over to where the oblivious Woodford was pummelling Devane frantically. With one huge wrench of his hand, Clark pulled Woodford away by the collar so fast that his feet actually left the ground. Staggering, Woodford turned towards Clark, incredulous and outraged.

"What the fuck do you think you're doing?" he demanded, his face red, his breathing heavy.

Clark stared hard at his colleague, his eyes as cold as his voice.

"I should be asking you that question" he said, his voice quiet but firm and accusing, "Now get out of here!" he shouted at Woodford, his voice brooking no response.

Woodford stood there for a moment, panting, out of condition, then he turned to look at Devane again, his expression filled with hate and contempt. Devane was breathing hard too, but still said nothing, looking Woodford in the eye.

"I'll be back to deal with you!" said Woodford, pointing at Devane aggressively, his voice almost rising to an hysterical scream, his eyes wild, his hand shaking with the pleasure of it all. He gave Clark one furious glare, and rushed out the door.

Clark turned to Devane.

"I'm sorry about that" he said, taking a handkerchief from his pocket, and beginning to wipe away the blood from Devane's face. He winced as he saw the full extent of the damage to Devane's face and the bruises on his body.

"Hold on a minute" he said, and walked to the door of the cell.

"Wilson!" he said loudly, then waited.

Moments later, Wilson appeared, frowning.

"What is it?" he asked, his voice irritated at the interruption to his TV programme.

"Release this man from the belt at once. I want to get him to the hospital wing" said Clark in a commanding voice. Not for nothing had he been an officer in the Welsh Guards.

Wilson looked over Clark's shoulder to where Devane was slumped, his face a bloody mess. He raised his eyebrows and whistled, but frowned again at Clark.

"I can't do that!" he said, his voice a whining protest, "I don't have the authority".

"I'll take the responsibility" said Clark, his voice getting louder and harder, "Do you want to be held accountable if anything goes wrong with this man's health?".

Wilson grunted reluctantly, but shuffled over to Devane, and with much clattering and fussing, eventually released him from the belt.

"Are you sure you know what you're doing?" said Wilson, both shocked and annoyed that one of

391

his colleagues would put himself out for a mere convict.

Clark's mouth tightened with impatience.

"Your job is done. Make your report. Meantime, I'm taking this man to the hospital wing, and that's that!".

Clark turned towards Devane. The man, obviously an ex-soldier himself, had obviously been in excellent physical condition before the beating.

"Just as well," thought Clark grimly, " He's in a hell of a mess".

Clark motioned to Devane, who gingerly rose, and wobbled towards him unsteadily.

Clark took Devane's arm and helped support him on the long trek through the gloomy corridors.

Finally, after what seemed to Devane an endless journey, they reached the hospital wing, where the Doctor was less than pleased to see them.

"What's the meaning of this?" his pompous face went into a pout. "You know that we don't receive inmates as patients at this hour!".

"This man needs treatment now, he can't wait for your blasted opening hours!" said Clark in indignation, "Would you rather I place it on report that you refused to see him?".

The Doctor visibly wilted. In this place of passing the buck, he knew whose career would be on the line if the man died, and the convict does look in a bad way, the Doctor noticed finally.

"Let's have a look at him" said the Doctor, annoyed at his loss of face.

Clark turned to Devane.

"You'll be all right now" he said, his voice sympathetic and reassuring.

Devane did not need reassurance, and in some ways would have preferred to deal with brutality rather than kindness. Nevertheless, he looked at Clark appreciatively.

"Thanks" he said, making eye to eye contact.

Clark smiled humourlessly.

"You've nothing to thank this place for" said Clark, his mouth tightening bitterly.

"I'll see you then" he said, as he made for the door.

Devane watched Clark leave with mixed emotions, then he fixed Woodford in his mind with a thought that did not auger well for the portly warder.

23

Rollinson rose at the despatch box, and the House, which had been a buzz of excited conversation, hushed to absolute silence. The Prime Minister looked around the chamber solemnly. Then he looked at the seats beside him, which should have held key members of his Government, including the Chancellor.

"Madame Speaker, I have a statement to make regarding the tumultuous events of the last two days. A scarce few weeks ago, her Majesty's Government was alerted to conspiratorial forces at work that threatened our very survival as a Nation. Evidence was placed before us which irrefutably showed that these forces had recruited members of the Government itself, indeed the conspiracy went to the very heart of not just the Government, but democracy itself".

Rollinson paused, and the House took the opportunity to simmer with excited but hushed gossip. The Prime Minister turned again to his notes, and looked over to Madame Speaker's chair with deference.

"Madame Speaker, we the Government – and myself, in particular – were placed in a unique dilemma. We could not consult cabinet to take the difficult decisions which had to be taken to protect our democracy, for members of that very cabinet had been shown to be part of the same conspiracy which they would be asked to judge and comment upon".

The House gasped audibly. Though the facts and accusations had been bandied about clearly enough in the papers, it was a different matter to hear the worst fears confirmed by the Prime Minister himself on the floor of the House.

Rollinson did not need to practice at looking grave; it was indeed a very serious matter.

"Madame Speaker, I am fully aware of my responsibilities to the House, and to the Country, and this great democracy of ours. Our Government lives and breathes by consensus and agreement, not by dictate, but in the light of what I had learned, I had little choice but to act as I did. As Prime Minister, I am expected to take difficult decisions, and none was more difficult than this one. This was, Madame Speaker, a situation as fraught with difficulty and constitutional concerns as was Cromwell's decision in an earlier and equally turbulent time, one which I would suggest is hardly likely to face another Prime Minister for a long time to come, by the grace of the good Lord".

"Hear! Hear!" echoed the House as one.

Slowly, the hubbub died down again, the House fell silent, waiting for Rollinson to speak once more.

The Prime Minister sifted through his papers for what seemed to everyone waiting an inordinately long time. Finally, he resumed.

"Madame Speaker, as I said earlier, there is ample evidence which involves senior Government officials including the Chancellor of the Exchequer and the Minister for Trade as well as several others accurately reported for the most part in the press. The evidence will all be revealed to honourable members as well as the general public through the auspices of the public enquiry I am setting in motion today. Obviously, I cannot comment on the individual cases of all who have been apprehended at this time, and enquiries will not be completed overnight, though the security services and the police are working at all possible speed to resolve these matters. Can I also at this time pay tribute to those officers who have worked long and hard on this and other related matters? Without the diligence and dedication of these officers and officials, we would not even be in a position to discuss this matter at this time. We indeed owe the security forces, the police, and the officers of APACS, the bank consortium group, as well as individuals from outside the regular security forces, more than we can ever repay in thanks for the work they have done. Indeed, the work they are still doing, to rid the Country of this insidious menace which has threatened each and every one of us".

The Prime Minister pause to take a drink of water. The House remained strangely silent, awaiting the return of his words.

"Madame Speaker, there are so many associated matters here, that it would take too long at one sitting to address them all. I propose that each department, will, over the next few days, address the concerns of those affected by the closure of I-Bank, the concerns over share ownership of our top companies, the internet implications and so forth. Each of these concerns will be addressed in full by the appropriate department in this House as soon as possible. For now, I will try to deal with the general situation, for time, Madame Speaker, is of the essence, and we are not yet out of the woods, by any means. If we are to protect our democracy and way of life, there are certain steps we – not just myself, or the cabinet, every member of this House must be involved – we must take decisive action now. The time for inquests will be when we are sure we have done all we can to minimise the damage to our democracy and way of life".

The House's voice was rumbling again, an awed whisper, till the chamber realised that the Prime Minister had paused, waiting for them to give him silence. Madame Speaker intervened gently.

"The Prime Minister" was all she said, in a authoritative voice, which was still somehow feminine.

"Thank you Madame Speaker" said Rollinson, "As I said, Madame Speaker, I-Bank will be dealt with in detail over the next few days, but I feel I should add something to illustrate the problem we faced. The evidence we were shown did not conclusively prove that I-Bank was involved in this conspiracy, but the signs were ominous. The bank had voraciously purchased – quite legally in so far as it goes – large stockholdings in all of our blue chip companies, principally the high street banks themselves. Their aggressive policies towards winning customers from the high street banks should have been of no concern to us. That is the nature of competition after all; but taken with the share purchases we saw, and the virtual monopoly over the internet, along with the fact that there were also mysterious purchases of these same blue chip shares by hidden offshore trusts, we had to act, we had to know the truth. With that in mind, the Governor General of the Bank of England took the decision to send in auditors, unseen and unannounced, to find out the truth behind the figures. What these auditors discovered, Madame Speaker, was a massive fraudulent banking operation whose illegal activities covered every financial crime conceivable. We have seen that happen before, have we not? But what made it more dramatic was the discovery that the bank was indeed both the engine room for the threat to our economy, and the paymaster of all of those in the Country who were not only working in Government, but working against it, the true enemies within. Among those arrested was Axel Margeles, a beneficial director of I-Bank, who has been the driving force in the run against the pound which has produced perhaps the major crisis in this Country's history."

The House could hardly contain itself. The Margeles connection had once again lit the fuse paper. The noise sprang up anew as the Prime Minister paused to take a sip of water and whiskey.

He stood at the box for a moment, hands resting on its sides, surveying his fellow members of Parliament gravely.

"Madame Speaker, these and other matters must, I agree, be investigated and reported to this House in full. In the meantime, I ask that this House grant me a mandate to continue as Prime Minister during what I hope and trust is the successful resolution of all the matters that trouble us. In the event of my endorsement by the House, I undertake to hold a General Election as soon as is practical following the resolution of these matters so that the Country can make its own choice, and properly preserve our principle of democracy."

"Hear! Hear!" roared the House, as one, conversations breaking out beneath the shouts.

Rollinson stood silent again, nodding his head solemnly, as if thanking the House for the support.

"Madame Speaker, there is one other matter, the matter which lies at the heart of all this, the source of our real troubles. During the past year, we have been at odds with ourselves. There have been two factions, not just in the Conservative party, but in the other parties too, with one grave exception. The Integrationists have been the only party with a clear agenda; that agenda was nothing less than the destruction of Great Britain. Because of this agenda, and the support engendered for it by fair means and often fowl, the Government of the day has been unable to take the sometimes harsh and unpopular decisions needed. Madame Speaker, if I am confirmed by the House as Prime Minister for the time being, I for one will not hesitate to do whatever I can to preserve our way of life, our great democracy, this I pledge to the House".

Rollinson looked up again from his notes.

"Madame Speaker, I am content to let the House speak for all of us".

As he sat down, somewhat exhausted, Rollinson looked out at the sea of faces, heard the reactions, soaked in the atmosphere. All of these things told him he would still be Prime Minister at the end of this momentous day.

24

The Chief was nervous. Sheila Remington wanted to see him. As expected, when he was ushered into her office, she wasn't in the least bit friendly. It was as if she hadn't despatched him so completely at their last meeting, for a mad moment, he was almost convinced he had imagined the whole thing himself, but then, he looked in detail at her mouth, and remembered.

"What is it, Sheila?" he asked, realising at once that the familiarity was not appreciated.

"Miss Remington to you, if you don't mind!" She exclaimed haughtily. Trust a man to think he owned you just because of one incident, she thought to herself. They were all the same! She fixed him with her steely glare and handed him a photograph.

The Chief looked in admiration at a beautiful redhead with enigmatic eyes. Remington glared at him again, seeing his interest with distaste.

"Here is your murderer. We traced her through her DNA. She uses the name Laura, among others, but she is a former East German spy called Larna Markov. She is wanted by Interpol in connection with various assassinations throughout the World".

The Chief was impressed. He opened his mouth, but Sheila had anticipated the question.
"We shall have her before the year is out" she said, knowing full well how little of the year was actually left. Finished with that, Remington reached for a tape recorder on the desk, and pressed 'play'.

There was a lot of surface noise, but through it, the Chief distinctly heard the voice of Jonathan Charles.

"………the Pound and the Country will be sunk beneath the waves before much longer if I've anything to do with it……."

Remington switched the voice off.

The Chief was impressed.

"So we have him," he finally said, looking at Sheila in appreciation.

Remington merely grunted, and handed him several sheets of paper.

"It's all in there," she said, her voice dismissive, "From the tapes we already had, the technical people cleaned up the sound until we finally pinned him down to this conversation. As you know, we arranged his hired car, which was, of course, fitted to our specification".

The Chief quickly glanced through the papers.

"Talk of money laundering, rigging votes, treason – you're right. It is all in here," he said admiringly.

"Unfortunately, as you also know, we were unable to trace the caller on the other end," said Sheila, the words almost choking her.

He pretended not to notice her discomfort.

"That's to be expected," he said, deliberately focusing his eyes on the paper again.

Then Remington played another trump card.

"The Right Honourable Jonathan Charles – I have his full details" she said, handing over a folder full of papers and photographs.

"Anything of interest?" asked the Chief, unfazed by Remington's cool demeanour, relieved if anything.

Remington narrowed her eyes, appraising his reaction as she spoke.

"Most of his life, uneventful, except that his mother – Mary, maiden name Porterfield – died when he was young; father away most of the time, the boy was mainly raised by Grandparents in Ireland. Went to Eaton, Oxford, nothing untoward in his life, a very respectable upbringing," [she paused, staring at the Chief with a hard gaze], "- on the surface at least".

Now what did she mean by that? The Chief looked at her, perplexed.

Remington, as with all things she did, delivered the coup de grace with full effect.

"Not born Jonathan Charles, but Jonathan Charles Devane" she said triumphantly.

The Chief's jaw involuntarily fell open, much to Remington's gratification.

"Devane is Jonathan Charles' father?" he gasped.

Remington spun a page at him from her folder almost as if it was a paper aeroplane.

"John Charles Devane, Lieutenant-Colonel, SAS regiment etc etc., photograph enclosed herein."

Still shell-shocked, the Chief stared dumbly at the familiar face. So Jonathan's mother was raped and murdered, and avenged by his father, thought the Chief. What had the boy made of all that? Obviously, he was still close to his Father, or he wouldn't be buried in this muck up to his neck, would he?

Remington was looking at him with amusement. He saw that glint in her eyes he recognised from their last meeting. It was his turn to shock her.

"We will leave it there for now, and retire to have a drink," he said.

Gratified, he saw the look of surprise on Sheila's face. It was time to deliver the second shock.

"I can't have full oral with you - I won't tell you why, it's none of your business, but I am willing to share a cup of coffee with you, if you are agreeable to that".

He paused, as if waiting for affirmation.

Remington's usually cold and serious face broke into a generous smile.

"Well, I'll settle for that," she said, "Though I would have preferred the original blend".

They laughed together and walked off to the lift, arm in arm.

25

"It has been an extremely interesting day," said the Chancellor, Adam Clayton, as he stood outside the Treasury with the eyes and ears of the World's press upon him. With an aristocratic hand, he swept his silver hair back from his forehead and smiled uneasily.

"The difficulties of the pound could not be allowed to continue any longer; I have therefore at this hour taken the decision to leave the exchange rate mechanism and devalue the pound..........."

Hardly had the magic words left his lips when the press pack howled like wolves and drenched Clayton with even more flashes of camera light. Half of them had already pelted off with their stories. At that moment too, TV studios were pounding into action, rounding up pundits and ex-Ministers to speak for and against the Government. It was certainly clear that the Government's credibility was seriously undermined following the many promises made in public that the pound would never leave the ERM and in particular, would never be devalued.

The Prime Minister had been a man of his word. He had undertaken to do what he deemed to be best for the Country, whatever it meant for the reputation of himself and his Government, for his party in general. As he watched the feeding frenzy surrounding the beleaguered Clayton grow, the Prime Minister knew better than anyone that he would not be Prime Minister for long. Thanks to his decision, he would be forever associated with vacillation and distrust, his meaningful political career was over, as was Clayton's, and everyone else associated with this time in Government.

A new era would enter, sweeping aside all others, but not necessarily a new broom, more like an old broom re-painted for effect. The Labour party, so long in the doldrums, caught up in its own internal factions, would be in the ascendant again. It would be the time of internet man, mobile phone man, politically-correct man, the most likely candidate being Terry O'Hare, the former shadow Home Secretary, a man of the times, the androgynous age.

To some it seemed a fate worse than death – but at least there was still a vote to be taken, and a reason for the vote in the first place. But for Rollinson at the helm, it could have been so different. Yet so many had so quickly forgotten just how much of 'a damn close run thing' it had been, nearly a Waterloo for Great Britain itself. There were some that wryly remarked that we had been saved from total loss of identity in Europe only to be subjugated by ideas from across the other side of the World. However flippant the tone of the remarks, there was some ironic truth to it.

American politics had finally arrived in Britain

26

From: lt@hotmail.com
To: comm@hotmail.com
Message: *'never despair; there's always a light at the end of the tunnel'*.
From: comm@hotmail.com
To: lt@hotmail.com
Message: *'the trouble is, it's usually a train travelling in the opposite direction'*.
From: comm@hotmail.com
To: lt@hotmail.com
Message: *'up and running; only one thing missing – you!'*
From: lt@hotmail.com
To: comm@hotmail.com
Message: *'rectified soon; axe at 121 07957 642348'*

Susan flipped through the reams of messages on her desk, handing one page to the Chief, who stood there silently, watching her.

"I've traced these," she said casually, as if it had been easy, "*lt* was set up from Standford Hill prison. Devane was there at that time, and was on Education, where he would have access to the computer and the Internet."

"What about *comm*?" asked the Chief, studying the paper in his hand.

"That was set up from Ford prison, and from there, it was linked up again outside, though the source is untraceable." said Susan, "As far as the Ford connection goes, it was obviously someone in Education again. We've narrowed it down to about twenty people, and we're tracing them as we speak."

The Chief nodded, preoccupied.

"Axe must refer to Margeles," he said thoughtfully, "It's obviously a contact number."

Susan smiled patiently. Did he think she wouldn't have checked that already?

"It *is* Margeles," she said, a little triumphantly, "The number goes right back to his first ventures into the financial world. It's linked to a back street office in New York, and from there, to one of his former homes in East Berlin."

He smiled at her, realising how patronising he had been.

"So, what else do we have?" he said, teasing her.

She pulled a face of mock fury, and threw a book at him.

"Study it for yourself!" she said, pushing him out the door as if furious with him.

"Hell hath no fury!" he said laughingly, briefly squeezing her hand as he left.

Back at his office, he spent hours trying to make connections. There were still so many loose ends. Staring at the book till his eyes began to blur, the Chief stood up and sighed. A series of photographs and a list of Devane's known associates and cellmates had revealed little. The man had made few friends, had kept any friends he had a secret, even to those around him. Susan and the rest of the team had managed to narrow it down to a short list of the twenty or so who were also connected to Education at Ford prison. None of them seemed memorable, and most had been traced.

It was time he paid a visit to Devane himself.

The day afterwards, the Chief wearily ploughed through the busy traffic to south London. He hated these visits. They were such desperate places, and Wandsworth had an aura of evil that was hard to wash off. The Chief shuddered involuntarily as he thought what it must mean to live in such a place. As a supposed paragon of virtue, he should have seen the situation as 'them' and 'us', but he was too wise to miss the fact that it could almost happen to anyone, given the right – or wrong – circumstances.

Finally, he drove through the formidable gates to the Victorian interior of the prison itself. After all the formalities with the grim-faced warders, the Chief was shown to a drab room, bereft of furniture apart from a table and two very basic chairs.

After a short wait, Devane walked in. The Chief noted that Devane was more powerfully built than he looked in his video and photographs. Nevertheless, he was startled to see the many deep cuts and bruises on Devane's face.

The two men sat facing each other in silence for a moment.

"No use asking if you're being treated OK," said the Chief, wryly nodding towards the other man's face.

Devane's mouth moved imperceptibly, a shadow of a smile.

"I didn't catch your name" he said softly, his eyes unfriendly, probing.

"I didn't give it," said the Chief, offering Devane a cigarette. The other man shook his head.

"You can call me Chief," said the visitor, giving a wry smile.

"I left the army years ago" said Devane, leaning forward, "But then, you know that".

The Chief lit his cigarette and paused, studying Devane for a moment.

"Yes, I know that. It won't surprise you to know that I've learned a great deal about you. I also know how your system worked, and where the money went", he said, almost triumphantly.

Devane smiled enigmatically.

"Do you?"

The Chief calmly took a puff of the cigarette. This man was definitely high up on the scale, he thought, probably second in line, top drawer.

"Well, it's true I thought you might help me with a few loose ends, now that the whole business is more or less wrapped up," he said, his face smiling, his eyes noting every expression of the other man.

Devane was thinking the same of the Chief. Here no doubt was the man who was responsible for the end of the system, sitting right here before him. His friend would have been fascinated, he thought.

"There's nothing I can help you with," said Devane, "Why should I anyway?"

"It could help you in court" said the Chief, knowing it was a futile thing to say to such a man. Devane merely smiled inscrutably again.

"We know all about your leader," said the Chief, slumping back in his chair as if unconcerned by Devane's lack of interest.

Devane gave another hard look. He knew the Chief was talking nonsense.

"I don't have any leader," said Devane, telling the truth. That one surprised the Chief. He had not expected Devane to lie, yet the Chief knew that someone else was the brains behind it all. Devane, as clever and as formidable as he obviously was in many ways, did not have the style or the intelligence to put together a system which would shake the world. Yet Devane seemed to be denying it. Was he protecting his friend? His friend – the Chief realised that was the definition, not leader.

"Your friend, then" said the Chief, catching Devane out.

The Chief noted with satisfaction the glimmer of surprise in Devane's face.

"Did your friend have Wife troubles too?" asked the Chief brutally.

Again, he was rewarded with a startled look from Devane before it was replaced by a look of anger. So, thought the Chief, a pattern emerges.

"I paid dearly in more ways than one for my Wife's death," said Devane in a rare moment of true feeling, his voice rising angrily.

The Chief knew this was true, but the professional in him took over.

"So did the man who killed your Wife," he said, standing up. This was as much as he could hope to get from this man. Satisfied, the Chief began to walk from the room.

"Giving up so soon?" said Devane sarcastically.

The Chief turned and looked hard at Devane, his mask of friendliness gone.

"We know what you did to Tremain, and given time, we'll prove it", he said, a bitter taste in his mouth. He sympathised with much of Devane's troubles, but totally disagreed with his remedies.

"How much time do you have?" asked Devane mockingly.

"Well, you for one have plenty of time - you're not going anywhere, are you?" said the Chief, wounded by the man's easy indifference to his plight.

Devane gave him a quizzical look. Something flashed in his eyes as he looked at the Chief, and then it was gone.

Later, back at the office, the Chief stared again at the rows of photographs in front of him. *His friend*, he thought. And yet, there were no known friends, only these contacts, tenuous at best. The team had tracked down and/or identified almost all of these, four had since died, some were back in jail, mainly for petty offences, some were living anonymously, pursuing relatively respectable lives. Of Devane's old army associates, all that were still alive had been contacted, and none of them seemed to know anything of Devane's whereabouts these last years.

Of the twenty from the prison Education department, the whereabouts of several were still unknown. At least three of them had emigrated, and had not yet been traced. The others were proving more difficult to track down, though it was an ongoing process. The Chief studied the details of the men again, as he had done so many times these past few weeks. His eyes stopped at a face that looked vaguely familiar, but he couldn't remember where he'd seen that face before. He looked at the man's details. Nothing memorable there, all petty stuff. Besides, the man in the photograph had died.

The Chief shuffled through the papers again. Nothing about a Wife who had died in unusual circumstances among this man, nor any of them. Yet Devane had definitely reacted to the suggestion that he and his friend had shared the same trauma. Sighing wearily, the Chief turned out the office light and reached for his jacket. That was enough for one day, he decided.

Unfortunately, when he had stared at the photograph of the dead man, his mind was not as selective and discriminating as a computer; it could not put its finger on that cold London day when two strangers had passed each other on an empty street.

They would never meet again.

27

It was another cold day in Wandsworth.
Sheltered in the doorway of the exercise yard, the
black-coated warders shivered and cursed in the
winter wind as their sparsely dressed charges turned
circle after circle in their shabby and ill-fitting
clothes.

One of their number was a special prisoner, a
category A, who was allowed exercise only rarely,
especially with other less infamous prisoners.
Devane was a bloody nuisance, thought one of the
cons. When Devane was around, security was so
much more stringent, a real pain in the arse. A
police helicopter circled low overhead, seeming to
emphasise the thoughts of the nondescript man who
gave Devane another black look.

Devane ignored the man's gaze. He had troubles
enough without him. An uneasy mutter sprang up
from the shivering warders by the door. The police
helicopter seemed to be dropping from the sky at an
alarming rate –was it in trouble?

The warders' anxieties turned to panic when the
helicopter was suddenly placed to land in the middle
of the exercise yard, scattering the prisoners like
rabbits. Only one prisoner didn't run.

Devane had been waiting for this moment. The
warders were approaching the helicopter as fast as
their bloated carcasses could carry them, but their
concerns were for the pilot and the policemen on
board, not the well-being of any prisoner in their
charge, they didn't matter. Devane still stood there,
not moving, waiting for the helicopter to land. The

leading officer in the pack was shouting at him, cursing, waving.

"Get out of there, you stupid bastard!" he said, his face a mask of fury.

He was the first to reach Devane, and as he did so, Devane hit him with a rabbit punch, knocking the podgy warder over like a skittle. He lay there unconscious to the World. The other prisoners looked on from the perimeter, awe-struck with admiration.

"He really nobbled that screw, didn't he!" said one black man with a bald head, his scarred and self-mutilated face a mixture of pride and wishful thinking.

The other warders were not so thrilled. They were like a pack of wild animals as they rushed both towards the helicopter and Devane, a mercy mission on one hand, the instruments of revenge in the other. The helicopter had not quite stopped, and the warders were almost upon it and Devane, when the helicopter doors suddenly sprung open, and a squad of men dressed completely in black leapt out, machine guns in their hands. These were clearly not police, they looked more like.........SAS.

The warders froze in surprise, their eyes wide with shock. Gone were the expressions of hate and revenge, the power visibly oozed from their faces, they were exposed as the cowards they really were.

Devane smiled at the leading man. He knew who he was, despite the mask.

"Which one?" asked the man brusquely.

John turned and pointed at the figure of Woodford, cringing at the back of the pack.

"Him" he said, his eyes like steel bullets as they fastened on the bully who had plagued so many already tormented lives in this hellish place.

"No! No! Please, No!" cried the whinging warder, begging on his knees for forgiveness as the man in black approached him.

There was no mercy. The noise of the machine gun echoed through the yard surrounded by the drab buildings, shocking every spectator there. The bullets smashed into the fat warder's legs, shattering his knees beyond repair.

The man in black looked at Devane again, his smoking machine gun still pointed at the crying warder.

"Are you sure?" he said, in his menacing voice.

Devane looked at the warder wearily. He would have wished for more – it would have been no loss to the World, he reasoned, but he had given his word. No more deaths.

"Leave it, " said Devane.

The man in black nodded, and made for the helicopter.

"John, let's go" he said, his voice respectful but firm.

Devane turned to look at the scene for the last time. He saw his fellow prisoners, the poor remnants of humanity they were, still condemned to this living hell. Some were genuine assholes, as Devane knew, but among their number there was also courage, dignity, and decency, ill served by society at their time of need.

He looked too at the warders, shivering even more now, and not just with the cold. He saw among them the figure of Clark, standing with his arms crossed, watching intently, calmly. Not all officers were bad, it wasn't that black and white, as Devane well knew. Clark had been decent, as had others. The trouble was, they were the exception rather than the rule. He and Clark studied one another.

Finally, Devane gave a short salute. Clark, unsure of how to react, merely nodded.

The man in black reached back and touched Devane's shoulder.

"We have to go," he said.

Devane nodded, and without further ceremony disappeared into the helicopter. The machine guns remained fixed on the crowd of warders until the last man was in, then the helicopter roared off into the sky, growing ever smaller and smaller till the ugly scar that was Wandsworth disappeared from view.

28

It was late that evening when the phone rang. Susan answered it casually.

"Oh no!" she suddenly shouted, startling the Chief, who rushed to her side.

"What is it?" he said, concerned.

"It's Devane," said Susan, her eyes tearful as she handed him the phone, "He's escaped".

The Chief was incredulous.

"Escaped? From Wandsworth?" he gasped, what the hell was going on?

McKay was on the other end of the phone.

"It's true Guv, he got away. A classic SAS operation. They nicked a police helicopter and bowled in to the exercise yard, as bold as brass".

"Was anyone hurt?" asked the Chief, realising it was hard to make an omelette without breaking eggs.

"One of the screws had his legs blasted away," said McKay unceremoniously, "He won't walk again, poor sod".

The Chief remembered Devane's battered face.

"He pays his debts," he said, to no one in particular.

"Sorry Guv?" said McKay, puzzled.

"Nothing Dave" said the Chief, distractedly, "Are the police on to it?"

"There's an all points alert at airports and ferries and the like," said McKay, his voice sounding doubtful, almost apologetic.

Dave was right, thought the Chief. Devane was well gone by now, and this time he would make damn sure they didn't catch him easily again.

His mind went back to Wandsworth, and his meeting with Devane. He remembered that flashing look in his eyes when the Chief had said he had plenty of time.

He knew now what that look had meant.

The stolen police helicopter was found abandoned in a field not too many miles away. Inside was the missing crew, securely tied and shocked, but otherwise unharmed. Obviously, the party involved had taken to cars, and then another air transport of some sort, which had whisked them out of the Country before a proper search was even underway.

Waiting for Devane at his new home was a new identity, and a series of bank accounts which used as its basis an impenetrable Liechtenstein trust called an *Anstalt*.

The funds available would provide a comfortable living for the rest of his life.

There was only one serious snag to this. John was a man of action.

Retirement would not suit him.

Nor would it suit his friend, but for different reasons. Only his friend's bitterness and sense of revenge had kept him alive these many years since Edith. Something had died inside him when she vanished from his life. Now, without his hate and determination to punish his perceived enemies to keep him alive, he would live like a zombie, functioning, but not really living.

Despite the massive loss of funds involved in the collapse of the system, such was his wealth that he and John would never suffer any kind of financial insecurity again. Indeed, they were now able to live like rich retired grandees, even though they would not be able to see each other or make contact for quite some time yet.

He could, in theory, do anything he wanted. He could survey the deserts of Sahara, or trek the frozen Arctic wastes. He could explore the Amazon, or sail the Nile, watching those fabulous Egyptian sunsets. But however beautiful those sunsets were, there was no one to share the sunsets with.

Edith was gone forever.

His enemies, on the other hand, were still out there, searching for him. They had not found him, and they never would. Nevertheless, he was locked in a prison of his own device, he would never be free.

Standing on his veranda, he stared in silence at the dark trees outside his window, stirring in the evening breeze. Somewhere out there, in the darkness, a solitary creature called.

His loneliness was complete

Epilogue

At the time of publication neither Devane nor his friend have been found; the other players in the drama were the ones who paid the price of society's wrath. Axel Margeles received fifteen years for his part in the drama; a mere pawn, he had nevertheless enjoyed all the trappings of wealth and influence, and his outer show counted against him in court and in the public eye.

James Germaine may have also been something of a dupe, but the court showed him little mercy, jailing him for twelve years. Pierre Arroneaux had to run the gauntlet of insults and anger from Billy Reynolds, among others, on his way to court. Perhaps he welcomed the relative safety of ten years in prison. In any case, he wasn't Pierre Arroneaux at all. His name was Peter Furneaux. One of those missing associates of John Devane, he was an ex-convict and accomplished con man. Even his name was misleading. In terms of birth, he was British through and through, the nearest he had ever been to France was on a few trips across the Dover ferry. On the other hand, he couldn't have been that close to Devane – there were no helicopters for him, he languished in the dungeon like the rest of the more humble miscreants.

There was also no hiding place for Larna Markov once she was positively identified. Her own lust and perversion had trapped her. Sheila was as good as her word. Markov was seized at Frankfurt airport, and at the time of writing, she is still in a German prison awaiting extradition to face a charge of murder in Britain. A queue of countries also await the outcome of any trial with interest. A number of previously unsolved murders and other crimes could now be safely laid at Larna or Laura's door. The appearance of her photograph in every national newspaper was also a source of considerable discomfort for Julian Somerfield. Laura's rise to notoriety brought painful memories back for him, though he kept unusually quiet about it.

Judges, barristers, lawyers, Council officials, and high-ranking civil servants also found their way into court, then beyond, to a world they could never have imagined existed. Judge Brooks received a typical sentence for those of his kind, three years, another comment on the inequality and injustice of the system called justice.

The prison population in general was greatly swollen by the ranks of the more lowly placed criminals who had worked within the system, and whose punishment was disproportionate because of their lowly stature in the social scale. As for the high ranking officers, the former Minister for Trade and the Minister for Employment were merely banished from office and from holding office or parliamentary position ever again, as were all former Integrationists, be they office holders or not.

To the outrage of the press and general public, this was also the fate of Jonathan Charles. Despite having much evidence against him, the powers-that-be decided that it would not be appropriate to send a former Chancellor to prison. Instead, using the excuse of his Canadian birth, he was deported in disgrace. His wealth was such that his financial future was assured, but his once glittering career lay in ruins forever. No country in the World would welcome him, and he was finally banished to a small island off the Jamaican coast, a modern Elba. There he could spend the rest of his empty days contemplating what might have been.

Henry Rollinson retired to the House of Lords, as did Adam Clayton, the former Chancellor. However unfair it was, their black day of devaluation and flight from the ERM would never be forgotten nor forgiven by the press and the public. As predicted, Farquhar-Brown was the one who given a knighthood, while his hard-working subordinate, the Chief himself, quietly received the MBE. Jim Barton became Editor of 'The Times', and was subsequently knighted in due course for the considerable part he had played in the downfall of the system.

The team itself was again sent their separate ways, McKay, Simmonds, Walker, and the others all joining various forces, working soldiers without due rewards for their efforts. Promotional carrots were dangled, but not often received, par for the course in a bureaucracy that was still itself corrupt, where rampant nepotism and unjustified awards were the order of the day. Susan was the only other member of the team who subsequently achieved high office, an event that was received cynically by some members of the team, though notably not by the loyal McKay.

All in all, the operation had been a success, though millions upon millions were still unaccounted for, and some of the leading participants had thus far never been found, principally the so-called Mastermind himself, a fact which the tabloid press never tired of repeating. Ironic, considering that they themselves had created the concept of Mastermind, the press now freely speculated that Devane had been the real ringleader, especially after his spectacular escape from Wandsworth. After all, there had never been any concrete evidence that such a Mastermind existed.

The Chief often worried and wondered about those loose ends, they played on and on in his mind late at night when he couldn't sleep.

On one such night, Susan stirred beside him, sensing his restlessness.

"Perhaps it was Devane. Perhaps he was the one after all," said Susan helpfully.

The Chief looked at her. She looked so beautiful there in the moonlight. He smiled at her, placed his hand on her head, stroking her hair gently.

"No," he said, "He's out there somewhere, dreaming of a lost paradise, I know he is".

Caught up as he was in his own earthly moment of happiness, the Chief could not yet begin to know just how transient such happiness was, and how easily that paradise could be forever lost.